LAURA LANDON'S
SEASONS

*Four love stories
in one great read*

BOOK ONE
WINTER'S COLD HEART

BOOK TWO
SPRING'S TENDER HEART

BOOK THREE
SUMMER'S DISTANT HEART

BOOK FOUR
AUTUMN'S WILD HEART

©2021
Lincoln, Nebraska

SEASONS
ISBN 978-1-952911-15-6
Lincoln, Nebraska

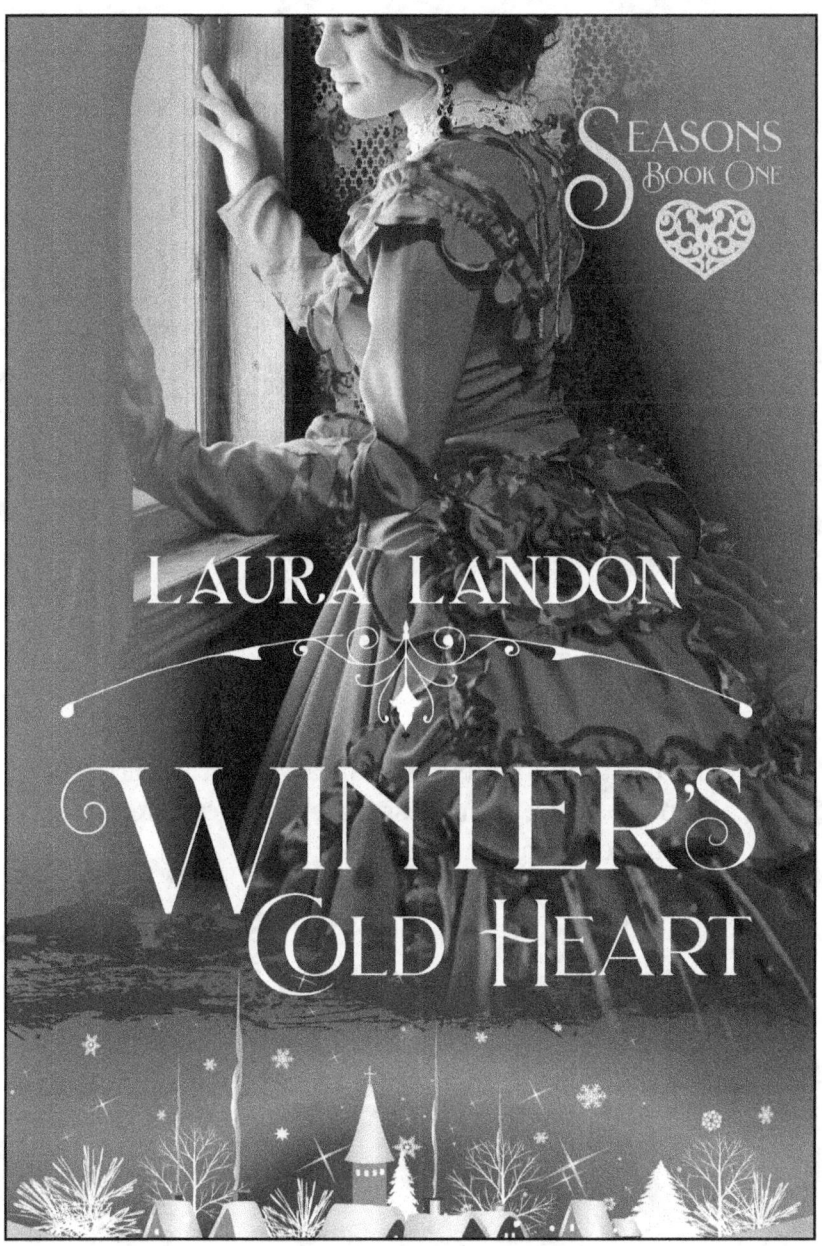

SEASONS
BOOK ONE

LAURA LANDON

WINTER'S
COLD HEART

LAURA LANDON

WINTER'S COLD HEART

*Only a poisonous rumor
stood between them.*

Could Lydia McDowell ignore an entire village
and trust the shamed Doctor Jarvis? Or would
doing so come at the cost of her brother's life...
and her own frozen heart?

Chapter One

LYDIA MCDOWELL PULLED THE HOOD of her cloak lower over her face. Sleet mixed with wet snow pummeled her eyes and stung her cheeks. She could no longer see where she was going.

Maybe she could use the storm as an excuse to return home and tell her brother that the snow prevented her from finding her way to the doctor's surgery, but she knew deep in her chilled bones that returning without a doctor wasn't an option. James was injured too badly. He needed a doctor's attention. And he needed it immediately. Her fear was that Doctor Joshua Jarvis wasn't the doctor she should be going for. She should instead be going to Doctor Elias Weatherby. But her brother had insisted he wanted Doctor Jarvis to tend to him.

Lydia stepped into a vacated shop doorway to gain her bearings and buried her face in the wet folds of her worn cloak. She wasn't sure where she was. She wasn't that familiar with the village yet. She'd only come to stay with James a few weeks ago—just long enough to hear the horrors of what Doctor Jarvis had committed. The deaths he'd caused.

Why on earth had her brother insisted that she fetch this man? He knew the rumors circulating around Jarvis as well as she did. Surely James knew the doctor was incompetent. Everyone in Middleton believed he was.

Lydia looked through the frosty glass panes in front of her and recognized some of the items inside. She was in front of Russell's Bakery.

Lydia shivered, angry at the cold, angry at the wasted steps, and angry at having to seek out the last man on earth she wanted tending her brother. She'd gone right past his door and didn't even know it.

Lydia stepped back into the raging snowstorm and retraced her steps. In a moment she stood shivering beneath the doctor's shingle that swung overhead, crusted with freezing snow that obliterated his name.

The windows were dark, but Lydia pounded on the door. Then again.

"Doctor Jarvis," Lydia implored as she pounded on the door one more time. She was relieved when a light finally glowed inside.

The door swung open and Lydia lifted her gaze to look at the tall, broad-shouldered doctor. She struggled to make out his features because the melted snow ran from her forehead and into her eyes, making it impossible to see him clearly.

"Come inside," a deep voice demanded. "What are you doing out in this weather? You're nearly frozen."

The doctor clamped his fingers around her arms and pulled her inside. The second he released her to close the door, Lydia nearly fell to the floor. He clasped his strong, sure arms around her again, then kicked the door shut before leading her to a chair by the fire and helping her to sit.

Lydia tried to speak, but her teeth chattered so violently she couldn't form any words.

All around her were the trappings of a well-ordered clinic—instruments neatly aligned on a tray, shelves stocked with bandages and medicinals, and a desk lined with neatly scribed notes. It was not what she'd expected from a man who was so careless with his patients.

The doctor hovered over her as he placed a thick woolen blanket around her shoulders, then disappeared into the kitchen. He returned a moment later with a cup of warm tea.

"I'm sorry the tea isn't hot. Nor is it fresh. It's left over from my lunch."

"Thank you," Lydia stuttered. With trembling hands she lifted the cup, but the tea sloshed wildly before she got it to her mouth. Doctor Jarvis knelt beside her and wrapped his fingers around hers to steady her trembling hands. He brought the cup to her mouth and Lydia took a sip of the welcome warmth.

She lifted her head after she'd taken a swallow and stared at the doctor's handsome face. When she realized she had watched him far too long, she lowered her gaze to where his hands still touched hers. An unexpected heat radiated from his touch and caused her frozen fingers to warm.

She allowed him to keep his hands wrapped around hers for several moments before slowly pulling away from him.

She didn't know what had caused such a wanton reaction to the man. Perhaps the cold that lingered in her bones had overtaken her good sense. Lydia straightened her back, refusing to believe there was any significance to the response his mere touch had roused.

"What's your name?" the doctor asked, interrupting her wayward thoughts.

"Lydia McDowell," Lydia answered through her chattering teeth. "My brother is James McDowell, at Cottage Hill. He's been gored by a bull. You must come quickly!"

Lydia lifted her head until her gaze locked with the doctor's. "There's no time to waste," she said as forcefully as she could.

The doctor sucked in a harsh breath then stood upright. His movement brought him to a towering threat. "Then you will want to see Doctor Weatherby. I'll take you to him."

"No. My brother wants you."

Lydia noticed the look of surprise and shock on the doctor's face.

"Well, I can't help you. I no longer practice medicine."

"You're a doctor, aren't you?"

"What I once was makes no difference. I no long practice medicine, so I'll take you to Doctor Weatherby."

Lydia threw off the woolen blanket and bolted to her feet. "I wish you would, sir. I certainly do wish you would! But the fact of the matter is that you will *not* take me to Doctor Weatherby. My brother does not want Doctor Weatherby. *Why*, I don't know. You're the last doctor in the world I would choose to treat him, but my brother doesn't feel that way. For some reason, you're the doctor he sent me for. So, whether you want to or not, you will accompany me if I have to drag you. Now, get your coat and your bag and come with me."

A shocked expression that covered the doctor's face lifted, then the corners of his mouth rose to form a smile. "Are you always this demanding?"

"When my brother's life is in danger, yes. Now please, hurry. Get your coat and your bag and come with me."

Lydia waited the few moments it took for the doctor to consider his actions before tipping his head. "As the lady demands," he said, then left the room.

Lydia released a breath she didn't realize she'd been holding and sank back into the chair. What had come over her? She'd never behaved so rudely in all her life. She'd never stood up to a man like she'd stood up to Doctor Jarvis.

When Lydia heard his footsteps coming toward her, she rose from the chair and stepped to the door. She'd left James alone too long already and was desperate to get back to him.

Thankfully, when the doctor returned he had his greatcoat and medical bag with him. He fastened the coat, then faced her.

"Stay in here while I hitch the carriage. I'll pull around front when I'm finished."

Lydia nodded, then watched Doctor Jarvis leave through a back door. When the door closed behind him, she walked closer to the fire to take in all the heat she could before she had to go back into the freezing weather. Too soon she heard his carriage stop in front of the surgery. Quickly she slipped on her wet gloves, then walked over to the lamp that was burning and extinguished it.

The door opened and he entered, stamping his feet and brushing snow from his lapel.

"Wear this," he said as he wrapped a heavy lap-robe around her shoulders. "The carriage is only partially enclosed, and it's getting colder by the minute out there."

The second his fingers brushed her arm a burning heat traveled through her body. Lydia tried to ignore it, but it refused to lessen. She thought he would pull away from her. Instead, he pulled the edges of the blanket tighter around her and kept his fingers locked beneath her chin.

"We need to be on our way," he whispered.

"Yes, James needs you."

Lydia looped her arm through his and together they walked through the snow. When they reached the carriage, Doctor Jarvis helped her inside. She sat as near to the enclosing canopy as she could while he hurried around to the other side and climbed up beside her. He secured the low doors that swung shut just in front of their knees, then pulled the brow of the canopy as low as possible to break the bitter wind. Satisfied, he hoisted the reins and tapped the single horse. The carriage lurched forward and he turned it toward the edge of town.

"Cottage Hill, you said?"

"Yes, on Littlegate Lane."

"You walked all the way into town?"

"I had no choice. I've never hitched a horse to a carriage."

"No wonder you were nearly frozen," he said, then tapped the reins on the horse's rump again to encourage the mare to move faster.

"Pull the lap-robe up around you, then lean behind me if you can."

Lydia did what he suggested but before she pulled the heavy blanket up, she did her best to place as much of it as possible over the doctor's legs. From everything she'd heard he certainly didn't deserve her thoughtfulness, but she would do whatever it took to keep the man in tiptop shape to treat her brother. When she finished, she leaned her head into the back of his shoulder.

"Why did your brother send you for me?" the doctor asked when they were on their way. "Doesn't he know everyone in town believes I murdered the last two patients I treated?"

"He's heard the rumors," Lydia answered. "Obviously he doesn't believe them."

"Rumors?"

"That's what James says they are."

"What about you?"

Lydia was silent for a moment. "An entire village can't be wrong. But anyway, it doesn't matter what I believe. What matters is that my brother doesn't believe that you killed Mrs. Smithers or Ivan Crumbly. He said Mrs. Smithers was nearing ninety years. James believes she wasn't strong enough to survive her illness. And, Ivan Crumbly has done nothing but drink for more than twenty years. Everyone knew it was only a matter of time until his body couldn't take any more."

"So you came obediently to get the disreputable Doctor Jarvis, without arguing?"

Lydia lifted her head to see the teasing expression on the man's face and felt herself blush in response. She was surprised by the gratitude that engulfed her. His playful tone seemed to calm her fear, even though she knew she had best not trust him. Somehow he had lulled her into a level of comfort that she knew she could never allow.

"No. I argued with him. But it did no good. His mind was made up."

"Are you saying he's as determined as you are?"

"He's definitely a great deal more obstinate. He said the people of Middleton are a close-minded lot and he refuses to listen to their nattering on about your unsuitability for the practice of medicine."

Doctor Jarvis looked at her sharply.

"Hmph. Your brother is probably the only one in Middleton who hasn't already sentenced me to the public pillory."

Lydia studied the tight clenching of Doctor Jarvis' jaw. He'd endured a great deal at the hands of the people of Middleton, yet he hadn't packed his bags and moved to a different area where he could practice medicine as he'd been trained to do. Now who was being obstinate?

"We're nearly there," Lydia said, struggling to see through the snow that came down even harder. She squinted her eyes so she wouldn't miss the corner where they needed to turn.

"Turn here," she said, and a few moments later they reached her brother's cottage.

Doctor Jarvis saw her to the front door, then took his horse and carriage to the cowshed.

Lydia rushed inside the cottage, then raced to the room where her brother lay on the bed. He was paler than he'd been when she'd left a short while earlier.

"James?" she asked, lifting his head for him to take a drink of water.

"Did Jarvis come with you?"

"Yes. He took his horse and carriage around to the byre. He'll be right here."

"Good."

"You can't leave me, you know, James," Lydia said as tears formed in her eyes. "You're all I have left. I won't allow you to abandon me."

"I won't leave you Liddy. Unless God needs me more than you do."

"He doesn't, James. I need you more. Just remember that."

"I'll try," her brother said, then closed his eyes, leaving Lydia to ponder a future without this good man in it.

Chapter Two

Lydia wiped the tears from her cheeks, then turned around to see Joshua Jarvis entering the room. She rose from where she'd been sitting and Doctor Jarvis came near to examine James. The doctor leaned over her brother and felt his forehead, then placed his fingers to the side of James's throat.

"Tell me how the accident happened."

"He was separating the stock and the bull just charged him. He tried to get over the stile, but the beast caught him and threw him into the fence. His leg looks terrible."

The doctor lifted the covers and his gaze lowered to the blood-stained cloths that covered James's leg. He lifted the cloths, then examined the wound.

"Does your brother have any Irish whisky?"

"Yes."

"Bring it to me and more clean cloths and water."

Lydia left the room and returned with what he'd asked for. When she entered the room, the doctor's medical bag was open and he'd removed several instruments as well as several jars of salve and medicinals.

"Will you need me to help you?" she asked, praying that his answer would be no. She'd never been squeamish when it came to blood, but the idea of watching Doctor Jarvis work on her brother was a different story.

"No," he said. "At least not now. I'll just need you to see that I have plenty of clean water."

Lydia sighed with relief. She left the cloths and whisky he'd asked for and went to get the water he would need.

Again and again she returned to her brother's bedroom with clean water and anything else Doctor Jarvis asked for. She tried not to look at the wound on her brother's leg as the doctor worked feverishly to clean the area where the bull had gored James, but her eyes refused to avoid the torn flesh and bony splinters. Instead, she rinsed a cloth in cool water and placed it on James's feverish forehead.

Her heart twisted each time she heard the clink of another splinter of bone dropping from the doctor's forceps into the porcelain bowl. As she rinsed the cloth for a second time, her gaze caught with the doctor's. "Thank you," he said. "You make an excellent nurse."

"I thought I'd handle this better, but it's different when the person who is injured is your favorite brother."

As an answer, Doctor Jarvis lowered his head and returned to his work. But not before the smile on his face caused her heart to trip over itself.

Yes, the man was handsome, but why in the world should she even care? He may as well be old with half his teeth missing and a wart on his nose. She didn't care a whit.

He'd rolled up his sleeves, revealing his tanned, muscular forearms. The top two buttons of his shirt were loose, revealing a scandalous sliver of his chest. In responding to her emergency, he evidently hadn't bothered with his cravat, and it startled her that she found the result most unsettling.

It wasn't that Lydia had never seen a man's chest before. She lived with her brother, after all, and had often seen him shirtless when he came in from the fields after a hard day's work. But even though her brother was a fine specimen of a man, with bulging muscles and bronzed skin, the sight of him shirtless didn't affect her like just a glimpse of Joshua Jarvis's chest had.

But of course it would not.

What was wrong with her? Where had these untoward thoughts sprung from? After all, she'd only just met the man.

"We're fortunate that your brother lost consciousness and I've been able to do at least some of the most painful work before he wakes," he said, jarring her from her imaginings.

"Will he be alright?" Lydia asked. She worried that her brother's skin seemed hotter than it had been earlier.

"I don't know," he answered. "He's been injured quite severely."

That wasn't the answer Lydia hoped for. She almost wished he had lied to her. Everything she knew about the man said she should not be surprised if he did lie. But although she had just met him, she already sensed lying wasn't in his nature.

Before gathering the bloody cloths and taking them from the room, Lydia held her brother's hand for a few moments while she said a silent prayer that he'd be alright. When she reached the kitchen she threw on her cloak and grabbed a wooden bucket, then walked out the door. The water she had wasn't cold enough to battle James's fever. Maybe if she used some melted snow to place on his fevered skin it would help.

She took one step out the door to fill her bucket. The wind was blowing even harder than before and the snow and ice pelted her face with stinging fierceness. Once she felt she'd found enough snow, Lydia turned toward the house.

As she lifted her bucket and took a step, Lydia stumbled, then lost her balance.

She reached out to break the fall she knew was coming, but there was nothing to stop her. She fell forward, bashing her head on the wooden bucket and landing face-down in the snow.

Lydia lay there for a moment evaluating her movements. Thankfully, all her limbs seemed to work. The only pain she felt was to her forehead.

Lydia got to her feet, then scooped up the spilled snow and took it inside. The minute she entered the cottage, the snow melted and ran down her face. She grabbed a cloth to wipe the moisture. When she removed it, the cloth came away bloody. She felt no pain, but she attributed that to the fact that her face was so cold she was probably numb.

She wiped the blood away again, then rushed inside James's bedroom with the bucket of snow.

"I brought in some snow to pack the towels with."

"Excellent," Doctor Jarvis answered as he continued to work on James's leg. "I'm almost done," he said, "which is a good thing. Your brother is starting to—"

Lydia wiped her forehead, then placed the bloody cloth on the bedside table. She didn't think he'd been watching, but he must have seen it.

"What the hell happened?"

"It's nothing," Lydia said turning her head so he couldn't see the extent of her injury. She didn't think it was too severe, but she was starting to get light-headed and her forehead throbbed.

"I asked you what you did."

"I fell getting the snow and hit my head on the bucket."

"Stop what you're doing and press a cold cloth against the cut."

Lydia knew better than to argue with him. She pressed the cloth against her forehead, then continued to minister to James.

Doctor Jarvis was correct. James was starting to wake. He thrashed his head back and forth and moved enough that Doctor Jarvis had a difficult time bandaging his leg.

"Here," Lydia said. "Let me help. I'll hold him still while you finish."

"I'm going to regret letting you help me," he said. "You should be sitting quietly until I can see how badly you're hurt."

"It's just a scratch. You know head wounds always bleed profusely."

"Let's pray that's right in your case."

Lydia prayed it was, too. Her head ached like bloody blazes and her stomach churned from the pain and a lack of anything to eat since lunchtime. She took in several deep breaths hoping her head would clear and she wouldn't embarrass herself by fainting.

She held her brother's leg while Doctor Jarvis finished. When he was done, he poured some laudanum into a glass of whisky and lifted James's head so he could drink. While he was tending James, Lydia gathered the soiled cloths and carried them along with a basin of dirty water to the kitchen.

Her head ached even more and the room spun in dizzying circles. She needed something to eat, yet she knew if she ate anything it would come back up. She tossed the water out the back door and dropped the soiled cloths into a bucket, then turned to make her way to the nearest chair.

She needed to sit. Her legs weren't steady beneath her and her entire body seemed to tremble uncontrollably.

She'd only taken one step toward the table when she lost her balance. Before she reached a chair, the room went dark and she collapsed to the floor.

. . . .

"Miss McDowell!"

Joshua heard the crash of a chair overturn and raced from his patient's bedroom. He knew he should have made the young woman remain in the bedroom and not overexert herself. The cut on her forehead was deep and still bleeding.

"Miss McDowell?" he said, kneeling beside her.

He felt her forehead and her cheeks. They were cool and clammy, but not alarmingly so. He brushed the hair from her face and placed a hand on her shoulder to keep her from trying to rise. Her eyes fluttered, then opened.

"Don't move. Just lie still."

"I'm fine," she said in a voice filled with pain.

"Of course you are. It's quite normal for people who are physically *fine* to faint and end up on the floor."

"I just—"

"Just relax," he instructed without giving her a chance to argue.

Joshua glanced around the kitchen and saw a cushioned rocking chair on the opposite side of the room close to the hearth. He scooped her up into his arms and carried her across the room. After he'd placed a blanket over her lap, he filled a basin of water and cleaned her wound.

As he touched her face he found himself fascinated by its porcelain smoothness, by her eyelashes that seemed impossibly long and full, by the softness of the moist curls that framed her face. His movements became less of a treatment and more of a caress. The emotion he experienced was foreign to him and he scarcely knew what had come over him.

"You're fortunate the wound isn't as deep as I feared it was. I don't think I'll need to sew your flesh together." He reared back and grinned. "Unless you want me to, that is."

Her gaze shot upward and her eyes locked with his. Joshua couldn't keep the humor from his eyes.

"That wasn't funny," she said, meeting his gaze and failing to hold a serious expression.

"It wasn't? And here I've been told I have a keen sense of humor." Joshua placed a folded cloth on her wound and brought her hand up over it. "Hold this but don't press too hard. The bleeding has stopped and I don't want it to start again."

She did what she was told.

"Do you have some wine here?"

"Yes. In the sitting room, in the cupboard."

Joshua left the room and returned with a bottle of wine and a glass. "Here," he said handing her a nearly full glass of wine.

"Hopefully, you don't have something else for me to do," she said when she'd taken a sip of the wine. "I've run out of hands."

Joshua couldn't stop the bark of laughter from escaping. "I see you're a match for my humor."

"I can give you a run, Doctor Jarvis," she said taking another sip of her wine.

"Joshua," he said. "You might as well call me Joshua, since it's not likely I'll be rushed with patients and have to leave. Nor will I be able to return to my surgery anytime soon. It seems to be snowing even harder, if that's possible, and your brother will need me to watch over him."

"Then you must call me Lydia."

Joshua kept his gaze focused on her and couldn't seem to turn away from her.

"Lydia. It's a lovely name."

Her cheeks turned a rosy red as if she was embarrassed he'd complimented her. She demurely lowered her gaze. But not before he noticed yet again the dazzling blueness of her eyes.

He thought if he could, he would like to stare at her features all day long, and deep into the night.

"You're staring."

Joshua recovered his wits and took a step away. Yes, he'd been staring. How could he not?

He returned to the sitting room and brought a pillow from the settee and placed it behind her head. "Close your eyes now and relax. I'll return after I've seen to your brother."

"If I close my eyes, how will I know you're not still staring?" She cocked her head and raised an eyebrow as if she'd just issued an unanswerable fact.

He laughed.

"Well, let's just assume I'll be staring."

He winked, making her laugh, and left the room.

Joshua walked down the hall to Lydia's brother's room. Before he entered, he braced his hand against the door frame and lowered his head beneath his outstretched arm. For a moment he'd actually forgotten how disrupted his life was. How uncertain his future had become. This woman had so easily diverted him from his own worry that something inside him felt like grasping on to her to keep that pleasant distraction close by.

But that was sheer folly. He could never do that to Miss McDowell. Even though he was drawn to her unlike he'd ever been drawn to another female, he sensed she regarded him with suspicion. And why shouldn't she? If the people of Middleton discovered he'd tended James McDowell, he was certain their reaction wouldn't be kind. They might even take their anger out on Lydia.

Joshua stepped into McDowell's bedroom and checked on his patient. Lydia's brother would be lucky if he didn't develop a fever. He would be luckier still if he survived.

The wound Joshua tended was deep and the flesh around it had been mangled beyond simple repair. Even if Joshua managed to keep McDowell alive, he doubted he could save his leg.

Even if he managed to save his patient's leg, he doubted he could ever restore his own former pride.

Chapter Three

LYDIA OPENED HER EYES and looked around the room. She'd fallen asleep. She wasn't sure how long she'd slept but it must have been well over an hour. She turned her head to look out the window but couldn't see anything but darkness and snow plastered against the panes. She placed her hands on the arms of the chair in an effort to rise.

"Don't try to get up without help," the doctor's deep, rich voice said from beside her.

Lydia turned her head and found him approaching her.

"How do you feel?"

Lydia lifted her gaze. She saw concern in his compassionate eyes. "Much better. My head hardly hurts at all." It was a small lie, but she abhorred the thought that he might view her as a simpering female.

"Good."

"How is James?"

"He's sleeping at the moment. But he's developed a fever. I've placed cold cloths on him and it seems to help, but that could change at any moment."

Lydia nodded and was about to speak, but Doctor Jarvis held up a hand in warning. "You'll smell alcohol on him, but don't be alarmed. I've dampened the towels with a modest amount of the whiskey, which may help. But you must not try to do this yourself. Too much alcohol soaking through his skin and he could slip away."

The doctor's words poured rampant energy into her worries. James could slip away? Then why would this man use such a dangerous procedure? Lydia rose without his aid and turned toward the bedroom, determined to remove the alcohol-soaked cloths. The man was known to be careless with his patients. How could she trust him to get the procedure correct when he'd already killed two people who seemed on the verge of recovering?

She rushed to her brother's room and began pulling the reeking towels from her brother's body.

"Lydia! What on earth are you doing?"

She refused to turn to the doctor but continued her mission.

"Lydia? Stop now. It was working, can't you see?"

She grasped the final towel but stopped, startled by James's peaceful sleep. In wonder, she laid her hand on his chest. It was very nearly the same warmth as her own hand. Swiftly, she moved her hand to his cheek and then his forehead, but there was no alarming warmth.

"Just a little longer, Lydia. To be safe." Joshua Jarvis walked to the opposite side of the bed. "Help me now. I'll show you how to arrange the cloths."

Lydia shrank away. She'd jumped to an unwarranted conclusion, as if she knew better than he how to treat her brother. Her eyes moved to the exposed wound on James's leg. It looked as wretched as ever, but the edges of the long wound that had been such an angry red were now less inflamed. He had a long way to go before the wound could truly be said to be improving, but this was a small step in the right direction.

Perhaps Doctor Jarvis did not deserve her suspicion after all.

Still…

Lydia squared her shoulders. "In future I'll expect you to explain your plan before you do anything further to my brother. Is that understood?"

Doctor Jarvis remained bent over James, still as stone. The only thing that moved was his hand that slowly smoothed the final towel in place. Then, as slowly as an awakening sphinx, he straightened to his full height.

And left the room.

. . . .

Lydia sat before the fire, agonizing over her brutal words to the man who was saving her brother. Why in God's name had she chosen to believe the townspeople—most of whom she scarcely knew—over what she'd witnessed with her own eyes? He'd been deathly silent for the last several hours, explaining in clipped terms every move he was about to make.

"Now I'll pour some weak tea into a cup and help your brother to drink it."

Lydia grimaced. "All right, all right. You don't have to explain every move. Just the medical ones."

"Ah. So you only wish to pass judgment upon things about which you know little or nothing."

She felt her eyes flare with annoyance.

"Really, now. Must you be so exasperating? Forget I said anything."

She waited for him to speak, and when he finally did, it was to change the subject. Perhaps she'd been forgiven. She couldn't quite tell.

"Do you and your brother live here alone?"

The change of subject threw her for a moment. But his neutral tone was welcome after the stony words that had passed between them for the last few hours.

"Yes, but we have a day maid who comes in each morning. I sent her home when it started to snow. James also has someone who comes to help him with the livestock, but he sent him home, as well."

The doctor nodded, then helped Lydia rise when she held out her hand for assistance. Her throbbing head made her secretly welcome his attentiveness.

The man was tall and muscular, his tendons rippling where his sleeves had been rolled up. She prepared herself for his strong grasp. But nothing prepared her for the welcome tingle that traveled up her arm when she discovered his touch to be once again gentle, steady, even comforting.

Then, instead of releasing her hand, he stepped even closer to her. She tipped her head to look him in the eyes and he focused his gaze on hers. She sat still as stone until ever so slowly, his gaze lowered to her mouth.

He was going to kiss her. Lydia knew it as surely as she knew her own heart was beating like a smithy's hammer. As his hand came up to her cheek she fought the panic rising in her breast.

And then his thumb stroked the tender skin below her eye, making her bite her lower lip to stop its quivering.

He drew closer, peering into the depths of her right eye as she held her breath. But an instant later the heat rose to her cheeks.

The man wasn't trying to kiss her. He was examining her. That was all. No kiss, no caressing thumb. Just checking to see that her eyes were clear. As any doctor would.

Yet her heart was slow to release its vision.

In her mind, the doctor lowered his head until his lips touched hers.

In her mind, Lydia skimmed her palms up his soft linen shirt, then wrapped her arms around his neck.

In her mind, her fingers tangled in the hint of curls that covered his collar. She could literally feel its soft thickness even as he deepened their imaginary kiss.

She'd never felt so forward. It was not her nature to be biddable where men were concerned. Even though she'd been engaged to be married, and had been kissed once or twice, the boys' affections had never moved her as this fanciful kiss with the doctor had. How could anything be so mind-altering?

With a smile, the doctor raised his other hand to her other cheek, cradling her face as he smiled.

"It appears you're on the mend, Miss McDowell."

As he began to withdraw his hands, Lydia hoisted herself from the chair and put several paces between herself and the man who still had her blushing.

But he hadn't seemed to notice. He merely turned, walked to the window, and wiped the glass. "I don't think the snow has let up any."

"Are you saying you're stranded here?" Lydia was suddenly ashamed of the disdain in her voice.

He turned his head to look at her over his shoulder.

"I promise I shall leave at the earliest opportunity so nobody will discover you've been sequestered with the village murderer."

Lydia gasped. "I didn't mean—"

The doctor looked at her for several heart-stopping moments. "Of course you did."

Lydia turned sharply toward the stove on the far wall of the kitchen. "I made some stew earlier," Lydia said after several moments. "It's in the cold cellar. I'll heat it so we can have something to eat."

"Tell me where it is and I'll get it," he said.

"The hatch is there in the floor, just to your left. It's on the first shelf at the bottom of the steps," Lydia answered.

Joshua Jarvis lifted the hatch and prepared to descend into the cellar. Lydia braced her hands against the back of a chair. That silly bump on her head must have sent her temporarily mad. No matter which way she turned her gaze, she saw the kiss that had never happened, felt the lips that had never brushed hers, relished yet again the flood of emotion the kiss had launched.

The imaginary kiss, that is.

Lydia pushed herself away from the chair and went to the bedroom to check on James. She pressed her hand to his forehead, then rinsed the towel that was drying there in fresh, cold water. His head turned when the cool cloth touched him.

"Lydia?"

"Yes, James." She leaned closer to him and brushed several strands of hair from his temple.

"Is Doctor Jarvis still here?"

"Yes, James. It's snowing so hard I doubt he'll be able to leave for at least a day or two."

He reached a finger to point at her bandaged forehead. "Are you… all right?"

Lydia smiled. "Yes, James. I'm fine."

"Good. Could I have something to drink?"

"Of course," she said, lifting the restorative glass of wine to his lips.

Before she'd placed the glass back on the table, Doctor Jarvis entered the room. He walked to the bed and lifted the sheet covering her brother's wound.

Lydia didn't look at her brother's leg, but she could tell that Joshua Jarvis wasn't happy with what he saw. Her brother must have thought the same.

"Is something wrong?"

"Your wound is showing signs of infection. I have a poultice ready to put on it. Hopefully, that will draw out the infection."

"And if it doesn't?"

"We'll cross that bridge when we come to it."

James grasped the doctor's wrist. "Don't take off my leg, Doctor."

"Hopefully, it won't come to that."

Her brother turned to Lydia with anxious eyes. "Promise me you won't let him take off my leg, Lydia. I don't want to live with just one leg."

"Oh, James—"

"Promise me, Liddy."

Lydia drew a calming hand across her brother's brow. "I promise, James. I won't let the doctor remove your leg."

Her brother closed his eyes and fell asleep again, clearly relieved by her words.

"I'll heat up the stew," she said, rising from the bed and walking to the kitchen. She didn't look into the doctor's eyes. She knew he didn't agree with the promise she'd made her brother. She also knew she wouldn't like the censure she would see on his face.

She'd had no right to make such a promise. She didn't hold the power to assure her brother that he would awaken with both his legs still attached.

. . . .

Lydia heated the stew, then served a bowl to Joshua Jarvis. She filled a bowl for herself and sat across the table from him.

"You shouldn't have made that promise to your brother."

Lydia absently stirred her stew which gave her something to do without facing the doctor.

"If the infection takes hold, the leg might have to come off in order to save his life."

Lydia shook her head, then placed her spoon on the table beside her bowl. "He won't survive if you take off his leg."

"He might not survive if I don't."

Lydia swiped at the tear that ran down her cheek.

The doctor reached for a slice of bread and proceeded to butter it. "We have time before we have to make the decision as to whether we can save the leg or not. So, try not to worry yet."

Lydia lifted her gaze and locked on to the doctor's empathetic expression. She saw a kindness she hadn't expected. A sense of understanding that didn't go with the rumors she'd heard about him.

She knew his talk of amputation was only realistic, but she couldn't bear it. Nor could she bear even speaking of it.

"How did you find yourself here in Middleton?" she asked.

The doctor paused eating the stew and looked at her.

"When I was studying anatomy, I formed a friendship with two other students, Bennet Chamberlain and Daniel Paulson. Bennet took a position in Russetsville, a village about an hour's ride from here. Shortly after he arrived in Russetsville, he wrote me that there was an elderly doctor here in Middleton who was contemplating retirement. He thought it was the perfect place for me to start a practice."

The doctor caught her eyes and smiled. "I thought it would be the perfect place, too. It was close to Bennet, and not that far from where Daniel had set up his practice. We could support one another. Plus, I never wanted to set up my practice in the city and Middleton seemed the perfect place to go."

"I imagine you've come to regret your decision, though," Lydia said.

"Let's simply say it hasn't turned out exactly as I thought it would."

"Well, it's hardly surprising given the unexplained deaths of your two patients."

Joshua lifted his cup to his mouth and look a long swallow of the coffee she'd just brewed, then set his cup back onto the table. "I'd like to say there had to be a cause other than my negligence, but I can't imagine what it might be."

"Why were you treating Mrs. Smithers?"

"She'd come to me with a cough that refused to go away. I'd given her an elixir to relieve her cough and she seemed to be getting better. Then, overnight, she must have taken a turn for the worse. When I went to check on her the next morning, I found her dead."

"What about Ivan Crumbly?"

"His death was more puzzling. He'd fallen off the back of a wagon and had broken some ribs. He also had several cuts and bruises from his fall, but nothing life-threatening. I bound his ribs and took care of his cuts and bruises and sent him home. He worked with his brother at the mill. When he didn't show up for work the following day, his brother went to check on him. He found him dead."

"What do you think he died from?"

Doctor Jarvis pushed his chair back from the table and rose. He walked to the window and wiped a pane of glass in order to look out.

"I know this will sound impossible," he said without turning to face her. "But I can't help but think neither Mrs. Smithers nor Ivan Crumbly died from natural causes."

Lydia struggled to take in what Joshua was saying, but it was difficult. Everyone else thought the two patients didn't die of natural causes. Now the doctor was admitting it himself? "What do you think they died from?"

"I think they may have been murdered."

Lydia sucked in a shuddering breath. Was he baiting her?

"I know," the doctor said. He turned to face her. "You think I'm imagining things. And I don't blame you. What I'm suggesting sounds impossible."

Not impossible, she thought.

"What brought you to that conclusion?"

"Several unusual happenings. First, the two deaths happened less than a week apart. And neither of my patients were so ill that they were at death's door. And…"

She watched his face change as if a deep worry had just traveled across his brow.

"There's another reason, isn't there?"

"Yes," the doctor said, then came closer to the table and sat. "Both of the bodies had a strange smell when I leaned close to them."

"What kind of strange smell?"

"The smell of arsenic."

"Have you told anyone this?"

Joshua shook his head. "Arsenic is a staple in any physician's chemistry cabinet. They were already hurling accusations, why would I give them my assessment and put the final nail in my own coffin?"

"And all of Middleton just turned against you?"

"It was as if I'd brought the plague to Middleton. No one came to me with even a scratch to take care of. They even stepped to the opposite side of the street when I approached."

Lydia shuddered. It must be a horrid thing to endure. And now she was adding her own condemnation, even after she'd watched him successfully treat her brother. And her own banged up head.

If she were honest with herself, her own observations coupled with her brother's clear support of the man were giving her every reason to admire Joshua Jarvis. Not condemn him.

"I'm sorry I said such horrible things to you earlier."

A sad smile lifted the corners of his mouth. "I can't blame you. I'm simply surprised that your brother insisted that you come for me."

"I'm not," she answered. "James has always been a good judge of character. He's never been one to follow the crowd mentality. He said he was sure Doctor Weatherby would take one look at his leg and cut it off, whereas he'd have a better chance of saving his leg if you took care of him."

"Good judge of character, eh? Then, I'd better do everything I can to live up to his high expectations."

The doctor rose from the table. "Would you bring in some of your stew and I'll see if I can't get your brother to eat a bit?"

Lydia watched the doctor leave as she filled a bowl with some stew, mashed it to a consistency easier for James to manage, then followed him.

What was there about this man that drew her to him even against her own suspicions? What was there about him that caused her stomach to churn and every nerve in her body to tremble?

She didn't know, but it had to mean something. The turmoil his very nearness prompted meant something she didn't feel equipped to battle. After the way she'd guarded her heart these many months, she felt it was only safe to resist any and all temptation. But in truth, if guarding her heart had been her mission, she feared she'd already surrendered.

Chapter Four

Joshua fed Lydia's brother as much as he could get down him. He followed that with anything liquid James McDowell would drink. When he finished providing as much nourishment as he could, he concentrated on changing the bandages on the fellow's wound.

He wouldn't fool himself. McDowell's wound was severe. Joshua had cleaned it several times, reaming out the most inflamed tissue in an effort to stave off infection. There was nothing more he could do to assure McDowell or his sister that he could save McDowell's limb. Not with the medicines he had at hand.

"Is there anything more you need?" Lydia asked from the opposite side of the bed.

"No. I managed to get him to eat and drink a little, so that's a good sign. I'll keep changing the bandages in hopes of stifling the infection."

Lydia rose from her brother's side and went to look out the window. "The snow has stopped."

"That's good. I need to go out to feed and water my horse."

"I'll stay with James until you return," she said, then walked to the basin and tidied the nightstand.

There was something very fragile in the way she moved, very delicate in her demeanor when she sat on the edge of the bed to place cloths on her brother's forehead.

"What made you leave your home and come to stay with your brother?"

Her hand paused in the act of rinsing a fresh cloth.

"I... um... James was alone, and needed someone to help him with the farm."

"I'm sure that's true," Joshua said. "But why do I think there is more to the reason you came here?"

"Why would you think that? Not everything is a puzzle, you know."

"If you say so," Joshua answered. He couldn't help but smile. "So your brother was lonely, and his good-hearted sister put her life on hold and rushed to his little cottage, just because he asked?"

The lady placed her trembling hands in her lap and clenched them tightly. Whatever her reason, it was no doubt difficult to talk about.

Joshua didn't think she was going to answer him and was just about to put on his coat and go to the barn when she breathed a deep sigh.

"He didn't ask. I came to live with my brother because I couldn't stay with my parents any longer."

"Because?"

"Because I found it impossible to face my mother's looks of pity and my father's expressions of frustration because he couldn't do anything to help me."

"Why did your parents feel pity and helplessness?"

"If you must know, I was engaged to be married to a man I'd known my entire life. We grew up together and never doubted we would marry. But..." Lydia paused, then breathed a heavy sigh and softened her tone. "The night before our wedding, the man I was to marry eloped with my best friend."

"I see."

She lifted her gaze and looked him in the eyes. "My father is the local vicar in Staybridge, and he and my mother have always been the most loving parents any children could ask for. There has never been a hint of scandal or disappointment attached to any of us."

Lydia rose from the bed and finished rinsing the cloth. "But, everything changed that day three years ago."

"Did you love him?"

Lydia shrugged. "To be honest, I'd never taken the time to think about it. I always thought I did, but now, I'm not sure what love is. I know I liked him. But now I…"

"You dislike him," Joshua finished for her.

She lifted her head and locked her gaze with his. "No. I feel nothing at all for him. Sometimes I can't imagine that I ever loved him."

Joshua studied Lydia's serious expression. There was something haunting and painful in her eyes. Something that told him she'd been hurt so badly that she'd lost much of her self-esteem. "So you came to live with your brother to start over."

A smile brightened her expression and her eyes shone with happiness. "I hadn't thought of it that way, but yes. I came to help James because I needed to start over. I needed to escape the expressions of pity, and find the happy, confident person I used to be."

"Then I hope you find that person."

"Thank you," she said in a firm, commanding voice. "I hope I find that person, too. I liked her much better than the person I've become."

Joshua gave her a comforting smile, then put on his coat, gloves, scarf, and hat and left for the barn. The snow had indeed stopped and the sun was shining.

He was surprised to realize that he felt better than he had in a long, long time, and he owed it all to Lydia McDowell. She wasn't nearly as forbidding as she'd led him to believe.

. . . .

Joshua watched Lydia tend her brother for the next two days, keeping him comfortable and forcing him to drink cool water even when he didn't want to. She cajoled him into eating more of the stew she'd made in an effort to keep his strength up. Outside the wind gained strength, whipping each new snow flurry into picturesque drifts of white that buried every pathway and lane.

He rejoiced at her pleasure when her brother woke and even spoke to her. They had an enduring bond of sibling love and support that was gratifying to see.

"I'm sorry you can't escape," James groused at her one morning after Joshua finished cleaning his leg and putting fresh bandages over his wound. The air was fairly blue from the epithets that spilled through James's gritted teeth each time they had to repeat the painful procedure.

"And just where would I go, I wonder?"

"Back to Mama and Papa, of course."

Joshua turned his head and looked at her over his shoulder, curious to hear her answer.

"Why would I do that?" she asked.

"Well, Jarvis's torture does bring out the worst in me. And whatever you do, do not tell Papa what you've heard here."

"You're right. I'm not used to hearing such language, but I'm certain even Papa would excuse you if he saw the dreadful state of your poor leg."

"Is your father so straight-laced?" Joshua asked.

Lydia turned her attention to where he stood at the foot of the bed. He was making more bandages from the sheet she'd given him.

"No," Lydia and James answered in unison. "But he's never allowed any of us to use profanity," James finished.

"So where did you learn such language?" Lydia asked.

"Where did I learn it?" James chuckled. "Do tell, sister dear, when did *you* begin to understand they were even off-color words? Hm?"

James grinned and dropped his head onto the pillow with a deep sigh.

Joshua stepped around the bed and placed his hand on her brother's forehead.

"Keep doing what you're doing and we may save that leg yet. That means rest."

Lydia walked over to the bedside table and mixed James something for the pain. She helped him drink it, then sat at his side until he fell asleep. When she seemed sure he was asleep, she and Joshua left the room. Lydia sank into her comfortable chair and Joshua walked to the parlor window.

"Is he going to be alright?" Lydia asked.

"Yes, he'll live. I'm not sure yet that he'll keep his leg."

Lydia looked weary as she brushed curling tendrils of hair from her pretty face. "James has never been one to sit in idleness. It will kill him if he can't work."

"Then let's hope we can save it."

Lydia lifted her head until her gaze locked with his. He slowly took several steps until he stood in front of her. Unable to stop his hands from reaching for her, he held them out.

Lydia placed her hands in his and let him pull her to her feet. He drew his hands slowly up her arms until they rested on her shoulders. How good it felt to draw her close.

"If I had a sister I'd want her to be just like you."

Lydia laughed. "You want a sour, bossy old maid for a sister?"

His smile felt a bit crooked. "No," he said. "I'd want a sister who cared about me as much as you care about James." His thumbs began to knead her shoulders. "I'd want a sister whose intelligence and wit would keep my days from such damnable boredom."

He lowered his chin, bringing his eyes closer to her, feeling the rightness of his words.

"I'd want a girl who—"

With the slightest pressure of his hands he urged her closer.

"You mean you'd want a sister," Lydia whispered.

"I mean...I'd want a woman," he whispered in return.

He lowered his head, and with her eyes riveted upon his lips, he touched her lips with his.

He forced himself to keep his hands from pressing her closer, but she came of her own accord. She placed her arms around his waist and leaned her face against his chest. There was no doubt that she must be able to feel the rapid pounding of his heart that raucously increased its pace until it raced as if there were a team of eight inside his chest thundering to win a race.

Joshua Jarvis gently placed his finger beneath Lydia's chin and pressed upward to encourage her to lift her head. He caught her gaze with his and slowly lowered his head until his mouth covered hers.

Her lips were warm, lush, soft, and alluring in a way that stirred him. His kiss escalated into the hungry melding of two people who had just discovered a passion that had lain dormant between them. A passion he knew he'd felt in the first hours she'd stood at his side tending her brother.

Joshua deepened his kiss, showing Lydia the magnitude of his feeling for her. He kissed her again and again as his arms kneaded her shoulders, causing her light shawl to slip away. He was aware of her in a way he'd never experienced before, barely controlling the desperation that threatened to conquer him. Like she was conquering him.

. . . .

Lydia tried to give reason to what was happening between them, but it was impossible to make sense of her confused thoughts. It wasn't as if she'd never been kissed before and yet that's exactly what it felt like. Any kiss she'd known previously now seemed like a feeble pretender.

Even though she'd been engaged to be married and the man she thought would be her husband had kissed her once or twice, he'd never kissed her like Joshua Jarvis was kissing her now.

Joshua opened his mouth atop hers and Lydia followed his lead. The sweetness of his lips left her craving more, and she pressed against him with abandon. Allowed him access without hesitation.

His arms tightened around her, clasping her to him as if he feared if he didn't hold her tightly enough, he'd lose her. But he would not. She knew that now. Had known it for some hours now. She couldn't imagine a place she'd rather be than in his arms, nestled close to him while he held her as if she were the most important person in the world to him.

Joshua kissed her again, then lifted his mouth from her.

A slight moan of protest echoed around her and it took a moment for Lydia to realize the sound came from her. It took another moment for her to realize Joshua had cut off their kiss because someone was knocking on the door.

"Shh," Joshua warned her as he placed a finger over her lips. "Give me time to get to your brother's bedroom, then answer the door."

Lydia nodded, trying desperately not to feel his absence so shamefully. After two long, chastising breaths she straightened her clothes as he walked away from her. When she was sure he was out of sight, she went to the door and opened it.

"Good day, Miss McDowell," a girlish voice said.

"Miss Carmichael? My goodness! Do come in."

Lydia opened the door and stepped back so Jenny Carmichael could enter. The girl stood on the door mat stamping huge clumps of snow from her trousers.

It was difficult not to stare at the girl's appearance. She was clearly wearing her father's clothing—an oversized coat and baggy trousers tucked into boots large enough for two feet. As she unwound the knitted muffler from her head more snow fell to the floor.

The young woman appeared ill at ease, much as she had appeared the one time James had introduced Lydia to her at the stile that separated his property from her father's holding. She and her father were James's closest neighbors.

"I'm sure you find it odd that I'm here, Miss McDowell." She stood on the doormat as she rather obviously fought to settle her nerves.

"Not at all," Lydia lied. "Are you in need of something?"

"Oh no. But father told me how grievously James was injured by the bull."

"We were so very grateful your father was there to help me get James into the cottage. He's very ill, but we think he's going to make a full recovery."

The girl's agitation seemed to escalate. "But that's just it, you see. You…you brought Doctor Jarvis to attend him. Instead of Doctor Weatherby. Papa saw Doctor Jarvis tending his horse."

"That's true," Lydia said. "In fact, Doctor Jarvis is here right now. He's barely left James's bedside since he arrived."

The Carmichael girl cleared her throat. As she shifted nervously, Lydia noted her bitten nails.

"Do you think that was wise, Miss McDowell?"

"What? Asking Doctor Jarvis to attend James instead of Doctor Weatherby?"

Jenny's cheeks darkened. "Well he's a murderer!" She blurted out the words and then clamped a hand over her own mouth. "Can I see him? I need to know that he's being taken care of."

Lydia assessed the concern on the youngster's girlish face. It was obvious she cared for James, but considering Jenny's age and lack of maturity, Lydia couldn't help but think Jenny had an awkward crush on her brother. From the comments James had made, he did not harbor any tender feelings for his neighbor.

The girl took a step closer. "Please, Miss McDowell. Please, allow me to see him. Just for a few minutes. I promise I won't bother him."

Lydia didn't have the heart to refuse the girl's request. "Only for a moment, Jenny. James is very ill. I don't want him to be disturbed."

"Oh, thank you. Thank you," Jenny repeated as she followed Lydia to James's bedroom. When the girl entered the room she froze and glared at Joshua Jarvis until he stepped back to give the girl a degree of privacy. But Lydia remained in the doorway while Jenny rushed to James's bedside.

Something compelled Lydia to stay at her post.

Jenny reached out to hold James's hand then whispered in his ear. "I love you, James. I'll love you forever, 'til death do us part."

Her brother's eyes widened, and something akin to alarm crossed his face.

A shiver ran down Lydia's spine and she stepped into James's room, indicating it was time for Jenny to leave.

The girl reluctantly followed Lydia to the door. Lydia breathed a sigh of relief when the neighbor was gone from their house. There'd been something about Jenny Carmichael's visit that made a slight shiver trace the base of her neck.

"Is your brother's visitor gone?" Joshua asked coming back into the room with a basin of fresh water.

"Yes."

"I'm glad. I need to leave for a while."

"Why? How long?"

"I'm not sure. I must go to Amesbury to get a solution I think will help your brother. I'm sure it can stem the infection. Depending on the roads, I might be gone a day or more."

Lydia thought of her brother lying still and pale on the bed. "He's getting worse, isn't he?"

"He's not improving like I'd hoped he would. He needs a stronger medicine than I have if we stand a chance of keeping the infection from spreading."

Lydia took a step closer to Joshua, praying that he would take her in his arms and hold her. She needed his strength more now than she'd ever needed it.

Without hesitation, Joshua reached out and pulled her to him. He wrapped his arms around her and brought his mouth down over hers.

"I won't be long," he said at last.

"Promise me," Lydia begged, more frightened over her brother's volatile condition than she'd ever felt before.

"I promise, Lydia. I promise," he repeated, then kissed her once more. "I'll return as quickly as possible."

In a rustle of coat and muffler he was gone.

. . . .

Not long after Joshua left, her brother's fever spiked and refused to go down. Lydia fought it with every skill she possessed. Then the edges of the wound turned an angry red, and nothing she did seemed to help. No amount of cold water eased her brother's fevered brow, and no careful application of salve quieted the enflamed wound.

James thrashed on the bed, flinging his arms to and fro, more than once striking her on the shoulder and across the face.

Lydia was desperate. She had no answers. She didn't know what to do that would ease her brother's thrashing. If only Joshua hadn't left her.

After flailing uncontrollably for what seemed hours, James finally collapsed from exhaustion, leaving the wound gaping and oozing from the stitches that had been torn free.

Where was Joshua? What should she do?

Before she had time to reconsider, Lydia retrieved her coat, tied a heavy scarf around her neck, and raced to the neighboring cottage for help.

Chapter Five

JOSHUA PUSHED HIS MARE through the heavy snow as fast as he dared. It had taken him longer than he'd anticipated to reach Amesbury and get the tonic he needed. It had taken his mount longer to travel through the drifts clogging the roads. At last he saw the smoke rising from the chimney on James McDowell's cottage. He was almost there. He was finally back to Lydia.

When he reached the little house on Carriage Hill, he jumped from his mount and raced to the wooden door. With a turn of the latch he shoved the door open.

"Lydia! I'm back, Lydia."

Joshua knew right away that something was wrong. The eerie silence that met him was a like a warning shot to alert him that nothing was as it should be. He raced through the house to the bedroom where Lydia's brother should be lying on the bed. But the covers were strewn about and the bed was empty.

"Lydia!"

Instead of hearing Lydia's voice, Joshua only heard James McDowell's painful moan coming from the far side of the room.

Joshua raced around the bed and knelt beside James McDowell. First, he checked Lydia's brother's leg, then he grabbed a sheet from the bed and wrapped it around the exposed wound. He'd torn open several of the stitches and Joshua worked swiftly to stop the bleeding. When he had the wound wrapped, he struggled to pick James up from the floor and place him back on the bed.

"Here," he said lifting his head and placing some laudanum-laced wine to his lips.

James drank a long swallow of the liquid, then sank back to the pillow.

"Where's your sister?" Joshua asked.

"Right here, Doctor Jarvis."

Joshua looked over his shoulder to where Lydia stood in the doorway with Doctor Weatherby at her side. He shifted his gaze from Lydia to the older doctor, then back again. Anger he failed to keep at bay reared its ugly head.

"You weren't here and I needed help."

Joshua glared at her. He refused to shift his gaze from her. Refused to forgive her for not trusting him.

"I didn't know what to do, Joshua. I was so afraid."

"You couldn't wait a little longer for me to return?"

"James became suddenly worse. I was afraid he was going to die. Mr. Carmichael got me through to Dr. Weatherby who…who was good enough to come."

Joshua had no choice but to shift his gaze from her. Not because of the tear in her eye, but because she didn't trust him. She no doubt hadn't trusted him from the beginning.

He couldn't look at her any longer. She'd admitted she didn't want to come for him but her brother had insisted. In his absence she'd managed to get her way. The doctor she'd wanted all along to tend her brother was here to take his place.

"I'll leave you with the doctor. You have what you've wanted from the beginning."

"No, Joshua. Don't leave."

"There's nothing for me to do here. I'm sure Doctor Weatherby can do anything that needs to be done."

"Joshua?"

There was a pleading in her voice. A desperation that tore through him. But he could not give in. She'd used him enough.

Without looking in her direction, Joshua shook his head, then took a step back when the older doctor took his place beside the bed. He bent over Lydia's brother's leg and lifted the bandage Joshua had just placed over the wound.

Joshua couldn't bear to watch someone else caring for his patient. He turned to leave.

"The leg has to come off or he'll die," Doctor Weatherby stated in an emotionless voice.

Joshua stopped and turned. "No! His leg does *not* have to come off."

"It does if you don't want him to die."

"No!"

Doctor Weatherby glared at him with a hostile expression. "It would help if you would assist me instead of arguing with me."

"No, I won't assist you in taking off his leg. It doesn't need to come off." Joshua knelt beside Lydia's brother and took his hand. "Your leg doesn't need to come off. I can save your leg."

"I don't want to die."

"You won't, James. I promise you won't."

"Lydia?" her brother pleaded.

Lydia turned her head until her eyes locked with her brother's.

Joshua waited. He waited until she gave the nod that she trusted him over Doctor Weatherby. He waited until she indicated she trusted Joshua's skills as a doctor. If she didn't, there could never be anything between them.

"Trust me, Lydia," Joshua pleaded softly.

Without lifting her gaze from his, she nodded. "I do, Joshua. I trust you."

Joshua's heart swelled until he feared his chest might explode. Before he could adequately respond, Lydia reached out and clasped her fingers to his. The feel of her flesh against his gave him a newfound sense of courage he hadn't realized he needed.

"I warn you, Miss McDowell," the elderly Doctor Weatherby said in a stern voice. "The longer you wait, you're sentencing your brother to certain death."

Lydia turned away from the doctor's reprimand, then heard the door close as Doctor Weatherby left. She kept her gaze focused on Joshua's until the house was quiet. "What do you want me to do?"

"I've brought the liniment we need to stop the infection from spreading. Help me clean your brother's wound again, then warm up this concoction. Once we've applied it, we bandage his leg again and wait."

Lydia took the foul-smelling pouch from him and warmed it on the brazier in the corner of the bedroom, then helped him tend to her brother.

They worked together in harmonious fashion. Joshua covered the wound liberally with the liniment, removed the most damaged flesh, then re-applied the remainder of the concoction he'd brought from the apothecary, while Lydia readied the laudanum and cut new bandages to wrap around her brother's leg. When Joshua finished sewing the jagged wound, he applied another hot poultice, stood up and rolled his stiff shoulders. "Now, we wait," he said as he washed his hands and cleared the soiled bedclothes and cloths from the bed.

Joshua watched her as she pulled the covers over her brother. There were tears in her eyes and Joshua knew the ordeal had been more traumatic than she'd let on. She was truly upset and on the verge of collapse.

He walked closer to her and turned her to face him. Then, he pulled her into his arms and held her.

"Your brother will be fine now," he said with more conviction than he felt. He walked with her to a large velvet wing chair and sat down, relieved when she allowed him to draw her onto his lap. He wrapped a blanket over her and held her while she softly cried.

When she quieted, he kissed her forehead, then watched until she closed her eyes and slept.

. . . .

Her brother's fever rose quickly, an initial response to the invasive treatment. Lydia and Joshua battled with everything Joshua knew to do. James thrashed so violently that Joshua was forced to throw himself over his body to keep the young man from falling from the bed. Then, just as suddenly, his thrashing stopped and he trembled from chills that attacked him.

Lydia gathered as many covers as she could find to keep her brother warm, but nothing seemed to help. And Joshua feared he couldn't keep his promise to save her brother.

The hours dragged on endlessly, and Joshua fought with all his might to encourage James McDowell to stay with them and not give in to death. The pale expression on Lydia's face told him she feared Joshua's promise had been a lie.

But finally, her brother's fever broke and Joshua knew he'd turned the corner and would live. Lydia sat on the edge of the bed beside her brother. With trembling fingers she brushed back strands of dark mahogany hair from her brother's forehead. Joshua had never seen a more tender sight.

Then slowly, she lifted her head and looked at him with tears of joy and relief running down her cheeks. "Thank you," she whispered.

"You're welcome," Joshua answered. There was no explaining the emotions he felt. He'd never prayed so hard in all his life. He'd never prayed more fervently that a patient would live. He knew if James McDowell died he'd never allow himself to hold Lydia again.

How could she ever forgive him if he failed to keep his promise?

Joshua checked the wound while Lydia straightened the room. When Joshua was sure his patient slept soundly, they walked arm in arm to the drawing room. Their immense relief seemed to unite them, and he sensed her pressing into his side as a silent thank you.

He turned, eagerly welcoming the gratitude he saw in her eyes as she turned her face up to his.

"We did it," she whispered.

Joshua wrapped his arms around her and lowered his mouth until his lips were just a breath away from hers.

"We did it," he echoed.

He was frozen in the moment, afraid to press for a kiss, afraid to back away. But a moment later she saved him from his agony. Ever so slowly she reached a hand to his cheek and laid it there.

"Thank you," she mouthed, no sound escaping from her lips that hovered so dangerously close.

It was apology and invitation all wrapped in two small words. Joshua felt the freeing force of them through his entire chest. He lowered his head and touched her lips that had been so tenderly tentative before. But this time they welcomed him with stunning eagerness. Her lips drew his into the kind of kiss that opened his heart. She returned his kiss with as much desperation as he felt. It was enough to carry him to the brink of control. And she answered his kisses with the same depth and desire as he commanded.

Lydia's arms wrapped around his neck and her fingers threaded through his hair. Joshua feared he wouldn't be able to stifle the passion that threatened to overtake him.

"We need to stop," he whispered as he broke their kiss.

"I know," she answered on a sweet moan.

They stood poised, whether for another kiss or to turn away. But Joshua couldn't bring himself to release her. He was too desperate to keep her in his arms.

Beyond the window he saw the sun, usually a welcome sight. But today it only signaled the melting snow to come, the opening of the snowbound paths so people would come now to intrude upon their privacy.

"I was afraid James wasn't going to live," she said with her cheek pressed to his chest.

"So was I," he answered.

"Were you?" she said, lifting her head to look at him. "You didn't seem as if you were." There was a look of astonishment on her face. "You seemed so in control. So sure of yourself."

Joshua smiled at her. "For your sake I had to appear as if I didn't doubt my abilities."

"You're a wonderful doctor, Joshua. Promise me you'll never doubt yourself again."

Joshua smiled down on her. "I'll try," he said. "But no matter how excellent the doctor, God may have other plans for the patient."

Lydia smiled, then returned her cheek to his chest. "You're right. I know you are."

Joshua kissed the top of her head and held her for a while longer. Finally, he broke their contact. "Will you be alright if I leave for a little while? I need to go home to clean up and change clothes. I also need to bring back more supplies."

"Yes," Lydia answered. "I'll be fine. James is sleeping peacefully, and I have plenty to do here."

"Good," Joshua answered. "I shouldn't be gone long. Only a few hours."

Joshua kissed Lydia's forehead, then left. He was in a hurry to leave so he could return all the sooner.

To know someone would be waiting for him when he returned was a wonderful feeling.

Chapter Six

ONCE JOSHUA LEFT, LYDIA SPENT most of her time in the kitchen baking bread she'd started earlier and baking an apple pie for her brother. Apple was his favorite and she knew when he woke he would be hungry.

She'd just taken the bread out of the oven when there was a rather timid knock on the door. Lydia's first thought was that Jenny had returned to call on James. This time she was determined not to let her in. She'd even find the opportunity to tell their young neighbor that her infatuation with James was nothing more than a schoolgirl crush. And that her imagined feelings for James were not returned. Nor would they ever be.

Lydia dried her hands on a kitchen towel, then went to the front door and opened it.

The visitor wasn't Jenny, but Doctor Weatherby's wife, Ethel.

"Good day, Miss McDowell," the elderly woman greeted. "May I come in?"

"Of course," Lydia answered. "Please. Come in."

Lydia took a step to the side and ushered Ethel Weatherby into the house. She was surprised to see much of the snow had been swept away from the stepping stones in the dooryard. *Dear, dear Joshua!*

"Would you care for a cup of tea? It won't take me but a moment to brew some."

"No. No. I can't stay. I just stopped by for a moment."

This was the first time Lydia had conversed with the doctor's wife other than a casual greeting after church on a Sunday morning. She studied the expression on Ethel Weatherby's face. She seemed a pleasant woman with a sweet smile and a bit of the faraway dreamer in her eyes. She reminded Lydia of her grandmother and Lydia felt an immediate kinship with the woman.

"I have come to make amends," the doctor's wife said, holding out a carefully wrapped parcel. "A sort of peace offering, you see. My husband described the conversation he had with Doctor Jarvis.

"Ah, yes. I'm sorry to say Doctor Jarvis left several hours ago. He did say he would call on my brother later this afternoon, so I expect him at any time. Would you like to wait and speak with him?"

"No... no. That's not necessary. I'll just leave this bowl of my favorite soup. I brought it for your brother."

Mrs. Weatherby held out the bowl of soup wrapped in newsprint and a kitchen towel to keep it warm. Lydia took the bowl and laid it on the sideboard before motioning Mrs. Weatherby to a seat in the drawing room.

"It smells delicious," she said with a grateful smile.

"I often take it to my husband's patients. He says he's not sure if it's his doctoring skills that heal his patients, or my soup."

Lydia smiled. What a generous way for the man to speak of his wife.

"I doubt that, though. My husband is an excellent doctor. He's cared for the people of Middleton for more than forty years and brought hundreds of babes into the world."

"That's quite an accomplishment," Lydia said.

"Yes, it is," Mrs. Weatherby agreed. "Now, I must be going. My son is waiting in the carriage. Please, be sure your brother has a bit of soup. It will help him get better soon."

"Thank you, Mrs. Weatherby. I'm sure he'll enjoy it."

"Good," the elderly lady said, then rose from her chair. "Just know that my husband meant no hard feelings, as I'm sure Doctor Jarvis didn't either."

"No, of course not. I'm sure you agree with me when I say that Middleton is a large enough village to keep two doctors busy."

"Hm. Yes. That's what Elias says. Middleton is large enough for both of them."

Mrs. Weatherby made her way to the front door, then bade Lydia good day and left.

Lydia watched the elderly lady's son help her into the little two-seater trap and click the reins. The horse took off at a steady pace as if it was used to taking the doctor or his wife about the countryside.

When Mrs. Weatherby had driven out of sight, Lydia carried the soup into the kitchen. It smelled delicious and she wondered what was in it to make such an appealing aroma. She would have to ask Mrs. Weatherby for the recipe, if she would give it up.

"Are you awake, James?" she called as she cut a piece of the bread she'd recently taken out of the oven. Unable to resist temptation, she tore off another small piece of bread for herself. She just wanted a small taste.

"Yes," his weak voice answered.

"I have a treat for you," she sang.

Lydia dipped the small piece of bread into the bowl and ate it. It was absolutely delicious. She would definitely have to ask Ethel Weatherby for the recipe. Heeding her growling stomach, she quickly downed two large spoonfuls of the savory broth.

Lydia placed the bowl of soup and the bread on a tray, then carried it to James's bedroom. Just as she crossed the threshold into James's bedroom, she was struck with the most wrenching pain she'd ever experienced. It began below her heart, then plummeted through her abdomen, stopping her in her tracks and stealing her breath.

She placed the tray on the bedside table, then doubled over in pain.

"Lydia, what's wrong?" her brother asked, but Lydia couldn't answer him. The pain was too severe.

"Lydia!"

Lydia cried out in an agonizing moan, then fell to the floor as the world went black around her.

. . . .

Joshua was gone longer than he'd anticipated, but now that Lydia's brother was out of danger, he didn't worry overmuch. There were several medicines he needed to add to his bag, including more laudanum, and creams to relax the damaged muscles.

By the time he hitched his horse to his buggy, it was nearing late afternoon. He'd been gone most of the day and wanted to return before nightfall.

He was glad when he saw James McDowell's cottage.

He pulled his horse and buggy into the cowshed and unhitched his mare and made sure his horse had plenty of food and water. Then, he made his way to the cottage.

"I'm back, Lydia," he announced as he entered.

No one answered his call.

"Lydia?"

"Help!"

Joshua heard James McDowell's call for help and raced down the hall. When he reached the bedroom, he found Lydia's brother on the floor next to Lydia.

"What happened?" Joshua asked as he knelt. He touched her forehead and her cheeks. She was pale and her lips were turning blue. She was cold and clammy and her forehead was dripping with perspiration.

"What happened?" Joshua repeated.

"I'm not sure," James replied. "We had a visitor. Doctor Weatherby's wife came to call and she brought over a bowl of soup. It's sitting on the bedside table. Lydia told me it was delicious so she must have tasted it. As soon as she set it down, she clutched her stomach and doubled over in pain."

Joshua leaned over and smelled Lydia's breath.

"No!" he cried out on a painful moan. "Lydia, wake up!" He shook her gently, then more forcefully. "Wake up, Lydia!"

The familiar smell of arsenic threw him into mild panic, but it was the underlying odor he hadn't detected before that caused his heart to shudder.

Belladonna. Or deadly nightshade as many knew it. Ten berries could kill a grown man.

The deathly combination set Joshua into swift motion. He pulled several pillows from the bed and propped Lydia into a semi-sitting position. Then, he reached for his medical bag and sifted through the items inside it until he found the bottle he wanted.

"What's wrong with her?" James asked. Fear and panic was evident in his voice.

"She's been poisoned."

"Poisoned?"

"Yes. I'm guessing from the soup Mrs. Weatherby brought."

"But why—."

Joshua opened a shutter and tossed out the water that was still in the basin on the bedside table, then placed it on the floor next to Lydia. With care, he held her head and poured a generous amount of ipecac syrup into her mouth. He had to be careful not to give her too much, but enough to induce vomiting. He had to empty her stomach or she would die from the poison she'd ingested.

"Swallow, Lydia," Joshua encouraged. "That's a good girl," he pleaded. "Swallow."

Most of the liquid he'd poured into her mouth escaped and ran down her chin.

"Drink, Lydia. You have to drink this."

He poured another dose of the ipecac syrup into her mouth. This time he held his finger beneath her chin to keep her mouth closed while he massaged her throat.

"That's good, Lydia. Now, get rid of the poison that's inside you."

He'd barely finished his sentence before Lydia's body jerked. Again and again she convulsed before giving up the contents of her stomach.

"That's my girl," Joshua said as he held her head over the basin. "Get rid of all of it," he encouraged.

She clutched at his coat, her eyes huge with fear.

"Joshua!" Her fingers tightened as she fought the demons that dueled inside her. "Joshua, I—"

"Lydia? Stay with me, now. Lydia?"

Joshua willed her to win her struggle, and for a moment it appeared she would though her eyes remained wildly dilated. Then, with no warning, her body went limp. Her eyes fluttered closed and her head lolled to the side.

"Lydia!"

Joshua was horrified. Had he given her too much syrup? Not enough? How could he know without being certain what she had ingested?

But it was the worst thought that stole the breath from him. Was she the third patient he'd failed to save?

Was he the one who had killed her?

Joshua let out a cry of denial.

With both arms around Lydia he rolled her from side to side, then lifted first one of her arms above her head, then the other. Twice he repeated the process, watching every second for a telltale sign that her heart would resume its rhythm.

Then, a moment before despair set in, he felt a quickening in her body. In the same instant she gasped and flung her hand to grasp his lapel.

She was breathing.

"Thank God," Joshua whispered. "Thank God!"

He sat on the floor rocking her back and forth.

His heart hammered at the thought that he had lost her, but her will to live had been stronger than his despair. All he could do was continue to rock her gently in his arms.

Eventually, she sank into exhaustion and Joshua reached for a damp cloth and wiped her face. Her eyes fluttered and she struggled to focus.

"You need to open your eyes, Lydia. You need to stay awake for a while."

Again and again he encouraged her to wake. Finally, she opened her eyes and stared at him.

"What happened?" she asked.

He nearly laughed like a lunatic at the dear sound of her voice.

"You were poisoned."

Her eyes narrowed and she shook her head in disbelief. Her confusion was obvious.

"My stomach hurts."

"I'm sure it does. And it will for a while."

Joshua turned to where James lay on the floor. "I'm going to get your sister to her bed. Then I'll come back and take care of you. Don't move until I return. You've done enough damage to your leg. You can't afford to injure it further."

"I'm all right," James answered. "But will she be?"

"Yes," Joshua answered as he rose from the floor with Lydia in his arms. "She's going to need to rest for a few days, but when her stomach has time to relax, she'll feel better."

Joshua coached Lydia to breathe deeply. In, out. And again. In out, until he was satisfied that her heart and lungs had emerged intact from the state of crisis. Then he carried her to her bedroom and laid her gently on her bed. He removed her shoes, then pulled the covers over her. The overwhelming enormity of his relief kept his own heart pounding long after he'd assured himself she was stable.

But at last his, too, quieted. It could do no less. Because the rhythm of his own heart now seemed impossibly joined with hers.

. . . .

She slept for a little while, then opened her eyes.

"Thank you, Joshua," she said in a trembling voice. "I'm glad you came when you did."

"So am I," he said, pouring some water in a glass and holding it to her lips. She drank a little, but not as much as he would have liked her to.

"Do I smell some fresh-baked bread?"

She nodded.

"I'm going to take care of your brother, then go to the kitchen and bring you some bread. It's the best thing to absorb whatever might be left in your stomach." He didn't tell her that after a brief time to allow the bread to absorb the dregs of the soup, he'd be giving her the ipecac elixir again.

"I'm not sure I can," she moaned.

"You will. It will make you feel better."

She didn't answer him, but he knew the idea of eating right now wasn't appealing.

"Don't go to sleep until I come back, Lydia. I'll just be a moment."

Joshua kissed her on the forehead, then left her to see to her brother and fetch the bread.

"How's Lydia?" James asked as Joshua entered his bedroom.

"She's hurting right now but she'll be fine."

Joshua helped James to his bed, then checked his leg to make sure he hadn't done any damage.

"Are you in pain?" Joshua asked.

"A little. But I don't want any more laudanum right now. I want you to tell me what happened to Lydia."

"She was poisoned."

"Was it the soup Mrs. Weatherby brought over?"

Joshua lifted the bowl of soup that was still on the bedside table and detected the unmistakable garlic smell of arsenic and the undertone of belladonna that made the soup lethal. Joshua set it back down on the table.

"Yes, it was the soup. Don't touch it."

"Why would she do something so horrible? She's a doctor's wife. Why would she poison Lydia?"

Joshua delivered the bread to Lydia, making her promise to eat at least half, then worked on James's leg. He made sure none of the deep muscle stitches had been pulled out, and hadn't caused any bleeding.

"I don't think she brought the soup for Lydia. I think she brought it for you."

James pressed his head into the pillow. "I think you're right. She did. Lydia said Mrs. Weatherby brought me a bowl of soup. And, Lydia told me it was delicious. So, she must have tasted it."

"She's fortunate that she didn't eat too much of it or it would have killed her."

His own words circled in his head. Indeed, that's what had happened. The soup *had* killed her. He felt the uneasy flutter as he realized he had actually lost her.

But she had returned to him.

Lydia's brother looked him in the eyes. "But why? Why would she want to kill me?"

"Because of me," Joshua answered. "You chose me to care for you instead of her husband."

"Why should she care what doctor I chose?"

"I'm guessing that she considers me a threat to her husband's practice. I should have realized it from the beginning. When Mrs. Smithers came to me, she poisoned her. And when I saw Ivan Crumbly she had another opportunity to make it seem as if I had no skill as a doctor. No skill to save her husband's former patients."

"And I was to be her third victim."

"Yes. I assume she thought if one more patient died at my hands, I would pack up my things and leave Middleton."

"What are you going to do?"

"I'm not sure yet. But one way or another I'll put a stop to it."

Chapter Seven

JOSHUA SAT AT LYDIA'S BEDSIDE and watched her as she slept. It had been two days since she'd been poisoned and an intense sense of fear and dread clenched inside his chest every time he thought what might have happened if he hadn't returned when he did.

A painful gnawing ate at his insides when he thought of how close he'd come to losing the woman he was just beginning to discover. It seemed that in her presence, the whole world opened before him in new and exhilarating ways. Without her? He just couldn't contemplate that. For the first time in his memory, he realized how shallow his life had been.

He reached out to hold her hand. As if she felt their connection, her eyes fluttered and she opened her eyes to look at him. A smile lit her face.

"Have you slept at all today?"

"I don't need any sleep. Don't you know doctors are like camels? They can go days without sleeping."

Now she laughed outright. "Water, silly. Camels can go days without water."

He faked a look of chagrin.

"Oh. Well. That I can't do. I must have my water."

"So you're not super human?"

"Well, I didn't say that," he teased, reaching for a glass of water and lifting her to a sitting position so she could drink. When she finished, she handed the glass back to him.

"How is James?"

"He's much better. He's no longer running a fever and his leg is beginning to heal."

"Good," she whispered. "I can't thank you enough, Joshua. Without your help I might have lost him. And I might have died."

He squeezed her fingers. "But you didn't. And he's as strong as you are. That gave him a head start."

Lydia looked at him and smiled and his heart thundered in his chest.

"Will you help me up?"

"You need to rest."

"I've done nothing but rest for two days now. It's time I got up and did something."

"There's nothing for you to do. Mrs. Childers came earlier this morning and is in the kitchen preparing meat pies she says are guaranteed to put flesh back on your brother's bones."

"Oh, I'm glad. I knew as soon as she could travel, she'd be here."

Lydia pulled the covers back and swung her legs over the side of the bed. Joshua had no choice but to help her to her feet.

"What are we going to do about Mrs. Weatherby?" she said as she drew a shawl around her shoulders and knotted it.

"I don't know."

"We can't let her get by with attempting to kill James. Or with poisoning any other patients that come to you rather than her husband."

"I know. But I can't simply tell her husband what she's done and expect him to believe me. Somehow, I'll have to come up with enough proof to convince him I'm telling the truth."

"You will," she said, stepping into his arms and standing on her tiptoes to kiss him. Part of him was stunned at how naturally she'd begun to show him affection, and another part of him told him not to question it. He felt the naturalness of their attraction himself, after all. From the moment she'd come back to life in his arms, his heart seemed to have claimed her as his own.

He returned her kiss, then stepped away from her. "I'm going to let you get dressed before Mrs. Childers catches us together. Besides, I know your brother is anxious to see you. He needs to know you've recovered."

"You're right. You go do that." She turned a sassy face toward him. "And take your time, because I'm going to lock myself in the closet and eat until I'm blue in the face."

She laughed, but he was completely puzzled.

"Why the closet, may I ask?"

"So I can eat without fear of you pulling out that bottle of ipecac again!"

"Ah," he smiled sagely. "But then, how would you know I haven't already laced the blueberry tarts with ipecac? Hm?"

Watching her face fall, he grinned a wicked grin and left the room just as a pillow hit the door behind him. The smells coming from the kitchen were making his stomach growl and he remembered he hadn't eaten since yesterday noon. He was desperate for a cup of coffee and one of the blueberry tarts that were cooling on the kitchen table.

And, he needed to think of how he dared tell Doctor Weatherby that his wife was a murderer.

. . . .

Lydia fidgeted at Joshua's side as he drove the one-horse buggy from Cottage Hill through the streets of Middleton. She cradled their precious cargo in her lap as if it held the answer to everything they intended to accomplish.

"What will we do if this doesn't work?" she asked when they pulled up in front of Doctor Weatherby's impressive brick home in the middle of a tree-lined block.

Joshua jumped down from the buggy then went around to lift Lydia to the ground. "We'll figure that out when we come to it."

Joshua cupped his hand beneath Lydia's elbow and escorted her up the walk to the front door. She gripped the bundle closer, careful not to let it slip from her hands.

Without hesitating, Joshua knocked on the front door and waited. After the second knock, a maid answered the door.

"Doctor Jarvis and Miss Lydia McDowell to see Doctor and Mrs.

Weatherby. Are they in?"

"Yes," the maid answered with a surprised expression on her face. "Please, follow me."

Joshua and Lydia followed the maid into a parlor. The room was decorated in maroons, grays, and pale greens, and, although the furniture was not extravagant or new, it was not overly worn.

"Please, have a seat," the maid said. "I'll tell the doctor and Mrs. Weatherby you're here."

"Thank you," Joshua answered, then sat down beside Lydia on the floral brocade sofa. It wasn't long before the maid returned with a tea tray and a plate of biscuits.

"The doctor and Mrs. Weatherby will be down shortly."

The maid served them and made her quiet exit.

Joshua drank his tea but smiled when Lydia didn't follow his lead. Instead, she let her tea sit on the low table in front of her and held the package in her hands.

"You can set that down now, Lydia. No one will steal it."

She turned to look at him, then shook her head. She obviously had no intention of letting go of the package.

Just as she was about to answer, the doctor and his wife entered the room. They sat in two chairs opposite Joshua and Lydia.

"Doctor Jarvis," the doctor greeted. "What a surprise. And Miss McDowell. A pleasure to see you. Ethel, have you met Miss McDowell? James McDowell's sister."

"No, we've not—"

"Yes," Lydia interrupted. "We've met. Just the other day, in fact."

A frown crossed Ethel Weatherby's forehead. Only then did the woman lower her gaze to the package in Lydia's lap. Her eyes opened wide and Lydia recognized fear and uncertainty in her eyes.

Ignoring protocol, the doctor poured a cup of tea and handed it to his wife, then poured a cup for himself. His wife, however, didn't hold her cup. Her hands trembled so violently she couldn't stop the liquid from sloshing over the rim and into the saucer.

"I have to admit that I'm surprised to see you, Jarvis. Although, I am pleased that you and Miss McDowell called on us today. I've wanted to apologize for my heavy hand the other day. We must put all this unnecessary suspicion to rest, I dare say."

"I must apologize, as well. I should have come by to talk to you long before now, but the weather…"

"Yes of course," Jarvis agreed. "The weather."

Doctor Weatherby took a sip of his tea, then set his cup and saucer next to his wife's on the table that sat between them. "I'm hearing that the people of Middleton haven't welcomed you as you hoped they would. It's unfortunate that Mrs. Smithers and Ivan Crumbly died just a day or two apart." He leaned forward. "I also know that their deaths weren't your fault."

Joshua seemed to study Doctor Weatherby. "No, their deaths weren't my fault. But their deaths were *someone's* fault. You see, both Mrs. Smithers and Ivan Crumbly were poisoned."

"What!" Doctor Weatherby's eyes opened wide. "Are you sure?"

"Yes. I'm sure."

"Do you have any idea who would have done such a thing?" Doctor Weatherby asked.

"Yes, I believe I do."

"Who would that be?"

"I think I shall leave you to discuss this matter," Ethel Weatherby said, rising to her feet.

"No, Mrs. Weatherby," Lydia said, standing in front of the sofa and stepping to the side to prevent Mrs. Weatherby from leaving. "Please, you must remain to hear what we have to say."

Lydia turned her head to look at Joshua as if she was asking for permission to take over their conversation. Joshua nodded his permission and Lydia continued where he had left off.

Her heart pounded at the thought of what she was about to say. And beneath its thunder lay the guilt she felt for holding two deaths against Joshua, against the man who sat just inches from her—the man whose very presence in her life had given her heart wings.

The man to whom she owed her very life.

She swallowed hard as she turned to face the woman across from her. The woman who had very nearly ended it.

Chapter Eight

LYDIA'S HEART SKITTERED MADLY as she sought the right words. She saw the guilt written on Ethel Weatherby's face, but behind it wavered an uncertainty that evoked a startling sympathy.

"You haven't asked how my brother is faring, Mrs. Weatherby. I'm surprised, considering how concerned you were when you called on him the other day."

"You didn't tell me you called on the McDowells, Ethel," her husband said.

"That's because it was nothing, dear. Just a benevolent call."

"Yes, Doctor Weatherby. Your wife brought my brother a bowl of her splendid soup."

The doctor smiled, but his smile was tense, unlike the jovial smile he'd worn earlier.

"Yes, my wife's soup has healed a great number of my patients."

"I'm sure it has," Lydia said. "It has also had the opposite effect on one or two. Hasn't it, Mrs. Weatherby?"

"I don't know what you're talking about. Everyone loves my soup. Don't they, dear?"

Doctor Weatherby reached a hand toward his wife and patted her arm.

"Well, it seems, Mrs. Weatherby," Lydia said quietly, "that you may have added a new ingredient or two."

"What are you saying, Miss McDowell," Doctor Weatherby asked, shifting his gaze from Lydia to his wife, then back to Lydia. Joshua had spoken of poison, and Weatherby was too astute to miss the accusation.

"My brother is well, Mrs. Weatherby. You see, he didn't eat any of your soup. But I did."

The doctor's wife's eyes opened wide. "But you weren't ill."

"That's quite true, Mrs. Weatherby. I wasn't ill at all. *Before* I ate your soup."

"Ethel? What does Miss McDowell mean?"

"I have no idea, dear. This woman is confusing me." She suddenly stood. "She must be in it with Doctor Jarvis."

"Ethel? Whatever do you mean?" Now Doctor Weatherby stood beside his wife, alarm etched across his face.

"Well, you know he wants to ruin you. He wants all your patients for himself. All those good people." She turned to her husband. "You know she's lying, Elias. There's nothing wrong with my soup. You love it, don't you, dear?"

Lydia's throat tightened as she realized what had happened. A woman who had at some point lost her grip on sanity had only been protecting her husband in her own crazed way. It was a grizzly outcome to her misguided mission of love and support.

Now all that was left was to bring her husband to that sad realization.

"I understand your motive, Mrs. Weatherby, but you see, I ate a bit of the soup you brought for my brother and almost died. If Doctor Jarvis hadn't arrived when he did, I would be dead."

"Ethel?" Doctor Weatherby asked again.

"That's just not true! She wasn't supposed to eat the soup anyway, Elias. Don't you see? It's her own fault if it made her ill. You really must tell her to stop lying!"

"Then, to prove I'm lying, you won't mind if your husband eats the remainder of the soup you brought over for my brother, will you, Mrs. Weatherby."

Lydia removed the towel from around the bowl of Mrs. Weatherby's soup. "I've tried to keep it warm, Doctor Weatherby," she said holding out a spoon for him to take.

She hadn't considered the woman's fragile hold on sanity, but now Lydia had to rely on the obvious love she saw between Mrs. Weatherby and her good husband. He needed to be convinced right here, right now, in the privacy of his own home. Requiring a coroner's analysis would expose Weatherby's wife's guilt, and ruin a good man. She couldn't have that. If Ethel didn't stay her husband's hand from eating the deadly soup, Lydia would have to.

The doctor took the bowl, then dipped the spoon into the soup.

"I do love your soup, dear." He touched the spoon to the side of the crock, then raised it to his mouth.

"No!" Mrs. Weatherby cried. She knocked the bowl from her husband's hands and stared at the soup that stained the carpet.

"Ethel? What have you done?"

"Don't be angry with me, Elias. I had to. Don't you see? Everyone in Middleton was leaving you and going to the new doctor. It wouldn't have been long before you would have lost all your patients."

"So you poisoned Mrs. Smithers and Ivan Crumbly?"

"I did them a favor, Elias. Don't you see? Mrs. Smithers was over ninety years and was on her deathbed. And Ivan Crumbly was drinking himself to death. Neither of them had much longer to live."

Tears filled the doctor's eyes and he gathered her in his arms. "Oh, Ethel. What have you done?"

"I did what I had to do to save you. I couldn't bear to see your patients leave you for...for *him*. Not after you've spent your entire life caring for them and bringing their babes into the world."

"I know, dear," he said, pressing his wife's head to his shoulder. He held her for several moments, then called for her maid.

"Mary, please take your mistress to her room. She needs to rest for a while. And please, don't leave her."

"Yes, Doctor Weatherby."

"Go with Mary, Ethel. I'll be up to see you in just a little while."

"Are you angry with me, Elias?" Her voice was pitiful, childlike.

"No, dear," he said then kissed her cheek. "I'm not angry."

"I'm glad, Elias. I knew you'd understand."

Doctor Weatherby watched his wife leave the room, then lifted his head and focused on Joshua.

"What do you intend to do?"

Joshua looked at Lydia and she reached for his hand.

"Your wife is ill," Joshua said. "You know that, don't you?"

"Yes. I know. I just wish I would have realized it before now."

"Do you have someplace to take her? Someplace where she can be watched and cared for?"

"Well, I . . ." He rubbed his forehead. "I have a friend who works in a sanitarium. He has wanted me to come work with him for years. He said there's a cottage on the grounds where Ethel and I can live."

"Then, I'll let you take her there. No one will ever hear of this. She needs help, as well as constant supervision."

With tears running down his cheeks, Doctor Weatherby nodded his agreement. "I don't know how to thank you, Doctor Jarvis. Or how to apologize."

"Just be sure she never does anything like this ever again."

"I will. She'll be well supervised."

Lydia watched the two men evaluate each other. She could imagine they would have formed a binding friendship if things had been different. But that had been taken out of their hands.

"We'll be gone by the end of the week," Doctor Weatherby said. "Before we leave, I'll recommend you to all my patients. I'll tell them that I know from experience that you are a gifted physician. I guarantee that in time you'll have more patients than you can take care of."

"Thank you," Joshua said, then he rose. Lydia rose to stand at his side. "You'd best destroy the crock, sir. And find that supply of belladonna."

He stepped forward to shake Weatherby's hand. "And if you ever have need of me, you have only to ask. The best of luck to you."

"Thank you," Doctor Weatherby answered, then walked them to the door.

As Joshua and Lydia left without looking back, the sun showed its face for the second time in ten days.

· · · ·

"Do you think they'll be alright?" Lydia asked Joshua that night while they were eating dinner.

James was sitting at the table with them. He'd healed remarkably well in the days since Joshua had administered the liniment he'd brought back from Amesbury.

"I'm sure they'll be fine. Elias truly loves his wife and will take excellent care of her."

"Do you have any regrets as to how you handled the situation?" James asked. "You could have brought Mrs. Weatherby up on charges, you know. She was responsible for the deaths of two people."

Joshua shifted his gaze from James to her. Then he shook his head. "No, I have no regrets. What good would it have done to bring Mrs. Weatherby up on charges? She's a sick lady, and considering what the people in Middleton think of her, the outcome would have been the same. A magistrate would have confined her to an institution. This way, Elias Weatherby can spend the remainder of his life with the woman he loves."

"I suppose you're right," James answered, then finished his coffee and rose from the table. He had a difficult time standing on his own and Joshua rose to help him.

"Do you want to retire now or go to the drawing room and sit by the fire?"

"I think I'll sit by the fire and read for a bit," her brother answered.

Joshua helped him to the drawing room while Lydia cleared the table.

"Would you like to go for a walk, Lydia?" Joshua asked when he came back into the kitchen.

"I'd love to," Lydia answered. "Let me get my coat and gloves."

The weather was crisp and beautiful. The moon was full and the wind was still. It was chilly, but Joshua wrapped his arm around her waist and pulled her to him as they stepped across the dooryard.

"This has been an interesting day, hasn't it?" Joshua asked as they walked down the lane.

"Very," Lydia answered. "I had no idea it would end like it did. When you mentioned that you thought someone had poisoned Mrs. Smithers and Ivan Crumbly, I have to admit that I didn't believe you."

Joshua's arm tightened around her waist and he slowed his pace. "Did you think that my negligence had caused their deaths?"

"Joshua, it breaks my heart to think that I fell prey to the village prejudice. But truly, you never gave me the slightest reason to doubt your ability as a physician. Never."

"Then what did you think?

"I honestly thought they'd died of natural causes but that you couldn't face that possibility."

Joshua continued their former pace. "I did think that was possible with Mrs. Smithers. She was over ninety years, after all. But when Ivan Crumbly died the following week, I suspected the two deaths were somehow connected. Other than being an alcoholic, Crumbly had no life-threatening injuries."

"Did you ever suspect Ethel Weatherby?"

"No. I didn't suspect her. But I have to admit that I suspected Doctor Weatherby."

Lydia stopped and turned to face Joshua. "You did?"

"Yes. When I realized my two patients had been poisoned, he naturally came to mind. He's a doctor, after all. He would know what medicines to use to end a life prematurely."

"That makes sense."

"If I had known the doctor better, I would have realized he wasn't capable of murder. He truly cares for his patients."

Joshua and Lydia walked on in silence until they reached the end of the lane where Joshua paused and turned to her.

"I would like to ask you something, Lydia."

Joshua's tone had taken on a serious note. Lydia turned to look at him but he wasn't looking at her. He was staring off into the starry night.

"Yes?"

"I know we haven't known each other all that long. Yet I feel as if I've known you for years. I feel as if I understand you as deeply as you know and understand me."

Lydia's heart beat faster in her breast. "I feel the same, Joshua. I feel as if we've known each other forever."

"I also know that I love you. And, that I want to spend my life with you."

"Oh, Joshua. I think I've loved you from the night you agreed to come with me to take care of James."

Joshua took her hands in his. He brought her closer, facing her with eyes full of hope. "Would you consider marrying me? I know I'm not rich, but if things go as I think they will, in time I'll be able to provide for you."

"Oh, Joshua."

"I know this is sudden, but please consider being my wife."

"I don't need to consider your proposal. I already know the answer. And yes. I would like nothing more than to be your wife."

"Oh, Lydia. I love you."

Joshua wrapped his arms around her and brought his mouth down on hers. His kiss was born of emotion, telling her without words how much he loved her.

He deepened his kiss and skimmed his tongue over her lips, causing every nerve in her body to sing for joy. Lydia wished she could put into words how much she loved him. How eager she was to become his wife. How certain she was that she wanted to spend her life with him.

There was nothing she wanted more than to marry him and have his children.

He broke their kiss and gathered her to him, holding her close for a while longer. They'd left the house two young people filled with hope for the future. They returned to the house knowing they'd found it in one another.

"Where will we live?" Lydia asked suddenly.

"Where would you like to live?"

"Do you think Doctor Weatherby would sell us his house? It's where the people of Middleton are used to going when they need to see a doctor. It's set up with a surgery, and you could spend a greater portion of your time with me than if you were off across town. I might even be able to assist you if I have time."

Joshua turned his head and looked at her. There was a smile on his face and a gleam of pride in his eyes. "I think that would be a remarkable idea. I'll talk to Doctor Weatherby before he leaves."

Lydia's heart swelled to the point of bursting. She had thought her life was over when she came to stay with her brother. Little had she known it was just beginning. Little had she known that it was Doctor Joshua Jarvis who had the power to change her life.

Little had she known that it was this one good man who had the power to melt her winter's cold heart.

SEASONS
BOOK TWO

SPRING'S
TENDER
HEART

LAURA LANDON

SPRING'S TENDER HEART

LAURA LANDON

She sought escape. He sought seclusion.
But an ill-timed near tragedy brought them together.

Jonah Mason, Earl of Glassborough, thought he had closed his heart to love. It would have worked, had a beautiful woman not fallen—literally—into his arms.

Finding no one to help her, **Lady Emma Randolph** had fled her stepbrother's grasp to avoid a horrid marriage and save her own fortune. When fate thrust her into the safe hideaway of the scarred Earl of Glassborough, she found herself questioning her decision to flee to America.

But... the day her demented stepbrother arrived on the earl's very doorstep, her only choice was to flee once again.

Yet, did she dare?

Chapter One

LADY EMMA RANDOLPH PUSHED HER HORSE to travel as fast as she dared on the rain- and ice-soaked roads. The rain had turned to sleet a mile back, and now a heavy, wet snow slammed against her. The wind was fierce as it pelted the huge flakes into her eyes with such brutality that she couldn't see her hand in front of her face. She had to trust her horse to stay on the road.

She reached behind her and felt for the two bags she'd tied to the saddle. They contained as many of her possessions as she could stuff into the large canvas satchels. She would purchase anything else she might need once she reached America. Once she was safe.

Emma's fur-lined gloves were no match for the blustery chill, and her shins above her riding boots now prickled with frostbite where the wind kept sweeping away the protection of her skirts. Her riding habit would have been warmer, but she had not dared to draw attention to the fact that she intended to leave.

"Just going for a short walk," she had said.

She drew her cloak tighter around her and prayed for the sun to peek through the roiling clouds.

Her hood was drawn as low as possible over her forehead, but already she could feel icy frost forming on her brows. The wind had escalated to a point where it was becoming impossible to protect herself.

Still, what she thought was a curse when it first started snowing had turned out to be a blessing. Drifts covered her tracks almost as soon as she made them. No one would be able to follow her. With any luck she'd be able to stay ahead of anyone who tried. Once she reached London she'd board the first ship to America and she'd be safe.

Emma leaned over the horse and buried her gloved fingers in the horse's mane. She gave the horse a free rein, praying the mare would instinctively find shelter somewhere. Her teeth chattered relentlessly now, and her body shook with jarring shivers. She was so tired she could scarcely keep her eyes open. But she needed to stay awake. She'd heard tales of people who had fallen asleep and frozen to death.

Emma forced her eyes to open and remain open. Then, from above her, she heard a loud snap followed closely by an even louder crack. Her horse shied, but Emma held the reins tighter to keep her mare from bolting. There was another loud snap and her mare reared, nearly unseating Emma.

In the next instant she heard an explosion, loud, like a booming cannon. Her horse bolted and Emma lost her hold on her mount and landed in the snow. She looked up just as a large limb crashed down on top of her.

The pain was unbearable. She pushed at the large branch, trying desperately to free herself, but it was no use. The branch was too heavy. And she was too weak.

Emma lay in the snow, exhausted beyond belief. She continued to push on the heavy tree trunk, but she was unable to move it. With a cry of frustration she dropped her arm in the snow and lay there. The more time that passed, the less her arm and shoulder hurt.

Eventually, a sense of peace wrapped around her. She'd never been afraid of death. She knew without a doubt that when she died God would take her to heaven. That when she died, she would no longer have to fight her stepbrother and the evil he intended.

Emma closed her eyes and accepted the peaceful rest. And she slept.

. . . .

Jonah Mason, Earl of Glassborough, filled his tumbler again and took a small sip of the fine brandy he kept in his wine cellar. Fine brandy was one of the few extravagances he afforded himself. One of the only extravagances he *could* afford these days, because it had been aging in his cellar for over a hundred years.

After he took an appreciative sip, he sat forward in his large leather wing-back chair behind his desk and lifted his pen to add the column of numbers in his ledger. This was his third attempt to add this particular column, and when he finished, he came up with a different total this time, too.

The oil lamp flickered. He'd meant to fill it earlier in the evening, but it was late now and he was tired. It was time to quit for the night.

He pushed away his ledger. He'd work on his accounts again tomorrow. He doubted any money would magically appear overnight.

Jonah placed his pen back in its holder and concentrated on watching the brandy swirl in his glass. He swiped his hand down his face and felt the scar that ran from his temple to just beneath his jaw. Even though the feel of it shouldn't shock him anymore, the puckering intrusion of his disfigurement was impossible to ignore.

His scar was just one more excuse the citizens of Glastonbury had to convince them that Jonah was a monster. It wasn't that it was such a hideous thing, really. It had more to do with the stories that had cropped up after the tragedy. All silly conjecture, of course. But in his own stunned grief he had let the stories run rampant so that now, six years later, nothing he could say or do would change the villagers' minds. The death of his fiancé on the day of their wedding was all the proof anyone needed to seal the belief that he was a beast with blood on his hands.

Jonah lifted the brandy to his mouth and took another large swallow, then paused, surprised by a knock on his study door at this late hour.

"What is it, Carter?"

"My lord," his butler said when he stepped into the room. "Farley requests a word with you."

"Send him in," Jonah said, then set his glass down.

Something must be amiss. He could count on one hand the number of times his stable master had come to the house to see him. It was the man's habit to conduct any business when Jonah went to the stables.

Which he did every day, except on days like today when the weather was so inclement it wasn't safe to take any of his horses out.

Jonah watched Patrick Farley enter the room. He held his cap in front of him and turned the sweat-stained felt cap in jerky circles. Something was definitely wrong.

"What is it, Farley?"

"A riderless horse, my lord. Galloped into the yard a few minutes ago."

Jonah sat forward in his chair. "A horse with no rider?"

"Yes, my lord."

"Have you seen the horse before?"

"No, my lord. It's not from around here."

"There's something else, Farley. What is it?"

"There were two bags tied to the saddle." Farley clenched his felt hat tighter in his hands. "I know I shouldn't have taken the liberty, my lord, but I opened one of the bags to see what was inside."

"No, that's exactly what you should have done."

Farley breathed a sigh of relief.

"What did you find?"

"Clothes, my lord. Lady's clothes."

Jonah sat back in his chair and considered his options. He wanted to remain where he was and forget Farley had told him about the horse that had ridden into his stable. But that wasn't an option.

He rose from his chair. "Farley, have Carter fetch some blankets, then saddle Jupiter."

"Yes, my lord."

Jonah watched Farley leave the room, then braced his hands atop his desk. He lowered his head between his outstretched arms and closed his eyes. Damn the female who left him no choice but to go after her. Damn any female for forcing her way into his life when all he wanted was to live the remainder of his days isolated from the outside world.

Jonah pushed himself away from the desk and stalked through the room. Carter was waiting at the front door with Jonah's heavy caped Ulster coat and gloves. Jonah pushed his arms through its sleeves, then raised the cape and buttoned it beneath his chin to form a hood before he stormed from the house.

"Would you want me or one of the boys to go with you, my lord?" Farley asked when he reached the stable.

"No," Jonah barked after he'd mounted Jupiter. And then he thought again. "You take the lane toward the ridge. Only that far, then right back. I'll go east, but only as far as the fork."

"Very well, my lord."

"You might tell Mrs. Jefferies to prepare a room in the event we bring someone back alive."

"Yes, my lord."

"And take the clothes to her."

"Yes, my lord."

Jonah rode from the yard considering what he'd just said.

In the event that we bring someone back alive.

If it was a female who had been thrown from the horse, what were the chances that he'd find her alive? What were the chances that even if she hadn't died from her fall, she hadn't frozen to death? Not that he cared. His life would be a great deal less complicated if she hadn't survived.

An ugly twinge of guilt assaulted him, then slipped away.

Jonah lowered his head to keep the brunt of the forceful winter wind and snow from pelting him in the face. He pushed Jupiter as hard as he dared through the mounting snow. The sooner he found the rider, the sooner he would find himself before a roaring fire with a glass of brandy back in his hands.

. . . .

The farther he traveled, the more convinced Jonah was that if and when he found the woman he was looking for—*if* he found her in the blinding snow—it was doubtful she'd be alive. If she'd been out in this weather any length of time, she was more than likely frozen to death. It was even more likely she was dead if she'd been injured.

Jonah pushed back the hood of his coat and looked as far as he could see into the distance. He scoured the ditches that lined the road and checked often to see if someone had tried to take shelter behind the rock wall that bordered the track.

Annoying clumps of snow kept dropping from the high branches that overhung the narrow road. They hit with a solid *thwack*, like the snowballs he'd launched at his schoolmates in better times.

As soon as he rounded the last curve before the fork he could see there was something ahead, in the middle of the road. He pushed Jupiter to wade through the drifts until it was possible to see that a large limb from a tree had fallen, blocking the road.

When he reached the fallen limb, he dismounted. That's when he saw it. A scrap of blue velvet visible in the blanket of white beneath the twisted limb.

Jonah's heart ramped up as it always had when a need for rescue presented itself. But this was no battlefield. The country lane was drifted hip-deep in places, making his progress maddeningly slow. At last he reached the spot where a woman lay tangled in the broken branches.

He removed one of his gloves and knelt in the snow beside her. Her face was visible. Her hair was wet and plastered to her forehead and her face was pale and lifeless. Jonah was certain she was dead, but when he pressed his finger to her neck, he felt a pulse. It wasn't strong, but weak and slow. At least she was alive. For now.

Jonah strained to lift the log that had fallen across the young lady's arm and shoulder, but it was too heavy to move. He slogged his way back to Jupiter and brought him forward. After securing a rope between the log and his saddle, Jonah urged Jupiter forward. The log moved enough that Jonah could free the woman from beneath it.

"I've got you now," he muttered, more to himself than to the woman who couldn't hear him.

Jonah untied the rope from around the log, then turned to lift the woman. No matter how gently he moved her, she cried out in pain. It wrenched his heart to know that he had no way to ease her suffering.

Her cry wasn't loud, nor did it indicate she had any amount of strength, but it told Jonah that the woman he'd found half buried in the snow was alive. Alive enough to feel pain.

Jonah placed her over his shoulder and mounted Jupiter, then lowered her to his lap and placed the blankets he'd brought around her. She was light as a feather, no more than a limp bundle in his arms, even with her sodden clothes that hung heavily about his boots.

Jonah nestled her close to him and cradled her in his arms as tightly as he could without causing her more pain. She was injured. How severely, he wasn't sure. All he knew was that when he lifted her from the ground, his gloves came away stained with blood.

Jonah pushed Jupiter to return to Glassborough Manor as quickly as possible. Already the familiar mantel of obligation was settling over him. He'd known it several times during the war, when he helped to recover a fallen man only to discover he now felt responsible for the man's entire future.

It was a familiar burden, yet unique. For some inexplicable reason he felt a strange connection to the woman in his arms. He didn't know her. He'd never seen her before, but he sensed a desperation in her. Only a desperate female would travel alone in weather as nasty as this. He looked down on her and wondered what was so important that she would risk her health and her life to flee from the safety of her home.

Jupiter stepped on a patch of ice that caused him to lose his footing and skitter a few steps until Jonah got him under control. The female in his arms shifted, then moaned in pain. Jonah held her tenderly until her breathing calmed and she seemed to rest more comfortably. He pushed Jupiter to continue on his way, then reached down to bring her velvet cloak over her face to keep the snow from hitting her.

If he were any judge, the clothes she wore indicated she wasn't a country lass, but someone from Society. Perhaps someone with a title. Perhaps someone who was running away from an unwanted marriage. Why else would she venture out in such foul weather? Why else would she risk her life?

If anyone knew the lengths to which a woman would go in order to avoid marriage with a man she could not tolerate, that man was Jonah. He had firsthand knowledge of what a woman might put herself through in order to escape marriage to a man she detested. To a man she considered a monster.

Chapter Two

JONAH SAT AT THE LADY'S BEDSIDE and watched her sleep. The fact that she hadn't wakened yet caused him to worry. The fact that her fever was still so high caused him even greater concern. Just as the fact that she shivered so violently from a chill was a telling sign. Not a good sign.

It had been four days since he'd found her and she didn't seem to be improving.

"Has she said anything, my lord?" Mrs. Jefferies asked when she entered the room.

Jonah only shook his head.

"I brought some broth and tea. Do you want me to try to get her to eat or drink something?"

Jonah shook his head again. "No, I'll try to get something down her when she stirs."

"Very well, my lord. I'll be back in a little while to sit with her. You've hardly slept since you returned with her."

Jonah didn't answer. He listened until his housekeeper left the room, then he lifted the lady's head and brought the tea to her lips.

"No," she moaned, then turned her head to the side.

"You really must drink something. You won't survive if you don't."

Jonah knew he must have been mistaken, but he thought he saw a smile lift the corners of her lips. The smile was ever so faint, but it was a smile.

Was that it? Did she welcome death?

"Here," he said more forcefully. "Drink this."

When she didn't turn her head to drink any of the tea, he spoke louder and more harshly. "You heard me! Drink this!"

She slowly turned her head and Jonah saw condemnation in her gaze. He felt contrite, and worked hard to soften his expression into something halfway encouraging as he held the cup to her lips. She opened her mouth and took a swallow, then a second swallow, then held up her hand to indicate that she'd had enough.

Her eyes opened fully and locked with his.

Jonah saw her surprise. Her shock. And it held no surprise for him. That was the usual reaction when anyone saw his scarred face for the first time.

"Now, get more rest," he muttered.

She closed her eyes and if Jonah hadn't been watching, he would have missed the tears that squeezed through her lashes and spilled down her cheeks. Were they tears of pain? Tears of regret that she hadn't managed to die? Tears of horror from the sight of him?

Jonah placed the cup back on the bedside table and retreated from the room. He'd had quite enough of women who longed for death. He took the stairs two at a time until he reached the bottom and met Mrs. Jefferies coming from the kitchen.

"Go see to our…guest," he bellowed, then stormed into his study and slammed the door shut behind him. He went to the sideboard and poured himself a glass of brandy. He took a large swallow, then filled his glass again.

He didn't know why he was angry. He didn't know why having the stranger in his house was so disturbing. Yet, he did. He knew exactly why.

He took another swallow of his brandy, then sat in the chair behind his desk. He dropped his head to rest on the back of it. The female's face flashed before him the second he closed his eyes.

Her hair was a rich, dark coffee, her lush curls spilling with abandon across her pillow. Her complexion was clear, except for the bruises she'd sustained from her fall and from the tree limb that had pinned her to the ground.

Her lips were full and enticing, her eyelids nearly translucent, closed over her large eyes that he knew were an arresting, vibrant blue. She was beautiful. One of the most beautiful women he'd ever seen.

Why she affected him as she did was a mystery to him. He had sworn he wouldn't be drawn in by another female ever again. Not after Constance. Not after the woman he thought he would marry had instead destroyed his reputation and his life. Not after the woman with whom he thought he would share his life had turned his heart into a cold, bitter stone that was incapable of emotion.

Jonah rose to fill his glass, then sat back behind his desk. He intended to drink until he couldn't remember that fateful day, until his past was nothing but a distant memory. Even though he thought he was beyond the need to drink himself into oblivion, he obviously wasn't.

And it was all her fault. The first time his house guest looked at him, tears had run down her cheeks, the same as tears of fright escaped the eyes of every woman who saw his monstrously scarred features. Why should he expect her to be any different?

. . . .

It had been more than a week since she'd seen Jonah Mason, Earl of Glassborough. Emma was glad. The longer he left her alone, the more peaceful her life was.

She only knew his name because the housekeeper, Mrs. Jefferies, had told her who he was. She'd also told her that his bark was worse than his bite, but Emma doubted that was true. She'd heard him bellow instructions to the servants in his deep, harsh tone.

At first she'd been frightened to death at the sound of his loud voice and abrasive tone. Yet, none of the servants seemed to mind. In fact, they entered her room each morning with smiles on their faces, giggling as if they considered their master's bad mood a hilarious joke.

Emma tried to recall his physical features. Other than to remember how large he was and how broad his shoulders were, she had little memory of the man. But she did recall how easily he'd lifted her in his arms and how effortlessly he'd placed her over his shoulder, then mounted his horse with her in his arms. She did recall how safe he'd made her feel.

Emma closed her eyes and tried to remember more but there was a knock on the door and Mrs. Jefferies entered the room with a tray in her hands.

"Good morning, my lady," she said placing the tray on the bedside table.

"Good morning, Mrs. Jefferies."

After the woman helped Emma sit, she straightened the bed covers and placed the four-legged breakfast tray across Emma's lap.

"How did you sleep last night, my lady?"

"Very well, Mrs. Jefferies. Thank you."

"Lord Glassborough asked after you."

Emma lifted her head and locked her gaze with the housekeeper's. "He did?"

"Yes, my lady. He wanted to make sure you were progressing."

"What did you tell him?"

"I told him you were progressing nicely, but you were far from ready to be up and about."

"Please tell him I shouldn't have to impose on his hospitality much longer. I feel much better and I'm sure I'll be well enough to be on my way in a day or two."

The housekeeper scoffed as if mocking a willful child. "You most certainly will not be ready to travel in a day or two, my lady. Perhaps in a week or two. But definitely not before that."

Emma remembered the Earl of Glassborough's harsh words and the angry tone of his voice as he impatiently scolded her to drink her tea. "I know how desperately his lordship wants me gone, Mrs. Jefferies. I will do everything in my power to comply with his wishes."

"Oh, miss. Don't be put off by his lordship's curtness. It's just that he's not used to having guests at Glassborough Manor. I fear he's forgotten how to conduct himself around company. Especially female company."

"Does he deal with the staff harshly?"

"Ach, no," Mrs. Jefferies answered on a laugh. "The master would never harm anyone. Even if the town fools think he might."

That was an odd thing to say.

"Why do they think that?" Emma asked.

"No doubt because of what happened some six years ago."

"What happened, Mrs. Jefferies?"

"'Tis nothing I can talk about. The master will tell you in his own good time."

"I doubt that," Emma said, taking a sip of the hot chocolate Mrs. Jefferies brought her each morning. "He hasn't called on me once since he brought me here."

"No doubt because he's uncomfortable talking to strangers. Especially female strangers."

"And the reason for that would be?"

Mrs. Jefferies paused straightening the bedclothes. "That will be for his lordship to share with you."

"I see," Emma said as she drank more of her hot chocolate and ate a piece of buttered toast.

"Can I get you anything else, my lady?" Mrs. Jefferies asked as she moved to the door.

"No, thank you," Emma answered. When she was alone, Emma sank back against the pillows. She couldn't remain in this position for long. There were several scratches on her back from the tree trunk that had fallen on her. The deep scratches prevented her from putting any pressure on her back.

Emma placed the breakfast tray to the side and gently turned in her bed. The mere effort of eating had completely worn her out.

She settled on her side to lessen the painful pressure on her back, then closed her eyes and slept.

. . . .

Jonah paced the hallway beyond the room where his houseguest slept. He stilled his breath, intent upon listening. He thought he heard a noise and stepped close to her door, in case she was calling out for help.

He was about to retreat when he heard it again.

She was crying out as if she was terrified of something. As if she was in pain.

"No!" he heard her cry out again. *"No!"*

He placed his hand on the latch of the bedroom door and pressed down. Another cry for help tore through the silence and he rushed into the room.

Lady Emma Randolph's hair whipped about as she thrashed from side to side. She raised her delicate arms to shield her face as if to protect herself from blows she anticipated striking her. Jonah felt a hitch in his own breathing as he viewed the desperate beauty of the scene playing out before him.

Without hesitation he rushed to her side and gathered her in his arms. "Everything is fine, my lady. You are safe."

She struggled a little while longer, then relaxed as he continued to comfort her. Her cries gradually lessened to whimpers that seemed to beg for protection.

"Help me. Please."

Jonah couldn't help but assure her. "You're safe now. No one can harm you."

The lady in his arms breathed a shuddering sigh, then struggled to return from the nightmare that had terrified her. Her eyes fluttered, then opened for a second. Then, longer.

Jonah knew the moment she realized he was holding her. He felt her stiffen.

"You have nothing to fear. You're safe now."

Her eyes closed and her breathing gradually calmed. "I'm sorry I disturbed you. A silly nightmare, I'm afraid."

"A very real nightmare, if I were to hazard a guess."

Her vibrant blue eyes closed tightly.

"Yes, a very real nightmare."

"Who are you afraid of?"

When she didn't answer, Jonah changed his question. "Who were you running away from?"

When she refused to answer a second time, Jonah gently released her and filled a glass with water. "You might as well answer me. I won't give up until you do."

He held the glass to her lips and let her drink. When she finished, he sat beside her on the bed. "Who?"

"My stepbrother," she answered without shifting her gaze from his.

"Why?" Jonah hardened his gaze and steadied her chin with his forefinger when she tried to look away from him. "Why?"

She breathed a steady breath.

"My father is…was…the Marquess of Willowbrook."

Jonah couldn't hide the surprise from his face.

"Did you know him?"

"Yes. I knew and admired him. As did most of London." Jonah also knew the marquess was one of the wealthiest men in England. As well as one of the most influential men in the House of Lords. "I was sorry to hear of his passing."

"Thank you."

"So why were you running away?"

"On my twenty-first birthday, I will receive a trust from my father worth several hundred thousand pounds."

Jonah couldn't stop the look of surprise.

"And when will that be?"

"In six months."

"Then, let me guess. Your stepbrother has arranged for you to marry someone you find unacceptable."

Jonah watched as Lady Emma nodded.

"Is the gentleman your brother has arranged for you to marry that reprehensible?"

"Yes, he is. He is one of the most disgusting men in Society. Not only do I refuse to marry him, but I decided years ago that I will never marry anyone."

"You don't intend to marry?"

"No."

"Must I guess the reason?"

The lady lifted her penetrating gaze but did not shift it from his face. "Don't say it as if it's some petty girlish whim. I have yet to meet a man who can love *me* and not just my money."

"I see," Jonah said.

"Do you, Lord Glassborough? How very astute of you."

Jonah chuckled. The woman was clearly convinced that a man's motive couldn't be trusted, so why should she expect him, an unworthy man, to understand circumstances that had brought her to that conclusion?

She couldn't know that she wasn't the only one in the room who had been betrayed in the name of love.

A memory of the heart-wrenching scream when a maid discovered Jonah's fiancé's dead body the morning of their wedding wiped the smile from his face. A vision of his last sight of his betrothed as she vowed to her mother that she'd rather be dead than marry a man she could never love—a monster of a man who frightened her to death—clouded his vision.

He heard Constance's trembling voice as she told her mother that she could never abide allowing such a loathsome monster to touch her. Let alone make love to her.

And she had put truth to her words by killing herself.

But that was his story, not Lady Emma's. He refocused his attention on her.

"Do you think it so impossible for anyone to love you for yourself?"

"Oh, they all profess their undying love. Until I tell them that the money they think they will inherit after we marry will not come with me."

"I don't understand," Jonah said.

"It's a choice I give them. They can marry me if they truly love me, but the money they've heard I will inherit will not come with me."

"So, you've managed to tie it up somehow?"

She saw the skepticism in his eyes.

"I had my father attach a codicil to the legal documents that stated no amount over fifty pounds could be withdrawn without my signature until I'm twenty-five." She smiled. "That had a remarkably cooling effect on their affections, I can assure you."

"Has no one agreed to your terms?"

"No, my lord. Money is a powerful magnet. Even men who have a great deal of their own wealth crave more. It kills them to let my wealth sit in idleness when they can become more influential and powerful if they can combine their wealth with mine. But those who are desperate for what I have are eager to pass me over when they realize they will have to wheedle it out of me a few pounds at a time. They are quite happy to turn away in search of a female desperate enough to marry them even though she will never be loved."

"Which you will never consider doing," Jonah said, not as a question, but as a statement.

"No. Which I will never do." Emma pressed her head into the pillow and closed her eyes. "Greed is a very powerful motive. I have found that words of love spill from their mouths quite easily when there is a possibility the money they will inherit when they marry me will make them rich."

There were so many arguments he could offer her, so many choices she could make other than the one she had set upon. But Jonah looked at her closed eyes. It was obvious she was tired. "You need to rest," he said, then pushed himself from the bed. "We'll talk later. If you will excuse me," he said, and left the room.

As he closed the door he knew he'd missed his moment. He should have told her she wouldn't have to worry about him wanting to marry her for her wealth. Love was too precious a thing to let something like money thwart it. Even though he was on the brink of losing everything he owned, he would never consider marrying another female for the money that would come with her.

Never.

At least, not a second time.

Chapter Three

EMMA TOOK A FEW STEPS ACROSS THE ROOM, then turned and made her way back to her bed. She rested a few moments, then repeated the trek from one side of the room to the other. After she'd rested a few more minutes, she rang for Mrs. Jefferies.

"Yes, my lady," the housekeeper said when she entered Emma's room. "Did you need something?"

"Yes, Mrs. Jefferies. I believe I'm well enough to get up for a while. Would you help me down the stairs? I'd like to visit the library and choose something to read."

"Are you quite sure, my lady?"

"Yes." Emma pushed herself from the bed. "I need to get stronger and I won't do that lying in bed all day."

"Would you like me to get one of the footmen to help you?"

"No, Mrs. Jefferies. I'm sure I can make it down with your assistance."

"Very well, my lady."

Mrs. Jefferies helped her to her feet, secured Emma's dressing gown at her waist, then wrapped an arm around Emma's shoulders to guide her from the room.

"The master has an excellent library, my lady. I'm sure you'll find something to your liking."

"I'm sure I will," Emma said as she made her way down the stairs.

Emma kept her hand looped through Mrs. Jefferies' arm as they made their way across the foyer.

"Careful now."

Mrs. Jefferies slowed their pace to guide Emma through the upheaval in the front hall. Everything was shrouded in tarpaulins that covered the floor and windows. Scaffolding reached from floor to ceiling, and a small stockpile of building supplies was neatly confined to the corner by the front door. Hearing a noise, Emma looked up and was surprised to see that at the very top, looking for all he was worth like Michelangelo painting the Sistine Chapel, the Earl of Glassborough lay on his back applying spackling mud to exposed joints in the beamed ceiling.

"My lord, whatever are you doing?"

She watched him carefully stow his trowel before he turned to his belly and greeted her. Her breath caught in her throat at the handsome sight. Creamy mud streaked his cheeks and jaw, highlighting his strong features that seemed practically rakish with a swatch of auburn hair plastered across his forehead.

"I almost had it repaired before this early spring snowstorm hit, but... now I have to do it all over again. The weight of the snow weakened my temporary mend, you see, and the roof seems to have landed there, there, and all the way over there."

He swept an arm downward, and now she saw the small drifts of snow that had collected in corners of the scaffolding. Bits of broken timber were littered across the floor, evidence of the collapse that must have happened sometime in the night.

Emma smiled.

"You're putting some poor craftsman out of work, my lord. Surely you should put this kind of job out for hire, I would think."

His pleasant, relaxed features transformed into something that spoke of discomfort.

"Yes. Well. Under normal circumstances one surely would."

With a gruff nod he flipped to his back and continued his work, slapping each beat of the trowel a bit harder than truly seemed necessary.

Emma glided away, feeling the need to tiptoe across the littered floor until they entered a long hallway.

That had been an odd encounter. She wondered what she'd said to cause such a reaction.

"I didn't mean to upset his lordship, Mrs. Jefferies."

"Ach, not to worry, my lady. The master meant no harm. He'll be pleased, he will, to find you in the library later. He does love his books."

Mrs. Jefferies reached a hand forward, beckoning Emma to continue, but a large double door on her right caught her eye.

"What room is this?" Emma asked.

"The drawing room, my lady."

"May I see it?"

Mrs. Jefferies hesitated as if debating whether Lord Glassborough would object or not. But in a moment, the housekeeper opened the door and let Emma enter the room.

It was dark and musty, the drapery drawn tightly across the windows and the furniture covered with dust cloths.

"Is this room never used?"

"No, my lady. There's no longer a need. His lordship doesn't entertain."

Emma stepped back quickly, pulling the doors closed against the chill that had pervaded the gloomy room.

"And this one?" she asked when they reached the next closed door.

"The morning room, my lady."

"May I see it?"

"It's much the same as the drawing room, my lady."

"The windows must face the east, though, if it's called the morning room," Emma said.

"Yes, my lady. When the drapery is open, the windows allow the morning sun to flood the room."

"But the curtains are drawn?"

"Yes, my lady."

Emma didn't wait for permission to enter the room, but turned the knob on the door and entered.

The high-ceilinged morning room was much the same as the drawing room they'd previously entered. The heavy window coverings were closed, there was no fire in either of the room's two fireplaces, and protective cloths covered the furniture.

"Does Lord Glassborough never have guests?"

"No, my lady," Mrs. Jefferies answered after a brief hesitation.

Something was amiss. Lord Glassborough was an earl. He was titled. Surely he was well thought of in the area.

"Why does he lack visitors?" Emma asked.

The expression on Mrs. Jefferies' face made it obvious that she had no intention of answering. Emma turned to exit the room and Mrs. Jefferies followed behind her. She led Emma to the library and opened the door.

"Oh," Emma said when the door swung wide. "What a beautiful room." Emma stepped to the center and turned in a slow circle to admire the magnificent collection of books arranged on beautifully polished carved wood shelving.

Two of the walls contained shelf after shelf of books covering all manner of farming practices and animal husbandry. The other two walls held everything from simple cloth-bound books to magnificent leather-bound tomes. "Lord Glassborough must love to read," she said when she reached shelves that contained the classics.

"Yes, my lady. He is an avid reader."

Emma continued to browse the shelves where, to her surprise, she even found several Gothic romances.

"I don't want to take up more of your time, Mrs. Jefferies. I'm sure you have other duties to take care of, and I can get along by myself."

"Are you sure, my lady?"

"Yes, I'm sure. But I would like to bother you for a tea tray before you go, if you don't mind."

A smile lit the housekeeper's face. "Of course not, my lady."

"And please, bring the tea into the morning room. I would like to read there."

The smile faded from the woman's face.

"Are you sure, my lady?"

"Yes, quite."

"Very well," she said, then bobbed a curtsy before leaving the room.

Emma considered the choices she might make. She could have taken a dozen or more books to read, but limited her choice to three that interested her. When she finished her selection, she left the library and returned to the morning room.

The tea tray, bearing scones and clotted cream, was waiting for her when she reached the morning room, but the heavy velvet draping was still drawn across the windows and the dust covers were still over the furniture. Emma wondered why the housekeeper hadn't at least uncovered one of the chairs or the sofa. But she shoved the question out of her mind.

Before Emma poured herself a cup of tea, she walked around the room and pulled back the heavy brocade drapery. The windows were massive and when she removed the elegant, dark fabrics, the sun flooded into the room. By the end of one circuit across the eastern wall she had freed each window from its dark shroud and felt the glorious, welcome rays of the sun begin to warm her shoulders.

She stepped back and brought her hands to her mouth to cover a sigh of great pleasure. The room was beautiful with the wood of the furnishings bathed in morning light. Emma couldn't resist rushing to a covered sofa to drag away its drab covering. But as the last corner swept away from the sofa, she gasped.

A huge gash had been cut in the fabric from the back of one corner to the front of the opposite corner. Its gorgeous tapestry had been rendered useless by the jagged gash, where stuffing and rope lacings protruded crudely.

Emma turned to what appeared from its shrouded shape to be a matching love seat. With a quick pull she dragged away its cover, revealing much the same vandalization. One damaged piece could have been an unfortunate accident. But two?

In a mere moment she discovered that no piece of upholstered furniture in the room had escape the brutal slashing. Stunned, she carefully straightened the covers, leaving bare only one overstuffed chair that seemed to have received the least damage. With great care she dragged it to a window alcove, covering its flayed seat with a low pillow.

It was here that she sat with her books, steadying her heartbeat as she set about breathing new life back into the room.

Jonah walked down the hallway to his study, rubbing at a kink in his back. He'd spent far too long up on that scaffolding, but if he hadn't made the repair when he did, the snowmelt would run into the walls and cause who knew how much rot. That would be a costly reconstruction he could never undertake by himself.

Startled by shafts of light illuminating the usually gloomy hall, he stopped short near the entrance to the morning room where the door stood ajar. He stepped inside. The sunlight that streamed through the undraped windows nearly blinded him.

He hadn't set foot in the room since the morning he'd drawn the curtains and ordered the furniture covered, desperate to blot out evidence of his late bride's rage. He'd spent a small fortune updating the furnishings in preparation for his new wife to occupy Glassborough Manor. And she'd shown him just how despicable she felt he was by decimating the first thing he'd ever chosen for her.

Jonah's stomach raged at the memory of it. So much so that he didn't see Emma at first. He only saw the open draperies. It wasn't until he stepped into the room that he noticed her. She sat in an overstuffed chair near the window with a book in her lap.

Her eyes were closed and her head rested against the chair.

Jonah had no intention of waking her. He couldn't. His tongue had turned to leather and his hands were frozen at his sides. The room seemed to have rendered him mute.

He could only watch her.

She slept soundly, her breast rising and falling in a peaceful rhythm that seemed to ease his own embattled heart. He had every intention of escaping before she woke. He just wanted to watch her for a few moments. He wanted to memorize her features so when she was gone, he would have a pleasant memory to replace the horrific nightmare that Constance had left him with.

He knew there was no explanation for what had happened when he and Lady Emma had first met, but the moment he'd lifted her in his arms, his entire body had reacted to her feminine softness. Every night his arms ached to hold her again, and now, it was impossible to tear his eyes away from her.

What was there about her that haunted him so? What was there about her that mesmerized him enough that he was finally able to forget Constance and how she'd chosen death over life as his wife?

A cold sweat washed over him when he remembered Constance's lifeless body on the morning of their wedding, sprawled across the bed alongside the open packets of sleeping draughts that had taken her from this world. He quickly shifted his gaze to the lady sleeping in the chair next to him and was engulfed by an overwhelming calm.

The woman he'd rescued from the storm hadn't chosen death to escape something she found unacceptable. Instead, she'd summoned the courage to solve her predicament. She'd shown a strength Constance hadn't possessed.

Jonah watched Lady Emma for several moments before he realized that her sleep was slowly becoming less restful, agitated, as if she remembered something she didn't want to recall. She sucked in a harsh breath, then stiffened in her chair. Her breathing escalated as her eyes opened wide in fright.

She sat for several moments without noticing that he was there, then slowly turned her head until her gaze locked with his.

"Oh," she said on a gasp. "Oh…I'm sorry. I fell asleep."

Jonah walked to the bell pull to summon Carter. "Perhaps a glass of wine, my lady?"

"Yes, thank you. I would welcome that."

Her answer drew a smile as Jonah relayed his request to his butler who appeared a moment later. Constance had refused to be in the same room with him. Not even long enough to enjoy a glass of wine. As soon as he suggested anything that would put them alone in the same room, she had made her excuse and escaped.

"Thank you," Emma said when Jonah handed her the wine that arrived swiftly.

"Are you the one who opened the room to the light?"

"Yes. It was I. This room is far too beautiful to keep it hidden in the dark, my lord."

"It meets with your approval?"

"Oh, yes," she answered on a sigh. "It's a beautiful room. It feels...I don't know, somehow as if it's seen tragedy it doesn't deserve. Or wants to forget."

"I suppose it has," he answered her, then turned away lest she see the emotion their conversation evoked. How was it possible to be so comfortable with this woman even when speaking of the most horrendous moment in his life?

"Why do you keep all your rooms closed off?"

Jonah was intrigued. She didn't seem the least frightened of him. Everyone in the countryside was. It wasn't that he hadn't heard the rumors that circulated about him. It wasn't that he didn't know what everyone thought. They all thought he'd killed his fiancé. Some of them had even guessed the truth—that his fiancé was so terrified of him that she'd killed herself rather than spend the rest of her life with such a monster.

Jonah shook off his thoughts of the past and remembered the question she'd asked. "Because there's no need to keep them open," he answered.

"Do you have no visitors?"

She wasn't shy, that much was obvious.

"No, Lady Emma. I have no visitors."

"Why ever not?" She took another sip of her wine, then locked her gaze with his as if waiting for an answer to her question.

"You don't know?"

"No, Lord Glassborough. I do not know. I asked Mrs. Jefferies but she refused to answer."

Jonah rose from the sofa on which he'd been sitting and walked to the opposite side of the room. He stood before the multi-paned French doors and looked out onto the garden. There were no flowers in bloom yet, only a blanket of slowly melting snow to make everything seem cold and barren.

"Do you mean to tell me that you are not frightened of me?" he asked.

"Frightened of you? Why should I be frightened of you?"

Jonah turned to face her. "Perhaps because of my size. Or my harsh features. Or my gruff voice. Or the scar that runs the length of my face."

"To be honest, my lord, I hadn't noticed such attributes."

"You hadn't?"

"No."

Jonah walked back to her and sat on the ottoman at her feet. "Then what have you noticed about me?"

"That you are a brave man who came out in the middle of a spring snow storm to rescue me. And that you are a very compassionate man who held me carefully while we made our way back to your manor house. A very caring man who encouraged me to keep breathing and not give up."

She tilted her head to the side as if evaluating every detail she could remember. "You are also the man who watched over me that very first night. And several after that."

Jonah was surprised. "How did you know I sat with you that first week? You didn't wake once."

"I felt your presence, my lord."

"It could have been Mrs. Jefferies. Or one of the maids."

She shook her head. "No, it was you. Your presence was too powerful. Too...comforting."

Jonah took a swallow of the liquor in his glass, then placed his glass on an ornamental table. "What are you running from, my lady?"

For a moment he thought she wouldn't answer. But when the lady's gaze shifted, then locked with his, her words were not what he had expected. "What are you hiding from, Lord Glassborough?"

Jonah couldn't stop the smile from lifting the corners of his mouth. He couldn't remember the last time he'd smiled. He couldn't remember the last time he'd sparred with a female. Both felt good.

"Perhaps you'd like to answer my question first," he said.

"Only if you guarantee you'll answer my question."

"I'll answer your question. Besides, it's only a matter of time until you discover why I live in solitude."

The lady emptied her glass, then set it on the table next to his tumbler. He expected her to lower her gaze or avoid looking directly at him. But, she didn't. She faced him directly and exhibited a strength he found admirable.

"My mother died when I was just a child, my lord. My father remarried when I was twelve."

"Did you dislike the woman your father married?"

"No, quite the opposite. The woman he married was kind and I believe she truly loved my father. And he loved her. Unfortunately, they were both killed in a carriage accident two years ago."

"The Marquess of Willowbrook and your stepmother. You lost them both in the same accident. That must have been very difficult for you."

He watched the subtle changes in her face as she fought to keep her composure. She was a grown woman, but it was clear the loss had taken its toll. And why wouldn't it? Willowbrook was one of the wealthiest men in Society. Everyone had heard of him. He was rumored to have the Midas touch. Every venture he undertook turned a handsome profit. Even the Queen asked his opinion when considering where to invest her money.

"Did you know my father?"

Jonah smiled. She didn't remember they'd had this conversation. But then, she had still been in quite a weakened state.

He nodded his head.

"I knew him, though not well. I only met him once or twice. My father was an acquaintance of his. They'd been in school together."

"Oh," she said on a sad sigh. "Then you probably know he was quite wealthy."

"And deservedly so. He was a brilliant businessman."

"When he died, he left his wealth to me in trust."

"Yes, you've told me as much. And of course, that means money will never be an issue for you," Jonah answered. He couldn't help but be a bit envious. Money had always been an issue for the Glassborough name, for as long as Jonah could remember.

"For me, the money father left me has always been a curse."

Jonah couldn't hide his confusion.

"Forgive me, Lady Emma, but earlier you indicated your father had restricted the funds that could be drawn by your husband, should you marry. Surely that safeguard protects you from the curse of scurrilous suitors."

The lady rose from her chair and walked to the window. "It did. Until Father died. My stepbrother Gerald has the authority now, and in his greedy haste to collect half my fortune he challenged the codicil, claiming he was obligated to draw adequate funds to see to my wellbeing. But," she said with a smug grin. "When I gain control I can turn off his spigot of free-flowing cash."

She faced Jonah.

"Do you know how many suitors have courted me?" she asked, her face barely masking her anger. "More than I can count. Not because any of them ever loved me, mind you, but because they were desperate for the wealth I would inherit at twenty-one."

She locked her hardened gaze with his. "If my father had known the true measure of his stepson he would have protected me. But Gerald is devious. Charming in a rather villainous way. So, until I am twenty-one, my stepbrother must give his permission for me to marry. And while he inherited quite a comfortable fortune from his mother, he has managed to fritter it away." Her hands fluttered about, underscoring her frustration as she related her dilemma. "So now he wants what is mine and he has refused to grant permission for me to marry any man except one of his choosing. And the man he has chosen is...is vile beyond words."

Lady Emma stopped to compose herself. "And why do you think he has chosen this particular person, pray tell?" She drilled Jonah with an intense glare, as if she were certain he could never guess the reason.

"It's rather obvious, I should think. The suitor has agreed to share it with your stepbrother."

Her eyebrows shot up. "Yes! Exactly!" She began to pace. "For two years I've held out, but now that I'm within six months of taking full possession of my inheritance they're getting desperate."

Jonah drummed his fingers on the arms of his chair.

"Just who is this desperado?"

"My stepbrother's choice is Viscount Charleton."

Now it was Jonah's turn to react with distaste. "Charleton!"

"It appears you know the man." Lady Emma wilted into a chair, clearly exhausted from the telling of her dire straits. "In which case," she continued, "you will understand my fear that it's quite possible I would not survive the first year of marriage with him."

She shook her head angrily.

"None of his previous wives did."

Chapter Four

JONAH STARED AT THE FEAR on his houseguest's face.

"How could your stepbrother agree to a marriage between you and Charleton? The man is widely known to have a violent temper."

She dropped her eyelids, gave a slightly tremulous sigh, then seemed to find her resolve.

"Half my inheritance was ample incentive. And I had proof that was their scheme! You see, I searched the house until I found the marriage contract Gerald and Lord Charleton drew up. When I turn twenty-one, my father's entire estate will come to me. But if Gerald can get me married to Charleton before then, control of the funds goes to Charleton. And Charleton is bound by the agreement to hand over half of it to Gerald."

"He'd sell you. Like a piece of chattel. That's monstrous." Jonah rubbed a hand across his forehead, realizing he'd entered into a similar bargain not so very long ago. Now he recoiled at the very thought of it. "I suppose it was an easy bargain to make, though. Even by gaining only half of your estate your stepbrother and Lord Charleton will both become very wealthy men."

"And I will live in fear for my life every day until Lord Charleton kills me."

The portent of her words sat heavily between them. Jonah leaned his elbows on his knees and took in a long breath.

"So you ran away."

"I had no choice."

"Where were you going?"

"To London. Then, to America."

"That is a wise decision."

Jonah watched Lady Emma as she reached out to the window ledge to steady herself. She swayed from one side to the other as if she had lost her balance.

He rose, then took several steps toward her.

"Come. Sit down."

But she resisted.

"You promised if I told you why I was fleeing from my home, you would tell me why you keep your rooms dark and why people think you are a monster."

"Perhaps another time."

"No, my lord. You gave me your word and I'm holding you to your promise."

Jonah took in a deep breath.

"Very well."

He leaned against the window frame and watched her reflection. He needed to see her reaction, but somehow couldn't look her in the eye.

"I will tell you what you want to know, but only after I've admitted that I am exactly like all the other men who have courted you. Except I must assure you that I am no longer interested in marriage. Not now. Nor ever. Please be assured, I have no designs on your wealth."

A frown creased her forehead.

"You are independently wealthy?" she asked.

Jonah laughed. "Far from it."

"Then why aren't you interested in the money that would come with me if I marry?"

"Because the price it would cost me is far too high."

She hesitated. "I'm afraid I don't understand."

"You wouldn't know," Jonah continued, "but neither my father nor my elder brother were good stewards of what they inherited. I tried to rein in their spending, but nothing I said or did made them change their wastrel living. I finally gave up trying. When the war started, I joined

Her Majesty's army."

"And came home with a scar on your face."

She said it in such a matter-of-fact tone, and yet one that was infused with notes of compassion, that he was momentarily startled. Her understanding loosed a cord deep within him that he only now realized had been strung as tightly as an archer's bow.

"Yes. It happened in the last battle of the war. A sabre wound."

Jonah found himself frozen in the moment as Lady Emma lifted her hand and pressed her fingers against the scar that ran down his cheek. Her touch was gentle yet clinical, probing as a physician might. He had never imagined that any woman would be brave enough to touch his pitiful, puckered flesh. And yet she had. With mesmerizing tenderness.

He dropped his eyes and continued speaking when she lowered her hand. "My father and my brother both died while I was gone. I returned to no family and an insurmountable pile of debts that I have yet to repay."

"I'm sorry," she said.

"There's no need to be sorry. My brother died the same way he lived. Reckless and in debt." Jonah paused. "He'd been accused of cheating in a card game, and died in a duel."

Jonah sensed her stiffen beside him. He knew he'd touched a raw nerve. He was admitting that his brother was exactly the kind of man she least wanted to know. Bloody hell, he was about to admit that he himself was no better.

"Two years ago, the Earl of Westshield offered me an enticing proposition. I had just returned from the war and was still recovering from my wounds. I hadn't been out in public yet and very few of the townspeople even knew I was home."

"What did Lord Westshield offer you?"

"He offered to pay all my debts if I would agree to marry his daughter."

"You were the man Lady Constance was intended to marry?"

Lady Emma gave him an incredulous look.

"Yes. I was the man. Except dear Constance was not pleased with our betrothal."

Lady Emma gave his arm a compassionate squeeze.

101

"The lady took one look at me and screamed in fright. Several times she refused to marry me but her father would not give in. When he demanded a final time that she had no choice but to marry me, she did exactly what you did. She ran away before spending even one night under my roof."

"But that should have put an end to it, surely."

"How many times I've wished it had. But her father found her at the inn in town and brought her back. After, of course, the lady had caused quite a scene. She'd informed everyone within shouting distance that I was a horribly disfigured monster and that I was mentally deranged from my time and experiences during the war."

"Oh, my lord," she said on a sigh. "How dreadful."

"As you can imagine, the people of Glastonbury believed what the lady told them. They feared meeting me, or even having me approach them."

"Is that why no one comes to call?"

"Do you blame them?"

She answered his question with a dismissing shrug.

"Was Lady Constance fleeing from here when she died in that carriage accident?" Lady Emma asked after a few moments.

"Carriage accident?"

"Outside London?"

"Ah," Jonah said. "I always wondered what reason her parents gave for her death."

"You mean, she didn't—"

"No." He could have left it there. He could have let her go on thinking that was the manner in which the distraught Lady Constance had died. But some force that now existed between himself and Lady Emma bade him to speak only the truth. And so he did.

"The lady took her own life."

This was the first time he'd related to anyone what had happened that fateful week. The look of shock on Lady Emma's face was evidence that much of Society had been spared the truth.

"Oh, my lord. I am so sorry. But not sorry that you escaped being married to such an unstable female."

"Perhaps. But there's also a certain amount of guilt that's associated with what happened."

"Please, my lord. The guilt is not yours to bear."

"Perhaps not entirely, but in part."

"Did Lord Westshield give you a reason why he was so desperate for his daughter to marry?"

Jonah shook his head. "I can only surmise."

A look passed between them, and he saw that she recognized his conjecture that his bride-to-be had been with child.

"But I never asked. I didn't care. I didn't love her. All that mattered at the time was the amount of money I would get if I married her and how many improvements I could make to Glassborough Estate."

Jonah felt again the anguish of that horrid time in his life and tried to forget it. The money he'd expected to receive had been so blasted important that it was all he could think about at the time. He had carelessly told himself that in time the female he was supposed to marry would become accustomed to his looks. That she'd find his grisly features less gruesome. He told himself that once they were married, he'd do everything in his power to make sure she didn't regret marrying him.

But nothing worked out the way he'd planned. The lady had chosen death rather than life as mistress of his household. Her mother had found her daughter's lifeless body the morning of their wedding.

Jonah caught Lady Emma watching him, and she quickly turned toward the room.

"She did this." Lady Emma swept her hand to encompass the room.

Jonah had been on the verge of assuring Lady Emma that while he had once been the very type of man she sought to avoid, she need never concern herself with any advances from him to marry her in order to get the money that would be hers. He wanted to assure her that he'd learned a harsh lesson from the last female who had been forced to marry him— that even death was preferable to spending life with a deformed monster.

But he could not.

He'd destroyed a woman once over money. How could he know he wouldn't do it again?

And then there was the matter of his temper.

"No. She didn't do this."

He strode to the door and turned sharply just before he reached the hallway.

"I did."

Chapter Five

EMMA SLOWLY OPENED HER EYES. Her afternoon in the morning room, with its soul-searching revelations by her host, had sapped her of energy. She wasn't sure how long she'd slept, but it must have been several hours. The sun was high in the sky, the same as it had been when she'd fallen asleep. From the way she felt, it may well have been an entire day.

She turned her head to watch Mrs. Jefferies enter the room after knocking softly at the door.

"Ah, you're awake," she said, then set the tray she carried on the bedside table.

Emma rubbed her eyes. "How long did I sleep?"

"A little more than a day, my lady. I haven't seen the master so worried ever. He checked on you more times than I could count."

"He did?"

"Yes," she said, then helped Emma to sit. She placed several pillows behind Emma's back, then handed her a cup of hot chocolate and a toast point laden with butter and jam.

"This is just what I needed," Emma said. "I can't remember when I ate last."

"That's what I thought," Mrs. Jefferies smiled. "His lordship wanted me to bring up a breakfast of eggs and bacon and ham and toast and sausage and pastries and kidneys and fried potatoes, but Cook told him you'd get sick if you ate that much after going without food for so long."

Emma smiled.

"This is plenty."

She finished her chocolate, set down her cup, and took a bite of toast.

"Thank you, Mrs. Jefferies. I appreciate everything you've done for me."

"You're most welcome, my lady. Just ring if you need anything else." The housekeeper pointed to a bell sitting on the bedside table.

"Perhaps in an hour or so, you'll help me dress so I can get out of bed."

"I'm not sure the master will approve of you getting out of bed."

"I won't get stronger if I stay in bed another day."

"We'll see," the housekeeper said, then left the room.

Emma knew she needed to begin moving about if she intended to get stronger. The same as she knew she needed to get stronger in order to be on her way. And she needed to be on her way before her stepbrother found her.

She had to be on the next ship sailing to America. She simply *had* to.

With great effort, Emma rose and dressed, then sat down in the chair beside the window. She had been forced to sit and rest several times while she dressed. It surprised her how exhausted she was. How weak she became from doing something so simple.

Emma sat in the cushioned chair and looked out the window.

The snow had stopped, but it was too deep to risk traveling. As if she were strong enough to travel, which she was not. Neither did she know how long it would be before she felt confident to travel on her own.

She was considering what lay ahead of her when a tentative knock sounded at the door.

"Come in."

The door opened to reveal the Earl of Glassborough standing in her doorway. He was dressed formally, now, not covered in work debris as he had been the day before. But there was little evidence of the confidence he'd exhibited atop the scaffolding and through the early minutes of their conversation in the morning room.

"When Mrs. Jefferies told me you intended to get out of bed, I had a feeling that I'd find you up and dressed." He clasped his hands behind his back. "And so you are."

She smiled.

"Yes, my lord. A testament to your magnificent care."

His lordship seemed startled by such praise, and covered his discomfort by stepping into the room to sit in a chair next to her, leaving the door fully ajar.

"May I"?

Her smile grew wider. "By all means."

"I brought the book you were reading yesterday."

Glassborough held out the small leather-bound volume of poetry and Emma took it. "That's very kind of you, my lord."

"Not at all." He looked about. "Have you any coffee in that pot?"

"It's chocolate, my lord. It should still be hot. Would you care for some?"

At his nod she rose and poured steaming cocoa into the second cup Mrs. Jefferies had placed on the tray.

"I must apologize for losing this lovely day to sleep," she said as he accepted the cup. "I thought I was stronger than I am."

"You were badly injured when that branch fell on you. You need time to heal."

Emma's heart beat faster. "But that's just what I don't have, Lord Glassborough. Time. By now, Gerald has returned to Willowbrook Hall and discovered that I'm missing. I'm sure he has begun his search for me."

"You are safe as long as you stay hidden. I doubt your brother will even think to look for you here."

"Why do you say that?"

"Because even if he inquires in the village, he will be told that everyone in his right mind avoids Glassborough Estate. The villagers believe that I am insane."

Emma's eyebrows shot upward. "That's ridiculous."

"You think so?"

"Of course I do. You're as sane as I am."

Lord Glassborough offered a crooked smile, then lifted his cup to salute her. "Thank you for the vote of confidence."

Emma returned Jonah's salute with a wink and a smile. She wasn't just being kind. She meant it, and infused her words with the weight of a mother telling her quaking child not to fear the dark. *You're as sane as I am.* She would say it as often as this good man needed to hear it.

A long moment later her host returned his cup to the tea tray and rose from his chair. He seemed deep in thought as he walked to the window where he braced his hands on either side of the window frame and looked outside.

Emma watched his shoulders stiffen as if the weight they carried was too heavy to bear. His fists tightened around the wooden window frame. Even though he pretended that what the villagers thought of him didn't matter, she could see that it did.

"I want you to know, my lady, that you need never fear advances from me with regard to the money that will rightfully become yours on your birthday. If I learned anything from what happened before, it is to be content with what I have and not rely on an unwilling female to free me of my debts."

"I have never considered you a threat, my lord."

"I am glad to hear that, my lady. I refuse to involve another female in resolving my financial dilemma. In fact, that whole ordeal thoroughly soured me on the very idea of marriage. We are of like minds in that regard, madam." He paused and ran a hand through his hair. "I cannot force another female to look at this face every morning when she wakes, or be forced to endure the looks of pity on the villagers' faces because the poor woman I married is saddled with such a monstrous man."

As she watched the tension in his face escalate, Emma was struck by Lord Glassborough's earnestness.

"Surely you exaggerate, my Lord. Certainly you have nothing to fear in that regard." She smiled. "You also have nothing to fear from me, my lord. I have made my intentions clear from the beginning. I am committed to making my way to America, and once there I intend to change my name and go someplace where Gerald will never find me."

"Do you know where you will go?" Lord Glassborough asked as he turned fully toward her.

Emma shook her head. "I'm not sure yet. I tried to discover places where I can get lost in the crowds, but I didn't have time to study too thoroughly. I couldn't risk Gerald discovering what I was doing for fear he'd realize I was planning an escape."

"What cities have you considered?"

"New York City, of course, the largest of American cities. It seems to offer the most opportunities for getting lost. Then, I've thought that Boston might do. Or Philadelphia. But I haven't researched the last two choices to become familiar with either of them." Emma lifted her gaze and looked at Lord Glassborough. "Have you been to America?"

He gave her a speculative look as he clasped his hands behind his back. "I have not. But I do believe you should avoid New York. Every immigrant passes through a place called Ellis Island. Surely all one had to do to discover you were in New York City would be to bribe the immigrant registrar or one of his minions. In fact," he continued, "the names might actually be a simple matter of public record."

"Really." Emma slumped in her chair. This was awful. She had no idea it might be so easy to detect her presence halfway around the world. What was she thinking? She'd escape her stepbrother's clutches here only to walk straight into his grasp in a strange and hostile country.

Slow panic began to trickle up from the pit of her stomach.

"I have an idea, though." Lord Glassborough took two steps and resumed his seat.

She heard him speak, even while her mind was still in the throes of dealing with the bubble of hope his words had just burst.

"Emma?"

Slowly she realized that Lord Glassborough had reached for her, and before she could think to move, his large hand covered her own. It was warm, roughened by work, and comforting in the most intimate way.

She looked up.

"Emma," he repeated.

"Yes?"

"Let me help you. I'll obtain passage on a trading vessel, a ship belonging to a friend of mine, Captain Russell, who takes goods to Virginia. His wife often goes to sea with him. She can be your companion."

"No, I couldn't involve you. I—"

"But you must." He moved to the edge of his chair and turned his earnest face toward her. "This way your name will never appear on any manifest. And Captain Russell will see you settled in Virginia. I promise you, he's a man whose character is above reproach. I served with him in the war. He was my commanding officer."

"I couldn't possibly, I—"

As she began to object, her eyes searched his, and the sincerity she saw there silenced her. In the next instant Emma felt him raise her hand from her lap. Ever so gently he turned her hand palm upwards and with immense care gently uncurled her fingers that had been clenched into a fist. His finger traced the marks left by her fingernails.

"Let me do this for you."

His voice was little more than a whisper, sending blissful waves of comfort traversing her veins, carrying this good man's promise straight to her heart. He was kindness personified. What great good fortune had landed her in his care?

His eyes glimmered like melting gold, stealing any reservations she might have had. He was telling the truth. He would orchestrate her escape.

"Thank you, my lord," she breathed. "I don't know what to say."

Her heart pounded in her throat, whether from the assistance he offered her, or his display of passion. Whatever the reason, she couldn't help but be affected.

"Just say yes. It will be my pleasure to help you escape the destiny your stepbrother intends for you."

Lord Glassborough rose to his feet, still holding her hand. "Now let's adjourn to the library and search for any books that might describe life in America. I may even have a map of America's eastern seaboard."

Emma rose, somehow regretting that now she would have to drop his hand that had seemed so perfectly natural joined with her own.

"Do you know when your Captain Russell will be sailing next?"

He shook his head as he led the way through to the hall and down the stairs. "I'm not sure if he's returned from his current voyage. If he has, I'll make arrangements for you to sail on his next trip."

When they reached the bottom of the stairs, Glassborough led her across the foyer, then down the long hall and into the library.

"I think you'll find books that contain the information you're searching for on these shelves," he said, pointing to the library's west wall.

Emma forced herself to concentrate on his books and not on his hands that gestured so expressively between them.

"Please, sit down and I'll hand you some books I think you'll find most helpful."'

Emma took a seat in one of the oversized upholstered chairs and placed the books he extended to her in her lap. Before long, she had more books in front of her than she'd ever be able to peruse in one sitting.

"Now," he said, walking away from her. "If you don't mind, I need to return to my ledgers. Call for Mrs. Jefferies if you require anything at all."

His departure seemed abrupt, but if he felt any of the electricity that was now charging through her own veins, Emma could scarcely blame him.

"Thank you, Lord Glassborough. You've been most helpful."

"You are welcome," he answered as he moved to the door. But when he reached it, he paused and half-turned toward her. He drew a breath, as if he were about to speak, then thought better of it. Instead, he gave her a small smile before stepping into the hall.

Emma watched him retreat. How comforted she felt, even with the riot of emotions that churned within her. The change in plans he had proposed gave her hope for the first time. She might actually be able to arrive safely in the New World.

Completely anonymously.

Chapter Six

EMMA WOKE EARLY THE NEXT MORNING. Refusing to spend another day resting in bed, she dressed, then went down for breakfast. She hoped that when she entered the breakfast room she would see Lord Glassborough and would have an opportunity to thank him for all he'd done for her. But he wasn't there. She asked after him, but was told he'd already eaten and left for the day.

When she finished eating, she went to the library to search for more books on America, then took the books to the morning room to read.

She was glad to find the draperies still open and the dust covers off the furnishings. The sun poured in through the windows and wrapped the room in sunny warmth. She had swiftly come to love this room. There wasn't a more beautiful room in Glassborough Manor.

Emma wouldn't have been surprised if Lord Glassborough had ordered the dust covers put back on the furniture to hide the shredded cushions, and the draperies drawn to keep the room in darkness. But instead, everything was perfectly in place. Where possible, the cushions had been turned upside down to hide the evidence of his temper, and to the unknowing eye, no one would ever imagine the master of Glassborough Manor had taken his anger out on the cushions in this room. The cushions would still need to be repaired, but that would come in due time. For now, the room seemed aglow with its reclaimed state.

It wasn't until mid-afternoon that Lord Glassborough returned to the morning room.

"Lady Emma," he said in greeting.

"Lord Glassborough. Have you finished with your ledgers?"

A smile lifted the corners of his mouth. That small movement transformed his features and caused a shifting in her breast. When he smiled, he was an incredibly handsome man. His features softened and he seemed caring. Protective.

Emma studied her host's features. There was a confident set to his shoulders, and his profile was strong and bold. The rugged angle of his rigid jaw exuded power while his firm features indicated an air of command. One would think he possessed a calm confidence, yet the inky darkness of his eyes allowed Emma to see something he tried to hide. A hurt that haunted him day and night.

His deep, rich voice pulled Emma back from her musing, "The first thing I learned when I took over the estate...," he said as an answer to her comment, "...was that one is never finished with the ledgers."

He walked into the room and stopped at the sideboard where he lifted a crystal decanter and poured some liquor into a glass. "Would you care for anything? A glass of wine, perhaps?"

"Yes, that would be lovely."

He poured her a glass of deep red wine and handed it to her.

"Thank you."

He unbuttoned his coat and sat in a maroon velvet chair next to hers. He stretched his legs out in front of him and took a sip of his liquor. Emma was glad he felt able to relax when he was around her.

"You seem to be improving, my lady."

"I am. It won't be long and I'll be well enough to be on my way."

"I know you are anxious for that day, but I doubt you'll be well enough to travel for another week or two."

Emma took a sip of her wine, then smiled. "I thought you would be eager to see me go," she said.

"Quite the contrary, my lady. I've grown accustomed to having you here. And, I enjoy our conversations."

Emma lowered her eyes to the wine glass in her hands. "I'm glad to hear that, my lord. I so hoped I wasn't too much of an imposition."

"You aren't. And since you'll be here a while longer, why don't you call me Jonah. That is my given name."

"Jonah," she repeated. "The name fits you."

He smiled again.

"Then, please. Call me Emma. My given name is Emmaline, but my father always called me Emma."

He nodded, then took another swallow of the liquor in his glass.

"Emma, then." He cleared his throat. "Would you care to take a walk in the garden? If you think you're up to it."

"By all means."

"We won't stay out long, just long enough to walk around the perimeter."

"That sounds perfect."

"I'll ask Carter to get your wrap," he said as he rose.

Nothing sounded more relaxing than taking a walk in the open air. It had been so long since she'd been out of doors, and the weather had turned so much nicer than it had been when she had her accident.

Spring was finally here after all, and some of the trees were starting to bud and the shrubbery was beginning to green. Even though dusk was approaching and she would not be able to see all the wonders of nature, she'd be able to imagine what the trees and flowers would look like in mid-summer.

Lord Glassborough returned with her wrap and helped settle it on her shoulders. Together, they walked out the paned double doors and across the terrace.

They descended the three steps to the garden, then walked down the path to their right.

"Once the trees leaf out and the flowers bloom, the east half of the garden is a masterpiece of vibrant colors that amaze the eyes. And the west?" With a small laugh Jonah swung his hand across the tilled soil of an untended group of plots. "Well, as you can see, it's a dismal work in progress." His self-conscious laugh held all the impatience she felt in him at having the project not yet completed.

"I can imagine what it will look like, though," Emma said, taking in the scenery around her. "Do you have a hand in caring for the garden?"

"Yes. I've always enjoyed planting the seeds and watching them grow."

"I admire you, Lord Glassborough."

"Jonah," he corrected.

"Jonah," she said."

"Why do you admire me, my lady?"

"Emma," she said with a laugh as she lifted her gaze to look at him.

He smiled, then looped her arm through his. "Why is it that you admire me, Emma?"

"Because not every man sees the beauty in nature. Because few men allow themselves to admire the beauty around them."

"That is probably true, Emma, but..." He paused for several moments. "...I will never forget the first sight I saw when I stepped off the ship after the war. I can't explain how I felt when I took my first step back on English soil. I wanted to weep. I had survived when so many others hadn't."

He took several more steps before he spoke again. "There was a young lass who met our ship. Her hands were full of flowers. She presented one to each of us. She handed me a yellow daisy. It was beginning to wilt and had several petals missing, but it was the most beautiful flower I'd ever seen. I can tell you with all honesty that it was the most precious gift I'd ever received."

He stopped walking and stared into the distance as though he were reliving that day. His hand clenched as if he still held that flower.

"After spending two years in a country where there'd been nothing other than mud and blood and the cries and screams of the wounded and dying, that daisy was the most hopeful thing I'd seen in months. That is why," he said looking around his garden, "much of my garden contains beds of daisies of every variety I can find."

"A veritable garden of hope," Emma sighed. "You know, old Henry VIII would have been thrilled to see your park filled with daisies."

"Gads," Jonah grinned down on her and winked. "He would probably have eaten them all!"

Emma looked at him quizzically. She'd recalled that the old king had a fondness for daisies, but was Jonah having her on?

"For stomach ache, you know. They're medicinal." He laughed. "Or at least Henry thought so."

Emma lifted a hand to cover her sudden laughter. She reached the other hand out to swat his arm, and she took a step closer to improve her aim.

He stopped. Then turned her to face him.

Emma lifted her head and her gaze locked with his. There was something immensely compelling in the look he gave her. Something that told her that his emotions were battling with his sense of propriety. Then, his gaze lowered to her lips.

He was going to kiss her. Emma knew he was. He was silently waiting for her to refuse his advances, or give him her permission. Waiting for her indication that she didn't object. Or that she did.

She should stop him. She only needed to turn her head and step away from him. But she didn't. It was as if something inside her refused to let this moment pass without experiencing what his kisses would do to her.

Emma focused her gaze on his mouth. His lips were full and kissable. She ran her tongue over her lips, then skimmed her hands upward over his chest. She didn't stop until her fingers were nearly to his shoulders.

With their eyes locked and their lips parted, he brought his mouth down to gently cover hers.

There was nothing demanding in his kiss, only a tender entreaty that begged permission to continue.

Emma wrapped her arms around his neck and pressed her mouth more firmly to his.

He answered her plea with another kiss.

The world spun in circles as the crystal moment lengthened. Their passion grew with unmistakable ardor before he wrapped his arms around her and held her closer still.

Emma heard a forlorn moan of distress. It was her own throaty affirmation of just how far his kisses had reached deep inside her breast to pull at her heart.

This shouldn't be happening. His kisses ought not to affect her like this. They weren't supposed to be so powerful that she would mourn the loss of them if he never kissed her again.

But they were.

In time, he broke off their kiss but didn't release her. Instead, he tucked her head beneath his chin and held her close. Emma was thankful. She wasn't sure her legs would support her if he released her, weak as they had become from his kisses.

"I should apologize, but saying I'm sorry would be a lie," he said without releasing her. "I'm not sorry. Not in the least."

"I'm glad you kissed me," Emma admitted. "Although, we must not give way to this…affection. You know that."

"I know," he said, then dropped his arms from around her. "I'll not forget what you said the other day."

"What was that?"

"You said that none of the men who courted you had loved you. What they loved was the money that would come with you. So I'll not forget that I am no different than any of those men. I need money as much as any of them did. Perhaps more. But I promised you then that I will not take advantage of you. I will not deceive you into thinking I love you just to gain your trust."

Emma heard disappointment in his voice, even as she felt it pinching her own heart. She turned to the side, hoping he wouldn't see the emotions with which she wrestled.

Jonah walked to the edge of the sidewalk and looked out over the garden. Instead of coming back to stand beside her, he walked a few steps down the path and stared out into the garden. "I think there could be something between us. I think that in time, we might come to care for each other. But neither of us can allow that to happen."

He paused for several moments. "I do not have a pound to my name, Emma, and if…" he paused. "…*if* something more developed between us, you would never know if I really cared for you, or if my words were lies like all the lies you heard before."

She knew he was right. She'd learned the lesson that she couldn't believe any suitor. And she'd learned it several times over.

"Thank you for understanding," she said quietly. "Now," she continued as she struggled to quiet her troubled heart, "I'm a little weary. I believe I shall retire."

"I'll see you in," he said.

Emma shook her head. "No need. I'll be fine by myself."

Emma turned away from him and walked back to the house. There was a very heavy weight inside her breast and a painful lump in her stomach, as if she'd just lost someone very special.

But she'd had no choice. She couldn't let any man in. At least not yet. Especially not someone who needed money as desperately as Lord Glassborough did.

Chapter Seven

EVERY DAY SEEMED ENDLESS. Jonah knew that was because of the effort it took to avoid running into Emma. And yet...she consumed every second of his thoughts.

He couldn't stop thinking about her. About what she was doing. Whether or not she thought about him even once a day. Or more. But most of all, he wondered if she relived the kiss they'd shared. And if it tortured her as much as it did him.

After Constance had chosen death rather than spend her life as his wife, Jonah was certain he would never find a woman who could overlook the rumors that surrounded him. Or the scar that marred his face. Or the recluse he'd become. Or any of a hundred other things about him that made him someone no female would want as her husband. And yet the kiss he and Emma had shared amid the spring's budding garden told him something altogether different. The kiss they'd shared woke emotions he thought were long dead.

But she had chosen escape, and he would honor that.

Jonah rose from his desk and walked out the paned double doors that led to the terrace. He braced his hands on the balustrade and looked out onto the garden. The weather had changed since Emma had arrived. It was warmer now. The sun shone with regularity and the crocuses and daffodils were peeking through the soil. Leaves were turning the branches green and buds were popping open.

Jonah had always observed the awakening of the flowers and the blossoming of everything that had lain dormant throughout the winter merely as a botanical event. But since Emma had come into his life, he felt that every part of him was awakening. That something inside him had come to life.

He pounded his fist against the railing in frustration. Such feelings were futile. Nothing could come of the emotions that blossomed inside of him. No matter how much he might care for her, he had nothing to recommend himself to Emma. He had nothing to offer her. Nothing at all. Not even a decent roof over her head.

Jonah pushed himself away from the railing and walked from the terrace to follow one of the paths in the garden. He needed to think. He needed to plan. He needed to do what was best for Emma. And only one thing was best for her. That was for her to get as far away from England as possible and make a new life for herself in Virginia.

He'd only taken a few steps when he saw her. She was sitting on a wrought-iron bench with a book in her hands. Her eyes weren't focused on the words in the book, but staring into space as if she were deep in thought.

Jonah knew he should make his presence known, but he'd rather use the little time he had until she saw him to study her. He wanted to look at her features and put them to memory so that when she was no longer with him, he could still recall every detail of her. The rich color of her hair and the slight tilt of her nose. The magnificent blue of her eyes and the proud lift of her shoulders. But most of all, her inner strength and the determination to do what she knew she had to do. And do it alone. He'd never met anyone like her.

Jonah thought it was best to turn around and leave before she realized he was there. He turned, but only managed to take one step back toward the house before her voice stopped him.

"My lord?"

Jonah turned. "I'm sorry, Emma. I didn't mean to disturb you."

"You didn't. I was just enjoying this perfect day. Please, join me."

Jonah made his way to the bench where she sat and took his place beside her. "It is quite beautiful, isn't it? The day, I mean."

She smiled and Jonah's heart flipped in his chest.

"Yes."

Jonah looked at the flowers just starting to bloom. "When I was young, I used to come here with my grandmother and she would sometimes read to me, or we would just talk. I thought she was the wisest woman in all the world."

"What did you talk about?"

"Everything. She would tell me about her mother and father and who they were. And she would tell me about my grandfather's family. She told me it was important to know where I came from."

"That is very important," she said. "I wish my father would have told me about my grandparents. I would have liked to know who they were and how they lived."

"Yes, I'm glad she told me about her parents. And my grandfather's. If she hadn't, I would have only known my father and brother, and they weren't examples I could be proud of."

She turned her head and stared at him.

"Does that surprise you?"

"Yes."

"My grandfather was a very intelligent member of Society. He was well thought of, and an excellent businessman. He took the little his father gave him and invested it wisely. He worked hard and was a very wealthy man when he died."

"What happened to his wealth?"

"It went to my father and my brother. My father was not blessed with a good sense of business and made one bad investment after another. My brother was a lazy wastrel. He enjoyed gambling and womanizing and spent far more money than he had."

"How did your father die?"

"He drank himself to death."

"I'm sorry," she said, and Jonah could tell from the sympathy in her voice that she truly meant it.

"They had both died by the time I came home from the war. Perhaps if I would have been here, things might have been different, but it's too

121

late to think of that now."

"Yes," she said. "You can't live in the past, or carry guilt for the choices your father and brother made. You only have to answer for the choices you make in the here and now." She gave him a piercing look. "As I am."

Jonah shifted on the bench to face her. "Is there not someone else you care for? Someone else you would like to marry?"

Lady Emma drew back, giving him an odd, almost questioning look, as if she were considering his own marital worth. And then she sighed.

"No," she answered as she rose from the bench and took two steps from him. "I have known I would not marry from the day Society discovered the amount of money my father had put in trust for when I marry. I remember that day vividly. Every man who had not so much as asked me to dance suddenly wanted to court me. There wasn't an empty set on my dance card from the moment rumors of my worth began to circulate. I felt like a prize horse at Tattersall's."

"I don't blame you," Jonah said, rising to his feet. "But speaking of horses, walk with me while we talk over a bit of business."

Emma lifted her gaze and took his arm. The corners of her mouth turned upward into a most appealing smile. To Jonah, her smile was her most enchanting feature. It might be winsome one moment, then pensive, inviting, or even intriguing the next. It could sit suspended upon her face while it lit her eyes, as if she were about to make a spontaneous comment. Or even a scandalous one. Her facial animations cast a prettiness over her features—a warm, smouldering welcome that invited closer study. The very effect of it tugged at his heart and refused to release it.

"Horses, you say?"

"Ahem. Yes. Your horse, in particular."

"My horse?"

"Yes. You won't be needing it, as I will be escorting you to London in the carriage. If you should require a mount, you're welcome to either of the two remaining in my stable." He cast his eyes away from her. He simply couldn't voice the real reason for wanting to sell her horse, so he fished about for a compelling reason. "But really, your stepbrother will have put out word that he's looking for a young woman on horseback, so you can't be seen out riding anyway. And I have a buyer if you give permission for me to pursue the sale."

The real reason for the sale stuck in his throat like a bit of bad fish. The funds from the sale of the horse would cover the cost of her passage on Captain Randall's ship. It was humiliating. He would give the world to gift her the price of her passage himself.

And if wishes were horses, beggars would ride.

They walked in silence a few paces down the path until Lady Emma stopped and laid a hand on his arm.

"Jonah, your kindness and hospitality have overwhelmed me. My horse is yours to do with as you please." She gave his arm a gentle squeeze. "With my deepest thanks."

Jonah smiled at her warm appreciation. "I'll see to it the moment I return."

An expression of surprise crossed her face. "Return? Are you leaving?"

"Yes. I must go to London. I'll find out if Captain Russell has returned and when he will be sailing again. If I'm lucky," he said, nudging her shoulder with his own, "he won't be sailing again for months. Maybe years."

She looked up in time to catch his dramatic wink. "You're flirting with trouble now, Lord Glassborough," she said with a wink of her own. "I think I must leave before I completely wear out my welcome."

Jonah stifled the words of denial that flew to his tongue and kept his answer light. "I imagine I can suffer through a few more days."

Emma paused in the middle of the path and turned to face him. "You were serious when you offered to find me passage on your friend's ship?"

"Of course I was. I completely understand why you're anxious to leave."

Emma lowered her gaze. "Thank you."

"You're welcome."

"I have no money yet. I can't pay you for my passage."

Without realizing it, Lady Emma had opened the way for him to confess without shame. He could not have been more grateful.

"That's not a problem. Your horse should cover the cost of it," he answered.

"Of course! Oh, splendid! I can't thank you enough, my lord."

Letting her regain her self-esteem by providing for her own need was an unexpected reward. Jonah locked his gaze with hers. He battled the ache inside him when he thought of how lonely he'd be when she was gone. He'd never taken such pleasure in each day as he had since Emma had arrived. He didn't want to think of how desolate he would be when she left.

"How long will you be gone?" she asked, looping her arm through his and making her way further down the path.

"Five days at the most, I would think. If Captain Russell is already in London and is preparing to set sail for his return trip to Virginia I'll return immediately to get you."

Jonah saw the excitement on Emma's face and the ache inside him hurt worse.

"Should I go with you? Perhaps—"

"No, you need to stay out of sight. The last thing we want is for your stepbrother to see you."

Jonah wasn't sure if Emma agreed with him or not, but finally she nodded.

"When are you leaving?" she asked.

"First thing in the morning. If I make good time, I should reach London before nightfall."

"Thank you," she said. Tears swam in her eyes but she swiped them away before they spilled over her lashes.

Jonah brought her close and placed a brotherly kiss on her cheek. He wanted to kiss her mouth as he'd done once before but he knew that would be a tragic mistake. Kissing her once had been a huge error in judgement. Kissing her a second time would be fatal.

"I need to return to the house. I have papers to organize before I can leave."

He gave her hand a warm pat and stepped away, letting the small pain of separation resume its place above his heart.

As he'd known it would.

Chapter Eight

JONAH PUSHED JUPITER as hard as he dared. His trip to London had gone well. First, Lady Emmaline's horse had brought a very fair price, sold to a fellow in the next village. He'd promised to keep the horse out of sight in his barn for ten days.

Next, he found that Captain Russell had docked several weeks earlier and was preparing to set sail in a week's time. That would give Jonah six days to return to Glassborough and escort Emma to London. Thankfully, the captain's wife agreed to accompany her husband as a chaperone for Emma. It could not have worked out better.

Or worse.

Jonah wiped a hand over his face. He was so tired. He'd been up since dawn and had traveled all day to reach home. When his eyes closed and he swayed in the saddle for more times than he could count, he decided to stop at the *Pig and Ale Inn* to rest for a moment and drink a pint of ale in an effort to revive himself. He only had a few miles to go until he reached Glassborough, but as tired as he was, he wasn't sure he could make it.

When he arrived at the *Pig and Ale,* the yard was thankfully empty. He wasn't in the mood to put up with a crowd of rowdy workers and tenants who'd stopped by for a pint before they went home.

He dismounted and tied Jupiter to a post.

The second he stepped into the taproom, he felt an eerie tension. Ordinarily he found the patrons engaged in jovial conversation. But tonight's small crowd seemed ill at ease. Jonah turned his attention to the man at the end of the bar and guessed that he was the reason for their unease.

"Surely one of you has seen her. She'd hardly blend in with you lot," he said, slurring his words. "She's a lady."

Jonah took a chair at a table in the corner of the room, far enough from the man that he hoped he hadn't been noticed. Unfortunately, before the barmaid even came to see what Jonah wanted to drink, the man staggered over.

"Are you from around here?" he asked.

Jonah lifted his head enough to look at the man. "Who wants to know?"

"Baron Marquardt. The woman I'm looking for is my sister."

"And you lost her?"

Jonah's comment earned him snickers from the few men in the room as well as a malicious glare from Emma's drunken brother. Jonah could see why Emma feared her stepbrother. He seemed a black-hearted excuse for a human being.

The barmaid approached with the ale and Jonah lifted the mug to his lips and took a long swallow.

"So, have you seen her? She's not much to look at. Dark hair, well-dressed. Rides a chestnut mare."

Jonah finished his ale and lifted his mug to indicate he wanted another tankard.

"I'm just returning from London where I saw several women who match your sister's description. No doubt they felt it safe to walk the streets now that you've vacated the city."

"You're a bloody smug toff," Emma's stepbrother hissed as he rose and kicked his chair across the room.

Before he could step away from Jonah's table, Jonah slammed his hand down and clasped Marquardt's wrist in an iron grip. "I'd watch my temper if I were you, Marquardt. We don't take kindly to pompous jaybirds from London causing trouble where there's no need."

Jonah gave Marquardt's wrist a cruel twist, then released him. Emma's stepbrother staggered across the room and took his place at the end of the bar.

"Thanks, my lord," the bartender said, bringing Jonah another mug of ale. "That bloody bloke's been nothing but trouble since he came."

"How long has he been here?"

"Two, three days. Been looking for his sister who ran away from him. Not that I blame her. I'd run as far from that one as I could get."

Jonah cast a glance at Marquardt. He'd knocked over a stool at the bar and was stumbling up the stairs to his room. "Hopefully, you won't be bothered by him any longer tonight."

Jonah reached in his pocket and pulled out coins to pay for his last mug of ale.

"No," the bartender said. "Last one's on the house. You earned it."

"Thank you," Jonah said, then finished his ale. The sooner he left, the sooner he'd get home so he could protect Emma. The man who threatened her future was altogether too close for comfort.

She was right. She needed to leave England as soon as possible.

Jonah mounted Jupiter and rode to Glassborough Manor. He handed his mount to Farley and strode to the house. When he reached the door, Carter was waiting for him.

"Has Lady Emma retired?" he asked as he entered the foyer. It was late, but not so late that he couldn't stop to bid her good evening. He needed to tell her what he'd found out from Captain Russell, as well as that he'd met her stepbrother. He knew she would be pleased to know he'd arranged passage to America. Just as she'd be more anxious than ever to be gone from Glassborough Manor. Even though he wasn't ready to see her go.

"Yes, my lord. The lady is in the library. She's waited up every night since you left."

Jonah couldn't help but smile.

"Would you like me to have the servants make up a tray, my lord?"

"Yes, please, Carter. And some bread and cheese and meat. I didn't stop to eat on my way home."

"Right away, my lord."

Carter turned away and Jonah turned toward the library. He couldn't wait to see Emma. He couldn't put into words how much he'd missed her. Now he looked forward to bringing that joyous smile to her face with his good news, even though it would crush him to do so.

He touched the inside pocket of his jacket and felt the books he'd purchased on his way out of London. He knew she would enjoy reading something more current than the books he had on his shelves.

Jonah walked down the hall and stopped before he entered the library. Emma wasn't sitting in one of the chairs reading like he imagined she would be, but was standing by one of the cushioned wing chairs, facing the doorway.

"Greetings, my lord," she said with a smile on her face. "I heard you enter. I can't tell you how pleased I am to see you've returned safely."

"Emma," he said, taking long, eager strides to reach her. He leaned close to her and placed a kiss on each cheek.

"May I pour you a glass of brandy?"

"With haste," he replied jovially, then sat on the sofa and stretched his legs out in front of him. He couldn't believe how good it felt to be able to stretch out after riding all day.

Emma brought the glass of brandy and he took it from her hand.

"I was sure you'd arrive home tonight."

"Were you?" he said with a smile, then took a swallow of the brandy. It was much more satisfying than the ale he'd had at the *Pig and Ale*. He took another sip.

"Yes I was. Did you have a successful trip?"

"If you're asking if I saw Captain Russell, then yes. I had a very successful trip. Captain Russell has been in England for nearly a month and is preparing to set sail in about a week."

"Oh, Jonah!"

There was the joyous smile, igniting dual flames within him and setting fire to his aching heart.

Emma breathed an audible sigh. "I can't believe it. It won't be long and I'll be where Gerald can no longer touch me."

"Yes. It won't be long now."

The expression on Emma's face was puzzling. But Jonah didn't have time to ask her what caused her confusion until the maids who had arrived with the tea service and tray left the room.

"You don't seemed pleased for me," Emma said.

"How can I be pleased when in less than a week you'll be gone? I'll miss you, Emma. Surely you know that."

"Jonah, don't."

Perhaps the thought of Emma leaving caused such a maudlin emotion because he'd been on the road all day and was tired beyond belief. Perhaps the thought of Emma leaving was more real now that the plans were in motion and the date of her departure was not that far in the future. Perhaps the reason was that Jonah didn't know how he would survive when she was gone.

"Never mind me, Emma. I'm just tired."

Emma piled meat and cheese on a slice of bread for Jonah, then poured herself a cup of tea and sat back in her chair.

"Here," he said, handing Emma the books he'd purchased by trading his watch fob to the bookseller. "I thought you might enjoy these."

Emma took the books. "Oh, Jonah. Thank you. You're too kind! But I'm the one who should be gifting my host."

"Your presence has been gift enough," Jonah said, then tried to cover his forthright words by taking a bite of his sandwich.

"I met your stepbrother tonight," he said when he finished his food.

Emma dropped the book into her lap and her eyes darted upward. "What? Where?"

The fear in Emma's eyes was plain to see.

"At the *Pig and Ale*. I was falling asleep and stopped to rest for a few moments."

"The *Pig and Ale*? Is that near here? Did you speak to him?"

"About twelve miles. And yes. He was far into his cups and was asking anyone within hearing if they'd seen you."

Emma rose from her chair and paced the room. She clutched the books he'd given her so tightly to her breast that her knuckles had turned white.

"He's found me. He's found me! What did you tell him?"

"Nothing, Emma. Nothing. Besides, he was so drunk he no doubt won't even remember he saw me when he wakes in the morning."

"I have to leave."

"And we will. Day after tomorrow. Farley has found two men who will accompany us as guards."

"But if Gerald's here, I need to—"

"You need to stay where you are. The longer he stays around, the easier it will be for Farley to keep an eye on him."

Jonah could see Emma wasn't convinced, and he knew she needed reassurance. He rose and walked to the sideboard, poured her a glass of wine and handed it to her. "Here, drink this. It will calm your nerves."

"But you don't know what he's like," she said when she'd taken a swallow of the wine.

"Yes, I do. You forget. I met him. He's got the devil in him. I saw it in his eyes."

She looked at him with the most terrified expression and Jonah pulled her close and held her in his arms. "Don't worry, love. Nothing will happen to you. I'll keep you safe."

Jonah held her for as long as he dared, then led her to the sofa. "Finish your wine, then it's early to bed. You can start packing in the morning. We need to be on our way in less than thirty-six hours."

She took another sip of her wine and nodded as if she agreed with what he said. But the fear in her eyes told another story.

It would be the longest thirty-six hours of her life.

Chapter Nine

JONAH SLEPT FAR LONGER than he'd intended, but he'd been so tired when he went to bed the night before that he was thankful he woke up any time before noon. He dressed, then went to the breakfast room. He wasn't sure what he needed more, food to put in his stomach, several cups of coffee to help him wake, or the sight of a beautiful woman.

After he drank his second cup of coffee and cleaned his plate of all the food he'd put on it, he realized he'd needed all three. As he finished, he looked up when Carter entered the room. "Mr. Farley to see you, my lord."

A flash of warning surged through him. "What is it, Farley?"

"It's the bay mare, your lordship. She's gone. I think her ladyship took the horse and left."

Jonah bolted to his feet. "What? How?"

"I was in the back paddock cleaning the troughs. When I came back to the stable, the horse was gone. My son says she had him saddle the bay. I just had Mrs. Jefferies check on her ladyship and she came back down to tell me Lady Emma is gone. And her satchels, too."

"Damnation!" Jonah muttered under his breath. "Saddle my horse. I'll get my cloak. She shouldn't be on the roads alone."

"Yes, my lord."

Jonah ran to the house to get anything he might need, including a pistol, then raced to the stable to get his horse. At least he knew what direction she'd gone. She was no doubt headed toward London.

He raced Jupiter over the road, hoping he'd see a sign of her up ahead. Surely she didn't have that ample a lead over him. He prayed he could catch up with her soon.

Each pounding hoof beat drove home to Jonah what life was about to become once Emma left. There would no longer be a reason to make plans. No longer a reason to work at retrieving his home's former glory. No longer a reason to smile.

Jonah pushed his mount. He could catch up with her and escort her on to London, but his solicitor was arriving that evening with the funds from selling his last bit of expendable property. It would allow him to give Emma enough to keep her comfortably in Virginia until she managed to get her own funds transferred.

He'd even arranged with his solicitor to handle that transfer for her, but she had to sign the documents first. And they were back at the manor on his desk.

He'd just have to force Emma to return with him. And when they reached Glassborough Manor, he'd lock her in her room until they were ready to leave for London.

Even as he formed the thought he dismissed it. He could never entrap her the way her brother wanted to. But he would distract her in every way possible. And if she still thought she might flee he'd take her to his bed.

Jonah urged his horse to travel faster. As tantalizing as the thought was, he knew it was a ploy he would never undertake. She was committed to her course, and he had promised to assist her in it. His own mounting need had no place in this unraveling plot. He may have behaved without honor in the past, but it would never happen again.

He pulled to a halt when he saw Emma sitting on the side of the road. The bay mare was grazing in the ditch.

Jonah dismounted and walked to where she sat. "Are you alright?" he asked when he reached her.

"Did you loosen this on purpose?"

She looked up as she tossed a horseshoe at his feet. Jonah bent to pick it up and saw the tears running down her cheeks. He turned the horseshoe over and over, at a loss for words in the face of her sadness.

"I shouldn't have left." A hiccup interrupted her words. "But I was so afraid. Twelve miles, Jonah! He's so close I can feel his breath on the back of my neck. I can't stand it. What will I do if Gerald finds me?"

"He won't find you, Emma. I'm here. I'll protect you."

"But he's so desperate there's no telling what he'll do."

"Trust me, Emma. I won't let anything happen to you. Now," he said holding out his hand to help her to her feet. "Let's go back to the manor. We'll stay with our plan to get you to London and onto the ship that will take you to America."

Emma took his hand and he tried to ignore the bolts of emotion that spiked through him.

Jonah brought her to her feet and she swayed enough that he gathered her to him to prevent her from falling. He held her for a few moments, then lowered his head. His gaze locked with hers, then lowered to her lips.

She was so beautiful. Her lips were made to be kissed and he couldn't stop himself.

He should release her. He should put her on his horse and take her back to Glassborough, but he couldn't. Not yet. He didn't have the courage. He wanted to kiss her. He wanted to experience the emotional upheaval that had consumed him the last time he'd kissed her. He was desperate to relive the mind-numbing turmoil kissing her caused.

He lowered his head until his lips touched hers. The feel of her lips pressed to his was pure heaven. Never before had he experienced anything so stirring. Not since the last time he'd kissed her. Not since the last time his lips had touched hers.

Jonah knew he should end their kiss, but he couldn't. Any strength he might have had to control his emotions was gone. Especially when her hands slid up his coat and her arms wrapped around his neck.

Her fingers raked through his hair and pressed his head closer to take in more of his kisses.

Jonah deepened his kiss. He wanted her more than he'd ever wanted any woman in his life. He wanted to touch her. He wanted to take her as a man takes a woman he cherishes. Because he loved her. Loved her more than he thought it was possible to love anyone.

He was lost. He had to stop now or he wouldn't have the strength to keep from taking her right here.

Jonah lifted his mouth from hers and pressed her head to rest beneath his chin.

She couldn't catch her breath. It was as if her legs had lost the strength to support her troubled heart. Jonah wrapped his arms around her more securely.

"Are you alright?" he asked in a voice that sounded ragged and heavy. She nodded her head.

"Oh, Emma. What power you have over me. Please, don't leave me."

"Don't, Jonah. Don't you understand? I don't have a choice."

"You do."

"No. I'm not safe here. I'll never be safe here."

Then, she turned away from him. And Jonah feared he'd lost her forever.

. . . .

Emma descended the stairs for breakfast. Her nervous hands smoothed her skirts as she went down to meet with Jonah at his request. He was there, but from the looks of him he hadn't slept any better than she had. It had been late when the solicitor arrived to sort out the necessary papers for transferring her funds to a bank of her choosing when the time came. It took a good bit of creative legal language, but at last all three were satisfied that the transfer of her fortune would be done safely. And secretly.

Jonah rose and pulled out the chair to his right.

"Good morning, Emma. I trust you slept well." He handed her a plate which Emma filled with more food than she'd probably be able to eat.

Emma was surprised to find that no footman was present to wait on them, yet there was a cup of coffee in front of her place that Jonah had undoubtedly filled.

Emma sat and began to eat, hoping her unexpected appetite might banish the gloom from Jonah's face. His features were set in a stern, determined expression—one that might intimidate her, but did not. Instead, it seemed to make him even more handsome. The scar down his cheek was as vivid as before, but she hardly noticed it any more. It was merely a part of him. The same as the color of his eyes and the waves of his thick dark hair were a part of him. His every feature was a unique part of him that she'd swiftly grown to love.

Emma concentrated on eating the food on her plate.

Jonah sat across the table from her while she ate, but didn't speak. It was as if he was intentionally waiting for her to finish before he broached the subject he knew she intended to discuss.

"You're a very patient man," she said when she laid down her fork.

"Does that surprise you?"

Emma shook her head. "No. It suits you."

He lifted his eyebrows in a querying expression.

"Are you finished?" he asked.

"Yes."

"Then, please. Come with me."

Jonah helped her to her feet and escorted her from the breakfast room to his study. When there, he saw her to a cushioned chair before the fire. Emma welcomed the warmth.

"I'm guessing you have something to add to our plan."

In response, Jonah went to his desk and opened the top drawer. He removed a folded piece of paper and handed it to her.

Emma slowly unfolded the heavy parchment and perused the writing. "What is this?"

"It's a marriage license."

Emma's heart slammed against her ribs. Surely he didn't intend for them to marry. "I can see that, but whose?"

"Mine. It's the license the vicar brought with him when he came to perform my marriage to Lady Constance."

"Oh," Emma said, unsettled by the notion of handling the unused document.

"That was, of course, before Constance refused to marry me. Once the vicar realized there might not be a wedding, he spent all of his time consoling the bride's mother, as well as trying to prevent the bride's father from killing his spoiled daughter."

"Could the mother not speak sense to her daughter? Or her husband, for that matter?"

The smile that lifted the corners of Jonah's lips contorted into a malicious grin.

"In truth, I think Lady Westshield fueled the torment. I wouldn't doubt that it was she who planted the idea in her daughter's head that I was to be feared."

Emma shook her head. "That can't have been the reason, Jonah. You are not a monster. Your quiet nature might have put her off at first, but that's only normal when two people first meet."

Jonah contemplated her for a long moment.

"What a forgiving and understanding woman you are, Lady Emmaline. You always look at things in the best light. How did your father raise a stepson so totally the opposite of you?"

"My father had very little to do with the rearing of Gerald. He was already grown and beyond influence when Father married Gerald's mother. She was a weak person who spoiled her son unmercifully. The damage was already done long before Father could influence Gerald."

Emma noted the marriage certificate's empty signature lines. It would be such a simple ruse to sign the paper so Gerald would believe that she and Jonah were legally wed.

"There had to be another reason Lady Constance objected to the marriage."

Jonah shifted in his chair, showing her just how uncomfortable he was with the memory of that dreadful time.

"In one of her rants, I overheard her tell her mother that she was in love with someone else. From what she said, I believe the man with whom she was in love was married. Her mother told her she was a fool if she believed that man would leave his wife and family for her, but of course Constance refused to believe her mother."

"It's obvious the girl was spoiled as badly as my stepbrother."

"I think perhaps she was not spoiled as much as she was desperate."

Jonah spoke with quiet certainty.

"What makes you say that?"

"I overheard her tell her mother that she was with child."

There was little Emma could do to hide her shock.

She refolded the unsigned certificate from the foiled marriage. Why had someone not counseled the young woman? Why had someone not spoken in defense of the good man who had been willing under the most dire circumstances to give her legitimacy?

But apparently nobody had.

And a misguided young woman had died.

Emma looked at the Earl of Glassborough with heightened compassion. How gravely it had changed him. How thoroughly it had cut him off from the community that could easily have been his salvation.

And how deeply it had touched her heart.

Chapter Ten

EMMA SAT BEHIND JONAH'S DESK and filled in the blank lines on the marriage license that would be their insurance against any claims on her estate. The small twinge of guilt that it was a sham license did not faze her in the least.

After she put in the bride's name and Jonah signed as her husband, Jonah's butler signed his name on the vicar's line. Cook signed as one of the witnesses and Farley signed his name as a second witness. The finished product looked real. It looked legitimate.

That thought shocked her to her very core. And not for the first time she wondered what it would be like to be married to Jonah. She wondered what it would be like for Glassborough to be her home. What it would be like if Jonah were her husband and he'd given her enough children to fill their home with joy and laughter. She wondered what it would be like if they shared a marriage bed.

"It almost feels as if we're really married," she said softly, not really intending for him to hear her.

"We can make that happen," he answered quietly.

"No, Jonah. We can't. I'm not safe until I am so far from Gerald that he can never find me. You don't know how his mind works. He's absolutely diabolical!"

"You could trust me to keep you safe."

"Or, Gerald could kill you and I would carry that burden of grief for the rest of my life."

Jonah turned his back on her and Emma realized the sooner they were separated, the sooner she could put this behind her. And the safer Jonah would be.

"I need to speak with Farley to make sure he understands our plans." Jonah walked to the door and left her.

Emma stared at his retreating back and knew she'd just lost a large part of her heart. She rose from behind Jonah's desk and sat in a chair before the fire. She pulled her legs up close to her breast and rested her chin on her knees. Tears she could no longer hold back streamed down her cheeks. She'd managed to get so little sleep the night before. The lonely hours had stretched endlessly forward as they crawled toward dawn.

She had spent nearly the entire night evaluating her feelings for Jonah. From the day she'd first realized that no man's word could be trusted, she'd lived with the knowledge that she would never give her heart away. But she'd done exactly that. Without even realizing what was happening, she'd given her heart to Jonah and it was too late to rescue it.

If only she hadn't let him kiss her. If only she hadn't experienced the passion he stirred within her. If only she hadn't placed her trust in his words. And his kisses.

She saw now that he may very well be the man who would shatter all her notions about men.

But as long as she remained single, she kept control of her wealth. And, as long as she controlled her wealth, she was guaranteed her independence. She would only lose her freedom if she gave her heart away.

Emma clutched her hand to her breast. She'd never hurt so much in her life. How could she have done exactly what she swore she would never do? How could she have opened her heart to a destitute man? A man who admittedly had tried once before to marry simply for want of a dowry? In truth, she had not seen such a weakness in him, but history could not be denied.

She felt deeply that his show of affection was genuine. But would it stand the test of time? Once he was on a sound financial footing, would he still feel that affection for her? She scarcely knew him. How could she possibly answer that question?

She couldn't have known it would hurt so much to give up Jonah. How was it that in just a few weeks' time she'd grown so close to Jonah that now a part of her trembled every time she thought of a future without him in it?

How had she fallen in love with him? How had she allowed him to take possession of her heart? She let the tears fall from her eyes. She hurt more than she could stand. Her only hope was that once she was away from Jonah she could start healing. Maybe in time she wouldn't hurt so much. Maybe in time her heart could begin the process of healing.

Emma rose from her chair and clamped her hands around her waist. The pain inside seemed to escalate. It could only mean that she loved him. She was coming to believe that she did, because life without him seemed a dismal prospect. Yet would her heart hurt any less if she trusted him with her love and he destroyed it? If he betrayed her love out of greed?

Emma left the room and went up to her bedroom. Tomorrow she would leave here and begin her new life. Tomorrow she could concentrate on mending her heart. There had to be a way to do that, and she was determined to find it.

. . . .

Jonah sat before the fire in his study that night and watched the embers in the grate slowly die. He reached for the brandy decanter and refilled his glass, then slowly lifted the tumbler to his mouth. His intention was to drink until he couldn't remember the emotions that tortured him every time he thought of Emma and a life without her. But drinking wouldn't erase the love he felt for her. Nothing could help him forget how indelibly she'd imprinted herself onto his heart. And deep into his soul.

It seemed ages since he'd last kissed her, but the feel of her lips against his refused to go away. The after effects of their kiss still burned deep in his heart until he thought it had just been a moment ago that he'd held her in his arms. And no amount of liquor could ease the pain of knowing how much he would miss her long after she was gone.

Jonah took a long swallow of the brandy in his glass, then turned his focus to the soft footfalls beyond the door where he found Emma standing in the shadows.

"Go back to bed, Emma," he said, thinking he could stop her from entering. "It's not safe for you to be here. Not tonight."

"Gone a bit tiddly have you, my lord?"

Oh, how he loved her for endeavoring to make light of his inebriated circumstances.

"No," Jonah said on a laugh. "But not for lack of trying." He raised his glass to her and swallowed the last of his brandy.

As if she didn't fear his words even a little, she walked into the room. She stopped in front of the cabinet where Jonah kept several crystal decanters of liquor and poured a small amount of wine into a glass. When she had her wine in hand she walked over to a second wing chair next to where he sat and joined him.

"Do you know if my stepbrother is still at the *Pig and Ale*?"

"Farley has a man watching who sent word that your stepbrother is still there. Evidently he's conducting his searches in larger and larger circles, using the alehouse as his center." Jonah shook his head sadly. "He's caused a fight almost every night since he arrived and the owner and patrons of the inn are anxious to have him gone."

"Why doesn't he leave?" she cried in frustration. "He should know that even if he finds me, I'll only run away again."

"Money is a powerful motive, Emma. You above anyone know to what lengths a man will go to get your wealth. You know what lies a man will tell to make you believe he loves you."

"Is that what you've done, Jonah? Lied with your kisses to gain my fortune?"

Her voice held a teasing, playful tone, but Jonah was halted by her words.

"Oh, Emma. How could I ever tell you anything but the truth? You've won my heart, it's as simple as that. I could never betray you. And I'll never let your brother harm you."

When she didn't reply, Jonah threw the remainder of his brandy to the back of his throat. He wanted to take her in his arms and hold her. And never let her go. He wanted to hold her so she couldn't leave him. But he'd promised himself that he wouldn't beg her to stay. Not again.

He'd already told her everything he needed to say. He'd told her that he loved her, and promised that in every way she was safe from him. But it hadn't been enough. She didn't trust him enough to believe he would protect her. And now it was too late. She would leave in the morning and he'd never see her again.

"Are your satchels ready?"

"Yes."

Jonah rose. He was afraid to look her in the eye, couldn't bear to see her eagerness to take leave of him. But the sadness in her voice made him turn.

She rose and took a step toward him, her hand beginning to rise as if she intended to touch him. He couldn't allow it. One touch and he would shatter completely.

"Good." He turned away. "We'll leave at first light. Now go to bed and get some rest."

It was so quiet Jonah thought he simply hadn't heard her leave, but long before the twisting pain eased in his chest, he heard the rustle of her robe.

She had left him for the last time.

. . . .

"Do you have your boarding papers?"

They'd finally arrived in London. Soon, Emma would board the ship to America and this nightmare would be over.

"Yes."

He knew she did, but he needed something to say. Their silence was driving him mad. He and Emma had never had a problem finding things to say to each other, but suddenly neither of them had the ability to carry on a conversation.

"Wait in the carriage while I find the captain and someone to take your satchels."

"Thank you," she said and Jonah left Emma behind while he went to find Captain Russell.

You can survive this, he told himself for the hundredth time since they'd left Glassborough Estate yesterday morning. *You can survive losing her.*

Jonah found Captain Russell and his wife and made arrangements for a deck hand to carry Emma's satchels to her cabin. He gave his old commanding officer the small cache of money and elicited a promise that he wouldn't give it to Lady Emmaline until they were well out to sea. When he was assured that she would be well taken care of on the journey to America, he returned to the carriage.

"Your cabin is ready," he said as he helped her to the ground. "Captain Russell and his wife will take care of you. Go to either of them if you need anything."

Emma nodded, then reached for his hand.

"Jonah, I'll never forget what you've done for me." A tear rolled down her cheek.

"Emma—"

"Don't, Jonah. We've said everything we need to say."

Jonah swallowed hard, then looped her arm through his and walked her to the ship. Captain Russell and his wife came down the gangplank to meet them.

"If anything goes wrong, send word. I'll find a way to get you the help you need."

Lady Emma gave him a sweet smile tinged with sadness. Her lips trembled as she whispered her reply. "I know you would, dear Jonah. But I'll be fine. Truly I will. Now please don't wait here until I'm gone. You have business to attend to." She laid her hand on his arm, and when it lingered there a moment longer he covered her hand with his. Their eyes met and held, and Jonah felt the urgent need to beg her to stay.

But she saw it in his eyes and gave a slight shake of her head.

Jonah nodded. With killing regret he forced his hand to ease away from hers, yet she didn't move. As her eyes communicated one last farewell, she raised her hand and cradled his cheek. Her thumb stroked the long scar, sending a powerful message of love and acceptance that nearly took him to his knees.

Jonah swallowed hard, choking off the pleas that threatened to escape his lips.

And then her hand slipped away. She turned toward the ship. Toward freedom. And left him standing there with a heart drowning in its own tears.

Somehow Jonah managed to find his carriage through eyes clouded with loss. It wasn't too late yet. He could abandon everything he knew and go with her. He knew she'd let him, though she never would have asked. All he had to do was—

Jonah braced his hands on either side of the carriage door and waited the interminable minutes until he heard the scraping sound of the gangplank being pulled from the dock. Heard Captain Russell bellow the final orders to set sail. Heard the ship's warning bell ring for a final time. Then, heard the sounds of the sleek ship moving away from the dock. Small waves slapped against the wharf as the vessel was released from its moorings and the sounds quieted as the ship slid out into the channel.

Jonah stood as if he'd turned to marble, unable to move or feel. His fingers clenched the sides of the carriage so tightly he couldn't force them to release the wooden frame. If he didn't move, maybe he could pretend Emma wasn't really gone. Maybe he could pretend he could turn around and she'd be there. But, he knew that was impossible.

At last he forced his fingers to release the side of the carriage and moved to step inside. He had one foot on the step and one foot still on solid ground when a voice spoke to him.

"Excuse me, my lord. But I seem to have missed the ship on which I intended to sail."

Jonah turned and his gaze rested on the most beautiful sight he'd ever seen—a sight he thought had been lost to him forever.

"Emma?"

"Yes, Jonah," she said, then took her first running step toward him.

Jonah met her with his arms open wide. He wrapped her in his arms and kissed her with the immense depth of passion that defied words. He kissed her once more, then deepened his kiss to emphasize how much he loved her.

"I couldn't leave you, Jonah," she said when he lifted his mouth from hers. "I love you. My life wouldn't be worth living if you weren't a part of it. I would miss you too much."

"Dear God, I didn't know how I'd live without you, Emma. Truly." He kissed her once more, then looked into her eyes. "You know that I will never betray you. I promise you will never regret marrying me."

"I know I won't. Just as you will never regret marrying me. Even if I gave everything away and we had to live like two foolish paupers."

"We'll be the happiest paupers ever," Jonah whispered.

He kissed her once more, then she looked up at him and their gazes locked.

"Take me home, Jonah."

Chapter Eleven

BUT HE DID NOT TAKE HER HOME.

Not immediately, at any rate.

Securing a special license to marry had been easier than either of them had anticipated, but it still took several days. In the intervening time before the marriage ceremony could take place, Emma had stayed with Mrs. Russell's housekeeper, and Jonah lodged in a rooming house across the street from Captain Russell's modest home. For five days the space between her door and his was the furthest they would allow themselves to be from one another. The world fell away, and nothing held their interest except the opportunity to know each other better. When at last they arrived back at Glassborough, they were truly husband and wife. The marriage license they had now was completely authentic.

The next few days were the happiest of Emma's life. Jonah had made her his wife in every sense of the word and for the first time ever she knew what it was to be truly loved. Her days were charmed and her nights were filled with wonder and amazement.

"Did you sleep well, my love?" Jonah asked when she entered the breakfast room the third morning after they were married.

Emma felt a blush rise in her cheeks. "Yes, very."

Jonah stood while she filled her plate, then helped her to a chair next to his. She'd put more food on her plate than she usually took, but she was starving. It wasn't until she looked at the food on Jonah's plate that she realized she had nothing compared to the mounds of eggs and bacon and ham and potatoes on his plate. She laughed aloud, loving the very sight of her husband eating his fill.

She and Jonah ate in companionable intimacy, sharing unspoken words with smoky glances. They had thoroughly discussed preparations for a small reception they were to hold the next afternoon to celebrate the announcement of their marriage. All was in readiness. The few landowners and village dignitaries they had invited had replied positively. Now it seemed to Emma that all they had to do was get through today.

After Jonah's valet—who also served as footman—removed their breakfast plates and refilled their cups, the newly wed couple were alone in the room.

Emma watched with curiosity as Jonah's face clouded. When his hand began to fidget nervously with the table linen, she could no longer wait for him to speak.

"Is something wrong?" Emma asked, praying there was not.

Jonah cleared his throat. "Your stepbrother has found your horse."

Emma felt the blood rush in her veins, setting her heart throbbing and her head spinning.

"My horse! Dear Lord, I...I had thought it would have been safe to sell." She stood looking frantically for a way out of the trap Jonah had unwittingly set. It should have been safe, since she had expected at the time to be a thousand miles away before anyone discovered the horse.

"Didn't you tell them—"

"Yes, luv, I told the buyer not to take the horse out for two weeks, until after the previous owner had left the area. He seemed to understand my feeble story that it might upset you if you were out and about and saw someone else astride your favorite mare."

"Then why would he—"

Jonah rose to stop her pacing and caught her gently by the arm.

"He didn't, luv. But his young son didn't get the message. He hitched the horse to a cart to deliver eggs to his customers in town. And Marquardt saw them. You can hardly blame the man for recognizing such a grand animal."

Emma slowed her breathing, trying desperately to feel the calm that

Jonah attempted to induce in her. His hands ran softly up her arms, leaving a trail of warm comfort that she wanted badly to absorb. But she could not.

"Jonah, what will we do if he finds out where I am?"

"He's already found out, luv. He—"

She stumbled out of his grasp. "How do you know that?"

Emma watched in horror as Jonah pulled a note from his waistcoat pocket.

"Because he wrote me saying he would be pleased to attend our Sunday reception."

"He what!"

Emma clung to her husband as he pulled her into his arms.

"He's coming, luv. I'm so sorry. But he's coming. Tomorrow."

. . . .

Emma dressed carefully for the Sunday reception. She had widened the pocket opening of her peach gown to accommodate the small handgun she intended to carry. But when she practiced drawing it out, the small pistol continually snagged on the fabric until she replace the pocket lining with a soft leather insert. Now she could draw it smoothly ten times out of ten, though she hoped she wouldn't need to draw it even once.

Jonah stepped into her dressing room, for a moment casting away Emma's dread as she took in his handsome presence. Even in his pre-war fashion he cut a stunning figure. He came close to draw her to him, even as he dropped his head to touch his forehead to hers.

He spoke again the simple words that had calmed her each time she'd wakened in the night shivering.

"Remember that you're my wife now. Nothing can harm you."

She relaxed her hands and brought them up to cup his face.

"I'm your wife now. Nothing can harm me."

She rose on tiptoe to kiss his cheek, but he stopped her and dropped his forehead to hers.

"All drama aside, are you happy?"

Emma smiled at the question and looked into Jonah's eyes. There was no fear, no worry. She saw only a reflection of her own happiness.

Her answering smile widened his grin as she moved a finger to trace the rough planes of his face. She loved it when he smiled, and kissed him softly. "And there, sir, is the answer to your question." She kissed him a second time, drawing her hand through his hair to press him closer. She wanted him to feel the full spirit of her reply.

"We have the upper hand, you know."

"Hm?" Emma had been fully distracted by his kiss and failed to understand his statement.

"We're in the right here, my love. And we're on our own territory. In our own house. Gerald will be the one who is out of place. We'll show him the license and he will not be able to deny its authenticity. He'll leave in a huff and we will put it behind us and enjoy our guests. Right?"

"Mm. Yes. Right."

With a sudden shift, Jonah sat on the bed and lifted her onto his lap. "Let's tell Mrs. Jefferies we'll take a light dinner in our room tonight, shall we?"

"You're like a little boy who can't wait to get out of his church clothes," she chided.

He kissed her gently. "After this afternoon's folderol I thought you might want me all to yourself." He sneaked another kiss as she gaped at his risqué statement.

Emma leaned away. "*Folderol*? Celebrating our marriage is *folderol*?"

She swatted him playfully on the arm and pulled him with her into the hallway. "Then let the folderol begin!"

As they reached the bottom of the staircase Emma was about to capture Jonah for another kiss when Jonah stopped her.

Carter stood in the center of the foyer, clearly distraught. "My—um, my lord?" His voice sounded strangely different. As if it contained a warning.

Out of instinct, Emma took Jonah's hand. They turned toward Carter, and Emma's heart catapulted in her chest when the saw the man crowding past their agitated butler.

"Oh my, sister dear," the man sneered. "You've been here all the time, have you? With that look of domestic tranquility you possess one might almost believe you *are* married."

Gerald Marquardt stepped across the vestibule, treading on Jonah's newly polished Italian slate with his muddy riding boots and bringing with him all the menace Emma had hoped to evade.

"But you see, I happen to know that no such marriage has been solemnized in the entire County of Essex in a fortnight."

Jonah drew Emma close, then stepped in front of her to protect her.

"I'm sorry, my lord," Carter said. "I told the gentleman you were entertaining privately, but he refused to leave."

"That's alright, Carter. We'll see to our guest. But do let Fielding know that I wish him to join us."

Emma felt a tremor of alarm. Fielding was the guard. Why had he allowed Gerald to come into the house unescorted?

If she hadn't been looking his direction, Emma might have missed the signal Carter gave in return. Something had happened to Fielding. They were on their own.

Carter hung back, looking as if he hoped to be swallowed up by the very wall near which he hovered. It was just the three of them in the foyer now. Emma stared at the man who had tormented her every day since her father had died. There was a wild look in his eyes as well as a gray paleness to his features. No doubt from too much drink and a lack of proper meals. If she had to find a word to describe how he looked, it would be *demented*.

"If you've come to see our marriage license, *brother*, we'll be happy to produce it for you," Emma said.

"Ha! Do you think I would simply take your word that you were married, *sister*? Do you think I would trust any flimsy document you tried to foist upon me to support your...your *fictitious* marriage?"

Emma bristled at his gleeful gloating.

"No. I had no delusions that you would be so trusting."

Jonah placed his arm around her waist and led her toward his study. "Please," Jonah said as he beckoned to Gerald. "If you'll follow me, I'll get our marriage license."

"So you insist upon carrying out this ridiculous charade, eh? Well then, by all means. Lead the way," Gerald said with a sweeping bow.

When they entered Jonah's study, Jonah led Emma to the chair behind his desk. But she couldn't sit. She need to stand in case it proved necessary that she retrieve her pistol.

"You may have a seat if you'd like," Jonah said, pointing to one of the wing chairs some distance from Jonah's massive oak desk.

"You'd like that, wouldn't you, Lord Glassborough? Get me off guard, relaxed, at a disadvantage. So thank you but no. I prefer to stand."

"As you wish."

Jonah stepped around Emma and opened the right-hand desk drawer.

"Be careful," her stepbrother said in warning. "Only remove a paper, Lord Glassborough. Nothing more."

Emma turned toward her stepbrother and froze. He had quietly moved closer, and held a wickedly long knife-blade in his hand.

Jonah gingerly removed the formal-looking document from the top drawer and held it out to her stepbrother.

Emma enjoyed seeing the look of surprise on her stepbrother's face when he viewed the marriage license with its official seal of London's Registrar General. She took pleasure in knowing he never expected her to have married. And most of all, she took pleasure in seeing his reaction when he realized he'd never get so much as a shilling from her.

"I don't believe this," he muttered beneath his breath, then snatched the paper from Jonah's hand and studied it. "You bitch!" he bellowed in a voice as hostile and vile as she'd ever heard from him. "You cunning bitch! You said you'd never marry! You swore it!"

Her stepbrother wadded the marriage license in his fist and threw it across the room. Then, before Jonah could react, Gerald lunged at Emma with a wild slash of the knife.

In a flash she understood his next move. If she were alive, marriage was the key to unlocking her wealth. But in the case of her premature death?

Emma darted backward just in time, even as Jonah leaped forward to protect her. The tip of the blade sliced through Jonah's jacket and reached the flesh of his chest.

"Run, Emma!" Jonah yelled as he fell to his knees and clutched his hand to his chest. "Run," he gasped.

Emma froze momentarily when she saw the look of shock and pain on Jonah's face. It was the terror she heard in his voice that jolted her into action.

"Jonah!" she yelled. Deep red blood streamed through her husband's fingers.

Fear grabbed hold of her and refused to release her. She wanted to run to Jonah, but knew it was useless to interfere. She was no match against Gerald.

Just when she thought that Gerald was satisfied with only wounding Jonah, he lifted his arm again to stab a final blow into Jonah's chest.

"No, Gerald! No!"

Her cry stayed his arm for the moment she needed to draw the pistol from its leather pocket. Her trembling fingers grasped frantically at it, finally losing their hold and letting the weapon tumble to the floor. She stared in horror as the gun skittered across the rug, just out of her reach.

"You may have been married for a few days, woman, but you'll be a widow the rest of your life."

Emma saw the knife in Gerald's hand begin its downward thrust and knew she had no time to consider what she had to do. She lunged forward, landing on her knees as she swept up the small handgun and fumbled it into both hands. Instead of weakening her position it seemed to give her an even more secure stance. Using both thumbs, she drew back the hammer and fired.

Her stepbrother's eyes opened wide in disbelief as he lowered his gaze to the scarlet blossom on his waistcoat. "What have you done!" he whispered, and clamped his hand over the wound. "What—" he muttered, then fell to the floor.

Emma trembled with shock as she saw the man who had tormented her so relentlessly suddenly collapse. The knife tumbled from his hand and lay harmlessly on the floor, no longer a threat to anyone.

The man who had wielded it a moment earlier was dead.

Emma rushed to Jonah and knelt beside him.

"My love, are you alright?"

"Yes, Emma. I'm fine."

But Emma knew he wasn't. She placed his head in her lap and brushed the hair from his forehead. "Go for a doctor!" she yelled when Carter tumbled into the room. "And find someone to carry his lordship to our chambers."

"Yes, my lady."

Emma clutched at Jonah and focused on his alarming loss of blood.

"Don't worry so, Em. I'm fine. It's only a flesh wound."

"Don't you dare leave me," she ordered through the tears that filled her eyes.

"I have no intention of…leaving you. I just…found you."

Emma leaned down and kissed him on the forehead. "I killed him," she moaned.

"To save my life," Jonah answered, which, when he put it in those terms, made her actions seem less horrific.

Emma gave him up reluctantly when Carter arrived with help to carry Jonah up the stairs. He helped her remove Jonah's jacket and blood-stained shirt. A knot clenched in her stomach when she saw the wound. Jonah's flesh was torn for several inches and would need to be stitched.

The doctor came shortly after, and when he finished sewing Jonah's flesh and left, Emma was at last alone with her husband.

"Here," she said, refilling Jonah's glass and handing it to him. He drank most of the liquor, then closed his eyes.

"Are the authorities here?"

"No, my love."

Jonah finished the liquor in his glass. "Then what's all that noise?"

"Um," Emma said, "the, um, guests. I'll send them away, Jonah. You need to sleep."

Half the countryside had responded to her invitation and were now assembled in the formal drawing room. On any other day she would have been thrilled with the success of their first reception. But not today.

As she watched her husband, she realized he could barely keep his eyes open. "Rest now, Jonah. I'll go down to make sure our guests are greeted and sent on their way."

Emma rose and walked to the door.

"Wait," Jonah said as he swung his legs over the side of the bed. "I'll need a clean shirt, waistcoat and jacket."

"But you can't—"

Jonah reached out and captured her hand. "I can. And I will." He drew her to him. "What I will not do is wait one day longer to introduce the world to my beautiful wife. Now be a good girl and get my clothes."

Chapter Twelve

THE DAYS FOLLOWING THE RECEPTION were surreal. Emma made a point of asserting herself in the community, and in no time was receiving invitations to afternoon tea. When the first invitation for the two of them arrived, Emma knew it was the beginning of a new and wonderful life for her reclusive husband.

Jonah was slower to believe their welcome would last, but when the men at the *Pig and Ale* drank a round to him and his new bride, he began to allow himself a degree of hope.

Three weeks after the Sunday reception, Emma wrapped her arms around his neck and kissed him good morning. "I received a letter from Mr. Jordan yesterday."

"Mr. Jordan?"

"My father's solicitor. He congratulated me on our marriage and informed me that according to my father's will, I am now in possession of the money Father left me in trust."

Jonah huffed in surprise.

"I didn't think you would receive your dowry until you reached the age of twenty-one."

"Twenty-one, or when I married. Whichever came first. Since I never intended to marry, I thought I would be forced to wait until my birthday finally arrived. But now we are set, aren't we, my love?"

"The money is yours, Emma. I've told you before, I don't want it."

"I know you don't." She kissed his cheek. "And I love you for that. But a certain portion of it is yours."

"Emma, you know I can't—"

She pressed two fingers against his lips to silence him.

"Until now that money has been a beacon for every rogue in the country to make my life a living hell. But now," she felt her face soften and welcomed the peace that flooded her. "—now it has a chance to work for good. For you, for me, for us, for everyone who makes Glassborough their home. You *must* see that Jonah. You really must."

She tightened her hold on him and he held her closer, pressing his silence between them.

"I've seen your plans, Jonah. You intend to fix the tenant homes on the estate and bring in even more tenants. You've figured out how to make Glassborough a profitable farm. You're going to plant crops on any lands that will grow them, and place cattle and sheep on any pastures that won't. You're going to raise barley that you'll sell to the brewery that makes such fine wine and ale, and see what would have to be done to increase the brewery's supply so they can sell it all over England. Such goodness, Jonah. Such honorable plans. And I refuse to let you lock me out of it."

"I won't, luv, and I have it in hand. Really, I do."

He seemed so earnest that Emma wondered if she had a right to assert herself into his plans. But it only took a moment's reflection to know she was right.

"But yours is a ten-year plan. And much of it can't be started for another three years until you're on a better footing."

She caressed his hand. "Jonah, think of the lives that can be changed if your plan starts now. The people whose lives depend on your success. The children who might have a chance at school instead of laboring in the fields with their families. Their lives could start getting better *today*!"

Jonah turned his face toward her and saw her eagerness. She had somehow righted all the things that had gone topsy-turvy in his world. Before she came into his home, he'd been a drowning man, flailing about for a way to save himself and his estate. And it was Emma who had thrown him a lifeline. Emma who had extended her hand to focus him on a future that had promise. Like a level-headed partner she was showing him a way forward that he could not hope to achieve on his own. But *with* her—

"Well, you've made a compelling argument, my dear. But it's an awful lot to consider." He sat up straight and pulled a studious look across his face. "Perhaps if I had a partner I might be able to manage all the work."

He heard her gasp and couldn't help the grin that seemed to spread wider across his face by the second.

"A partner," she whispered.

"Yes," he whispered back. "Know where I might find one?"

Now she was beaming as broadly as he was. "A partner! Yes! Oh, Jonah, we'll be partners!" She grasped at his hand and stood up, dragging him with her.

A moment later she thrust out her hand.

"Let's seal our partnership with a handshake," she said. "Isn't that how it's done?"

Jonah just gave a slow shake of his head as he closed in to take her in his arms.

"Sorry, partner," he whispered. "I prefer to seal it with a kiss."

Epilogue

"ARE YOU SURE THERE WILL BE ROOM for so many?"

Jonah gazed around the ballroom that had never looked better thanks to his wife's keen instinct. Glassborough Manor had not housed a ball in his adult lifetime. Now Emma couldn't wait to banish that dubious record.

Emma laughed. "I will be terribly disappointed if it's not the crush of the decade."

"Surely some of them won't come," he argued.

"Won't come? How could they not?" Emma gave him her most glorious smile. "They admire you, darling, whether you know it or not. Have you forgotten that in the past year, you've turned Glassborough into a thriving estate? Tripled our staff? That you've given jobs to many of the locals who desperately needed work, and that you purchase lumber and farming supplies from the local merchants, causing their profits to soar? That we purchase the food that goes on our table from the shops in the village? And," Emma continued, "that you were very generous to the church when they asked for donations?"

"My partner is the one who was generous. I wasn't even aware the reverend was taking collections for the orphanage."

"You would have been had you listened closer when Reverend Smithey made announcements after Sunday service."

"It's difficult to listen when all the parishioners sitting around me are staring at my wife."

"Nonsense."

Jonah rolled his eyes then looked at Emma. She seemed a little pale tonight. "Feeling alright, Em?"

"Yes, I'm fine. It's your babe that's letting me know I've been on my feet a little longer than usual today." She patted her stomach that had not yet begun to show evidence of the coming joy.

"Then I will make sure you spend the entire evening seated."

"You will *not*. You are going to dance with me at least a hundred times. I didn't hire a London orchestra for the evening so I could sit on the side and listen. I'm going to dance like I haven't had the opportunity in years."

"Do you miss living in the City?"

"Heavens, no! I wouldn't be anyplace but here. With you."

"I love you, Em," Jonah said.

Emma leaned on the tiptoes of her most comfortable dancing slippers and kissed him on the cheek. "You have to, sweetheart. You're stuck with me whether you want me or not."

Jonah returned Emma's kiss and tried desperately not to leer. "Oh, I want you. Have no doubt of that, lassie."

She gave him a playful swat of the glove she had still to put on. "What a cheeky thing to say to your business partner."

He took her breath away when he pulled her suddenly into his arms. Jonah lowered his head until his lips brushed hers and her eyes fluttered closed.

"I want you a great deal. Wife."

BOOK THREE

SEASONS
BOOK THREE

SUMMER'S
DISTANT HEART

LAURA LANDON

SUMMER'S DISTANT HEART

Victorian Romance by
LAURA LANDON

*Two wary souls, one tyrannical father,
and no way to avoid a deadly clash.*

Amelia Halloway has lost her sister and gained an infant
nephew. She knows she can keep him safe, as long as
the child's grandfather never hears of his existence. And
it's working, until the babe's uncle, **Hunter Montclaire**,
the new Lord Atherton, arrives on her doorstep—a
handsome devil whose father wishes the child dead. He
says he's there to save the child. But can she trust him?

Chapter One

HUNTER MONTCLAIRE KNELT AT HIS BROTHER'S BEDSIDE and reached for his hand. His brother's palm was damp, his skin hot and clammy. He'd been in the throes of a violent fever for more than a week, and the physician who had just left gave him little chance of recovery.

"Hunt?" his brother whispered.

"Yes, Evan. I'm right here." Hunter took a wet cloth from the bedside table and wiped his brother's brow. "You must fight to get better, Evan." He struggled to keep the desperation from his voice. But it was close to impossible.

"I'm afraid the choice is out of my hands, Hunt. I'm afraid only God knows how long I have left on this earth."

Hunter stood to rinse the cloth in the fresh cool water a maid had arrived with a short while ago. It was important that his brother didn't see the worry on his face. It was hard enough to keep the terror from his voice.

Hunter wrung out the cloth and placed it on Evan's forehead.

"Is Father gone, Hunt?"

"Yes. He went down to his study. I think he could not bear to watch you struggle to catch your breath any longer."

"Good. It's you I need to speak with."

"Don't get maudlin on me, Evan. I refuse to let you speak as though you won't see morning."

"Perhaps I won't," Evan said, then struggled to pull in enough air to fill his lungs. He failed.

"I refuse to listen to you talk like that, Evan. I won't allow it."

"I have something to tell you, Hunt. It's important."

Hunter pulled up a chair and sat at Evan's bedside. "Very well. What is it you need to say to me?"

"First, I want you to know how much…I love you. How very important you have always been…to me. How much I regret…the way things have always been…between you and Father."

Hunter's throat thickened with emotion. He couldn't speak.

"I know Father has always favored me…over you, Hunt, and I know why. He blamed you…for every bit of trouble…I got into. Even when he knew I was at fault. But don't let his words…or his actions…get the better of you. You have…nothing…to fear…from him. Stand up to him…as you have always done, and be your…own man."

Hunter tried to smile. "You know how he hates it when I do that. It always infuriates him."

"Then you must continue to do it. It will keep him on his guard. Never allow him to…think he has the upper hand over you. He'll destroy you…if he thinks he can…master you."

Hunter could see how parched his brother was and rose to get him something to drink.

"You might be the next Earl of Atherton."

"Stop talking like that. I don't want to be the next earl. I have never wanted the title."

Evan ignored his demand and continued. "I know you've never wanted it…but it will be yours, brother. And you must take over…the duties at which I have…failed."

"You're the epitome of successful earldom, Evan. You've never failed at anything."

"Yes. I have."

His brother gasped for air, then reached for Hunter's hand and pulled him closer. "I grieve that you've never met the woman with whom I've fallen in love, Hunt. Janice Halloway. Professor Halloway's daughter. I love her with my whole being, Hunt, and we were…married."

"What?"

Hunter couldn't believe Evan's words.

"We married in secret because…Father proved he would never…accept her. And I could not live without her." Evan stopped to catch his breath. "Find her, Hunt. Promise me that you will…take care of her. She may be carrying…my heir. The future Earl of Atherton. If the babe is a girl…Father will not lift a finger to help my wife or the child. You know that. He would rather see them starve…than provide for them."

Evan clutched Hunter's hand harder.

"Don't let Father find out…about the babe. He will not accept it. His anger could well put the babe in danger."

Hunter couldn't find his voice. He couldn't answer his brother because he knew Evan's words were true. Their father would never accept a child whose mother was a commoner. He'd treat her and the babe as he would an unwanted pest. Or a litter of kittens for which he had no use.

"Promise me you'll…find her and…take care of her…and the child, Hunt."

"I will, Evan. I promise."

His brother's head sank deeper into the pile of pillows that allowed him to sit almost upright. It was the only way he could breathe.

"Where is this lass you married, Evan?"

Evan shook his head slightly. "I…I can't be sure. I doubt…she's with her family…any longer. She said she had some…relative she could stay with until…until she knew if she was with child, but I don't know…who that…relative is…or where they…live. We arranged to meet. At Christmastime. Once I recovered. But now—" Evan's voice dissolved into a painful bout of coughing.

"Don't worry, Evan. I'll find her."

"And promise you will not…let Father…know of her."

"I promise."

Hunter watched his brother and saw the tears that filled his eyes, then trickled down his cheeks. Before his illness, he'd been a handsome man, so hale and hearty. His hair was golden blond in color and his eyes a vibrant midnight blue, very much like their father's. It was quite the opposite of the coloring that Hunter was blessed with, thanks to their mother.

Hunter's hair was as dark as roasted chestnuts and his eyes were a brown so rich they were almost black. His coloring did not help disguise the anger he wore like a shield to protect him from appearing overly friendly. Tonight the frown that deepened across his forehead make him appear even less approachable. His father had taught him to wear the scowl as a badge of honor. Hunter was not allowed to appear weak, and a smile gave him too gentle an appearance. It had been his father's mission to erase it from his son's face. In short, Hunter had been reared to be the brutal dragon who protected the favored son and stayed out of his father's way.

Altogether, it gave him an aloofness that females found intriguing. Something that drew them to him the same as a moth is drawn to the flame.

"Would you...sit with me...for a while, Hunt? Talk to me...like you did...when we were younger. Tell me the latest...scrape you've managed to get yourself into."

Hunter couldn't stop a smile from lifting the corners of his mouth. "I'm afraid I've outgrown the scrapes of our youth, Evan, and have turned to other indulgences."

"Do you...still have...your mistress?"

Hunt chuckled. "I still have a mistress, Evan. It's just not the same one."

"Is she a...redhead like you...prefer?"

"I'm afraid my tastes have gone from ginger to raven."

"How...revealing," Evan whispered.

His voice was losing strength and his words slurred more than they had earlier.

"My wife Janice...has hair the color of...ripened wheat...and eyes... as blue and mesmerizing as the...sky after a summer...rain."

"She sounds lovely."

"She is."

Evan turned his head and locked his gaze with Hunter's. "There's a... letter for her in the top drawer...of my desk. Will you give it to her... when you find her? I want her to know...how much I...loved her and how…deeply I'll regret not living my life…at her side."

"Don't talk like that, Evan. I won't allow it. I can't let you leave me alone with Father. You've always been the buffer that saved us from doing each other harm."

"Now that…duty will…fall to you…Hunt. You'll have to…devote less time…to your estate…and help Father manage…Trentridge Park."

"Do you honestly believe Father will allow me to have anything to do with Trentridge Park? Don't you know that's why I spent all my inheritance from Mother in purchasing Rainwood? I was not assured of a place here even with you as his heir. If you abandon me like you're threatening to do, there's not a chance I will be allowed to darken Trentridge Park's door ever again."

"You must…take an interest…in the running of…the estate, Hunt. For your sake…as well as…my child's…should it be a…boy."

"Don't worry, Evan. I will see to your child and raise him as if he were my own."

"Yes," Evan sighed. "Now…get the letter from my desk," Evan demanded as his eyes threatened to close.

Hunter rose to retrieve the letter from Evan's desk and put it carefully in the pocket of his waistcoat.

"Will you take…Janice and the babe to your estate…then?"

Hunter sat down again and reached for his brother's hand.

"Yes. They'll be safe at Rainwood. Father doesn't know it exists. Or that I even own it, for that matter."

"Thank you…Hunt. I knew I could…count on you."

"You can, Evan. Always."

"Don't let…Father ever…have my child, Hunt. Promise…me."

"I promise, Evan. Father will never lay hands on him."

Hunter sat at Evan's bedside and watched his brother's breathing become more shallow with each breath.

The candles at the bedside burned down until there was nothing left of them but small stubs. But Hunter couldn't bear to leave his brother's side.

His father looked in on Evan once, but didn't stay for any length of time. Nor did he speak. After a few moments, he left the room and didn't return.

Hunter wasn't sure when Evan took his last breath. It was sometime before the sun rose in the sky. Sometime before the dark of night had lightened to gray.

Evan's breathing had become so shallow and quiet that Hunter didn't hear his final breath, but he somehow knew that his brother was gone. A blackness unlike anything he'd ever felt consumed him with a painful emptiness that would have brought him to his knees had he been standing.

Tears he'd never before allowed to spill from his eyes fell like rivers down his cheeks.

If Hunter knew anything for sure, it was that he would never be the same again. The only kind thing that had kept him balanced had just left this world.

. . . .

The day they buried Evan was damp and dreary. Hunter thought how appropriate it was that even the heavens were weeping.

But Hunter didn't weep. He didn't want to show such weakness in front of his father. He stood at Evan's graveside with a stoic expression on his face and a rigid stiffness to his shoulders. It took every ounce of composure to keep from releasing the pent up tears that threatened to fall. He knew if the first tear fell it would be impossible to stop the river from bursting through the dam he'd erected to prevent himself from falling apart.

His father's face was colorless and his eyes had a haunting depth to them as if he was intent upon ignoring any sign of what was going on around him. Hunter understood the source of his anguish. The man had, after all, placed all his hopes in his golden-haired son. And though he had been blessed with the coveted 'heir and a spare', he had never really recognized Hunter as such.

The crowd of mourners that had gathered was large. The Marquess of Trentridge was an influential member of the House of Lords, and as his firstborn son and Earl of Atherton, Evan had been considered one of the finest catches of the Season. In sitting rooms far removed from Trentridge Park, many a damsel mourned him. None of them knew that his heart as well as his name had already been taken by another.

Hunter stole a glance at the mourners to notice that several of them were evaluating him, probably comparing him to his brother. Where Evan had been jovial and popular with both male and female alike, Hunter was considered moody and lacking approachability. Hunter had also been thought of as lacking a business head on his shoulders.

Little did they know. Little did his father know. Nor would anyone here ever know if he could help it. Hunter had more of his father's business acumen than he let on. He was already a wealthy man with several profitable investments and an enviable estate of his own.

As Hunter pondered the dismal state of affairs, the graveside service ended at the doors of Trentridge Park's impressive stone mausoleum. After quietly greeting the mourners who had remained to pay their respects, Hunter and his father led their guests to the mansion for luncheon. Hunter would be glad when this was over. He looked forward to the moment he could escort the last of the guests from the house.

And yet, he also dreaded that moment. It meant that he and his father would be alone together. It meant that he could no longer avoid the serious conversation he needed to have with his father to decide what exactly was expected of him. If anything.

Hunter entered his father's study after the last of the guests were gone and poured himself a glass of brandy.

"I would like to discuss a few matters with you before I leave, Father."

"You intend to leave yet today?"

"Yes. I thought I might return to London. Unless you have need of me here?"

"God, no. The sooner you are gone the sooner I can put things to right."

Hunter threw the contents of his glass to the back of his throat and filled his glass again. "I thought that's what you would want."

The Marquess of Trentridge sat in the chair behind his desk and feigned interest in some papers before him. "So," he said, shuffling the papers closest to him. "How does it feel to wear your brother's title?"

It was the first time anyone had mentioned the title that had fallen to him upon his brother's death. Earl of Atherton. Hunter couldn't ease the pain from the fist that clenched inside his chest. "Like a weight around my neck. I have never desired Evan's title, nor wanted it."

"You expect me to believe that?"

"Believe what you want, Father. You have always thought the worst of me."

"You have always shown me your worst side, as well as your lack of what it will take to assume your brother's title."

"Well, Father," Hunter said, draining the brandy from his glass and setting it down on a nearby table. "You can always take solace in the fact that there is your younger brother's son, Winston, standing in the wings to replace me. You have always treated him more like a son than you treated me."

"That's because he has always been more of a son to me than you have."

"And whose fault is that?"

"Don't lay the responsibility for that at *my* feet, blast you. I am not to blame. You are."

Hunter's temper rose to a dangerous peak. "The only thing for which I am to blame is that I lived and my mother did not."

"Don't you dare speak of her!"

"Why? Isn't that what you've repeatedly told me? Well, with Evan gone, I give you permission to call on Winston to serve as your heir. I have no doubt that in the end you will leave everything not entailed to him."

"You can be assured that I will."

"It's a pity that Trentridge Park is entailed and you cannot leave that to him as well."

His father's glare turned dark and deadly.

"Oh, how I hate having to call you my son. Would that you had died instead of Evan."

"I know, Father. More's the pity."

Hunter turned to leave. He couldn't escape his father's bitter hatred quickly enough. "If there's any need to reach me," he said as he stepped to the door, "you may contact me through my solicitor. Although I doubt you'll have need to reach out to me for any reason."

"No, I doubt that I will," his father said looking back to the papers on his desk. "Nor do I anticipate you coming to me when you find yourself lacking funds. You will get nothing from me. Do you hear? Nothing."

"What will be different then, I wonder? Since I have never asked anything of you, nor received it."

"And you never will. All you can ever expect from me is that when I am gone there will be a small amount in trust to keep Trentridge Park solvent."

"You lack faith in my ability to keep the estate profitable?"

"I have faith in nothing but my ability to keep Trentridge Park in the Montclaire name. Without the amount I intend to leave in trust for the upkeep of Trentridge Park, I fear all will be lost of the wealth that generations of Montclaires before you have worked so hard to amass."

"I'm overwhelmed by your confidence in me," Hunter said as a rebuff. He actually relished hearing his father admit that he had not one shred of faith in Hunter's ability to manage Trentridge Park.

"You expect me to tell you I believe you will be as prepared and able to run the estate as your brother was? I am not that blind to your incapabilities."

"I expected as much. But, when have you shown me anything different?"

"You had no need. Your mother's trust has allowed you to live the wastrel lifestyle you're accustomed to living. But even that much wealth will run out eventually and you'll be forced to fall back on what I've earned. I only hope I'm alive to refuse you."

"Then you will wait in vain. That day will never come, my lord. I would rather starve to death than have to rely on you for a crust of bread."

Hunter gathered his cloak, hat, and cane and stormed from the mansion. It would be the last time he would darken its doorway while his father was still alive.

Chapter Two

AMELIA HALLOWAY SAT IN THE WOODEN nursery rocker and lulled the babe to sleep. Four-month-old George Hunter Montclaire, future Earl of Atherton, was the most contented baby any mother could ask for.

"Is the babe asleep?" Lia's Aunt Mildred, the dowager Viscountess Collinson asked as she tiptoed into the room.

"Yes." Lia smiled and stared down at the blond-haired, blue-eyed child. "I do so love rocking him to sleep."

Lia's aunt sat in the over-stuffed chair next to her and placed her hand on Lia's knee.

"What is it, Aunt?"

"I've had news." She held up a letter written on crisp parchment edged in funereal black. "News that could threaten the child."

Lia's heart pounded harder in her breast and her breathing quickened. "Is it about the babe's father?"

Her aunt nodded. "As we feared, he has died."

Lia tried to take in what her Aunt had just said but her mind refused to absorb what that might mean. "Lord Evan Atherton is dead? How do you know?"

"My sister has sent me several papers with the accounts of his death from a fever."

"When did he die?"

"According to the articles, he passed away more than two months ago.

Lia rose from the rocker and placed Georgie in his cradle. He stirred, but didn't wake. Lia returned to her chair and reached for her aunt's hands. "What are we going to do? Do you think his grandfather will come looking for him?"

"Wouldn't you if you knew you had a grandchild you'd never seen?"

"Oh, Aunt Mildred. He mustn't find the babe. You know that was the only promise Janice asked of us—to keep the babe hidden from the Marquess of Trentridge. She was sure he would do the babe harm if he knew of the child's existence."

"I know," her aunt said worrying her bottom lip.

"Perhaps no one will ever know about George. We can only hope Janice hid her tracks well enough that nothing leads to your door."

"It was very clever of her to reach me by such a circuitous route, though I think it weakened her in the last days of her pregnancy. Still, anyone trying to find her is probably wandering around Scotland at this very moment. If they even know about the babe, that is. We can only hope. But we mustn't let our guard down. It all depends on what Lord Atherton told his father before he died. Perhaps he told him nothing. Then, no one will know."

"But we must have a plan in case the marquess does know," Lia said. "We have to be prepared in case we are discovered."

"Do you have an idea?"

"Yes, although I'm not sure how adequate it is," Lia said, praying that her plan would work. If it didn't, she could lose the babe, and that was something she refused to consider. She'd sworn she would raise the babe as her own. She'd promised her sister on her deathbed that no one would take the babe away from her. Especially someone from the Marquess of Trentridge's family.

And she vowed she would keep her promise.

. . . .

Scarcely a week later, Lia sat in the library with a book in her hands. There was nothing she enjoyed more than a good novel—especially one of the romance novels that were becoming so popular. She was ever so fortunate that there was a book store in the village not far from Collinson Manor. Mr. Hodges, the store owner, had a surprising cache of the latest gothic novels.

"Have you begun reading again, Lia?" her aunt asked as she entered the library.

A maid followed with a tea tray and set it down near Lia, who set aside her pen and poured each of them a cup of tea. "Just writing a note of thanks, Auntie Mildred. Hodges' Book Shoppe has sent me an absolutely tantalizing note to inform me they've received a new selection and I have pleaded with them to send the lot to me forthwith!"

Her aunt smiled. "I have no doubt that you are his best customer."

"Do you think I'm spending too much of your money on books, Aunt?"

"No, no, my dear. That is what I asked you to do. My library is in need of refreshing, and you're the perfect person to satisfy that need. I have no idea what books to choose."

Her aunt took a sip of her tea. "Now, if I were in need of new horse flesh to fill my stables, I would have no problem filling that order. I'm quite knowledgeable in equestrian affairs. My late husband had a keen eye for horses and he taught me what to look. But I daresay, books are beyond my understanding."

"Then I will continue to visit Hodges' and add to your woefully lacking selection of literary fiction."

Her Aunt Mildred smiled. "You do that, my love." The Viscountess took another sip of tea, then set down her cup and saucer. "Is the babe asleep?"

"Yes. Mrs. Rodgers fed little George, then put him down for a nap. I daresay he'll sleep for an hour or more."

Aunt Mildred began to reply but stopped when her ancient butler rapped at the open door.

"Yes, Hobson. What is it?"

"You have a guest, my lady."

"Who is it, Hobson?"

"The Earl of Atherton, my lady. I told him you were not receiving, but he insisted he needed to see you."

Lia's heart lodged in her throat and she looked at her aunt, whose expression was filled with the same alarm Lia felt.

"Give us a moment, then show his lordship in, Hobson."

"Very well, my lady."

"Let me do the talking, Lia."

Lia nodded, then sat rigidly in her chair. She rehearsed the plan she and her aunt had formed weeks earlier.

"The Earl of Atherton, my lady," Hobson announced, then stepped aside to admit the man who, in their minds, posed a most dangerous threat.

"Bring in a fresh tea tray, Hobson."

"Yes, my lady."

Lia wasn't sure what she'd expected. Perhaps a man who resembled the babe. Someone blond with blue eyes and a ready smile on his face. The man who stood before her, however, was the opposite of anything she'd conjured in her mind.

"Lord Atherton," Aunt Mildred greeted.

Lia stared at the dark, imposing figure as he lowered to a respectful bow.

Lia took in his height and the breadth of his shoulders that nearly filled the doorway. Much taller and he would have had to lower his head to enter the room. He wore a formidable frown that made him appear angry and…dangerous.

His hair was as dark as little George's was light and his eyes were equally dark and lacking any softness. He stood as an unreadable sphinx, hardened with lethal calmness.

His shirt and cravat were a pristine white and his jacket, trousers, and waistcoat were funereal black. But his perfectly tailored attire wasn't what drew her eye and refused to allow her to look away from him. The deep bronze of his rugged features is what caused her to keep her gaze focused on his face. His profile was sharp and confident. His high cheekbones were strong and rigid. His jaw was sculptured in captivating lines that evidenced a formidable strength.

He seemed all ruthlessness, danger, and unapproachability.

Lia shivered.

There was nothing soft or yielding in the man who stood before them. In his black gloves and his coat with its black armband he should have presented the sympathetic picture of a gentleman in deep mourning. But to Lia it made him simply intimidating. Lia knew it would take all her courage to stand up to him. All her fortitude and determination to protect herself and the babe if she intended to succeed in keeping Janice's babe safe.

"Lady Collinson," the man greeted with a sharp bow.

"Lord Atherton. Allow me to present my niece, Miss Halloway."

"Miss Halloway?" he questioned. "Don't you mean Lady Atherton?"

A terrifying silence stretched throughout the room. He knew. He knew Janice and his brother had married.

Hobson and a maid arrived with the tea tray and placed it before her aunt. Thankfully, the interruption gave Lia a moment to gather her courage.

Her auntie had not corrected his assumption that he was meeting his late brother's wife. Lia swallowed hard. Could they? Did they dare? Was it possible they might deceive the man into thinking she was Janice? In truth, it could turn the table in her behalf. It was one thing to try and take a child from his aunt. But his mother? Surely they would be much less willing to take such a drastic measure. Lia's mind raced forward, seeking to identify every aspect of their secret if she was to carry it off.

Aunt Mildred poured tea and handed Lord Atherton a cup. Then she handed Lia a cup before pouring one for herself. The china teacup that had always felt substantial in Lia's hand looked miniature in the large, steady hand of Lord Atherton.

Lia placed her cup on the table in front of her without taking even one swallow. She knew if she tried to take a sip her hands would shake so badly Lord Atherton would know how severely his presence affected her.

Their guest finished his tea and placed his cup and saucer on a side table, then let his gaze focus on Lia's attire. She wore black today as was only appropriate in mourning Janice's death. But he wouldn't know of that. He would think that somehow she had heard of her estranged husband's death.

Fortunately she had dissuaded her aunt from decking the house in high mourning for Janice. That would have been quite a bit more difficult to explain, in light of the deception they were prepared to carry out.

"May I presume you know of your husband's death, Lady Atherton?"

Lia lowered her gaze to her lap. He'd merely stated a cold, hard fact. No commiseration. No effort to express sympathy. "Yes, my lord. I have been so informed."

She was so very grateful that she didn't have to try to look the part of the grieving widow. She was terrified enough to play the role without any effort.

"May I ask you a question," she said, lifting her watery gaze.

"Yes, my lady."

My lady. It would have been Janice's place to be spoken to in such elegant terms. The very idea brought her loss very close to the surface and sent a tear to trickle down her cheek.

"Did he...did Evan suffer at the end?"

"No, my lady. He did not."

"I'm glad," she answered, even though she believed he was lying to her. Perhaps there was a softness in him somewhere, although from every indication if there was, it was hidden perilously deep.

"Did he die alone?"

He drew a deep breath. "No, my lady. I was with him when he died."

"Thank you," she answered. "I would hate to think that he died alone."

Lia couldn't stand his evaluative stare and rose to her feet. She walked to the window and stared out into the garden. Summer was in its full glory. Color filled the garden and climbed the stone walls that enclosed it.

Janice had loved the out-of-doors. She'd spent hours in the garden while waiting for her child to be born. She'd been so excited not only for the babe's arrival, but for the man she loved to come for her at Christmas. She never doubted that he would. She never lost faith in the love they shared for each other. Even at the end, when she struggled to give birth to their son.

How Amelia missed her sister. How she wished she could have her back. How she wished Jannie were still here to watch her child grow. But that was no longer possible. Both Janice and the man she loved had left their babe in her care.

Lia wiped her eyes before she turned to face the dangerous man who dominated their library. "I take it your brother told you about us. What did he say?"

"He said that he loved you with all his heart. He told me that you and he had married and that you were carrying his child. Is his child alive?"

She was going to lie. She intended to tell him the babe was dead. It's what they had planned, to tell the Earl of Atherton's family that the child had not survived a difficult birth. That would solve all their problems. If he thought the babe was dead, he would leave and she would never see him again.

But at that exact moment, George cried out loudly in one of his most demanding bellows.

Lia stared at Lord Atherton but he was not watching her. His eyes were looking toward the closed door, in the direction of the upper floor where the babe had been sleeping, but was no longer.

Lord Atherton rose and took his first step to leave the room.

"No, my lord!" Lia said more forcefully than she'd intended.

The earl spun around and glared at her. "Is that my brother's child?"

"No. It is mine!"

"And my brother's," he said. "The child is—"

"He is nothing to you but a relative. He is my son!" she repeated. "*My* son."

The Earl of Atherton took but a few long strides to reach the door, then he was out of the room.

Lia followed him almost at a run but she could not catch him. He took the stairs two at a time and was at the top before she reached the landing that marked half way.

"No!" she cried. "Leave him be. Don't touch him. He's not yours!"

Lia's advantage was that Atherton did not know which room the babe was in. She took the opportunity to race ahead of him to the nursery when he paused at the top of the stairs. When she reached the babe, she gathered George in her arms as Atherton entered the nursery. She cradled the babe closely, determined to protect him with her last breath, if need be.

"He is not yours!" she insisted, turning her back to him so he couldn't reach the babe,

Atherton was silent. He didn't speak, nor did he move. When enough time had passed that Lia no longer felt threatened, she slowly turned.

Their gazes caught and held. The inky blackness of his eyes bore into hers. Anger showed clearly in his eyes, in his expression. Her heart hammered in her breast and it was all she could do to take in a breath and release it.

Lia looked around the room and saw Aunt Mildred standing close by. Her presence caused Lia to feel a small bit of relief.

"May I see him?" Lord Atherton asked softly, almost in a whisper. And yet, his voice held a threat. There was a demand in his tone.

Lia turned with the babe in her arms. She made sure to stay far enough away so Lord Atherton could not snatch the babe. She slowly lowered the blanket from around the babe's face and turned him so Lord Atherton could get a good look at his brother's child.

"It's not possible," his lordship whispered in a muted hiss.

Lia snuggled the babe against her breast and turned as if to protect him. "What is?" she asked.

The Earl of Atherton slumped against the wall, then swiped his hand over his face.

"It's like looking at a portrait. The child is a replica of my brother."

Lia turned back toward him, offering the man a second look at his nephew.

"What did you name him?" he asked in a weak voice.

"He is named after my father, George, and yourself. George Hunter Montclaire." Lia lifted her gaze. "It's what Evan would have wanted."

Atherton reached out and touched the babe as if he were made of glass. As if he would break. He touched little George's cheek with the back of his finger, then Atherton held out that same finger for the babe to take. The child wrapped his tiny fist around his uncle's sturdy finger and held on tightly.

The expression on Atherton's face filled with wonder. It was obvious he wasn't accustomed to being in the presence of babies. Obvious he didn't have the slightest idea how to act around a child this small.

"May I hold him?"

Lia turned her head and focused her gaze on her aunt. There was a frown on her aunt's face as if she didn't trust his lordship. Lia didn't trust him either.

"Sit in that rocking chair," Lia said, pointing to the chair in the far corner of the room.

Aunt Mildred walked to the door and called for the butler who appeared within moments.

"Hobson, come in and guard the door."

"Yes, my lady."

Hobson closed the door and stood in front of it so the Earl of Atherton couldn't escape if he tried to take George. Lia prayed the old fellow was stronger than he looked. Still, being seated in the rocking chair would slow Lord Atherton should he try anything.

When the Earl of Atherton was seated, Lia held George out and placed him in the earl's arms. He held the babe awkwardly, as if the child were a fragile piece of china.

"He won't break," Lia said.

"I've never held a babe before."

Atherton adjusted George and even became brave enough to reach for the babe's hand and hold it.

Lia watched as George stared at the stranger holding him and frowned. Then, the babe reached up and grabbed Lord Atherton's cravat in his fist and graced him with a bright smile and a giggle.

His lordship didn't stop his nephew from pulling on the elegantly-tied fabric. He let him pull until the knot was undone. When the babe tired of undoing Atherton's cravat, he cooed, then wiggled in boredom.

Lord Atherton gave what nearly appeared to be a smile as he reached into his pocket. Lia gasped, unnerved over what he might withdraw. But before she could contemplate his intent, Lord Atherton drew a small object from his pocket and dangled it on a slim black ribbon above the baby's face. It twisted and turned, catching the light and eliciting all sorts of delighted burbles from the baby.

Lia stepped forward to see the object more clearly, and recognized it as a funeral brooch—a beautifully faceted piece of jewelry with a glass center that held a twist of blond braid.

The late Lord Atherton's hair.

Georgie reached for it, intent upon capturing the gleaming object that held a lock of his father's golden hair.

The sweetness of the scene brought tears to Lia's eyes, until the new Lord Atherton snatched it back up into his hand and thrust it toward Lia.

"I trust you'll keep this for him," Atherton said in voice that seemed brusque with indifference.

The abrupt disappearance of the shiny object and Atherton's harsh voice set the baby fussing. Lia reached down and took George back. The earl willingly gave him up, then stood.

Lia separated herself from him enough that she was out of the Earl of Atherton's reach. She lifted her head and their gazes locked. His eyes held a dark, unreadable expression. There was nothing that hinted at softness or understanding, but only a burning lethal resolve that indicated there were many battles ahead of them.

Battles he intended to win.

Chapter Three

HUNTER LEFT HIS BROTHER'S WIFE with the babe and escorted the dowager Viscountess Collinson to the drawing room. But his mind lingered in the nursery. He could certainly see why his brother had loved the fetching woman. She was lovely in every way, even though she carried herself with what could only be described as strength of will.

"Would you care for something stronger than tea, Lord Atherton?" Lady Collinson gave a flick of her wrist toward the sideboard as they entered the room.

"Yes, I believe I would," Hunter answered, then stopped at the modest arrangement of crystal decanters. "If I may?"

Receiving the lady's permission, Hunter lifted the brandy decanter and filled a glass. "Would you care for anything?"

"Yes, I believe I'd like a glass of sherry."

Hunter handed Lady Collinson her sherry, then sat in the chair opposite her.

"Thank you, Lord Atherton."

Hunt took a small swallow of his brandy. He refrained from drinking the entire glass like he wanted to do. He refrained from drinking the entire decanter like he wanted to do. Instead, he took another small sip.

"Montclaire, if you please," he corrected. "I am no longer the Earl of Atherton."

"Yes, but surely you see that you must retain the title," a voice said from the open doorway. His brother's wife entered the room and closed the door behind her. "For all intents and purposes, you must remain the Earl of Atherton for the foreseeable future."

Lady Atherton paused at the sideboard and poured herself a glass of wine. She sat in the chair between himself and her aunt.

Hunter tried not to stare, but he couldn't take his eyes from her. She wasn't at all like the woman he thought his brother would marry. Every bone in her body exuded courage and determination. He thought the woman his brother would be drawn to would be softer, more naïve. This woman had a strength that Hunter couldn't help but admire.

His brother's widow took another sip of her wine, then placed the half-empty glass on the table before her. She sat back in her chair and leveled him a hard look.

"Why are you here, my lord?"

"That should be obvious, my lady. To discover if my brother had a child and if that child was his heir."

Lady Atherton's eyes closed for a moment as if his directness pierced her resolve. "How did you find out about the child?"

"My brother told me."

Her eyes widened.

"He knew he was dying and asked me to give you this." Hunter reached into his pocket and took out the letter Evan had written. When she took it, he turned his gaze away from her to offer what little privacy he could.

She didn't open the letter while seated there, but rose from her chair and walked to the window. He heard the paper rustle when she unfolded it, then waited in silence while she read.

He heard the silent sobs and saw her shoulders shudder in pain. He should have known how upsetting it would be to read her husband's letter. He was sure his brother had poured his heart and soul out in the words he wrote.

After several long moments, his brother's widow turned to face him. "Does your father know Evan and…I…were married?"

"No. He doesn't."

"You know he can never find out, don't you?"

Hunter closed his eyes and took a deep breath. "Yes, I know. Neither you nor the babe will be safe if he becomes aware you and Evan were married and there is a child."

Lady Atherton folded the letter and placed it in the pocket of her skirt. "What are your intentions, Lord Atherton?"

"I intend to take my brother's child and keep him safe."

"That, sir, I cannot allow. I will not permit you to take George away from me. He is mine. *Mine!*"

Somehow her anguish startled him. Hunter blanched. He wasn't a completely unfeeling cad, even though he'd just indicated he intended to remove her child from her care.

It was the child he'd been concerned for. He could provide for the child's safety, ensure the babe grew into manhood prepared to carry his title. It hadn't for a moment occurred to him that the solution he offered would rend in two the heart of the babe's own mother, the woman his own brother had loved with his whole being.

What a brute he was. How could he have been so single-minded as to even think such a solution might be even remotely acceptable?

"But Lady Atherton. You can't keep him safe."

"I can! No one knows I am here."

"How long do you think you can stay hidden? It didn't take me but a few weeks to discover your whereabouts."

"That was only because your brother told you about me."

"And how long do you think it will be before my father discovers your existence? I knew my brother better than anyone. I can almost guarantee you that in his letter he explained that he would take care of you. Did he promise that he'd left money so you and the babe would be looked after?"

The swiftness with which the lady's eyelids lowered answered his question.

"Yes," Lia said, recalling the words in Lord Atherton's letter. "He said he opened an account in a certain bank in London. He instructed me to withdraw the money and deposit it in any bank I chose."

"How long do you imagine it will take my father to discover Evan's money has been placed in an account bearing your name?"

Evan's wife staggered forward and sank into her chair. The little color she'd previously had in her cheeks faded until she was as pale as the white plaster of the marble statues in the hallway.

She turned her gaze to her aunt. "What are we to do, Aunt?"

"I'm not sure, Janice. I was certain I could hide you here and keep you safe, but now I'm not sure."

Hunter reached for his sister-in-law's glass of wine and filled it, then handed it back to her.

"There is only one choice I can think of, Lady Atherton."

She took a sip of her wine, then looked at him. Her eyes were wide with fright and her hands trembled so violently the wine in her glass sloshed back and forth.

"What is that?"

Hunter made sure her aunt was included in the conversation. He didn't want her to feel left out. This had as much to do with her as it did with her niece.

"My father and I have never been able to tolerate one another. Evan was his favorite and I was...well, I was a failure in his eyes." Hunter took a sip of his brandy and kept his gaze focused on the ladies. "I knew the day would come when I would be forced to escape his wrath, so I took my inheritance and purchased an estate of my own. Father has no idea I own it. He thinks a town house in London is my only place of residence. I intend to take you to my estate, Rainwood Place. You'll be quite safe there."

She bounded to her feet. "No. I cannot share a home with you. That's impossible. I will stay here with my aunt."

"I'm afraid I can't let you live on your own. There's no telling what might happen to you."

"Then I will write to my brothers and ask one of them to come stay with me."

"What good will that do, my lady? Are they acquainted with my father?"

"Of course not."

"Do they know any of the men my father might send to find you?"

"No, but—"

"But nothing, my lady. You may have one of your brothers accompany us, but you will stay at my residence and I will look out for you and my nephew."

The look on Lady Atherton's face as she stared at her aunt tore at his heart. Staying with him wasn't an option she wished to consider but she knew how limited her choices were.

"How long will it take for one of your brothers to join us?" he asked.

"If it's Miles, he can no doubt be here in a matter of a day or two."

"Then write to him and ask him to make all haste."

Hunter watched as George's mother clenched her hands tightly in her lap and worried her bottom lip.

"Is there another way, Aunt?" she asked looking at the dowager viscountess with desperation in her eyes.

"If there is, my dear, I do not see it."

The lady's beautiful brown eyes filled with tears.

"There isn't," Hunter said, the finality of his words ringing harshly even to his own ears.

"There has to be," she implored. There was a frantic quality in her voice.

"There isn't," he repeated. "And I cannot understand why you are so desperate to avoid doing the one thing that will keep your baby safe."

Her head shot upward. Her gaze when she looked at him nearly took him to his knees. Because her eyes were filled with terror.

. . . .

Of course he couldn't understand why she was so hesitant to do the one thing that would keep the baby safe. He had no idea the babe was not hers, and if he ever discovered that fact there would be nothing she could do to keep him from taking her sister's child.

Even though he was just an infant, little George was now the Earl of Atherton. He'd inherited the title from his father. He was next in line to be the Marquess of Trentridge. There was no court in the land that would side with Lia if the Marquess of Trentridge tried to take the babe away from her.

Lia rose from her chair and paced the room. No matter the choices she gave herself, none of them protected the babe from the marquess. The man standing before her was the only man capable of protecting her sister's child.

"Very well, my lord."

Lia felt as though a heavy weight had descended on her and had pressed the air from her body.

"My lady," he said as she continued her nervous pacing. "There are several other matters I need to discuss with you. In private. Perhaps in the garden?"

Lia turned her gaze to her aunt who nodded her approval for Lia to join Lord Atherton in the garden. Lia dreaded the thought of being alone with him. The more they conversed, the greater her chances were that she would reveal something that would cause him to question what she told him. The greater her chances of revealing even the smallest detail that might give him cause to question her claim that she was the baby's mother.

Yet, what choice did she have?

Without acknowledging him, she walked to the glass doors that led to the terrace, then descended the three steps that led to a cultured, walled garden. The night was perfect, a beautiful summer's evening.

Lia had always been fond of the out-of-doors. Of all manner of flowering plants. The garden was rich with blooming shrubs and flowers of all kinds. She and her sister had spent many hours sharing the swing that hung from the garden's central shade tree when they'd come to stay with Aunt Mildred for Jannie's confinement.

Janice had shared whispered details of her time with Lord Atherton, and how and where they met. She'd told Lia of the exact moment she knew she loved her blond earl. Lia was sure she knew as much about their relationship as there was to know.

"Where did you meet my brother?" he asked.

"At university, my lord. My father is a professor at Cambridge and Evan and I met at a musicale. We happened to sit next to each other and we struck up a conversation that I found engaging. Your brother was one of the most interesting men I had ever met."

"Did you ever hear him play the pianoforte?"

Lia smiled and lifted her gaze. She remembered how Janice talked about the man she loved and how much she admired everything he did. "His music was as charming as he was himself." Each time she thought of Janice's description of her husband's musical skill, she wished that she herself could have heard him play.

"Yes," Lord Atherton said on a sigh.

"Do you share that same gift, my lord?"

"Alas, no, I do not. I play tolerably well until I'm put up against an eight-year old. Then, I'm found quite wanting. To be bluntly honest, there weren't many things I could do equally as well as Evan."

Lia stopped. "Are those your father's words, my lord, or your own?"

His eyes narrowed and the darkness in his gaze caused her a moment's pause. "And what, pray tell, do you know of my father?"

"Only what Evan told me, but that was enough to know you were constantly the recipient of all manner of criticism. You were also at loggerheads with your father on a daily basis. Which is why you went out on your own at such an early age." Lia prayed she'd remembered that part right.

"I think if my brother were here at this moment I might rebuke him for his openness when discussing me."

Lia lowered her gaze, relieved to know she had, after all, remembered correctly. "Evan and I shared everything, my lord. I think he wanted me to know everything about him. It was as if he knew he wouldn't be here to watch his son grow to manhood and he wanted someone to be able to tell him everything there was to know about him."

"How long did you know each other before you married?"

"Nearly a year."

"Where were you married?"

"In Scotland. It was quite simple to arrange it there."

"Were you carrying his son before you married?"

Lia paused in her circuit around the shade tree. What good would it do for Lord Atherton to know Jannie was pregnant with his brother's child before they wed?

After a short hesitation, she stepped forward and sat in the swing. Lord Atherton stepped aside and leaned a shoulder against the tree's trunk.

"Do you think it's possible that your father won't find out about his grandson?"

"Do you want the truth?"

"Yes."

"Then, no. Eventually he'll find out about you and your son. And when he does—"

Lia thrust herself from the swing and lost her balance as her feet sought purchase. Before she could right herself, Lord Atherton's hand reached out and he caught her. His arm wrapped around her waist and he pulled her to him.

Every muscle in her body stiffened. Every nerve sparked as if struck by lightning. She experienced the strangest pull on her heart when she clasped her hands around his arms in an effort to support herself.

Their gazes locked in shock and surprise. His brows lowered and a lethal frown deepened across his forehead. His eyes turned dark and dangerous. His arms held her firmly for several moments, then he dropped his hands from her body as if she'd burned him.

His body stiffened and he took a distinct step away from her.

The electric moment defied belief. Lia forced herself to banish the unwelcome sensation that lingered on her flesh. She couldn't be affected by something as simple as his touch.

Not by *him*.

Not by a man with a title.

Janice may have found her great love in the arms of her handsome young earl, but Lia's experience had not been so kind. Never again would she expose her heart to a man who might steal it, then stomp it beneath the heel of his boot. A man who might leave her for a prettier woman with a fine name and a huge dowry. A woman whose father boasted a far grander title than university professor.

Lia turned and walked away from Hunter Montclaire. This time she was certain he had no intention of following her. But his voice called to her as she entered the house.

"How soon can you and your aunt be ready to travel?"

She didn't turn. She didn't want to answer his question but she didn't have a choice. She didn't have a choice in anything. Not if she wanted her son—no, her *sister's* son—to be safe.

"Soon," she answered, then stepped into the dark cool of the drawing room. Thankfully, her aunt was no longer there and Lia could escape to the nursery.

She picked up little George and held him as the reality of her situation enveloped her. She had no choice but to go with Atherton.

It was the only way George would be safe.

Chapter Four

Hunter fumed his way across Lady Collinson's terrace. His steps were long and angry.

What the hell just happened?

He raked his hand down his face as if he could wipe the events of the last fifteen minutes from his memory.

Just the feel of his flesh touching hers through layers of clothing had caused a tumultuous reaction that he'd never experienced before.

He couldn't allow himself to unleash emotions like this. He was incapable of caring for anyone. Caring for someone meant you could not live your life without them. Just like his father hadn't been able to live without Hunter's mother and had spent the rest of his life hating the son who was responsible for her death.

No. He would not allow himself to care for anyone.

"Lord Atherton?" a soft voice said from behind him.

Hunter turned to find himself looking into the concerned gaze of the dowager viscountess. The lady's butler followed her carrying a tray with crystal decanters and glasses. He placed the tray on the terrace table and left them.

"Lady Collinson," Hunter answered, executing a perfect bow. "I didn't expect that you'd still be about."

"I was waiting for you." She pointed to a nearby chair. "Please, sit down."

Hunter waited until Lady Collinson sat, then walked to the table.

"Would you care for something to drink?" she asked.

"Yes, my lady. I would. May I pour you something?"

"Yes. Sherry, please."

Hunter poured Lady Collinson a glass of sherry, then poured a snifter of brandy for himself. He needed something strong after the conversation he'd had with his sister-in-law. And after the way he'd reacted to her nearness.

"My maid tells me my niece was upset when she returned to the house."

Hunter took a swallow of his brandy. "Yes. I'm afraid the outcome of our conversation wasn't what your niece wanted to hear."

"Do not judge her too harshly, my lord. This hasn't been easy for her. She has found herself in a position she neither wanted nor expected."

"No, I don't imagine she did want it. But neither did I." Hunter watched the liquid slosh as he turned the glass in circles with his thumb and forefinger.

"Of course not, my lord."

"Why do you insist on referring to me by my brother's title when you know I am no longer in possession of it?"

"Because we cannot risk anyone knowing you are no longer the Earl of Atherton. A four-month-old babe can hardly object to you borrowing his title for a few years."

Hunter couldn't stop a smile from appearing on his face.

"She will go with you, you know."

"I would hope so, but I cannot be sure. She seems determined to send me on my way and try to handle this on her own."

"Janice would never put the babe in danger. If that means going with you, she'll do it."

"Will you accompany us?"

The dowager viscountess hesitated a few moments, then said, "If Janice wants me to, I will. It will be her decision."

"She mentioned something about asking one of her brothers to go with her."

"That would be Miles. He served in the war and has experience with weapons."

Hunter nodded. If his father sent men after them, Hunter would appreciate having someone at his side with military experience. He was surprised, though, at the dowager's ease at mentioning the possible need for weapons.

"How soon do you think she can be ready?" Hunter asked.

"A week from today," Lady Collinson answered. "That should give Miles enough time to get here."

"Very well. We'll leave in a week. Would you speak to your niece for me? Have her write to her brother at once?"

"Of course. Is there anything else?"

"I know Lady Atherton might not feel that she can impose on you more than she already has, but I would ask that you seriously consider accompanying us. Your niece needs a sympathetic friend right now. She has just lost her husband, and from what my brother told me, he and your niece were quite in love."

"Yes, they were."

"I would also ask that you and your niece take only one maid each. The fewer people who know where we're going, the safer we'll be."

"You're quite right. We should be content with my lady's maid and the wet nurse, of course, and Janice's maid."

Hunter nodded once, then watched Lady Collinson rise to walk to the house. She paused before she entered through the French doors.

"Thank you, Lord Atherton. I am acquainted with your father only enough to know I must be wary of him. He has a cruel streak running through him. I've heard rumors of the little regard in which he holds you. Neither do I doubt that he would do anything in his power to rid the Trentridge line of an heir born to a commoner. Although, I wager that you are more aware than anyone of the anger that courses through him."

"Did you know my father before I was born?"

"Yes, my lord. He was a different man in those days. But that man died with your mother."

Hunter watched Lady Collinson leave, then refilled his glass. This was the reason he could never love someone. If he ever fell in love it would be forever. It would be completely. And if he lost the woman he loved, what guarantee did he have that he wouldn't turn into a man as bitter and demented as his father. Or treat the child who caused her death as cruelly.

He wouldn't want to wish such evil on any child.

He had his nephew to think of now. He would focus his love and attention on him. And teach the child to take after his father instead of his grandfather.

That would be his goal in life. He would not fail.

. . . .

Lia sat in the nursery while Marjorie Rodgers fed little Georgie. Lia couldn't get over how he'd grown in the last month.

"There's a possibility that my aunt and I will be leaving within the week, Marjorie."

Marjorie Rodgers' head shot up to look at her. "Will you be taking the lad with you?"

"Yes," Lia answered. "I could never leave him behind. Not for any reason. He's mine and I intend to raise him."

"Does his lordship know you're not the boy's mother?"

"No, Marjorie. And you must never tell him that I'm not."

"Of course, miss. You can trust me to never say a word. I know how important it is that his lordship never realize that you're not the child's mother. I fear he would think he has more right to the babe than you do and he would try to take little Georgie away from you."

"That's exactly my fear. He can never know that I'm not George's mother." Lia worried her lower lip. "I know it's quite impossible for you to come with us, Marjorie, but do you know of anyone who could? Someone who's recently had a babe and would be willing and able to leave her home?"

Marjorie thought for a moment, then focused her gaze on Lia. "There might be someone, miss. There's a girl in Abbotslede who is rumored to have had a babe two weeks ago, but the baby died."

"Oh, how sad."

"Yes. But if her milk is still flowing, she might be able to help you. Would you like me to speak with her parents? I don't know them well, but mayhap they'd be willing to let their daughter leave until rumors die down."

"How old is the girl?"

"She's coming up on sixteen."

"Oh. She's so young."

"Yes. It will be good for her to have something else to do other than think on the babe she lost. I'll speak to her and her parents tonight."

"Thank you," Lia said as she walked to the nursery door. George had fallen asleep and was breathing slowly and deeply. Thankfully, he was unaware of the turmoil that threatened his young life. Hopefully, she would always be able to protect him.

Lia went to her room and penned a letter to her brother. She was sure Miles would agree to go with them. He was a different man from the day he left for the war. It was as if he'd seen and done things that had made him age far past his five and twenty years. He no longer seemed to fit in with the young men his age.

Lia had no doubt he'd be glad to escape the watchful, worrying gazes of their parents. It was only that they were concerned over their son and hoped that he would regain the cheerful optimism they'd known in him before he went to war. Now that she was in many ways a mother, she began to understand why they were on tenterhooks over her handsome brother.

When Lia finished, she went down to give her letter to Hobson and asked that someone deliver the missive. She turned to go back up the stairs when a deep, commanding voice stopped her.

"Do you have a moment, my lady?"

Lia turned and found herself face to face with the man who unsettled her so. "Yes, my lord. Did you wish to speak with me?"

"Yes. I have several matters to discuss with you. Would you join me in the library?"

"Of course."

Lia walked past him and entered the library in front of him.

She chose to sit in one of the two brightly woven brocade wing chairs that faced each other with a round tea table between them. It seemed the safest way to avoid contact with the man. She didn't want to relive the reaction she'd experienced the last time they'd accidentally touched.

"A fortifying drink, my lady?"

"No, thank you. But please, help yourself."

He did. With the glass in his hand, he settled his tall frame into the chair opposite her.

"What was it you wished to speak with me about?"

"Our journey." He shifted so he could face her directly. "We don't have much time to prepare, as we shall need to leave within the week. Have you made all the necessary arrangements for the babe?"

"I believe I have. I just posted a letter to my brother Miles. I doubt he'll answer. Instead, I look for him to arrive ready to travel with us. If that is his choice, he should be here in three or four days."

"And Lady Collinson?"

"Aunt Margaret has already instructed her maid to begin packing. There's no doubt she will be ready well in time."

"And you?"

"I shall be ready, as well."

"That only leaves young George."

"Marjorie can't come with us, of course. She has a husband and family here that she can't leave. But she suggested a young girl who recently lost her babe at birth. She will speak to her to see if she might agree to take the post as wet nurse for the babe."

"Very good."

Lia couldn't help but study her sister's brother-in-law. There was something very serious about him, as if his father's hostility toward him had indelibly marked him.

"Is your estate very far from here?" she asked when a long period of silence stretched between them.

"Not far at all. Only a half day's ride. Far enough that my father should not think of looking there, should he have reason to search for us. Yet close enough that if we leave in the morning, we can reach our destination well before tea."

"Do you fear your father that much?"

He lowered his snifter and rested it on his knee. "Did you ever meet my father?"

Lia had heard every horrid detail of Jannie's few moments in the presence of the Marquess of Trentridge, but the very recollection of it stilled her tongue.

"Surely Evan wouldn't have introduced you to our father. He surely would have known that would be the worst of mistakes."

"Actually, we did meet briefly, and it went badly. Evan was mortified."

"No doubt. I'm actually appalled that Evan put you through that. Father would never accept his heir marrying beneath him. He would have objected to your lack of station and made no bones about it."

"He did rather colorfully express his objection to our association."

"I'm sure he did. He would have had a difficult time accepting that his heir wanted to marry the daughter of a mere professor. A common man can hardly compare to Society's titled nobility, no matter how intelligent or knowledgeable he is."

Lia felt her temper rise as she searched for a touch of irony in his tone and heard little. "No. They hardly compare. Is that your impression, as well, my lord?"

His expression turned dark. "Are you asking if I object to you marrying my brother as emphatically as my father did?"

Lia knew it was important that she stand up to him now. If she didn't, he would have the power to destroy her. "That's exactly what I'm asking."

"I don't see where my opinion matters one way or the other."

"I think it would matter a great deal to your brother. I believe he would want to know if you could come to terms with his choice of wife, or if you would always hold his wife in contempt, as does your father."

"Perhaps he would, but since he is no longer here to object, I don't find it important."

"Lord help us!" She huffed as she rose angrily from her chair. "Are you always this obtuse? Perhaps you aren't that different from your father."

"Enough!" His voice took on a harshness that he seemed to try hard to soften as he continued. "You know nothing of me or of my father. I would ask you not to assume that my father and I are alike in the least."

"I will speak because I am about to put my life and my…my son's wellbeing in your hands." Now it was she who felt the need to soften her tone.

"Then perhaps we should make an effort to learn to tolerate one another. At least for the child's sake. The last thing I want is to have to fight you and my father at the same time."

"Then I suggest we avoid each other as much as possible, my lord."

The man sitting next to her put a harsh expression on his face. "I agree wholeheartedly."

Hunter Montclaire rose to his feet. "If you'll excuse me, my lady. Suffice it to say that I expect to be on the road one week from today. Until then I expect you to conduct yourself with the greatest of caution."

"But what if my brother isn't here yet? Or a wet nurse hasn't been secured? We would have to delay our departure."

"As to your brother, I'm afraid we'll be forced to leave without him. As to the wet nurse, it should be no hardship to procure one when we reach our destination. I'm sure we can find one in the village or among my tenant families."

A wave of panic surged through her. If need be, she was sure a wet nurse could be found when they arrived at Lord Montclaire's estate. But she didn't want to leave without Miles. She needed him to protect her from the Marquess of Trentridge, should he find out about George's existence.

Even more importantly, she needed her brother to protect her against Lord Hunter Montclaire.

Chapter Five

HUNTER SAT IN THE LIBRARY nursing a glass of brandy. His sister-in-law stood watching out the window that faced the drive. She was waiting for her brother. It had been one day shy of a week since she'd written him.

Hunter was serious when he'd told her they would leave tomorrow morning. If her brother didn't arrive yet today, they would leave without him.

He heard a carriage pull up and saw her reaction.

"Is he here?" Hunter asked.

She shook her head. "It's Mrs. Rodgers. She's here with the girl to interview for the position of wet nurse for George."

"Did you want to meet with her in here?"

"No. I'll take her to the nursery. I want to see how she interacts with George."

Hunter watched her leave. Her shoulders looked as if they carried the weight of the world. He regretted the harsh words they'd shared earlier in the week, yet he had no choice but to hold her at arm's length considering the way his body reacted to her.

It was exasperating.

He couldn't contemplate anything coming of a friendship between them. He wouldn't risk falling in love with the woman. Not after he'd seen the bitterness and hatred that ate away at his father after he lost the woman he loved.

Even if he didn't have that to look back upon, the woman standing at the window was the last person with whom he could entertain thoughts any deeper than friendship. England's affinity laws forbade it. A man could never marry his brother's widow.

Well, he could, but anybody who objected could bring suit and void the marriage. He had no wish to enter into such a tenuous predicament.

Hunter swiped his hand across his face. How the hell could his mind entertain such thoughts? Since he'd met Janice Montclaire his errant mind traveled to places where he didn't wish it to go. Places that were totally foreign to him. If it hadn't been for that heart-stopping reaction he'd had to her, he wouldn't be giving her a second thought.

In fact, she created a reaction that caused him to become even more hostile than he usually was. But to his surprise, where she should have cowered in his presence, she stood with complete ease. Even the men in his regiment hadn't shown the courage she did when his temper showed itself.

There was no denying that she was quite a remarkable woman. But, he couldn't allow himself to be affected by her. Instead, he had to figure out what there was about Janice Montclaire that caused him to be drawn to her.

Yet each time he thought he had hit on the answer, she changed. Like a chameleon, she could blend seamlessly into whatever new scenario presented itself. As if she kept herself one step ahead of him. Had planned her moves or her words in advance. As if she was hiding something, a secret that kept her at arm's length from him.

Yes, something was askew. Perhaps it resulted from having had to keep her marriage to Evan secret. But somehow, it seemed more than that. It was almost as if the lady had been lying to him. He'd swear that once or twice something she had said did not quite ring true.

He tried to remember every word Evan had told him about his wife. He'd said how beautiful she was, and Lady Atherton was indeed beautiful. Then too, Evan had professed how fair and delicate she was.

Hunter considered Lady Atherton's regal bearing that he had so often admired. Little Georgie's mother was anything but fair and delicate.

Although she could be called delicate in the sense of feminine grace, she certainly was not fair. Her coloring was certainly closer to Hunter's warm coffee undertones than Evan's almost translucent fairness that Hunter had expected her to have. The same fairness as the babe's. But she looked nothing like what he expected.

He would indeed watch her. What if his father had already discovered the babe and planted an imposter here to care for it?

Hunter raked his fingers through his hair. No. That couldn't be. She knew too much about Janice's family to be an imposter. And the dowager viscountess was too comfortable around her.

All he knew for sure was that he would have to be on his guard. If his suspicions proved false, all would be well. But if not, someone was sure to slip up.

. . . .

Lia greeted the young girl Mrs. Rodgers brought with her, then led the way to the nursery. When they reached the room, the girl went right to the cradle where little George was playing with his toes.

"I'd like to introduce you to my son, George Hunter Montclaire. Look here, Georgie. This is Frannie McTavish. It's possible she might be your new nurse." Lia reached down to tickle the child. "If you don't frighten her off," she said with a smile.

"Oh, he'd never frighten me off," the young girl said, lifting George from his cradle and holding him in her arms. "He's beautiful. A right nice gentleman, aren't you, Lord George."

The young girl held George in her arms and played with him as if she'd held and cared for several babes all her short lifetime.

"We are about to travel to a different estate, Miss McTavish. Do you have any concerns about moving away from your family?"

"None whatsoever," she answered. "And please, call me Frannie."

"Very well, Frannie. Could you be ready to leave by tomorrow morning?"

"I can leave this very moment, my lady. When Mrs. Rodgers came to tell me about this position, I packed the few belongings I possess and brought them with me. I've already told my family farewell, so there's nothing for me to return for."

Lia studied the girl, impressed with her forthrightness. Her openness made Lia realize that the girl had a right to know what she was getting into. But did they dare reveal their fear for George's safety?

"Miss McTavish. Frannie. You should know that a certain…relative poses some concern for George's safety." She took a breath before continuing, but Frannie seemed to need no further explanation.

"Tis always so, isn't it, Lady Atherton? Rest assured no mischief will come to the babe while I live and breathe."

Her bold declaration was both stunning and reassuring, and put an end to Lia's worry that anything further needed to be said.

Lia and Mrs. Rodgers spoke with Frannie McTavish for several more minutes and by the time George had been fed and laid down for his nap, Lia was certain the girl was perfect for the position.

She was young, that was for sure, but she held and ministered to the babe as if he were her own, yet not in a possessive way that caused even the smallest alarm. Lia watched as she cared for the babe, and felt a pang of sorrow that little George wasn't her own. The little scene made her grieve for the pain and suffering young Frannie had endured already. It must have been heart-wrenching to have lost a babe before it had drawn its first breath.

"May I ask," Frannie said with a slight blush to her cheeks, "why you haven't nursed the babe yourself, Lady Atherton? Nothing is more special for a mother."

Frannie's question shouldn't have taken Lia by surprise, but it did. She swallowed several times before she came up with an answer. "I was ill in the first weeks after George was born, and have not been able to nurse him. I don't have enough milk."

"I see," Frannie answered. "Well, I'll have no problem on that score. Since I lost my babe, I've helped out several women whose babes want more than their mothers have."

"Then we are fortunate that you can help us out."

"Oh, aye. I'll be happy to give your lad as much as he needs to grow strong and healthy."

"Then I'll be grateful to you."

When Lia had discussed all the details of the girl's employment, she left Frannie with Mrs. Rodgers to explain Georgie's daily routine.

She walked down the stairs and returned to the library. It was the room that held the best view of the front drive. Lia wanted to stand watch for Miles. If she was lucky, Hunter Montclaire would have retired and she would have the room to herself.

But luck, it seemed, wasn't with her. He sat where she'd left him as if he'd been waiting for her.

. . . .

"What did you think of the young girl Mrs. Rodgers found?" Hunter asked when she returned.

"She will do very well."

"Good," he said. "Please, have a seat. Will you join me in a glass of wine?"

At her nod, he rose and poured her a glass of wine then handed it to her.

She'd walked to one of the two wing chairs set before the fireplace. But before she sat, she looked out the window. He presumed she was checking once again for her brother. Unfortunately for her, the drive was empty. Hunter watched her shoulders drop as the lady breathed a heavy sigh of disappointment.

"I owe you an apology, my lady," Hunter said as he took his seat in the chair opposite her.

"As I do you," she answered, taking a sip of her wine. "I shouldn't have spoken to you as I did. Although I have to admit that you were right when you said it might be best for us to avoid one another."

"Why do you think that is?" he asked her.

At first Hunter thought she didn't have an answer for him. But she did. From the expression on her face she was debating whether she wanted to share it or not.

"Go on, my lady," he said as he relaxed in his chair. "Tell me why you think it wise of us to avoid each other."

She took another drink from her goblet. "Perhaps because we seem to rub the wrong way."

"Yes," Hunter answered in a harsh whisper. "We do seem to rub the wrong way."

"And the solution for this would be?"

Hunter shrugged his shoulders. "Perhaps there is no solution," he said. "Perhaps we will only need to make an effort to tolerate each other as much as possible."

"Yes," she answered, then stopped when she seemed to hear a noise from the drive in front of the house. A noise Hunter hadn't heard. She rose from her chair and went to the window, standing in the same spot where she'd stood the day before as she watched for her brother.

He didn't want to remind her that they would leave in the morning whether this brother of hers was here or not.

She clasped her hands so tightly at her waist that her knuckles were white. Her muscles were braced so tautly he was sure if he walked up to her and pressed against her shoulders, the muscles beneath would shoot like springs from her flesh.

"Come and sit, my lady. Watching will do no good."

She shook her head. "I'm fine."

"What is it you're so concerned over? That your brother won't come and you'll be left to face me alone?"

"He'll come. I know he will." She looked out the window yet again. "And even if he doesn't, I won't be alone with you. There's Aunt Mildred, you know."

Hunter walked to the window and stood beside her, though careful not to crowd. She didn't notice him at first, and when she did, she jumped.

"Blast it all, what the devil is the matter?" he muttered.

"Excuse me?"

"I asked you what the matter was. You seem terribly nervous. And if I'm any judge of character, I would say you were hiding something from me."

She spun to face him. The terror in her eyes told him he'd hit an exposed nerve.

"What is it you're keeping from me?"

"I don't know what you're talking about."

"I think you do, Lady Atherton. And I'm not about to give up until I find out what it is."

Her face lost what little color it previously possessed. His brother's wife had a secret she was guarding and he would pursue her until he discovered what it was.

"Would you like to save us both a great deal of time and tell me now what you're keeping from me?"

"Leave me alone!" she cried out.

She clutched the side of the window as if she needed to hold on to something solid to steady herself.

"Isn't it enough that I have to worry about your father and what he will do if he discovers he has a grandson he wants to eliminate?"

"That won't happen. I won't let it."

"You can't make that promise. Your father wields too much power and influence. What match are you against his authority and manipulation?"

"Do not underestimate me, Lady Atherton. I have spent my whole life battling my father. The years I spent fighting the enemy in the war were not nearly as treacherous as one day battling my father."

Hunter watched her eyes open in fright, then her hands clasped around her waist as if she needed to hold herself together. For a moment he regretted his harsh words, but he couldn't allow himself to soften toward her.

"Do you really think your father would do his grandson physical harm?"

Her words reverberated in his mind, words he dared not answer. The admission seemed too outrageous. Too inconceivable. Too deadly.

How could he answer her question when he didn't doubt for a moment the lengths to which his father would go to make sure the son of a commoner would never inherit the Trentridge dynasty?

Chapter Six

IT WAS A FOOL'S ERRAND, but try as she would, Lia found it impossible to abandon her post. For what seemed hours, Lia waited impatiently at the library window. She abandoned her watch long enough to go to the nursery to check on the babe, then returned to keep her vigil. It was nearly dark outside. Time was running out.

She didn't know what she would do if she had to match wits with Lord Hunter Montclaire by herself. The only thing she could think of that would be worse would be if his father knew of the baby's existence. Her world would be altered irreparably if the Marquess of Trentridge and Montclaire both demanded possession of the babe.

She looked out onto the empty graveled drive. Thankfully, Montclaire had left her in peace for much of the afternoon. Thankfully, she hadn't had to battle his unpleasantness. She didn't think she could manage that right now. She'd never been so frightened in her life.

Tears filled her eyes and spilled over her lashes. It had been difficult enough to assume responsibility for her nephew, after having watched while her sister lost her life birthing him. Then, to discover that Lord Atherton had asked his brother to take care of his son so their father would never gain control of him only added to everything she'd been forced to deal with.

To be uprooted and moved to a place that was unfamiliar. To live with a man whose hostility toward her was unrelenting, and who wanted possession of the babe as desperately as she did, was almost more than she could cope with.

Lia swiped at a second tear that trickled down her cheek, then turned her gaze to the window. The sight before her blurred and she was forced to blink several times before she clearly saw a figure riding toward the manor house.

"Miles," she whispered, then raced toward the front door.

Hobson opened the door and she ran through it on her way to meet her brother.

"Miles!" she called out.

Her brother leaped from his horse when she reached him and gathered her in his arms.

"Lia," he said wrapping his strong, muscled arms around her. "I got here as quickly as I could. Are you alright?"

"I am now, Miles. Oh, I can't tell you how glad I am that you're here."

Her brother brushed a tear from her face and held her for another second.

"Your letter was a bit sketchy, I'm afraid. What's going on?"

She nodded. "Come in and I'll explain everything. But, you have to remember to call me Janice."

"Janice? Why?"

"Because Lord Hunter Montclaire doesn't know Janice died giving birth to a son. He thinks his brother's wife is still alive."

"Oh, Lia."

He gathered her close again.

"And you've been living as Janice?"

Lia nodded.

"Let's get you inside, sister. You're trembling like a leaf."

Her brother wrapped his arm around her shoulders and led her into the house. They stepped into the foyer and Lia lifted her head. Her gaze locked with Lord Hunter Montclaire's.

Lia stumbled and Miles steadied her.

"Miles, I'd like you to meet Lord Hunter Montclaire, Georgie's uncle. Montclaire, my brother, Miles Halloway."

"How do you do, Halloway," Montclaire said.

"It's a pleasure," Miles answered.

"Please," Lia said. "Let's go into the drawing room. I'll send someone for Aunt Mildred. I know she'll want to see you. It's been quite a while since you were last here."

"Yes. And you need to sit before you fall," her brother said.

"Are you unwell?" Montclaire asked. There was concern in his voice and in the expression on his face.

Lia didn't like it that he might think she was ill. Or weak.

She glanced over to where he stood. "I'm fine. Just a little tired." She hadn't been feeling herself all day, but she was not about to let them know it. "Come," she said and led her brother to the drawing room.

A footman opened the drawing room door and Miles led her to a chair. Montclaire poured a glass of sherry and handed it to her.

"Thank you, my lord."

Montclaire nodded, then shifted his gaze to Miles. "Brandy or port?"

"Brandy, if you please."

Montclaire poured two glasses of the good French brandy then sat, after he'd handed one of the glasses to her brother.

"Has Lady Atherton explained our plans?" Montclaire asked.

"Not fully. She only said that it was imperative that you move the child someplace where he won't be found."

"Yes, that's true."

"Found by whom?" Miles asked.

"By the boy's grandfather. By my father."

"He's in danger from his own grandfather?"

Lia intended to answer Miles' question, but Aunt Mildred rushed through the door and all conversation ceased. The topic went to their aunt telling Miles how good he looked, which he did, and how glad she was to see him. He'd always been a strapping boy, but the war had molded him into a handsome fellow who exuded strength. Lia was surprised that he wasn't married, but like many men who'd survived the war, they came home with memories that haunted them. It took some of them a long time to adjust to normal life.

After they'd conversed a while, Lia set her glass down. "Would you like to see your nephew, Miles? He should still be awake."

"Of course I want to see him."

They rose and climbed the stairs to the nursery. When they entered the room, Miles stepped to where Frannie held little George in her arms. "Oh, Li— Janice," he corrected. "He's beautiful."

Lia tried to cover Miles's near mistake. "Lord Montclaire says the babe resembles his father, the Earl of Atherton. I agree. He does."

Miles held out his finger and the babe clasped onto it.

"Oh, what a grip he has, Janice. He's going to be a strong lad."

Lia stepped close to her brother and her nephew.

Miles reached out his hands. "May I hold him?"

"Of course," Lia answered. "Miles, allow me to introduce you to Frannie McTavish. Frannie, this is my brother, Miles Halloway. He will be traveling with us."

"It's a pleasure, Miss McTavish."

"Likewise," Frannie answered, then held the babe out for Miles to take.

Miles cradled little George closely as if he'd held dozens of babies in his life. "How old is he, Janice? I wasn't home when he was born and I've lost track of when that was."

"He's just four months. If you hold his little fists he tries to pull himself up."

Lia watched while little George lifted his tiny fingers and touched the stubble on Miles's chin. He made a cooing sound, then touched Miles's chin again.

"How long have you been home from the war, Halloway?" Montclaire asked.

"The same. Nearly four months."

"I thank God you came back to us, Miles." Lia reached out a hand to touch her brother's arm. "So many didn't."

"Far too many," Miles agreed.

"Come," Lia said when the conversation threatened to turn too serious for her. "Dinner should be ready soon, and we'll need to retire early if we intend to get a decent start tomorrow."

"Yes," Montclaire said, then led the way from the room.

Aunt Mildred kept the conversation going through dinner. She was interested in everything that had happened to Miles since she'd last seen him. Even Lord Montclaire joined in the conversation with interest. Under different circumstances, Lia could imagine her brother and Lord Montclaire becoming fast friends. But that was hardly possible when chances were likely that they would have to watch one another to make sure the other didn't gain control of the babe.

Before they left the room, Lia found a moment to whisper to Miles that she would meet him in the garden later, after everyone else went to bed.

She couldn't wait to share her burden with Miles. The weight she carried was so much heavier than she thought she'd be able to sustain on her own. She was glad he was here with her. Glad she would be able to have another set of shoulders with which to bear her burden.

. . . .

Lia slipped down the servants' stairs to reach the side door to the kitchen garden. Once she opened the door, the cool air hit her and brought welcome relief. She'd done nothing but pace back and forth in her room until the house was quiet and she was assured everyone was asleep. By the time she'd taken a few steps, she realized she should have brought a wrap against the cold, damp night air. But in fear of looking as though she intended to leave the house, she left it behind.

Now, just steps away from the door, she already shivered.

She walked around the corner of the house, crossed the terrace, and took the steps that led to the formal garden. She hurried down the path, praying she'd chosen the right one to where Miles waited for her. She'd gone several feet into the garden before she heard his voice.

"Lia."

She stopped, turned, then toppled into her brother's arms. "I'm sorry, Miles. I can scarcely hold myself upright these past few days." In truth, her lack of balance of late had actually begun to annoy her.

Her brother held her close and rubbed her back with his strong, sturdy hands.

"Are you sure you're well? You seem terribly pale."

"Yes, Miles. I'm fine." She swatted him playfully. "When have you ever known me to be ill?"

That should have brought a smile, but didn't.

"Then what is it, Lia? Has Montclaire hurt you?"

"No, no. It's just that so much has happened. You must forgive me, I'm just a watering pot these days. I was so worried you wouldn't come in time and I'd be forced to leave with Lord Montclaire without anyone with me."

"You're afraid of him, aren't you?"

"I'm not afraid *of* him, Miles. I'm only afraid of what he has the power to do."

"Come," he said as he led her to a corner bench. "Sit with me and tell me everything. Why are you pretending to be Janice?"

Lia sat beside her brother and leaned against him. He draped his arm around her shoulders and rested her head against his chest.

"Lord Montclaire arrived last week. He had been searching for his nephew."

"Why does he call you Lady Atherton?"

"Because that's what Janice would be if she were alive. She and the Earl of Atherton, Lord Montclaire's brother Evan, were married."

"They were married?"

Lia felt her brother's arms stiffen at the shocking revelation that his youngest sister had been secretly wed.

"Yes, Miles. Lord Atherton married Jannie when he discovered she was carrying his child. But he contracted a terrible fever and died about the same time the babe was born. He made his brother vow to take care of Jannie and the child before he died. If the babe had been a girl, I doubt there would be much fuss over her. But—"

"But the babe was a boy," Miles finished for her. "The Earl of Atherton."

"And, the future Marquess of Trentridge."

"Bloody hell," Miles hissed through his teeth.

Her brother sat forward and turned to face her. "Are you afraid that Montclaire intends to do the child harm?"

"No, not him. He isn't at all jealous of the child. He never relished the idea of being the next Earl of Atherton. In fact, he doesn't want the title."

"And you believe him?"

"I think so...no, I actually do."

"Then why is he here?"

"At his brother's request. To protect the babe."

"Protect him? From whom?"

"From George's grandfather. From the Marquess of Trentridge."

"Why?" Miles asked in disbelief. "You'd think the marquess would be ecstatic to have an heir from his firstborn son."

"He might be if Jannie had come from a titled family. But she was a commoner. The Marquess of Trentridge refused to allow them to marry. He forbade them from ever seeing each other."

"So, Lord Montclaire is here to protect the babe from his own father."

Lia pressed deeper into Miles' shoulder. "He intends to take us to his estate north of here so we can hide George there. His father knows nothing of the place."

"For how long?"

Lia breathed a heavy sigh. "I don't know. I imagine until his father has come to terms with the fact that his heir is a child of less than six months and the son of a commoner. Or, until his father is dead."

"Oh, Lia. What a mess you've been thrown into."

"Yes, Miles. This is why I am forced to pretend to be Jannie. If Lord Montclaire discovers I'm not George's mother, I will have no hold on the babe at all. I'm only his aunt, after all. Lord Montclaire is the next in line to the earldom after George. And the third in line to the Marquess of Trentridge. He has more right to the babe than I do and can take him in the blink of an eye."

"So, the babe in the nursery is the Earl of Atherton?" Miles said rubbing Lia's arm.

"Yes. He is the earl."

"And you're sure the babe is in no danger from Montclaire?"

"It may seem strange, but I feel he's been absolutely truthful about it. He has no love for his father. According to Montclaire as well as what Jannie told me, the Marquess of Trentridge and Lord Montclaire have always been at odds. There's no reason for him to want to turn the babe over to his father. In fact, I believe he is certain his father will do the babe harm."

"Oh, Lia. No wonder you've been so worried."

"Things will be better now, though. You're here. Everything will be fine."

The reassuring smile she tried to give her brother failed to reach her eyes. And she knew it. Perhaps she just needed a fortifying night's sleep. Morning would come soon enough, and at least now she would have an ally when she faced the looming problems—the most worrisome of which seemed to be the formidable Lord Hunter Montclaire.

Lia shivered. Why was she so damnably cold?

Chapter Seven

HUNTER ROSE THE NEXT MORNING to find Lady Atherton's brother at the breakfast table.

"Good morning, Halloway," he said in greeting. "You're up and about early."

"Army habit, no doubt. Now that it's actually possible to indulge myself with a lie-in, I find it absolutely impossible to do so."

Hunter filled a plate and sat down across from Halloway.

"My sister tells me you'll be taking us to your secret lair."

Hunter chuckled, enjoying Halloway's easy humor.

"Yes. We'll leave for Rainwood as soon as we're ready. If we can be on our way before noon, we should arrive before nightfall."

"And you are sure your father doesn't know about this place?"

"As sure as I can be about anything where my father is involved."

"And if he discovers its existence?"

"He has not done so in the past six years. If he does so now, we'll cross that bridge when we come to it."

Hunter turned his direct gaze on Lia's brother. "Make no mistake, Halloway. We don't know that my father has any idea that the babe exists. We don't know that there is any kind of plan to harm the child. But," he paused to make sure his next words were heard, "we don't know that there is not."

Halloway nodded, his eyes communicating that he clearly understood. He continued to eat his breakfast as he brooded over the malevolent possibilities. Neither of them spoke again until Lady Atherton entered the room.

Everything about her showed careful attention to propriety, and she carried it off with a grace that quite charmed Hunter. Her bearing showed that she was still on guard around him, and yet her face revealed a serenity that seemed impossible for a woman in her situation. Either she had come to terms with his need to keep her child safe, or she was a marvelous actress.

As he watched her, he was stricken by an uncomfortable clench of his stomach. She was a most entrancing woman—alluring in a way he'd not noticed until this very moment. Even as his mind assessed her in these calculating terms, his body responded in a much more human fashion.

The men stood.

"Good morning, Lady Atherton," Hunter said with a bow.

"Good morning, Jannie," her brother said.

"Good morning, gentlemen."

She walked to the sideboard and placed a sparse amount of food on her plate, then sat beside her brother.

"I'd ask how you slept last night," her brother said, "but it's obvious by the darkness beneath your eyes that you didn't get enough sleep."

The lady blessed her brother with a smile. "Thank you for your compliment, Miles. I've always been partial to blues and grays. I wear them with pride."

Her brother raised a glass in toast and winked at her rebuttal.

"I have had a thought, my lord," she said, turning her attention to the Earl of Atherton.

"And that is?" her brother prodded.

"I tire of using titles. I find them bothersome. From now on, please call me Jannie. It is what I am accustomed to being called."

Hunter eyed her. It was a bit soon for such familiarity. What was she playing at? He swallowed his suspicions and decided to play along. "And please, call me Hunter. Or Hunt, if you prefer."

"There, now that we have that settled, we should be more at ease with one another."

Hunter watched as Lady Atherton ate a few more bites, then rose to take her leave. "I must go to the nursery and make sure Frannie has everything ready for the trip."

"Yes," Hunter said, then rose, too. "I'll go with you if you don't mind. In case there's something that needs tending to."

"Of course," she answered.

"After I finish breakfast," Miles added, "I'll check on the horses and get them saddled. Unless you arrived by carriage?"

"Mine is the gray gelding," Hunter answered.

He walked from the room at Lady Atherton's side. When they reached the stairs, he held out his hand for her to take.

He noted the merest breath of hesitation before she placed her hand on his arm and he waited, positive that this time when she touched him he would feel no attraction to her. But his certainty merely proved just how wrong one poor fool could be. When her hand touched his, Hunter's flesh warmed as if on fire. The feel of her flesh against his was almost more than he could bear.

She felt it, too. Her eyes lifted to lock with his and her cheeks darkened. The startled expression on her face was nearly his undoing.

"Excuse me," she whispered. "I...I..." She lifted her hand from his arm and dropped it her side, then stumbled and he was forced to wrap his arm around her waist and assist her to the top of the stairs. She separated herself from him the second they reached the landing.

She shook her head. "I don't know what came over me," she said as an apology. "I believe the lack of sleep is catching up with me."

"And lack of food, I daresay. You ate like a bird this morning. Might you ask your cook for a basket to take along in the carriage?"

"No need. I'll be fine."

"But you are not fine, my lady."

She gave him a disapproving look and he rephrased. "Jannie. You are exhausted. The last thing we need is for you to become ill. Come," he said and led her to the nursery. He took her to the nearest chair. "Sit here," he ordered.

"Is the mistress ill?" Frannie asked rushing to Jannie's side.

"No, I'm fine," she answered. "I only need to hold the babe."

Frannie handed the babe over to his mother.

"Leave us, please," Hunter ordered, and Frannie hurried from the room.

Hunter poured some water into a glass and handed it to her. She took a swallow and handed the glass back. When he'd set the glass back on its pewter tray he knelt at her side. "Are you well enough to travel?" he asked. "We can wait until—"

"I'm fine," she answered. "The sooner we get on the road the sooner we can settle in at Rainwater."

"Rainwood."

She looked at him in momentary confusion.

"Ah yes. Rainwood."

He nodded, surprised at her brief lapse.

She nestled the babe in her arms and little George looked up at his mother, then reached for the locket she wore.

"How are you today, George?" she asked, talking to him as if he could understand every word she said. "I'm glad to see you're awake. We're going on a trip and you can sleep in the carriage the whole way there. It will make the time pass more quickly."

Hunter looked at the paleness of her features and experienced a worry he couldn't ignore. "Excuse my boldness, my lady, but..." Without warning he reached out and placed his hand on her forehead.

She pulled back, but not before he had time to feel her skin. She was warm, but not too much so. Perhaps she was just overly tired. And overly concerned. This had to be difficult for her. Being warned of the danger her child was in and being uprooted from her home had to be a challenge. But when he looked at her, he didn't see her weakness. He only saw anger.

"How dare you. You had no right," she said indignantly. "Please, my lord. I'd appreciate it if you would not be so forward ever again."

"I know you would, Jannie, but I had to know that it was safe for you to travel."

"And what did you discover?"

"I believe it's safe for you to travel, but the minute we reach Rainwood you will be confined to your room until you are completely rested."

Her expression turned defiant and if Hunter was impressed by her strength and determination before, he was doubly so now.

"Is there a reason you accompanied me to the nursery? If so, what was it?"

"Yes, there was a reason. Rainwood Place is not equipped for a baby. I therefore wish to know what furniture we might take with us. I assume we will need the babe's cradle, and perhaps that rocker," he said pointing to the chair in the corner.

"Oh. Yes, of course," she said in a calmer tone.

It seemed to pacify her to know there was a reason for his presence. The frown on her forehead eased.

"But first I would like to get Aunt Mildred's permission to remove anything from the house."

"Of course. I'll send one of the maids to fetch your aunt right away."

"Thank you," she said, and Hunter noticed her gaze resting on him. He wondered what that meant, and if he liked it or not. But the question did not need answering. The tripping of his heart was answer enough. Evidently a traitorous part of him like it well enough, indeed.

Hunter nodded, then left the room, telling himself in the most brutal way possible to get a grip.

He forced his mind to deal with the matter at hand. But as was his habit, dealing with a problem meant looking into the future before charting a course of action. And each time he looked, he saw only a lively sweet face set about with lush brunette curls.

How was this dilemma to be resolved? How could it end? He could not hide her away at Rainwood forever. It was inevitable that before long his father would discover that Evan and Jannie had married. And because of that union they had borne a son—the future Marquess of Trentridge. And when he did discover it, Hunter truly didn't know what his father would do.

There were two options open to the Marquess of Trentridge. He could reject the fact that the next heir to Trentridge Park was the son of a commoner and do everything in his power to get rid of the boy. Or, he could move heaven and earth to take the child away from his mother and raise him as he had raised Hunter. Either would be a living hell for the child, to say nothing of what it would do to the child's mother.

Hunter knew he could not let either of those possibilities happen.

. . . .

They had been on the road for over an hour and Lia thought someone had beaten her body with a large stick. She ached all over, from the top of her head to the tips of her toes. Every rut in the road caused her body to groan.

Several miles earlier, she'd had the carriages stop and she put Aunt Mildred in the carriage with Frannie and the baby. If she was ill, she didn't want Aunt Mildred or the babe to get ill, too. She tried miserably to convince herself she wasn't ill but simply overly tired.

"Are you alright, Lia?" Miles asked as he rode up beside the carriage.

"I'm fine, Miles. Why does everyone keep asking me that?"

"Because you don't look well."

"I'm fine. I simply thought perhaps Frannie might need help with the baby and Aunt Mildred volunteered to take the first trek of the journey. I intend to relieve her in an hour or so."

"Maybe you can get some rest now that you're alone."

"I'm fine, Miles. Just fine. You're as bothersome as Lord Montclaire. He's convinced that I'm at death's door, which I'm not. I'm just tired."

"Very well. Close your eyes and rest for a while."

"I will," Lia said, then watched her brother ride away.

A small voice inside her wanted to call her brother back. Her head pounded like a dozen church bells were pealing between her ears. Although she'd been overly hot a few minutes before, now she was shivering with cold. She pulled out a blanket they'd brought for the babe and draped it over her shoulders. She barely had it in place before she became so hot she tossed it aside.

She couldn't be ill. There was too much to concern herself with.

Including keeping an eye on Hunter Montclaire.

Lia closed her eyes and darkness consumed her.

. . . .

Hunter rode past the carriage several times to check on his brother's widow. He knew she wasn't well. Why she denied it was another mystifying aspect of her aloof nature.

It had been more than an hour since the carriages had stopped and her aunt had gone to the carriage with the babe and the nursemaid in it. He was glad she'd made that decision. If she was alone, it was more likely that she would not be bothered and could sleep.

The first time he rode close enough to catch a glimpse of her, she sat with her head leaning into the corner of the carriage. Even though it was a warm summer's day, she'd pulled a blanket up over her and tucked it beneath her chin as if she were cold. The thought that her sickness had developed into chills concerned him even more.

The second time he managed to get close enough to see her, she'd pulled the blanket away from her body and opened her gown at the neck as if she were overly warm. He rode his horse close to the lady's brother to voice his concerns.

"Halloway," he called out. "I'm going to go check on your sister. My estate is about an hour away just down this path. Turn to the right as soon as you go over a bridge. That will take you down the lane to the manor house."

"Do you want me to see to her?" Halloway asked.

"I'd rather you guarded your aunt and the babe. Is your weapon ready?"

"Yes."

"Good."

"Do you anticipate I'll have to use it?"

"No, but you're no doubt a better shot than I am, should the need arise."

Halloway nodded and Hunter made his way back to the carriage. "Halt for a moment," he ordered the driver.

When the carriage stopped, Hunter tied his horse to the back of the carriage and stepped inside. When he was seated, he pounded on the side of the carriage and the vehicle resumed its journey.

"I hope you don't mind if I ride with you," he said, then looked at Lady Atherton. She didn't move. Neither did she open her eyes as if she'd heard him.

"Bloody hell," Hunt hissed, then moved to the seat beside her. He placed his hand on her forehead and issued another swear word more violent than the first. She was burning up. Her forehead was streamed with perspiration, yet when he pulled her to him she was trembling like a leaf.

"My lady," he said, grabbing the blanket that had fallen to the floor and wrapping it around her. "Wake up, my lady," he said, holding her as close as he could. But she said nothing, stirred not at all, her head lolling awkwardly to the side.

With stunning clarity, Hunter absorbed the urgency of the situation. He knew now why the woman hadn't called for help. She was quite unconscious.

Hunter wrapped his arms around her and tucked her head beneath his chin. He rubbed her arms and back in an effort to stimulate blood flow, but her body didn't react to his ministrations. He stuck his hand out the window and pounded on the side of the carriage. "Faster, man. Go as fast as you can."

When Lady Atherton's brother realized they had sped up, he rode toward the carriage. "What's wrong?"

"Your sister has lost consciousness. We need to get to Rainwood Manor as quickly as possible."

At this speed, the rocking carriage nearly threw the poor woman onto the floor. Hunter caught her up and held her on his lap.

"Jannie?" he asked, brushing several strands of damp hair from her forehead. "Stay with me. We're almost home. I'll get you into a nice soft bed and you'll be better in no time."

Hunter prayed he was right. He prayed that she would be better in no time. But she was burning with fever. And each mile felt like ten.

"We're almost there, my lady. We just turned into the drive. A short jaunt up the lane and we can get you to bed."

Hunter was never so thankful as when the carriage pulled up in front of Rainwood Manor. He stepped from the carriage with her in his arms and raced through the door his butler held open for him.

"Send for a doctor, Mason, and send up some cool water and cloths."

"Very well, my lord. Right away."

Hunter carried her to the first guest room he came to and laid her on the bed. He'd be glad when her aunt caught up with them. They needed to get her out of her clothes and dressed in a nightgown. He didn't dare undress her by himself, even though it had felt to him that her bodice was soaked through.

At that moment the viscountess bustled into the room with a worried frown on her face.

"Oh, dear heaven, Lia! What is wrong with her, Lord Montclaire?"

"Lady Atherton is ill. I've sent for the doctor but it will take time for him to arrive. I'll leave you and your maid to look after her."

"Of course. Of course. We will manage."

"Good. I'm going to make arrangements for your trunks to be brought up. Then I'll send a tea tray for you, and inform Miles of what has transpired."

"Very well, my lord."

Two maids rushed in to help, leaving Hunter free to step out of the room. He made sure the babe was settled and rooms prepared for Lady Atherton's aunt and her brother. He met Miles in the foyer and invited him to join him in his study.

The first thing he did was pour two glasses of brandy and hand one to Miles.

He took a healthy sip, then turned to face Miles Halloway. He couldn't hide the anger that welled inside of him.

"Who the bloody hell is Lia?"

Chapter Eight

THE LOOK OF SURPRISE on Miles Halloway's face told Hunter he'd stumbled onto something monumental.

"What did you say?"

Hunter took a threatening step closer to Halloway. "I asked you who Lia is and why your aunt called Lady Atherton 'Lia.'"

Miles Halloway finished his brandy in one swallow, then rose and walked to the other side of the room.

"No lies, Halloway! Why would your aunt call Lady Atherton 'Lia'?"

Miles braced his hands against the window frame and lowered his head between his outstretched arms. "I shouldn't answer you. It's not my place to tell you. It's...Lia's."

"I presume Lia is the woman who is lying unconscious upstairs?"

"Yes."

"Since she is unable to speak, Halloway, the responsibility falls upon you."

Miles Halloway turned away from the window, then reached for his glass and filled it again before returning to his chair. "I told Lia she wouldn't get away with her lie for long, but she said she couldn't risk you finding out until she was sure of your intentions."

"What is it she couldn't risk me finding out?"

"I have two sisters: Amelia, who is upstairs, and Janice. My sister Jannie was married to your brother. She died shortly after giving birth to young George, so Lia has pretended to be the child's mother."

"Why?"

"Why? Good god, man. Because she was afraid you would take George away from her. She thought if you knew that she wasn't George's mother her chances of keeping the babe would be nil."

"She thought I would take the babe away from her?" Hunter asked, unable to believe she trusted him so little.

"You or your father. She didn't think there was a chance that she could keep the babe when your father discovered there was a Trentridge heir."

Hunter tried to digest the information that was thrown at him, but before he and Miles could discuss matters further, the doctor came from seeing Lia.

"How is she?" Hunter asked rising to his feet.

The doctor shook his head and Hunter's heart clenched in his chest. "What is it? What's wrong with her?"

"An inflammation of the lungs, it seems, though not tuberculosis. That coupled with exhaustion has laid the good lady quite low, I'm afraid."

His assessment made all kinds of sense to Hunter. She'd spent days caring for her sister, then managed the travails of her death. She'd cared for the newborn babe, and had gone night after night with little or no sleep. Add to that the worry of losing the babe and it was no wonder she'd taken ill.

"With rest and the proper care, she'll be good as new."

"Thank you," Hunter said handing the doctor a few coins. When the doctor was gone, Hunter turned to Miles who stood silently beside him. He put a compassionate hand on the worried fellow's shoulder.

"I need to see her," Lia's brother said.

"Go on up. I'll check in on her later."

Hunter watched as Miles left the room. He felt as if a huge weight had been lifted from him. He'd never been so concerned in his life. He recalled the sight of her slumped over in the coach and his heart skipped a beat. Try as he might he could not erase her paleness from his memory.

He rose with his glass in his hand and walked to the multi-paned doors that opened onto the terrace. It was frustrating to think she'd felt compelled to go to such lengths to play the impostor, just to keep his nephew safe. Carrying out her preposterous plan had taken a bitter toll on her health. Hadn't she known that eventually she'd be found out?

He took a sip of the amber liquid in his glass. In the days of their brief acquaintance, Hunter had come to know Lady Atherton's nature reasonably well. Her commitment to the babe and the courage she'd shown in facing the challenges of keeping him safe had impressed Hunter greatly. But now that her plan was fully exposed, he had to wonder. Was she truly on board with his effort to hide the babe at Rainwood? Or was she merely biding her time until she found an opportunity to disappear once again?

The very thought stole the breath from him as Hunter realized he must not let her out of his sight. Or he'd lose her.

. . . .

Lia woke two days later with a throbbing head and a body that ached all over. Her aunt told her she'd lost consciousness and had slept forty-eight hours without waking. By the time she was able to open her eyes, the sun was well up in the sky and Lia had lost all track of time.

She lay still, taking in the strange room. It was prettily appointed with chintz fabrics on the window seat pillows that livened up the robin's egg blue wallpaper. The furnishings were cleverly arranged and the bed, oh, the bed was so comfortable she thought she might never leave it.

Her maid brought in a tray, then dressed her hair and helped her into her robe. She felt much better when Frannie brought little George in to see her.

"Oh, George," she said taking the babe into her arms. "How I've missed you."

"I think he missed you, too, mistress. He was wakeful half the night."

"Did you miss me, my sweet?"

Lia had been fussing over the babe for a short while when Frannie interrupted.

"Would you mind if I saw to my needs, my lady? I won't be long."

"Of course, Frannie. Take as long as you like. George and I will be fine here."

"Thank you, my lady."

Frannie left the room and Lia almost didn't notice that the door hadn't closed behind her and that Hunter Montclaire stood in the open doorway watching her.

"My lord," she said when she looked up and her eyes locked with his.

Her heart raced and she fought with its wish to leap from her chest. The man had startled her. Or rather, the devastatingly handsome man had startled her. She'd never known anyone who could cause her cheeks to warm the way he did. There was something so intriguing about the chiseled cut of his cheekbones and jaw that she had a hard time looking away from him. Or, perhaps it was the dark, captivating look in his eyes that mesmerized her.

"How are you feeling, Miss Lia?"

The pain of discovery shot through her skull and worked its way down her spine. He knew! How? When?

His gaze grew more intense. He took a threatening step into the room and stood in front of her. It was obvious that he wasn't about to avoid confronting her with the fact that she'd tried to deceive him.

"How long did you think you could get away with pretending to be your sister?"

"How did you find out?"

"That hardly matters. The point is, I know."

He knows.

The very words should have sent her screaming from the room, but oddly, they brought an unexpected breath of relief. Of safety.

"What are you going to do now that you know?"

He stepped further into the room and sat in the chair beside the bed.

"I don't see that the fact that you are George's aunt instead of his mother changes anything. At least as far as I'm concerned. The courts or my father finding out would be another matter altogether."

"Yes," Lia said on a sigh. "I'm sorry I tried to deceive you, but..." Her voice trailed off. Partly because she didn't know what to say in defense of her actions, but partly because his dark, threatening gaze stayed focused on where she sat and refused to move.

He looked at little George playing in her lap. Then, without asking, he reached out and took the babe into his arms.

"Hello, George," he said, placing the babe in his lap. "Have you adjusted to your new home?"

The babe gurgled and cooed, then reached out to grab the ends of his uncle's perfectly tied cravat. Hunter didn't stop him.

"And you, Miss Halloway. Are you improving?"

Lia didn't answer him. She didn't know what answer to give. But she was saved from having to answer him at that moment when Frannie entered the room.

"Frannie, would you please take George back to the nursery?"

"Of course, my lady."

The nursemaid took the babe and left the room, leaving Lia alone with Hunter.

"I owe you an apology, Lord Mont—"

"Hunt. Call me Hunt."

Lia lowered her gaze to the cravat George had untied. "Hunt. Yes. I owe you an apology."

"Your brother explained in part your reasoning. I can't deny that I might have made the same decision had I been in your position. I can't imagine what it was like to be weighted down with the responsibilities that were forced upon you."

"I wish I'd have had the strength to carry the weight the world placed on my shoulders, but I did not. I never thought I would have to watch my sister die in front of me. Nor did I believe I would ever know what it felt like to be truly alone. But that is how I felt when Jannie died. More alone than I had ever been."

"I know it's not the same," he said taking her hand, "but that's how I felt when Evan died. As if I had just lost my best friend, for in truth, that's what he was. No one knew me or understood me like Evan did. He was the only person in the world who knew what it was like having to live with my father. He was the only person who understood what it felt like to be rejected by the one person a child should never be rejected by."

"I understand," Lia whispered. "Jannie told me about your father. Your brother had explained what your father was like. She told me how mean and cruel he was and how unaccepting he was of anyone he considered beneath him."

"And that was most of the world," Hunter added. "Did your sister tell you the details of their meeting with my father?"

"Yes. She said it was horrible. Your father called her everything from an interloper to a whore who had no love for your brother but only wanted his title and his wealth."

"I know that wasn't the truth. I know she truly loved my brother and he loved her. I know that they would have done everything possible for each other."

"You're right," Lia answered, then tightened her grasp on his hand.

"What's wrong?" There was a frown on his forehead as if he realized something was not right.

"Nothing," she lied. "I just felt a little dizzy."

"Here, lie down."

He settled her in the bed and brought the covers up around her.

"You're not well enough to overdo. You need to sleep."

Lia closed her eyes and took a deep breath. She hated that she was ill. If there was ever a time when she needed to be strong, this was it.

"Would you like me to send for your aunt?"

"What time is it?"

"It's midmorning."

"Then, no. She'll be out walking. Don't bother her."

"Then I will sit with you until you feel drowsy."

"That's not necessary, Lord— Hunt."

He ignored her dismissal and stayed right where he was, just smiling like a Cheshire cat.

"As you wish," he whispered, though he didn't move an inch.

Lia focused her gaze on Hunter Montclaire's handsome face. There was a note of compassion in his eyes that tugged at her heart. "Thank you," she said softly, then closed her eyes, feeling safer than she had in months.

She didn't go to sleep immediately. How could she, with the blood still singing in her veins.

Hunter stayed at her side most of the day and night. He watched her sleep and held her hand when she became restless. Each time she roused he became more and more aware that some awareness deep within him had been freed, something that allowed him to appreciate her like he'd not appreciated other women in the past. He was happy to wait while she slept, knowing that when she woke she'd think of some new and engaging bit of conversation. She was so widely read, so fascinated with things he'd not expected, that her commentaries never ceased to delight him. He'd always enjoyed witty banter in the gentleman's rooms at Whites, or in the bidding booths at Tattersall's. He considered himself well versed and with a natural wit, when he chose to expose it. But this woman had him beat in spades. And he loved it.

Shortly after the sun rose, he found himself roused from drowsing as her aunt entered the room.

"How is she?" the dowager viscountess asked.

"Much better. She was wakeful from time to time through the night."

"Thank you for taking such good care of her."

"It was my pleasure."

"May I discuss something with you?" the dowager viscountess asked, beckoning him to join her in the hall.

"Of course." Hunter stepped from the room and led Lia's aunt to a pair of chairs arranged on each side of a painted Bohemian chest. As he passed the mirror that hung above it, he swept his unkempt hair from his forehead. She must think him a veritable country bumpkin.

The venerable lady wasted no time getting straight to the point.

"It has been obvious to me that you have feelings for my niece."

He opened his mouth as if to object, but she raised a regal hand to silence him.

"And now Miles tells me you are aware that she is in truth my elder niece, Amelia."

"Yes, I am aware."

"What resolution do you seek with regard to your feelings for her?"

Laura Landon

"I'm not sure I understand you, my lady."

"Then let me be absolutely clear, Lord Montclaire." The dowager Viscountess Collinson leveled him a look that left no doubt of her seriousness. "I lost one niece to your family. And the result of that tragedy was terribly hard on Lia. For a while, I was afraid I might lose both of them. And perhaps I would have, had it not been for the babe Jannie left behind. But Lia stepped up when she had to and took over the care of your brother's heir."

"What is your point, my lady? What is it you wish to know?"

"I want to know what your intentions are where Lia is concerned. If you intend to use her, then cast her to the wind, I will fight you every step of the way. But, if you intend to be a helpmate to her and assist her in her efforts to protect the babe and secure the future of both Lia and the child, then I will stand at your side and help you in any way possible."

"I assure you, my lady, my intentions are both principled and honorable."

"Very well," she answered. "But be warned. It shall go badly for anyone who causes her harm or distress."

"Then I have no cause to fear you, my lady. I have no intention of hurting her." Hunter rose. "Now, if you will excuse me, I will meet your nephew for breakfast to discuss what needs to be done should my father's threat become imminent."

Hunter excused himself, then left Lady Collinson.

A smile crossed his face as he descended the stairs. The dowager Viscountess Collinson was as formidable a threat as his father. He was thankful she was on his side instead of working against him.

Chapter Nine

LIA HAD BEEN DESPERATE FOR A CHANGE of scenery after several days in bed, and when the doctor gave permission for her to spend several hours in the solarium, she was thrilled. Restricted to reclining on the chaise as she was, her favorite distraction was the few hours Frannie brought little George to see her each day. She played with him and talked to him to give Frannie a break, yet the maid didn't seem to mind being with George all day long. She seemed as attached to him as Lia was.

Lia had held the babe until he fell asleep and was about to call Frannie to put him in his cradle when footsteps sounded on the cool tile. Lia looked up as Hunter Montclaire neared the chaise.

With each step he seemed to survey her wellbeing and judge it acceptable, which made her oddly happy. She took delight in the hint of a smile that tipped the corner of his mouth. His handsome good looks had not ceased to affect her, and today there was such an ease about his gait and posture that he quite took her breath away. She'd never met such a fine specimen of male perfection. Rarely had she even seen a fellow so perfectly formed, with such broad muscular shoulders and thighs. Rarely had her eyes had the opportunity to linger on a face so strong and perfectly chiseled. Even though she tried not to let him affect her, just looking at him stole her breath.

"May I join you?"

"Of course." She pointed to the chair nearest the chaise.

"I see he's asleep," he said, lowering his gaze to where little George lay peacefully tucked beside her.

"Yes, I was just about to call Frannie to put him down for his nap when the little rascal nodded right off."

"Allow me."

Hunter Montclaire rose to tug at the bell pull, and moments later a footman appeared. "Send Frannie to us, if you would please," he said.

He turned to retrieve the infant's rattle that had fallen to the floor and Lia could not help but reward him with a smile. Most men would have merely kicked it away. "Thank you, my lord," she said.

"Hunt," he corrected, turning to her with his eyebrow cocked in a winsome way. "You promised to call me Hunt."

She blushed. It was true. She had promised. But each time her tongue sought to form the familiar name, such amorous feelings cascaded across her mind that she found herself blushing furiously.

With great effort, Lia swallowed her hesitation. "Yes. Hunt. Thank you." She found it quite exhilarating to speak his name, and her smile broadened further at the small joy.

"Ah," Frannie said as she scurried into the solarium. "You tuckered the lad out, my lady. I'll see him to his cradle. Hopefully he'll sleep for a long while."

"Yes, Frannie."

The nursemaid picked George up and carried him from the room.

"How do you feel?" Hunter asked when they were alone.

"I'm much better. Completely recovered, I must say."

"Are you?" he asked with a questioning voice and inquisitive look.

"Yes. Truly, I am. And I daresay it's none too soon, if you intend to keep up your witty midnight repartee." She grinned when he flinched dramatically.

"Alas, I fear it is I who cannot keep pace, my lady. You are far too quick-witted for me."

Their laughter echoed happily in the high-ceilinged room, a welcome sound that almost seemed to startle them both.

The Earl of Atherton stretched his muscular legs out before him and relaxed against the back of his chair. "I've been wondering, my lady. That is...Lia. Was your sister's coloring the same as yours?" he asked.

Lia couldn't stop the smile from lifting the corners of her mouth. "Goodness, no. She was as light as I am dark. The babe is a replica of his mother, with hair of gold and eyes as blue as the sea."

"Then she and my brother would have made quite a stunning pair. He also had hair of gold and eyes a startling blue."

Lia turned her head and her gaze locked with Hunter's. Before she could respond, a strange emotion stole her breath. Without reason, she suddenly wanted him to see *her*. Amelia. Not Janice. Not the sister whose future had been cut short, but Amelia, who had a whole life ahead of her.

"I would ask a favor," Lia said in a breathless voice that quite surprised her.

"Yes."

"You see, I am quite desperate to move about. Just for a bit."

"Well, then, let's give it a try. But you must be sure to keep hold of my arm." He rose and extended his hand.

Lia smiled and nodded. "I shall appreciate your support."

She extended her hand which he clasped with his own, adding just enough of a pull to help her slip off the chaise with what almost felt like grace.

"I can't believe how weak I am," she said once she had steadied herself. "I'm going to have to work to regain my strength."

"And how do you intend to do that, Jannie—" He stopped and turned an apologetic look in her direction. "Lia. Sorry. It's going to take me a day or two to accustom myself to thinking of you by your real name."

Lia lowered her gaze, somewhat chagrined at the reminder of her earlier deception. "It's understandable."

Hunter Montclaire turned toward the door that led to the garden. "Perhaps a few minutes in the sunshine?"

She laughed. "You have no idea how positively wonderful that sounds!"

Acknowledging her enthusiasm with a grin, he led her out onto the terrace that was set about with lush Grecian planters. With each step she felt stronger, more sure-footed, and without a thought, she urged him down the three steps to the garden path.

"I refuse to allow you to overdo the first time you think you are strong enough to get out of bed. It's growing late, and it won't be long before it will start growing dark. We'll make sure we've returned to the house before then."

Lia made a face and nodded as she secured her hand more snugly through his bent elbow. It felt natural to walk next to him. She felt safe when she was near him, as if she belonged next to him.

"Have you seen Miles today? It's quite unusual for him not to visit. I thought for sure I would see him."

"The truth is, I sent him to the village."

"For what reason?"

"To see if he could discover anything concerning my father. I didn't want those kinds of questions being associated with me. With Miles asking the questions, there's no reason for folks to make a connection with Rainwood."

"You think your father might be searching for you?"

"Not that he wants to have anything to do with me. Only that he wants to know where I am and keep watch on me. When I stopped taking his allowance several years ago he began making veiled inquiries around London. He was merely curious how I manage to exist without his help." Hunter raked a hand through his hair. "Now, however, he has reason to think I know something about Evan's marriage. I would imagine he will escalate his search soon if he hasn't already."

"Forgive my, my lord, but how is it that you manage if, as you say, you hold yourself apart from your family estate?"

He chuckled. "Not every man fritters his days in the gaming hells, I assure you. I for one have found industry to be the most satisfying way to occupy my time."

It was a vague answer, but as Lia took in the beautifully manicured grounds and sizeable, well-kept household, she could believe that he was indeed, as he said, a man of means. And the respect shown him by his staff was a most telling clue to the fact that he looked after them with as much care and concern as he exhibited for his estate.

"I do not believe I like your father," Lia said with a grimace.

"Then you are very wise. He is not someone anyone would wish for a father."

"Why does he dislike you so?"

"Because he is a man of deep cravings and he loved—or rather coveted—my mother more than anything in the world. Many men had vied for her hand, but he had won her. He took immense pride in her. And then she died giving birth to me."

Lia stopped in the middle of the path and lifted her gaze to look at him. "And he blames you for her death?"

"Yes. That plus the fact that Evan had my father's hair and eyes, and I inherited my mother's."

"So, every time he looks at you, he is reminded of what he lost."

"Yes. You're quite perceptive."

"I'm sorry," Lia said.

"Don't be. I stopped seeking his love years ago. The price of groveling for it became too high."

They took a few more steps down the path, then Lia saw what she was looking for—a bench beneath a rose-laden arbor. "Would you mind if we sit for a moment?"

"Of course not. Forgive me. I wasn't thinking. You're probably tired. Here." He drew his arm around her shoulder to turn her toward the bench. As warm ribbons of comfort cascaded about her, Lia became aware that it was more than a bench she'd been hoping to find. Much more.

She relished the feel of him close beside her as they sat.

"I didn't think I would tire so quickly. But it seems..."

Quite without realizing it, Lia's mind withdrew from her worries and focused on the soft, slow, rhythmic stroking of Hunter's hand that had quite successfully robbed her of words. She doubted he even knew he was doing it, but she prayed her shoulder would hold the memory of it for a long, long time.

What was there about him that consumed her with this welling passion? She had no wish to feel this way. Once before, she'd fallen in love with a man who'd carried a title. And she'd been abandoned by him because she wasn't a member of the *ton*. Her hopes had been dashed as thoroughly as her heart had shattered.

But then, it had always been important to the nobility that they not marry beneath them. Montclaire's brother and her own sister were rare exceptions in their determination to stand against the *beau monde*. And yet, in the end even her dear sister had hidden from Society's scorn. As for herself, Lia did not want to put herself through that turmoil ever again.

She shivered, and felt her heart shift in concert with the soothing fingers that gently stroked her arm.

"Are you alright? Or would you rather go back into the house?"

"No. I'm fine. Truly." She turned and found him facing her. "I don't want to go back…yet," she said softly. Though she did not feel weak, she certainly was atremble, and the thought of walking seemed more than she could manage.

It was quite another thought that invaded her conscious mind at the moment—the thought of what it might feel like to touch his lips with hers. He dropped his head, bringing his mouth tantalizingly near as he sought to look her in the eye.

"Are you feeling faint?" His concerned gaze was locked with hers and his arm stretched more securely around her.

"Yes," she whispered. "I mean, no. I mean…that is…"

Keeping his arm around her shoulders, he lifted his other hand to cover her clasped hands. His touch caused her to take an involuntary gasping breath.

He tucked his head lower, searching her eyes for a caution she knew she should issue, but could not.

Instead, she kept her gaze locked with his as he brought his face closer. His gaze lowered to her mouth, to her lips. The very nearness betrayed his intent. He was going to kiss her. She knew it without a doubt and she wasn't going to stop him. She should, she knew. But she wasn't going to.

He brought his mouth down on hers and kissed her. Softly. Sweetly. A tender touch that launched a most welcome flood of longing.

He deepened his kiss as if he'd wished for it for some time but hadn't found the opportunity. Lia reveled in the sweetness of it, and then his kiss turned more sensual. Yet it was not in the least intrusive or demanding.

She turned and lifted her hands to his chest as she answered his kiss. She couldn't deny him. She wanted him too badly. Far too badly.

. . . .

There was no way for Hunter to know how long the kissing lasted. All he knew was that he never wanted to let her go. The emotions that roiled within him were powerful and pleasant. Now that he knew she wasn't his brother's wife it was as if the doors had been thrown wide and he'd been given permission to unleash his ardor.

He lifted his mouth from hers and drew her to him.

She rested her head against his chest, pressed closely enough to hear his heart thunder beneath her ear.

"I should apologize, Lia, but I cannot. I wanted to kiss you too desperately."

"As I wanted to kiss you," she whispered. "But it cannot happen again."

"Why?"

She pulled away from him. "Because it cannot. Your father would not allow it."

"Damn my father! I refuse to let him ruin my life like he did Evan's."

"Only, this time I would ruin your life."

"How could you possibly ruin my life?"

She scoffed. "You know well the brutal arm of the *ton*. The day will come when you will be expected to take your place in Society. If not for your own sake, then for George's. How can you expect to be accepted if the woman you marry is a commoner? How can you expect George to be accepted when it becomes known that his very mother was a commoner as well as the woman his uncle married?"

"Damn Society! I don't care a whit what they think."

"Enough!"

Hunter knew Lia's demand was meant to stop the discussion they were having as well as to make him believe such talk was impossible.

"We're getting ahead of ourselves," she continued, then lowered her gaze to her clenched fists in her lap. "I would like to return to the house, Hunt. I'm tired."

"Of course you are."

He rose and helped her to her feet. She stumbled and he pulled her against him and held her.

She lifted her gaze and he lowered his head to kiss her once more. She met his kiss, but did not encourage him to continue.

"Let me get you into the house."

He'd kept her out too long. He'd asked too much of her. Hunter vowed to see her right upstairs, but when they entered, Miles was walking through the solarium toward them.

"Miles," she said reaching for her brother.

"Are you feeling better, Lia?"

"Yes, much."

"You gave us quite a fright."

"I'm sorry. I didn't mean to."

"Well, you look much better than you did the last time I saw you."

"I am. Have you had something to eat?"

"Not lately."

Hunter greeted Miles. "I'll have the staff prepare the table, then have Cook send in something to eat."

"I'd appreciate that."

"I'll be happy to relay the message on the way to my room," Lia murmured. "You must excuse me, gentlemen. I feel the need to retire."

Hunter nodded and Lia left the room. He studied Lia's brother, curious over the tension he saw in the man's bearing. "What have you found out?"

"There are several men staying at the Carbury Inn." Miles drew a weary hand through his hair and took the seat Hunter offered.

"That's not twenty minutes from here. How many?"

"At least three. Perhaps more. I believe they've been sent by your father. They're asking questions concerning you and my younger sister."

"They know about Janice."

"Yes. Of course, nobody around here even knows the names. And from what they're asking, I don't think they know that Jannie died in childbirth. Or that Lia is here with you. But from their inquiries, I believe your father knows there is a child. They seem to be preparing to travel with an infant."

A gasp from the doorway caused the men to turn to see who had overheard their conversation.

"Frannie?" Hunter said, rising to his feet. "Did you need something?"

"I was looking for her ladyship."

"I think you will find her in the dining room."

"Thank you, my lord." Frannie bobbed a polite curtsy, then hurried away.

"Should we worry?" Miles asked. "Should we tell Lia?"

Hunter shook his head. "I don't believe so. She's going to know soon enough. And if we have to move the child, she will have to go with him."

Miles agreed just as Lia re-entered the solarium.

"Did Frannie find you?" he asked.

"Yes. It seems your nephew wants more to eat than Frannie can provide," she said with a smile. "She asked if I thought it would be alright if she fed him a little porridge, or mashed vegetables. As if I'm an expert on raising babies."

"You've done an admirable job so far, Lia," Miles said. "Don't doubt yourself now."

"What did you find out, Miles?"

Miles looked at Hunter for approval to tell Lia what he'd discovered. Hunter nodded. It would be impossible to keep her in the dark. What good would that accomplish?

"Lord Trentridge has suspected you might be in the area and has sent several men to investigate."

The color left Lia's face and she reached out to steady herself.

"Lia?" Hunter watched abject fear drain the color from her face and an instant later raced across the floor to reach her before she collapsed.

Chapter Ten

LIA OPENED HER EYES TO SEE HUNTER and Miles standing over her.

"Are you alright?" Hunter asked, kneeling beside the chaise where he'd placed her. He took her hand in his and held it.

"Don't worry, Lia. We won't let him take George."

"How are we going to stop him?"

"I can't say at this moment," Hunter answered, "but we'll keep him at bay. We won't let him find the babe. It's hard telling to what lengths he'd go to rid the world of the next Trentridge heir. All I know is that he'd never accept a commoner's son as his heir. I have no doubt he'll do anything in his power to keep the Trentridge line pure, even if it means something as drastic as ridding the world of his legal heir."

"What of you?" Miles asked. "What if something were to happen to you? Who would your title go to?"

"A cousin. Winston. Father has always favored him over me."

"Surely your father would not harm his only son," Lia said in disbelief.

The smile on Hunter's face sent a chill down her spine.

"If you think that, you obviously do not know my father. He will do everything in his power when it comes to the Trentridge line."

Lia moved restlessly on the chaise. "Help me up. I cannot stand to lie down any longer."

Hunter took her hands and helped her sit, then stand. "When is the last time you had anything to eat?"

Lia shook her head. "I'm not hungry."

"You may not be hungry, but you have to eat. You'll become ill if you don't and you'll be no use to us or the babe."

"You're right." She moved with them into the dining room.

As they ate, Miles tried to keep the conversation neutral. Hunter asked about the events he'd experienced during the war without referring to the more horrendous incidents. When they finished, Hunter's staff served coffee in the drawing room. Or rather, Lia had coffee while Miles and Hunter had brandy. But nothing seemed able to dull the tension that filled the room, the anxiety lurking just below the surface.

"I think I should go up to check on George. Frannie should be about to put him down for his afternoon nap."

Hunter and Miles stood when she rose.

"Will you come back down, Lia?" Hunter asked.

"I think I shall. Perhaps I'll spend the afternoon in the library, if I may."

"By all means." Hunter gave a lavish bow. "Feel free to plunder my shelves."

Lia blushed, then hurried up the stairs. First she walked to the nursery, but it was empty. Frannie must still have little George in her room. It was her habit to let him play there and tire himself out.

She went to Frannie's room but it was empty, as well.

"Frannie," she called out, but there was no answer.

"Frannie!" she called again.

She retraced her steps, knowing the young girl had to be somewhere close by. But she found her nowhere.

"Frannie! Frannie!"

Nothing.

Lia ran to the top of the stairs. "Hunt! Hunt! Come quickly!"

. . . .

Hunter heard the terror in Lia's voice and took the steps two at a time.

"She's gone, Hunt. Frannie's gone. And she took George!"

Hunt clasped her by the shoulders and pulled her against him. He wrapped his arms around her and held her close. She trembled so badly

241

he could hardly keep her in his grasp.

Miles came up behind him and raced to the nursery. "She's not in there," he said when he returned.

"Search the downstairs and the kitchen," Hunter said. "Maybe she took George for that porridge she was speaking of."

"Yes!" Lia said as her brother left to follow Hunter's orders. "Oh, yes! That's got to be it."

"I'm sure, sweetheart," he said, taking her by the hand to start searching the nearby rooms. But he was afraid that wasn't what had happened. If it had been, surely Frannie would have heard them calling out for her.

They finished looking in each room on the floor, then went down the stairs.

"She's not in the kitchen," Miles said when he reappeared from below stairs. "I have the staff searching every room in the house."

"Where could she have gone, Hunt? Why would she take him? Why?"

Hunter held her close and rubbed his hand up and down her back. Before he could say anything more, one of the footmen raced in from outside.

"There's a horse missing from the stables, my lord."

"No!" Lia cried out. "Why would she do that?"

"To protect him," Miles answered. "She heard us talking when we said your father had sent men to search for the babe, and if he found George, he would no doubt get rid of him."

"What are we going to do?" Lia cried out.

"We'll go after her. We'll find her and bring her home. She can't have traveled too fast with the babe or gone too far."

"Let's go," Miles said racing for the front door. "I'll have our horses saddled."

"I'm going too," Lia said rushing for the front door.

"No, Lia. You can't."

"I can't stay here, Hunt. Please, don't ask me to. You know I won't."

Hunt leaned toward her and kissed her forehead.

"Yes, I know you won't."

He turned to Miles.

"Have a carriage readied. We'll need the carriage to bring Frannie and the babe home."

Miles nodded, then raced from the house.

"Collect a blanket and follow me," Hunter said before he followed Miles.

Lia joined him by the time they had the horses saddled and the carriage ready. "Careful now," he said, handing her into the carriage. A footman was on top with the reins in his hands. As soon as Lia was inside, they were off.

"This way," Miles called out. "Tracks go this way."

Hunter admonished himself to stay calm and alert. Losing his head would wouldn't help anyone if he let the crisis cloud his thinking. But all he could think about was the promise he'd made to Evan that he would take care of his child and not let anything happen to the babe.

Hunter clenched his teeth. This was yet another thing he'd failed to do.

. . . .

All Lia could think was that she'd failed to keep the promise she'd made her sister. She'd promised her that she would take care of her child and not let anything happen to him. But she'd failed to keep her promise.

Lia looked out the window, praying she'd see Fannie and the babe up ahead. But the road was empty.

Suddenly, the carriage slowed, then came to a halt. Hunter appeared beside her and Lia leaned out to see what had caused them to stop.

"Lia," Hunter said, stopping beside her.

Lia's heart raced faster in her breast. "Do you see her?"

"Yes, she's up ahead. Miles scouted ahead of us and saw her."

"Then why are we stopped. We need to catch up with her. We need to get George before she gets too far away from us."

"We can't."

"What do you mean, we can't."

Hunter reached through the carriage window and took her hand. His grasp was solid in hers and he squeezed her fingers as if to tell her he was with her and everything would be alright.

"The men my father sent to find me have Frannie. Apparently she stopped at the inn to borrow money from a friend. A friend with a loose tongue, it seems."

Lia couldn't stop the small cry that escaped her. "What are we going to do? We can't let them take George. We can't!"

"We won't. We'll do whatever we have to do to get him back."

"How?"

Before Hunter could give her an answer, Miles rode up beside them. "There are five of them. They have Frannie and the babe, but they are safe."

Lia refused to release Hunter's hand. The strength of his warm flesh against hers was all that was keeping her from falling apart at this moment.

"Lia." Hunter's serious gaze locked with hers. "You have to promise me you'll stay in the carriage and not get out."

Lia shook her head. "I can't. I—"

"You have to. I can't worry about you and deal with Father's men at the same time."

"But what if—?"

"Please, Lia. The only way you can help George is to do exactly what I ask you to do. Promise me you will."

Lia hesitated. How could she stay here not knowing what was happening? He was asking the impossible.

"Promise me, Lia."

"I promise," she whispered, knowing that she probably would not be able to keep her promise.

"That's my girl."

"Are you armed?" Miles asked.

Hunter pulled a gun from a pocket in his jacket, then opened the carriage door and drew a gun from beneath the carriage seat.

"Take this," he said and handed Lia the pistol. "Use it if you have to."

"Set it like this."

He showed her the mechanism.

"Point. Shoot. Got it?"

Lia nodded.

"Are you ready?" Miles asked.

Hunter nodded.

"Good," Miles said. "Let's go."

Lia watched as Hunter mounted his horse, then followed Miles and the footman who had been driving the carriage.

· · · ·

Leaving Lia was more difficult than Hunter had imagined it would be. Expecting her to stay hidden inside the carriage was the one thing he didn't expect her to do, even though she had promised him she would. He knew it would not be possible for her to keep her promise. He only hoped she would stay hidden long enough for him to reach his father's men and assess the situation before she followed.

They rode close to a copse of trees and dismounted. With extreme care, they slowly crept through the saplings and shrubbery until they had a clear view of the men holding Frannie and George. They were safe... so far.

Hunter recognized one of the man, and the man's distinctive voice confirmed his identity.

"What should we do with them?" one of the kidnappers asked.

"You know what Trentridge said. He wished the whelp never born."

"I ain't killin' no babe, Hank," one of them said.

"Me neither," a second man was heard to say. "I just thought we were supposed to find them. Not get rid of them."

"Well, Trentridge changed his mind. He said if something happened to his son and the babe he wouldn't mind."

The full force of the words sickened Hunter. He'd known his father was capable of such thoughts, but hearing them put into action drew the despicable act out of the realm of possibility and into the here and now.

"What kind of man intends to kill his own grandson?"

"The kind of man whose twenty quid is waitin' for ya once the deed is done."

"Well, I ain't gonna do it."

"*Fine. I'll do it,*" the first man said, and stepped out to where Frannie stood holding little George.

Hunter's mind raced, seeking a strategy to foil the man's intention. At the same moment, the second man stepped in the leader's way. He held out a hand to stop the leader's action, but the burly man knocked him to the ground with a beastly punch. With a kick to the downed fellow, he turned and strode toward Frannie.

"Halt!"

With a loud bellow, Hunter rushed forward with his gun drawn. He fired once, then twice, before his fire was returned and he felt a sharp pain in his side.

Miles fired at the same time and so did the footman. One of the kidnappers went down, then a second. The footman tackled a third man and Miles went after the fourth. The leader had managed to dodge them all.

The pain in his side caused him to stumble, but Hunter couldn't give in to it. He needed to reach the baby before his father's man did.

Hunter ran as fast as his wound would allow him to go and he reached the babe just as the last gunman pulled the trigger of his weapon. Hunt waited to feel the burning pain of a bullet going through him, but there was none. The man's pistol was either jammed or out of powder.

Hunter rushed him, thankful for the reprieve, but when he reached him, the man swiped a long-bladed knife through the air. The tip of the blade tore through his jacket and reached the skin beneath.

His gun had fallen to the ground as he plowed into the man, and Hunter scrambled to recover it. But the man slashed his knife again and this time cut through the fabric on his arm.

Hunter knew he didn't have much strength left and wouldn't be able to hold the murderer at bay.

The man lifted the knife in the air and with a loud bellow lunged at Hunter. Reeling, Hunter held out his arm to ward him off, but before the man reached him, a blast of gunfire echoed in the air and the man froze with his arm extended.

A large circle of blood stained the man's shirt and he looked at his chest in disbelief. The man sank to his knees and locked his gaze with that of his killer, then fell to the ground.

"Lia?" Hunter called out, then staggered to where she stood. She looked at the man lying dead on the ground, then stared with incredulity at the gun in her hand.

As if the gun had burned her fingers, she dropped it and clamped her hand over her mouth.

Hunter knew she wanted to scream in fright, but she didn't. She raced to him and wrapped her arms around him to hold him up.

"Are you alright?" Hunter draped his arm across her shoulders and leaned against her.

"I'm fine. But you're not. You're hurt."

"I'll be fine."

"Of course you will. You have to be."

Hunter looked around to where Miles and the footman stood over the two men they'd overpowered.

"How badly are you hurt?" Miles asked, looking at the dark red circles that spread across Hunter's shoulder and side. They were getting larger by the second.

"Not bad enough to kill me."

"Lia," Miles said. "Get Hunt to the carriage. I'll see to Frannie and the babe."

Hunter looked to where Frannie was huddled behind a tree with little George. The babe was crying with fright over the noisy chaos, but he was safe. He hadn't been hurt.

Lia ducked beneath Hunter's arm and he placed his arm across her shoulders. He hurt more with every step he took and feared he might lose consciousness before he reached the carriage. But when he finally reached the open door, the footman moved swiftly to help him inside.

"Please tell me you're going to make it," Lia begged when he was settled inside.

"Yes, thanks to you."

The footman was dispatched to town with the dead kidnapper across his horse and his three injured cohorts in tow. The authorities would mete out justice. When Miles arrived with Frannie and George, Lia took the babe and had Frannie ride atop with the footman. Miles climbed inside to care for Hunter.

Lia gave the excuse that with Hunter injured and Miles caring for him, it would be too crowded for Frannie inside. But Hunter knew that wasn't the reason. He knew Lia was so angry with Frannie that she didn't want to be confined with her.

"That girl!" Lia fumed. "After everything we've done to keep Georgie safe she went and, and—"

Hunter took a slow, shallow breath and reached his hand to cover hers. "Lia. She didn't know what else to do."

"She could have told us!"

"No." He shook his head. "She couldn't." He drew something from his pocket. "I found this in the stable. I didn't tell you because, well, because it scared the bloody hell out of me."

He unfolded a crumpled note and handed it to her. "Frannie must have dropped it."

Lia shifted the babe a bit so she could read the blood-stained note.

> *You have the babe we want. Bring him to the old mill by six o'clock and you will be well paid. Fail to bring him and both you and the babe will die. Tell anyone and you'll all die.*

"She took him to that broken down mill? She just handed him over?"

Lia was incredulous. She'd had every reason to trust Frannie and what had the girl done? At the first hint of reward she handed him right over.

Beside her Hunter groaned and clutched his shoulder.

"No, Lia. She didn't."

"But—"

"She went the opposite direction. It must have been the so-called friend, the one she went to for money, who gave her away."

He watched Lia sit back against the squabs as the full weight of the revelation chastised her. She'd been so very wrong. What else would a girl in Frannie's position have done?

As the carriage rocked crazily along, the babe began to whimper. Lia raised him in her arms and tucked his face into her neck. Her soft clucking quieted him as they raced toward home.

But nothing could quiet Hunter's escalating fears. They'd saved the child this time, but what would his father do next? He'd just declared himself. His lethal intent was no longer mere conjecture. The Marquess of Trentridge wouldn't rest until the child was out of the picture.

Completely.

Chapter Eleven

THE BABE FINALLY FELL ASLEEP and Lia had time to relive everything that had happened.

Frannie had taken George to the nursery to feed him and put him down for the night. Miles was keeping watch in case there were any more of Hunter's father's men around. Aunt Mildred had gone to bed after making sure there was enough food to feed everyone, and the doctor had come to take care of Hunter's wounds. Now Lia sat at Hunter's bedside, waiting for him to regain consciousness.

The knife wound to his arm was minor. The doctor had cleaned it, sewn the flesh together and bandaged it. But the lead ball that had drilled into his shoulder had caused more severe damage. The doctor was forced to work a long time before he was able to dig the ball out. Hunter had been in a great deal of pain throughout the ordeal.

Lia reached out to hold Hunter's hand, then moved from her chair to the edge of the bed. She needed to be close to him.

This had been the most horrible day of her life. The terror she'd felt when she realized that George was missing caused her heart to want to stop beating. Then, when Hunter had been shot and she feared he might die, a part of her wanted to die, too. She'd suffered the same emotions as she had the day Jannie took her last breath. It was an emotional tempest that was difficult to explain.

She took a damp cloth from the bedside table and wiped the perspiration from Hunter's face. Then, she sat back down beside him and held his hand, refusing to let him go.

"You can...go to...bed," he whispered hoarsely. "I'll be...fine."

"Oh," Lia said in surprise. "Oh, Hunt. I didn't mean to wake you."

She tried to stop the tears from rushing down her cheeks but she couldn't. It was as if the river of tears that had been dammed up were suddenly released.

"You...didn't."

"Would you like something to drink?"

"Something...cool and...wet."

Lia rose and poured some fresh water into a glass and held it to his lips. "Not too much," she said, taking the glass away from him.

"Where's...George?"

"Frannie has him upstairs. She fed him and put him to bed."

"You...trust...her now?"

"More than ever!" The relief was apparent on her face. "Miles is keeping watch in case your father sent more men to harm the babe, or to prevent Frannie from falling into another trap. She's promised to come straight to us with even the smallest concern and I believe her."

"We need to...talk, Lia."

"I know, Hunt. But not now. You're too weak. You need to sleep. You need to heal. We can talk tomorrow."

"Yes," he whispered, then fell into a laudanum-induced sleep.

She sat at his bedside and held his hand while he slept. As the minutes crept by she began to understand that this was no ordinary compassion that she felt for the man. This was love. How it had happened she couldn't say. Perhaps it had begun in that initial electric moment that had passed between them the first time he'd touched her.

Whatever its origin, she knew without a doubt that it was love, and that she loved him more than she had believed it was possible to love anyone. She loved him with her whole heart and soul.

Tears ran down her cheeks when she thought of what was ahead for them. There was Hunt's father to deal with, and Lia couldn't think of any way out of the mess they were in as long as his father remained in the picture.

And she couldn't think of any way they could eliminate his father and live with themselves after it was over.

. . . .

Hunter healed slowly. His entire body ached for days as he fought to conquer the pain caused by the lead ball that had penetrated to a dangerous depth.

He was actually grateful that Miles stayed around. He took over when Hunter couldn't even manage to get out of bed. He watched the babe and made Lia rest when she stayed up night and day keeping watch over the babe, calming Frannie, and caring for the Earl of Atherton.

Disjointed thoughts of having children with Lia peppered his drug-laced dreams. He wondered what it would be like to have a child with her. He wondered what it would be like to have a family filling the halls of Rainwood Place. A need deep inside him ached to find that out, ached to have children of his own. With her.

"Are you awake?" she asked entering the room. She carried a tray laden enticingly with small meat and cheese sandwiches.

"Yes, I'm awake. And starving."

"Then you will love what I've brought with me."

She set the tray down beside him on the bed, then poured him a glass of water.

"I think I would like something stronger than water. Ale, perhaps?"

"Are you sure?"

"Yes. Or maybe a glass of brandy."

She smiled and poured him a glass of brandy from a decanter he kept on the highboy.

Hunter took a sip, then leaned against the headboard and sighed with pleasure.

"Oh, Lia. That tasted good."

He reached for one of the sandwiches and devoured it in two bites. "And so does this. I can't believe how hungry I am."

"You're getting better, Hunt. Much better."

"Yes, I am."

Hunter finished the plate of sandwiches, then drank the brandy. When he finished the first glass, she filled it partially for a second time.

"Do you feel up to talking about your father?"

Hunter paused. He had known this day would come. He had known the time would come when they would have to discuss how to handle his father. He was surprised his father had waited this long before sending more men to finish what the last ones had failed at.

"We can't put it off any longer, can we?"

She shook her head.

"Would you call Miles? I want to get his input on the matter."

She nodded again and rose to her feet. She left the room for a few minutes and came back with her brother in tow.

"How are you doing today?" Miles asked brightly when he'd closed the door behind him. "You certainly look greatly improved from when we brought you back."

"I am, thanks to you and Lia."

"Lia deserves the credit. She's the one who refused to let you give up. I just sat in the study and drank your expensive brandy."

Hunter smiled. He doubted that was true, but he appreciated Miles' attempt at humor.

Lia moved to sit on the bed, leaving the chair free for her brother.

"Do you have any ideas how to handle my father?" Hunter asked.

Miles took a moment to settle into the chair. "Do you want my honest advice or a piece of advice that will be pleasing to your ears?"

"Let's start out with your honest advice. If I cannot accept that, we'll go to what will be pleasing."

"Very well," Miles said, stretching his legs lazily in front of him. "He could die."

Lia's hand flew to her throat.

"When you said honest advice what you really meant was honest and blunt advice."

"You already knew this wasn't going to be easy," Miles continued. "You already knew there wasn't going to be a different outcome. The man tried to kill his own son. And his grandson, the heir to his name. The law would sentence him to the gallows. Besides, what makes you think he won't try to kill again?"

Hunter grabbed the bedclothes in his fists and wadded them into a tight ball.

"Bloody hell, Miles! I can't just walk up to him and put a lead ball in his brain."

"No, you can't. No man could do that to his own father. I would not have expected you to see that as a solution."

"So you were just checking, eh?"

"I thought it prudent," Miles chuckled. "But I believe Lia might have a suggestion she thinks you'll like."

Hunter looked at Lia. She was still recovering her composure after hearing the men speak of cold-blooded murder.

"Lia?"

"I have an idea, but I would like to hear what Aunt Mildred thinks of it first."

Hunter looked at Miles and Lia's brother nodded. "Very well. Miles, would you help me dress, then take me down to the study. We'll meet you there in half an hour, Lia."

"Don't be silly," she said. "Just throw on a robe. We'll expect you in five minutes." She swept off the bed and made her exit.

Hunter considered disregarding her and getting fully dressed. But the mere effort of climbing out of bed changed his mind. "Just give me my trousers, then."

He grunted his way into his trousers and robe, then asked, "What do you think she has in mind?"

"I haven't the faintest idea, but I hope it's something we can carry off."

"So do I," Hunter said, then turned to leave his room for the first time since a gunshot paid for by his father had laid him low.

. . . .

Lia watched Hunter enter the study. He leaned heavily on Miles' arm and Lia knew he was in a great deal of pain.

Hunter reached for her hand and Lia eagerly grasped his.

"You cannot kill your father, Hunt. If you do, you won't be able to live with yourself."

"I know that," Hunt answered squeezing her hand in reply. "I trust you believe that I could never have considered it. But I am curious what you have in mind?"

"I suggest a death of sorts. But not a mortality. Merely a death of standing, a mortal blow to your father's reputation." She smiled, and Hunter felt the weight of the world begin to lighten with it. "I suggest we take the babe and Aunt Mildred and go to London."

"What good will that do?"

"Aunt Mildred?" Lia smiled. "Tell them our idea."

Aunt Mildred chuckled and held up her elegant, ringed hand. "It's really quite simple, you see. My oldest son is Viscount Collinson. It's well known that he has the ear of Queen Victoria."

The men nodded their agreement.

"Then, my brother-in-law is the Duke of Natchess, who controls grain prices in southern markets." As she spoke, she ticked off a finger with the mention of each new influential name. "And, one of my sons-in-law is the Duke of Palmery, whose subsidiary manages shipping permits for the government. Another is the Earl of Wentbury. He's not particularly influential, but he has most folks fooled in that regard. Some think that no matter of business takes place without Wentbury's approval."

"I'm impressed, my lady," Miles said with a growing smile. "I'd forgotten you were so well connected."

"Don't ever forget it, nephew. There is hope yet for advancement in your future."

Miles laughed. "Yes, my dearest aunt."

Their laughter broke the tension in the room.

"The purpose of calling upon this long list of nobility is to impress and, shall we say, potentially hobble your father," Aunt Mildred said looking at Hunter.

"I'm sure it will do exactly that," Hunter said. He looked at Lia and smiled.

"Once we reach London," Lia said, "Aunt Mildred has offered to host a dinner party. The guest list will be small, but impressive, and will include your father, Hunt.

"What will be the purpose of this dinner?" Hunt asked.

"To introduce the *beau monde* to the current Earl of Atherton, and the future Marquess of Trentridge."

"We're going to take George with us?"

"Yes."

"What good will that do?" Miles asked.

"You'll see," Lia answered. "You'll see."

"I already see," Hunter said with a smile on his face. "And it's brilliant, Lia. Positively brilliant."

Chapter Twelve

Two weeks later, Lia sat at Hunter's side as they waited in a secluded gathering room at the dowager Viscountess Collinson's London town house. Even her worry about what was ahead had not spoiled the perfection of each day spent with Hunter Montclaire in her aunt's gracious home.

Whether it was she who softened toward him, or he who shed his cautious attitude toward her, she could not say. Perhaps both. Happily, the air between them had warmed in a way that caused them to seek it out every moment they could. They seemed to thrive within it, bask in the comfort of it, treasure the gift of it.

They would face their futures in the dowager viscountess's drawing room before the night was over. And this night would either be the best or the worst night of their lives.

Of course, Aunt Mildred's brother- and sister-in-law, the Duke and Duchess of Natchess would be there, as well as her two daughters and their husbands, the Duke and Duchess of Palmery, and the Earl and Countess of Wentbury.

To make the dinner party an even dozen, Aunt Mildred had also invited one of the Queen's most relied upon advisors, Sir Henry Panden and his wife, and another very influential member of the house, Lord Franston and his wife, Lady Franston.

Then, of course, there would be Hunt's father, the Marquess of Trentridge. His acceptance of the invitation made it clear that if he was aware of the dowager viscountess's network of influence, he had seen no reason to be suspect of it.

As agreed, Hunter, Lia, Miles, and baby George remained secluded while the group gathered. Several servants brought dinner to them, but none of them were overly hungry and much of the food went untouched.

Hunter stayed close to Lia, grateful for every opportunity to graze her hand or brush her shoulder, anything to remind her that he was near. Each time he was rewarded with a small smile.

Lia stepped close. "Gracious, I'm a nervous Nellie tonight."

Hunter noted her small shiver with a compassionate look.

"Your plan is brilliant. I know my father will see the only course open to him, which is retreat, if not abject banishment from Society and destruction of his business empire."

"You're certain of that?" Lia reached a hand to his chest, her eyes showing how clearly she understood the impropriety of her action. But he needed to touch her as badly as she needed him, and he covered her soft hand with his own, pinning it near his heart.

"What do you think they're talking about in there?" Miles asked.

"Nothing important," Hunter replied. "The conversation at gatherings such as this requires more diplomacy than it does intellect. Women, you know, are not prepared to engage in conversation that requires forethought or intelligence."

He winked at his own sweeping statement and dodged the playful swipe of Lia's hand.

Miles howled. "Pish-tosh. It's a good thing they're not sitting around our dinner table then, isn't it Lia?" he said with a smile.

Lia looked at Hunter and raised her eyebrows. "In our home it was required that we engage in thoughtful conversation, with facts and opinions to back up any comments we made."

"Members of the *ton* would definitely be out of place in your abode," Hunter said on a laugh.

They stopped talking when a soft knock sounded at the door. A moment later, Hobson appeared in the doorway.

"Her ladyship says to inform you that the meal has concluded and the ladies are going to the drawing room while the men have their port. I will return again when you are to join them."

"Thank you, Hobson," Lia said, then watched the butler leave. She breathed in a heavy sigh, then turned to her brother. "Would you go through to the study and make sure Frannie has George ready, Miles?"

Miles nodded, then went to the next room where Frannie had been caring for George.

Hunter rose from his chair and walked to the far side of the well-appointed room. He moved past her aunt's priceless collection of clocks, seemingly unaware of their ominous ticking. From the rigid set of his shoulders and his clenched hands that hung stiffly at his sides, it was obvious that he was as nervous as she was about this evening.

But he shouldn't be.

In the intervening days she had watched him carefully, listened to the beat of his words, experienced the strength of his touch. Each look from him had drawn her closer. Each touch had lifted her further out of fear and into reassurance.

Lia rose from her chair and went softly across the room. When she reached Hunter, he draped his arm around her shoulders and pulled her close to him. She rested her head on his shoulder.

"I love you, Hunt," she whispered as she looked up at him.

He cast his eyes downward, then lowered his head and kissed her. "And, I love you." He kissed her again and she returned his kiss. "Did I tell you how beautiful you look tonight?"

"Yes, you did, but as I told you the first time, flattery will get you...," she stood on her tiptoes and kissed him, "...anything you want."

His smile proved to her that hearts could actually melt. Her heart shifted in her breast as he gave a lazy wink. It wrenched from her a silent prayer that this night would go well. For his sake as well as the babe's. Their futures depended on it.

"And have I told you how very special you are?"

"Yes, but I never tire of hearing it. There's nothing I want more than to be someone you know you can trust and rely on."

"Stay by my side, Lia. Tonight and always."

Lia looked him fully in the face, and found his sincerity untangling a knot that had bound up her heart for years.

He leaned down and kissed her again, then they broke apart when another knock sounded at the door.

"Lady Collinson is ready for you to join them in the drawing room."

"Thank you, Hobson."

As if he'd heard the butler, Miles brought Frannie and the babe to join them. Little George was asleep in Frannie's arms.

Hunter held out his arm for Lia to take and together they walked down the short hallway. Miles and Frannie followed.

When they reached the drawing room, Hobson stepped inside and announced them.

"Lord Hunter Montclaire and Miss Amelia Halloway."

There were several small gasps, then everyone turned to look at them. Aunt Mildred stepped over to them. "I'm not sure you know everyone," she said to them, "so let me introduce you."

Aunt Mildred did the honors and introduced Hunt and Lia to everyone in the room. Even the Marquess of Trentridge. His eyebrows shot upward when Lia was introduced to him. His face reddened at mention of the Halloway name and his lips clamped tight.

"I have formed this gathering tonight for the express purpose of introducing you to my niece, Amelia. She is the daughter of my oldest brother, Charles."

Everyone was too polite to show anything but kindness or deference to Lady Collinson, and hence to Lia.

"And of course you all know Lord Hunter Montclaire, Earl of Atherton and son of the Marquess of Trentridge."

Everyone uttered their assent. Yes, they all knew Lord Trentridge's son.

"Lord Montclaire has something he would like to tell everyone here. Or would you like to do the honors, Amelia?"

"No, Aunt Mildred. This is Lord Montclaire's news to share."

"Very well, then. Hunter?" Aunt Mildred gave Hunter the floor.

"Thank you, Lady Collinson." Hunter took a step forward. "And thank all of you for allowing us to interrupt your gathering. Please sit, if you care to."

Anyone who had been standing and wanted to sit did so while two footmen walked about the room refilling glasses. As they finished, Hunter began to speak.

Lia watched Hunter face the gathering, squaring his shoulders and lifting his chin—not in superiority, but in determination. Pride welled in Lia from a place that had seemed so bruised of late, and it was so very welcome. This good man had been sorely abused by his father. But now he faced the man without a trace of vengeance. Without a trace of hate.

"I know many of you believed that upon the death of my brother, I assumed his title as Earl of Atherton, but that is not so. You see, my brother Evan married before he died."

"What?" In a corner of the room, Hunter's father bolted to his feet. His voice was tight, blistering with surprise and laced with shock.

"Yes, Father. One year ago Evan married Miss Janice Halloway, the dowager Viscountess Collinson's niece. Miss Amelia Halloway's sister. I have their signed marriage license with me as proof." He waved the parchment before tossing it onto the sideboard.

"Liar," Trentridge muttered. "Your brother was not married before he died."

"Oh, but he was, Father. And from that union was born a son. The new Earl of Atherton. The future Marquess of Trentridge."

"Stop your blaspheming prattle!" The Marquess of Trentridge lurched toward Hunter, looking as if he intended to do him harm. But Viscount Collinson, the Duke of Palmery, and the Earl of Wentbury stepped together in a united front to stop him.

"What sort of lie is this?" he growled as he struggled to get past. "Another of your childish deceits?" Trentridge scoffed. "You and the truth never did see eye to eye!"

There was a loud murmur of confusion as the members of Society whispered to each other.

"It's no lie, Father. And though you wish it would be, you know it's not."

"Lying devil." Trentridge seethed. "I have no grandson."

"You do, my lord. And nothing would please me more than to introduce you to the woman Evan loved more than life itself. But I cannot. She perished bringing your grandson into the world." Several women uttered a startled gasp, giving Hunter a moment to slow his breathing. "But their son survived. Would you like to see him?"

"Conjure what you may, boy, I'll have none of it."

Lia watched as Hunter moved to the doorway and took the babe from his nurse's arms. He turned toward the room to a chorus of startled gasps.

"Allow me to introduce George Hunter Montclaire, Earl of Atherton."

"No!" Trentridge cried out and staggered backward.

"Look into his face, Father, and tell me you don't recognize his features. His likeness to Evan is uncanny, is it not? His likeness to yourself is equally unmistakable."

"No!" his father uttered, shaking his head as if to deny any family resemblance.

Hunter turned with little George and faced the group of people in the drawing room. The babe was awake now, but focused on the people in the room as if they were there for his amusement. He was quite content, until he saw Lia. Then his little face scrunched and he held out his arms to be held by her.

Hunter stepped to her and handed the babe over, then he turned to face his father once again.

"I am sure you're wondering why I've chosen this occasion to introduce you to my nephew, the true Earl of Atherton." He drew a long breath as if it might be laced with courage. "It's because my father has left me no choice but to do it in this manner. As you've seen and heard, he has no intention of accepting his heir. Nor does he have any intention of introducing him to Society when he comes of age. But I want those of you gathered here tonight to know of young George's existence."

"How dare you," Hunter's father hissed. "What are you trying to do?"

"I am attempting to thwart your plan to pretend to the world that my brother's son does not exist. I am making sure that any more attempts on his life or my own will not be ignored."

The group of people in the room gave a collective gasp.

And so did Trentridge. His face paled and he staggered back a step.

"I would never..."

"But you did."

"Never! How can you think that?" Trentridge sank into a chair, his legs clearly having given out on him.

"It was the five men who kidnapped my nephew and abused his nursemaid who make me think that's exactly what you intend to do. Make your grandson disappear."

A hush fell over the room, a deeply uncomfortable silence.

"That's absolutely diabolical, Trentridge. You sent men to take the child?" the Duke of Palmery asked.

"No. Yes. It wasn't like that," Trentridge sputtered.

"Wasn't like what," Hunter asked.

"I didn't *send* men. I...maybe I gave the impression. *Bloody hell.* I didn't know they'd actually do it."

The Duke of Palmery asserted himself at Hunter's side. "You'd best explain."

The Marquess of Trentridge heaved a mammoth sigh and swept a hand across his brow. "I'd been drinking. With some of the tenants. I said..." He paused, the look on his face showing his sickening realization of what he'd done.

"You said?" Hunter growled, not wanting to hear the explanation and at the same time desperate to know it.

"One of the hands asked when they might meet my grandson. Of course I said there was no grandson. Still, he...he seemed so sure. The bloke's own brother was married to a woman who swore she'd given midwifery services to birth the future Earl of Atherton. Over in Middlechurch. It was impossible, don't you see? Evan had just died. I was...I was angry that he'd left me without..." He looked at Hunter. "Without a suitable heir."

Lia felt the room's scrutiny as if it were she herself at whom every gaze was directed. But Hunter didn't flinch.

"And?" Hunter prodded.

"I said as much. And I said it would be worth a hundred quid to me if that babe had never been born." He dropped his chin. "That's all I said."

"That was enough," Hunter groaned. "Enough to send five men to make an innocent babe disappear."

Hunter stepped forward until he was just a pace from his father.

"Hear me now, old man," Hunter said, his tone communicating the full measure of condemnation he intended. "Your careless brutality with words flogged me my whole life and nearly got your grandson killed. I had no choice but to believe you meant it." He moved a half step closer and enjoyed the way his father shrank away. "In future, should anything happen to either the babe or to me, I would beseech these good people present tonight to seek out the cause of our deaths."

"Surely you're not insinuating that your father would intentionally harm you or his grandson?" the Duke of Natchess asked in disbelief.

"I am only asking for your assistance should anything suspicious happen to either of us."

Lia watched the remaining color leave the Marquess of Trentridge's face and his eyes widened in shame. Even so, he still managed to direct a goodly amount of scorn at his son. A lump formed in her chest and pressed painfully against her heart. No child should ever see that look from their parent.

With a jerk of his shoulders, Trentridge seemed to rally. "By God, how do I know this is my grandchild?" he blustered. "For all I know it's some brat you stole from an orphanage."

Such hateful words. Lia listened to Trentridge deny the existence of his own grandchild when it was obvious to anyone who knew the babe's father that this was his son.

"This is your grandchild, Trentridge," the dowager Viscountess Collinson announced. "I was witness to his birth, and to his mother's death. She lived only long enough to see her son for the briefest of moments and bestow his name. You can be immensely grateful that his mother's sister, my niece here, has cared for him like her own."

Several of the women in the room dabbed at their eyes.

"If this is my grandchild, then I will take him."

His words struck like a knife, and Lia felt her world crash around her. No, he couldn't take the babe. That would be like signing his death warrant. She stepped close to Hunter and he put his arm around her to steady her.

"No, Father. You will not take the child. I have in writing from both his father and his mother that he is not to be raised by you, but by us."

Spittle dripped from the corner of the old man's mouth as he spat back. "Who? You? I've seen to it you don't have a penny to your name. How the devil could you possibly raise a child worthy of carrying a title?"

"Now hold on, Trentridge." Sir Henry Panden stepped forward from the fireplace where he'd been observing and commanded the attention of the room. "Rainwood is one of the most profitable estates in my valley. Why, Montclaire here has built an enviable success, and in just a few years, I might add. To my way of thinking, the boy couldn't do better."

Trentridge looked confused.

"Rainwood? Never heard of it."

"You will now, Father, because Rainwood is my home." He turned to Lia. "Our home. Miss Amelia Halloway and I intend to marry and raise Evan and Janice's son as our own. You see, my experience growing up in your care is far from recommendable. As you have refused to acknowledge me as your son or treat me as any loving father would, I have no doubt that you would do the same to Evan's son. I will not permit you to have any hold over the boy."

"How dare you," Trentridge hissed. "This is not over. I intend to take whatever legal action is needed in order to gain control of the boy. You are not worthy of having him."

Lia watched as the Marquess of Trentridge realized the guests were staring at him with revulsion and disbelief on their faces.

"Surely you know I'm correct," he said to the room. "Surely one of you will assist me in my quest to gain custody of my grandson?"

The Duke of Palmery stepped forward, his hands clasped thoughtfully behind his back. "I'm afraid your attempt—whether intended or not—to take the boy away from those both his mother and his father requested as guardians before they died will be met with disappointment, Trentridge. I believe I speak for everyone here when I say we will stand with your son should you attempt any further action, legal or otherwise."

Trentridge sagged. "Damned traitors, the lot of you."

"That may be, in your estimation," Palmery said standing up to Hunter's father, "but we're only doing what we think is in the boy's best interest."

"You all feel this way?" Trentridge asked.

"We do," they answered in unison.

Without another word, Hunter's father staggered in disgrace from the room, flinging epithets every step of the way.

No one spoke for a long moment until the Duke of Natchess turned to Hunter. "The truth is out now, Montclaire. The boy is no longer in danger."

He reached out a hand and Hunter shook it.

"Thank you."

"And Montclaire? Miss Halloway?" Palmery laid a hand on Hunter's shoulder as he shook his hand. "I'd be honored to take a seat at your wedding."

Lia blushed at the kind words of a man asking for an invitation to a wedding that Hunter had drawn from thin air. How she was going to deal with explanations that no such wedding was planned—though perhaps in a corner of her heart it had been pondered—was too much for her brain to consider at the moment.

As if sensing her discomfort, Georgie squirmed in her arms and she made her excuses to leave the room.

Hunter led her across the foyer to transfer the babe into Frannie's arms.

"It's over," he said, drawing Lia to him. "The Earl of Atherton is safe now."

Lia wound her arms around Hunter's neck and stood on her tiptoes. His mouth came down over hers and he kissed her tenderly.

How she loved him. It was impossible to think that she had ever thought any feelings she had for Hunter were wasted. It was impossible to believe that he could love her as much as she loved him. But he did. She knew it in the way he held her. In the way he kissed her. In the way he cherished her. It was a feeling she never thought she'd experience. An experience that had set her blood tingling.

"What, pray tell, was that folderol about our getting married?" she asked with a coyly innocent grin.

"Folderol? I meant every word! If you'll have me, that is."

And then his face fell.

"You will have me, won't you?" The hint of a plea made his voice crack unexpectedly. He swept a hand across his forehead, pushing his thick dark hair from his brow. He grasped her hands. "It's the only way, Lia, don't you see? If you won't have me I'll wander the world half a man, I'll—"

Lia laughed with an unrestrained delight that welled up from a place within her which a moment ago had seemed impossibly distant. She thrust her hand up to cover his lips and rob him of speech.

"Half a man, is it, Hunter Montclaire?"

He gave her a sheepish smile. "Nearly half, I should say. Bordering on three-quarters on a good day, though."

He lowered his head to catch her lips in a tender kiss. Rightness flooded her veins, and a moment later she forced herself to pull away to catch her breath.

"At half a man, my love, you are head and shoulders above any other. Now kiss me properly."

With her hands on his chest Lia allowed him to crush her. As his kiss began to ply her eager lips, she knew this was the only distance she could ever allow between herself and the man who filled her heart with such joy. But long before she was ready to let even the smallest space come between them, Hunter reared back.

"Does this mean—?"

His eyes drilled hers as if he could ferret out her answer to his proposal merely by looking deeply enough.

And then his boyish hesitation set her laughing. Lia strove to offer her answer with a modicum of decorum, but he would not allow it. With a rakish wink he coaxed the words to gush from her.

"Yes, my Lord Atherton. I shall indeed have you."

No sooner had she breathed the words than he took away the remainder of her breath by twirling her right there in the grand foyer.

"Then we will marry as soon as I can procure a license."

He set her back on her feet, though he seemed unable to let her go.

"Wait, my love. Would it be possible to wed while we're still in London? Might we marry here, at Aunt Mildred's house?"

She prayed that the hopeful look in her eyes would prove to him that she was as eager to become his as he was to become hers.

"Of course we can. Nothing would please her more, I'm sure. We shall ask her this very moment."

Lia's heart burst with joy. With his heroic care and his eager, heartfelt proposal, Lord Hunter Montclaire unleashed in her the confidence that a wish she thought had been a distant impossibility would now become reality.

. . . .

A whirlwind of special licenses, nuptials, and private celebrations consumed the following weeks. Hunter often found himself standing apart from the groups of well-wishers, simply watching them interact with his beautiful bride. She charmed. She cajoled. She employed a clever wit that kept them supremely entertained. And inevitably, it was she who would draw him back into the group with a teasing look or a melancholy gaze.

Hunter found it impossible to remain far from her. His solitary nature had swiftly crumbled—at least when it came to her. He went to ingenious lengths to manage his business matters in ways that allowed him to indulge his need to remain near Lia. As he was tonight.

"Are you happy," he asked, after they'd loved one another more than once.

"I've never been happier in my life. I can't wait to return to Rainwood and put everything back to normal."

"And what," he asked, "do you consider normal? I daresay we haven't experienced a day that's been normal since we met."

Hunter stroked her fair skin and nuzzled his cheek against the cascading tendrils of her hair. No, nothing about their time together had been remotely normal.

He sighed. "I would give the world to have presented you with a family, dearest. At the very least, a doting grandfather for our children."

"Hush now," she said as she laid a finger against his lips. She drew a breath as if to say more, but no words broke the tender silence.

"What?" Hunter turned to see his wife contemplating the rich tapestry that hung over their bed. "Darling? What?"

Now it was Lia's turn to utter a sigh. "I wrote your father a letter."

Hunter drew himself up on one elbow, unable to reconcile the shocking effect her words had on him.

"You wrote my father?" Hunter was incredulous. "After everything he did?"

Lia turned to him. "Yes, husband. I wrote him a letter."

He started to speak but she shushed him and sat up. "I told your father that I understood the early breech that was allowed to fester between father and son until it seemed impossible to heal. I told him that even though he was unable to mature in his thinking, his son had. And for that reason I thanked him for bringing you into the world, a man so rooted in kindness that I knew my future and the future of our son would be not only secure, but blessed."

Her words drilled through layers of bitterness and seemed to open a festering vault in his own heart. As his feelings of resentment poured from it to disappear in a mist of forgiveness, he felt renewed. Cleansed. Her words had done that. Such a simple act, writing a letter. But how it had begun to free him from years of acrimony toward his father.

An image of who he might become if he continued to harbor such thoughts loomed in his mind. He'd grow old and angry, bitter and defeated. Like his father.

But she was saving him from that.

Hunter wondered at this newly revealed dimension of his wife's character—this compassion for a soul that deserved none. He looked up and saw apprehension on her face as she waited to see his reaction to her boldness in writing to his father.

He reached a hand to take hers. "Come here, my love. You're too far away." She responded to his gentle pull and laid her head on his chest, but not before marking his heart with the softest of kisses.

"I shall never be more distant than this, my dearest love."

He felt her smile as her cheek tugged against his skin. And he agreed. "Never."

Epilogue

HUNTER PACED THE STUDY FLOOR waiting for Lia to present him with another son or daughter. He looked toward the door when it opened and saw Frannie enter with the children. Aunt Mildred was not far behind. She'd come to be with Lia for the birth of their third child.

"Papa!" young George cried out as he ran to Hunter. He was four already and reminded Hunter more of Evan every day. His hair was the same burnt gold that had crowned Evan's head and he'd been blessed with the same adorable curls that Evan had always hated, but all the females loved.

Then, there was Charlotte, Hunter and Lia's firstborn. She would be three in a few short months, born exactly nine months after they were married. She ran to him with her arms outstretched, calling out to him. Hunter scooped her up as he always did.

"The children wanted to come down to see you before they went to bed. I told them you would have a surprise for them when they woke in the morning," Aunt Mildred said, trying to keep up with the rambunctious duo.

"Is it Christmas, Papa?" Charlotte asked. "We only get presents at Christmas and on our birthdays. And none of us have our birthdays tomorrow."

"No, it's not Christmas," Hunter said placing her on his knee. "But your present will have his or her birthday tomorrow."

"That doesn't make sense," George said. "How can our present have a birthday tomorrow?"

"Because your present will be born tomorrow," Hunter answered. "It will be his birthday."

"Is it a puppy?" Charlotte asked, jumping from his lap to the floor.

Hunter couldn't help but laugh. "No, it's better than a puppy."

"What's better than a puppy?" Charlotte asked.

"A new brother or sister, that's what."

"But I'd rather have a puppy," Charlotte said with a frown that puckered her sweet cherub lips.

Hunter laughed, then gave his daughter a hug.

"Is that where Mama is?" George asked. "Did she go to buy our new brother or sister?"

"Yes," Hunter answered. "That's exactly where she went, to get your new brother or sister."

"I wish she would have asked us first," George said. "I'd have told her to get me a brother. I like brothers every so much more than sisters."

"I'll wager Charlotte doesn't agree with you," Miles said from across the room.

"But you like boys better don't you, Uncle Miles?"

Miles gave Hunter a wink. "When you get to my age, George, you'll realize you like girls better."

"Yuck," George said. "Girls are bossy. Boys are more fun to play with."

"Well, some day you'll outgrow playing and that's when girls are more fun."

"That's enough education for one night, Miles. Your sister won't thank you for putting such ideas into her children's heads."

"Very well," Miles said, then rose to his feet and held out his hands. "First one to reach me gets to go up the stairs on my shoulders."

Charlotte was the first to reach their Uncle Miles and he put her on his shoulders and let George ride on his back. Frannie followed close behind.

"I think I'll go up. The doctor said it won't be long now," Aunt Mildred said.

Hunter watched Lia's aunt go up the stairs and went back to his study to wait. This was the worst part of having children. The waiting. The worry. Knowing that Lia was going through unimaginable pain while he was spared the agony.

He poured himself a tumbler of brandy and drank it slowly. Miles returned shortly after and sat with him to offer moral support. But there was something about the waiting that no amount of moral support could make better.

It wasn't until Hunter heard the cry of his child that he ran up the stairs to be with his wife.

"Are you alright, sweetheart?" he asked when he entered their bedroom. He knelt at his wife's bedside and looked at the bundle in her arms

"I want you to meet your new son, Hunt."

"A son?"

"Yes."

Lia pulled away the blanket so Hunter could see the babe's face. He wasn't beautiful. No newborn was, he'd come to believe. But he was a miracle.

"I love you, sweetheart," he said kissing his wife on the forehead. "More than I ever thought was possible to love anyone."

"And I love you," she answered. "I only wish things had been different and your father could have accepted the gifts he's been given."

Hunter smiled, wondering if he should tell her, then deciding that he must.

"Interesting that you should say that, my love. Because Georgie was the recipient of a gift today, although he doesn't know it yet."

Lia smiled. "A little brother."

Hunter took his eyes off his new son long enough to answer his wife's smile. "A little pony."

Lia raised her eyebrows in surprise. "I thought we were waiting until he was a bit older for that."

Hunter shook his head. "It wasn't from me."

Now Lia looked puzzled. "Then…"

"My father."

The two looked at one another in silence.

"Your father gave Georgie a pony? Just like that?"

"Um-hm. Out of the blue."

Lia sighed as she played with Hunter's hand that was tangled in the folds of the baby's blanket.

"So perhaps he's changing?"

"You mean perhaps he's grown a heart?"

Lia sighed. "Perhaps."

Hunter leaned over to kiss his wife and then the babe. "It will take a lot more than a pony to convince me he's changing."

Lia brought her hand to Hunter's cheek. "At least see it for what it is—an overture of sorts. A first step toward reconciliation."

Hunter tried to see his father in the positive light Lia had cast upon him. But too many bitter words had left their blistering effect for too long for him to be very eager about it.

"I'll tell you what. On the day my father comes to Rainwood with hat in hand and an apology on his tongue, that's the day I'll consider the remote possibility that the man might be changing."

"That's all I ask, my love." Lia dropped her hand to Hunter's chest and grasped the buttons of his waistcoat. "Now come here." She gave a gentle tug. "The mother of your son is in need of a kiss."

Hunter smiled and felt the wetness that dampened the corner of his eye. For so many years the beautiful picture before him had been too elusive to even consider. But now he was the luckiest of men. Because of her. Because of this beautiful woman who walked into his life on a summer's day and reshaped his world with hers.

She'd dragged him from doubt to belief, from denial to faith, turning a once distant hope into his forever home.

LAURA LANDON

AUTUMN'S WILD HEART

SEASONS
BOOK FOUR

AUTUMN'S WILD HEART

Victorian Romance by

LAURA LANDON

She was invisible to him, until her loving betrayal opened his eyes…and his heart. Can a forced marriage destined for loneliness become a match made in heaven?

The fact that the eldest daughter of the Earl of Shelton is no match for the dashing Earl of Danvers does not mean she can't fall hopelessly in love with him. But love from afar is enough for Lady Petronella Westerly. When she discovers a plot to trick him into a compromising situation, Nella's heart tells her only one thing—she must save him.

But while she is in the act of saving him from his cruel destiny, fate trips her up—literally—sending her tumbling to the bedroom floor and into the arms of her secret love.

Now her predicament is even worse. How in the world is she to save the young earl from an even worse fate? Marriage to her!

One plus-sized wallflower plus one dashing bachelor equals one compromising situation. And one great read!

Chapter One

"Nella, look."

Lady Petronella Westerly, eldest daughter of the Earl of Shelton, lifted her gaze to the spot where her best friend, Rosamonde, pointed.

"He's here," Nella sighed.

"Oh, doesn't he look handsome tonight?" Nella's second best friend whispered from Nella's other side. Nella didn't have to look to know that Patricia was gawping in a most unseemly fashion, because in truth, Nella couldn't blame her. The man was indeed a vision of masculine perfection.

Ask anyone and they'd tell you Lord James Carmichael, Earl of Danvers was the most handsome man in all of London. No, she corrected her thoughts, in all of England.

Nella took the opportunity to study him as he stood at the top of the stairs. He certainly knew how to make an entrance. He seemed to pose there, as if allowing every female in the room ample time to take in his presence. From his towering stature to the confident set of his broad shoulders that were the envy of every man in the ballroom, to the muscular strength of his arms and legs, to his narrow waist and muscled thighs, he cut the quintessentially heroic figure. And Nella hadn't yet dared to gaze on his face.

His profile was utter perfection, from the high cheekbones to his noble square jaw, to the inky blackness of his eyes and brows. His features were strong and captivating, and the look in his eyes a mixture of intelligence and assessment, as if he evaluated every person in attendance. And yet, when he smiled, every lady in the ballroom was captivated by the mischievous glimmer in his eyes.

Nella included.

Her response to the handsome earl had become proof to her that there was such a thing as love at first sight. From the first moment she'd seen him at her come-out ball five years past, she had never been moved as grandly by any other. That had been the night Nella realized the Earl of Danvers might well be her first and only love.

If she closed her eyes, she could relive that most embarrassing scene. It was her first ball, and Nella was more nervous than a cat in a kennel. Perhaps if she hadn't been so terrified of having everyone stare at her, she wouldn't have been so clumsy.

She'd entered the ballroom on her father's arm—after enduring his lecture to try not to embarrass him—and instead of staying at her side to see her settled, he had led her to a chair against the wall and abandoned her.

And there she had sat—at her own come-out—for hours, watching the dashing young men ask female after female to dance, while she went ignored. Oh, she did dance twice—with the two fellows whose mothers had required them to do the polite thing and dance with the maiden of honor at her own come-out. They seemed so embarrassed to be seen with her that she fairly prayed nobody else would ask her to dance.

And of course they hadn't.

She had thought her heart might break, and finally, when she couldn't bear it another minute, she had risen to her feet and exited the ballroom as quickly as she dared. By then, tears blurred her vision and she couldn't see where she was going, but she was in too much of a hurry to stop. And that's why it happened.

In her headlong race to the nearest exit, Nella had seen her father step into the ballroom. *Don't make a scene*, he'd warned. She'd promised him, and the memory of it nearly took her to her knees when one slippered foot slid out from beneath her. She had felt herself falling to the floor, but was miraculously stopped from going down when strong arms came around her and pulled her upright. She grabbed on to the man as he brought her against a wall of muscled chest as if she weighed nothing.

"Careful, my lady." He said, his deep, masculine voice laced with concern. His arms came up and held her until she regained her balance. "Are you all right?"

"Yes, my lord," she answered, then looked up to see who she'd nearly run over.

It was him. James Carmichael, Earl of Danvers.

For just the briefest of moments, his hands clutched her arms and he held her. Then, he lowered his gaze and smiled.

Nella had never known a face could arrange itself in such a heart-stopping manner. Nor had she ever known her own heart to tumble in such a way that she found it impossible to breathe. But in that moment she experienced a world of sensation.

She'd never been so affected in her life, and it was in that moment of discovery that she fell in love. It was in that moment that she knew there would never be anyone in all of England who she could love as much as she loved the man who'd saved her father from humiliation. And herself from disaster.

It had all happened so fast she knew he would never remember her or the event of that evening. But she owed him for saving her from the most horrific embarrassment imaginable. And she relived that memory every time she saw him and imagined him noticing her. Just as every other female in London wanted to be noticed by the dashing earl.

Half the eligible females in London searched for a way to lure him into a marriage trap. Not only was the earl the most handsome man in all of England, he was also rumored to be wealthy beyond compare.

Nella snapped her fan shut, determined to chase the unbidden images from her wandering mind. For pity's sake, wasn't five years long enough to moon over an unattainable fellow?

"Look at the preening debutantes moving to the front of the room," Rosamonde said, casting her glance in the direction of three of the Season's most glittering debutantes. All three of them—Lady Penelope, Lady Blanche, and Miss Melanie Franks—had taken London by storm. "They're making their way to the bottom of the stairs so Danvers will have to walk through them to enter the room."

"Don't they realize everyone knows what they're doing?" Patricia scoffed, giving the trio of preening flirts a narrow glare.

Nella stepped back into the shadows to watch Lord Danvers descend the stairs. He was nothing but natural poise and masculine grace and her heart flipped in her breast.

"I don't know why you're hiding, Nella," Patricia said on a laugh. "It's not as if he'll notice us."

"I know that, silly," Nella answered. "I just don't want him to catch me staring at him."

"Do you think that will bother him?" Rosamonde asked. "He's quite used to being stared at."

Nella knew that, too, yet she couldn't take her eyes off him. The Season was nearly over and her father had already informed her that this would no doubt be her last Season. She wouldn't put it past him to marry her off to a vicar in some remote provincial village. This could well be her last opportunity to lay eyes upon the object of her affection.

She had three younger sisters and her father had been blunt in saying that he couldn't outfit all four of his daughters next year. Since this was Nella's fifth Season without even one suitor showing any interest in her, they would just have to face the dismal truth—Nella's too-generous figure and her lack of comeliness left her an unsuitable marriage prospect. For the London set, at any rate.

Nella peeked around one of the large columns that lined the ballroom and watched as female after female vied for the earl's attention.

She knew how futile her feelings were, but what was left to her if she couldn't dream? What remained of life if she couldn't fantasize a future where she was loved? A future where one man thought she was the most special person on earth?

"Come along," Rosamonde said, pulling her by the arm. "There are three chairs together where we can watch the dancing."

Nella followed Rosamonde and Patricia to the other side of the room.

"Who do you think he'll ask to partner first?" Rosamonde asked.

"I'd expect him to ask Lady Melanie first," Nella said.

"Why her?" Patricia asked. "Obviously Lady Blanche has the most to recommend her. Her father's a duke, after all, and he's said to be worth as much as the Queen."

Nella shook her head. "She's making her quest too obvious. He intends to put her off as long as he can. He doesn't want her to become too self-confident of his feelings for her."

The three wallflowers watched as the object of their interest strode over to Lady Melanie and invited her to dance.

"It's unsettling how well you know Danvers, Nella," Patricia said. "So which one of them will he eventually ask to marry him?"

"Oh, that will be Lady Blanche. She has plans to be the next Countess of Danvers. And nothing will stop her from attaining her goal."

Both her friends looked at her with their mouths gaping open.

"What makes you think it will be Lady Blanche?" Rosamonde asked.

"Because she's the prettiest and she will not give up until she has him in the parson's net," Nella answered. "Even though I will hate to see that. Marriage to Lady Blanche will cause Danvers a lifetime of unhappiness and misery."

"Well," Patricia said. "If all he's interested in is beauty, he deserves a lifetime of misery."

"That's cruel," Nella said. She was enamoured of him enough to want only happiness for the young earl.

She watched him dance several sets and didn't move until it hurt to realize nearly every other female had danced with at least one partner. Except her.

. . . .

Nella made her way up the stairs to the retiring room. She only needed someplace to hide for a while. She couldn't even think of asking her father to leave until he'd had at least an hour in the card room.

Tonight had been especially depressing because Patricia and Rosamonde had both been asked to dance a number of times, where Nella had not been asked even once.

When she reached the retiring room, she made her way to a chair set conveniently behind a disrobing screen. Thankfully, no one else was in the room and she could sit in silence.

She was about to leave when the outside door opened and what sounded like several women entered. She recognized their voices immediately and pressed her back into the corner so she wouldn't be seen. If anyone peered behind the screen, she would merely be seen adjusting her stockings.

"*You know what to do, don't you?*" one voice whispered.

Nella couldn't miss Lady Blanche's superior tone even when she whispered.

"*Yes, we know,*" two other voices said.

"*I'll go up right now and put this sleeping draught in the brandy. My maid confirmed that the decanter was delivered to the bedchamber.*" Lady Penelope was so excited she actually giggled.

"*And I'll give your note to a footman to give to Danvers,*" Lady Melanie said. "*You watch for Danvers to leave the ballroom, then give him fifteen minutes before you go up. That should give him enough time to find the brandy and drink a glass or two. Any longer and he might get bored and leave.*"

"*Oh, this has got to work,*" Lady Blanche said. "*If it doesn't, I'm going to be forced to marry Lord Wexley. He's already asked for my hand and I have to marry soon. You know I do.*"

"*Tell me again. Second bedchamber on the left?*" Penelope Knight asked. "*I want to make sure I drug the brandy in the right bedchamber.*"

"*The second room on the left after you climb the stairs.*"

"*Yes.*"

"*Very well. Let's go.*"

The three conniving females left the room and Nella came out of hiding. She was more than a little stunned that Lady Blanche was going to make it appear as if Danvers had compromised her. But no, it was worse than that. The conniving trollop was going to trap him into marriage.

Nella slapped her fan against her hand. She couldn't allow it. She couldn't let him be trapped into a marriage. She had no doubt that he would probably end up marrying Lady Blanche in the end, but she didn't want him to be forced in a way that would forever taint his honor.

She made her way to the door, then peeked out into the hall to make sure no one saw her leave the retiring room. When she was free, she went up one more flight and stood on the balcony that overlooked the ballroom.

It didn't take her long to find the earl. He was one of the few men in the room taller than she, making him easy to spot. That and his rich, brown hair that flowed enticingly over the back of his pristine collar, and his princely posture, and—

Concentrate, Nella.

She watched until a footman approached him and held out a silver salver. The earl took the folded paper from the tray and read it. He appeared to frown, then crumpled the paper and dropped it into his coat pocket.

They were actually doing it! Those three meddling misses were actually putting their devious plan into action.

Nella wondered what the message said. She wondered if Lady Blanche asked to meet him, or if they'd used someone else's name to lure him upstairs—someone like Lady Winterbourne, with whom Danvers was rumored to be having an affair.

Nella kept her gaze focused on him. He danced one set, then left the ballroom. As he did so, Nella turned away from the balcony rail and raced down the hallway, then turned to go to the second level.

"Where are you going, Nella?"

She turned to see Rosamonde and Patricia coming up behind her.

"Uh…um…nowhere. I was just…going to find my father. I'm ready to go…home."

"Already?" Rosamonde asked.

"Yes. I'm not feeling very well. My head aches like Sunday's church bells are clanging away in it."

"Do you want to go lie down?" Patricia asked. "We'll come with you."

"No, no," she said, stepping away from them. "I'll be fine by myself. I just need to go."

She turned away.

"Nella?" Rosamonde sounded worried. "Your father would be in the card room with my father, wouldn't he?"

She stopped. "Well, yes, I imagine so."

Rosamonde hooked an arm through hers. "Then I'll go there with you."

"But, I—"

"Nonsense, we'll all go."

"Stop!" Nella pulled her arm away. "For once, may I just do something by myself? Please?"

Rosamonde and Patricia looked startled, confused, and then affronted.

Patricia cleared her throat, obviously uncomfortable at the highly unusual kerfuffle between the three great friends.

Nella softened her face and her tone. "Please. You two go on back to the dance. I'm going to feel awfully bad if you don't. And I want to be alone."

She fluttered her fingers at them, playfully shooing them back the way they'd come. She could see in their expressions their disappointment, but she had no choice. If she didn't go now, she'd be too late.

If she wasn't already.

Nella watched them walk away for a moment, then she sped up the stairs. She needed to get to the second bedchamber down the hallway on the left before Danvers arrived and drank any of the brandy.

With unladylike speed she reached the second bedchamber, then opened the door and rushed in.

"Lord Danvers," she whispered, then looked around the room.

He wasn't there. Thankfully, he hadn't arrived yet.

She breathed a sigh of relief and turned to leave. That's when she saw him sitting on the floor, using the side of the bed as a backrest.

Nella ran to him. "Lord Danvers," she said, struggling to lift his head. Struggling to waken him. Could the sleeping draught have worked that fast? She assessed the amount of time she'd been waylaid by her friends and realized that if enough of the sleeping draught had been used, he could already be feeling its effects. In fact, combined with the alcohol it could even deliver a lethal dose!

She crouched beside him, noting the glass of brandy that was tipped over and had spilled on the floor.

"Wake up, Lord Danvers. You must get out of here."

"I can't," he moaned. "Something is…wrong." His eyes rolled back and his head lolled to the side.

Nella shook him again. "Lord Danvers. Wake up. You have to get out of here."

His only response was a pitiful moan.

She shook him again and again. Nothing.

"Wake up, my lord. Wake up."

"Nooo," he slurred. "Tired. Sooo…tired."

"You've been drugged. You have to wake and get out of here before someone finds you."

"You found…me," he said, then smiled.

"Yes, but you don't want anyone else to find you."

"Who…are you?" he slurred.

"That doesn't matter," Nella said, then placed her hands on his shoulders and tried to lift him to his feet. He was impossibly heavy.

"Can you help me?" she said, struggling again to make him sit.

"No, I don't want…to help you. I want to…sleep."

"You can't! Get up!"

He opened his eyes and looked at her, then smiled. "Do I…know you?"

"No, my lord. You don't know me."

Nella put her hands behind him and lifted with all her might. He shifted and she almost cried for joy. But her relief was short lived. He went from sitting to falling to the side. He hooked his arms over her shoulders and fell.

Nella couldn't keep from toppling over with him. She landed on her back with the earl on top of her.

She pushed him as hard as she could but he didn't move. Instead, he lifted his head and brought his mouth down over hers.

He kissed her. He cupped her cheeks in his palms and kissed her again.

Nella had never been kissed, but that didn't matter. Danvers was an expert. He kissed her a third time and a fourth, and Nella kissed him back. God help her, she knew this was a once-in-a-lifetime experience and shameless harlot that she was, she took full advantage of it. But when his hands began to wander, reality came back with a jolt and she turned her head to break off the kiss.

She wrapped her arms around his waist and rolled with him to her side. "Get off me, my lord. Please."

His eyes opened. "I'd rather sleep," he slurred. "You're so soft. So very…comfortable."

"No. Please, wake up."

He would have none of it and rolled her onto her back, preparing to ply his kisses. But this time his eyes opened and he looked at her. Confusion filled his gaze. He had no idea who she was. Where he was. How he'd managed to find himself here.

"Please, let me up," she begged, and he started to obey her, but not in time.

At that moment the door flew open and Lady Blanche stepped inside. "No!" she cried, her voice reaching hysterical heights.

Suddenly, a growing crowd of nobility stood inside the room, filling it with their stifled gasps, their mouths hanging open.

"Who is she?" someone in the crowd asked.

There were several who answered they didn't know who the girl was and Nella was thankful. She crawled gracelessly from beneath Lord Carmichael and thought perhaps she could escape without being identified. But that wasn't about to happen.

"She's the Earl of Shelton's eldest daughter."

There was a chorus of 'oos' and 'ohs' followed by the suggestion that someone fetch her father.

Nella wanted to run. She tried to make her way to the door, but a hand reached out to stop her.

"Oh, no you don't, young lady. You will stay to face the consequences."

Nella looked up into the face of the woman who had proclaimed herself the arbiter of Nella's fate.

"Nothing happened, my lady. It isn't at all what it seems."

"That's hardly likely," clucked Lady Gladmoore, the *ton's* biggest gossip. "Considering your torn gown, flushed cheeks, and swollen lips."

"Petronella?" her father said as he entered the room. "What is going on here?" he added in an angry tone Nella rarely heard him use.

"Nothing, Papa. Nothing. It's not at all what it seems. Nothing inappropriate happened. Nothing at all."

As she spoke, she began to slowly realize her lie. Something inappropriate had indeed happened—as was evidenced by her torn gown. She raised a hand to cover her bared shoulder.

Lady Gladmoore stepped forward. "That's not what we saw, Lord Shelton. Your daughter's been ruined. The lot of us opened the door to discover your daughter on the floor with the Earl of Danvers on top of her."

Every pair of eyes turned to stare at her. The earl's head swung in her direction, as well.

Nella thought she might die of embarrassment. Not because of the condescending looks from the members of Society. But because of the look of horror and disgust she saw in Lord Danvers' eyes.

The man of her dreams raked his hand down his face and shook his head. He was slowly coming awake and stared at her as if nothing made sense. She realized he couldn't believe what had just happened.

Nella had never been so humiliated in her life. She knew what he was thinking. Knew from the expression on his face that he realized his world had just crashed down around his feet.

He slowly rose and turned to face her father. "Lord Shelton?"

"Yes, Lord Danvers."

"Please, allow me to call on you tomorrow afternoon."

"No!" Nella cried. "Nothing happened, I tell you."

"I will be expecting you," her father answered to Lord Danvers' retreating back.

"No," Nella whimpered, but her father clamped his fingers around Nella's arm and ordered her to keep quiet.

"No, Papa. I will not! Because nothing happened."

But no one heard her entreaty. And just that fast, it was over. She was ruined...

...and so was Lord James Carmichael, Earl of Danvers.

Chapter Two

DANVERS, WOKE WITH A STAMPEDE of renegade beasts thundering between his ears.

"The Lords Candleton and Pomeroy are waiting in your study," his butler announced in a voice so loud it echoed in the room.

"Very good, Hudson."

James reached for the coffee Hudson had placed on his bedside table and took a hefty swallow.

He swung his feet over the side of the bed, then stood.

The room spun in circles going to the right while the floor seemed to move in the opposite direction.

"Bloody hell," he growled, pressing a hand to his head. He dropped back down on the bed and waited for the room to stop spinning. When he thought he might have the movement under control, he rose to his feet and called for his valet.

He quickly washed and dressed, then went down the stairs and walked to his study. His longtime friends Richard Willoby, Earl of Candleton, and Vincent Scotshire, Viscount Pomeroy, sat in two of the three chairs clustered before the fire.

When Danvers entered the room, Candleton and Pomeroy broke out in wide smiles.

"I say, Danvers. You look like hell."

"That's much improved from how I feel."

"That bad, eh?"

"What happened last night?"

"How much of it do you remember?" Pomeroy asked.

"Very little before I returned home."

"Oh, then you missed the good part," Candleton said on a laugh.

Danvers poured himself a steaming cup of coffee. What he wanted was a glass of brandy, but the thought of drinking so early in the day turned his stomach. "What's the good part?"

"You've become an engaged man, my friend," Pomeroy announced.

"Bloody hell. I'd hoped that was only a nightmare."

"You might think so when you hear who you got yourself engaged to," Candleton answered.

James lifted his gaze. "Who?"

"Should we tell him?" Lord Pomeroy said. "Or keep him in suspense a while longer?"

"He looks like he's in enough misery," Candleton said on a chuckle. "I think we should—"

"Who!" James bellowed, and his head felt as if it might explode.

"Lady Petronella Westerly," his friends said in unison.

"Who?" James tried to put a face to the name but couldn't.

Candleton leaned forward in his chair. "Lady Petronella Westerly. The Earl of Shelton's eldest daughter."

"I'm afraid I can't place her. Describe her to me."

Candleton began the description. "About five foot seven. Twenty-three, maybe twenty-five years old."

"So far so good," James said. "Although I'd rather she were a little younger. Go on."

"Fair hair, the color of year-old straw, dark eyes and a turned up nose," he continued. "Are you sure you don't know her?"

"I'm sure. Go on. What is it you're avoiding?"

"She's considered one of the wallflowers. I don't believe I've ever seen her dance."

James frowned. There was something Candleton avoided telling him. "Go on, man. Tell me the worst of it."

"She's not exactly ugly..."

James closed his eyes. He wasn't sure he was prepared for this. "But she's not considered a beauty," he finished for his friend.

"Definitely not a beauty," Candleton said on a sigh. "And…"

"There's more?"

Candleton nodded.

A weight fell to the pit of Danvers' stomach. "Out with it."

"She's…um…she's…"

"What!"

"Not thin," Pomeroy finished.

"What does that mean? She's not thin?"

"It means she more than likely outweighs you by a stone," Candleton finished.

"What!"

"She's quite round," Pomeroy said to soften Candleton's description.

Danvers rose to his feet and walked to the fireplace. He braced his hands on the mantel and dropped his head between his outstretched arms.

"How am I going to get out of this, my friends?"

"I don't know," Pomeroy offered. "I'm afraid you might not be able to."

Candleton leaned forward and added to the conversation. "Rumor has it the chit hasn't had a suitor in her five London Seasons. No doubt her father is more than pleased that he can finally get her off his hands and concentrate on marrying off her four other sisters."

"There is no doubt that you compromised the lady good and proper," Pomeroy added.

"Explain good and proper."

"When we walked through the door, you and the lady were on the floor and you were lying on top of her."

"Bloody hell!" James closed his eyes and let the damning truth sink into his brain. "Why don't I remember this? What happened?"

"We think you were drugged."

"Drugged? By whom?"

Candleton shook his head. "I don't know. The lady says she didn't drug you but—"

"Well, someone sure the hell did!" Danvers yelled, clutching his head.

"I know. But, she and her friends claim it wasn't her."

James raked his fingers through his hair. "What am I going to do?"

"If you want my opinion," Pomeroy said, "you only have two choices."

"What two choices?"

"You can either sail on the first ship out of England. My suggestion is to go to France or America and stay there for several years, until this entire scandal is dead and forgotten. Or…"

"Or?" James asked.

"You can marry the chit."

Danvers stared at his two friends as if they'd both grown two heads. "I am not the sort to run and you know it."

"Oh, and Danvers, you should stop by your aunt's town house on your way to Lord Shelton's. She was there, you know," Pomeroy said.

"My aunt was there last night? She saw…"

"Everything," Candleton confirmed. "And I daresay she wasn't pleased."

James raked his fingers through his hair and sat in the chair between his two friends. He placed his forearms on his thighs and stared at the carpet until the paisley pattern swam before his eyes.

"She asked us to give you a message," Pomeroy said. "She said she wanted you to talk to her before you did anything irresponsible."

Candleton and Pomeroy got to their feet. "We'd best be on our way, Danvers. You have a busy day ahead of you."

He heard his friends walk across the room, then close the door behind them. And James was alone.

Alone with his nightmare.

. . . .

James dressed in his finest dark blue frock coat, checked that his top hat was meticulously brushed and his lavender gloves spotless, then traveled to his aunt's town house. Having to speak to Lord Shelton after he'd ruined the man's daughter wouldn't be half so difficult as having to face his aunt.

His aunt, Lady Angela Morningside, dowager Countess of Newbury, was his sole remaining relative. She was his father's sister and had been a mother to him after his own mother died when James was only twelve. She'd also been more of a father to him than his real father had been. He'd died five years after his wife.

If it hadn't been for his Aunt Angela, James wasn't sure what would have become of him. If there was one person in the entire world he didn't want to disappoint, his Aunt Angela was that person.

His carriage came to a stop in front of his aunt's town house and James stepped to the curb. He took a deep breath, then walked to the front door.

It opened before he had to reach for the knocker and James stepped into the foyer.

"Her ladyship is expecting you, my lord," her butler said, then closed the door and led James to the drawing room.

"Thank you, Perkins."

Perkins rapped on the door once, then opened it.

"Lord Danvers to see you, my lady."

"Thank you, Perkins. No need for tea."

"Yes, my lady."

The butler nodded respectfully then backed out of the room, and James was alone with his aunt. She hadn't asked for tea. This was going to be an upbraiding and nothing more.

James was suddenly even more uncomfortable.

"Sit down, James," she said pointing to the chair next to hers.

He walked to where she'd indicated and sat.

"Well, my boy. You're in a fine pickle, I must say."

James opened his mouth to speak but closed it again. He didn't have a leg to stand on.

"Why don't you explain what happened last night?" his aunt said.

"I wish I could, Aunt. But I don't remember the happenings of last night."

"What was the cause of that, do you think?"

"I believe I was drugged."

"By whom?"

James brushed a hand across his temple. "I don't know."

"Do you think it could have been Lady Petronella Westerly?"

James shrugged his shoulders. "Most likely it was. Who else could it have been?"

"So, what is it you intend to do?"

"What options are open to me, Aunt?"

"Come, walk with me," his aunt said, more as a command than a request.

James rose and led his aunt to the double doors that led out to the garden. It was early autumn and the flowers that had been in full bloom throughout the summer were losing their vibrant colors as well as their fullness. It seemed appropriate to James' bleak mood.

When they reached the cobblestone path, they walked deep into the garden. A white wooden gazebo overlooked a pond in the middle of the garden. His aunt stepped up the two narrow stairs and sat on a wooden bench that outlined the perimeter of the small pavilion he'd practically lived in as a child.

"You have always been as a son to me, James." She spoke with a wistful smile.

"As you have been mother and father to me, Aunt."

She reached over to pat his hand.

"You know I love you and only want you to do what will make you happy."

"Yes, I know."

"Although I've heard rumors of your ill-disciplined lifestyle and have been aware of the scandals in which you've involved yourself, I have tried not to interfere in your life. I considered your escapades part of a young man sowing his wild oats."

James flinched. "Yes, I have sown my share of wild oats, Aunt. But I'm afraid last night had nothing to do with sowing wild oats. I truly believe I was tricked."

"And if you were?"

"Then I must consider calling the girl out and forcing her to publicly admit she intentionally drugged me to force a marriage."

"No."

James jerked his head to the side to look at his aunt. He was sure he'd misheard her. Surely she didn't intend to force him to marry the girl. Not after what she'd done. Not a girl he'd never met before and had nothing in common with. Not a girl who was someone he could not tolerate looking at every morning and evening for the rest of his life.

"What?" he asked. "Why?"

"Because your good name will be ruined if you fail to do your duty. Even if you can force her to publicly admit she tricked you, your reputation will be forever tarnished. Besides, I'm told the girl in question is a young lady of culture and refinement. Under the circumstances, you could do no better."

A rock fell to the pit of his stomach and he found it difficult to breath. He had known his aunt would be disappointed in him but he had been certain that once she understood what had happened she would agree with his decision not to fall into the maiden's trap. Instead, she intended to force him to marry.

"And if I don't?"

"You will force me to do something I never thought I would consider doing."

"What is that, Aunt?"

"You know that as you are my closest living relative, I intend to leave you my fortune and estate."

"Are you saying that if I don't marry the girl you will disown me?"

After a slight hesitation his aunt answered. "Yes. That is what I'm saying."

James rose to his feet, desperately controlling the panic that welled within him. He walked to the edge of the gazebo and braced his hands on the two wooden beams that lined the open entryway. "May I ask why?" he ventured.

"Because you are the only one who can keep the girl from being cast on Society's dung heap. Because you are the only one who can save your own future from being consigned to tittle-tattle."

She gave him a piercing look. "And because I think marrying the girl is the only decision you will be able to live with."

Chapter Three

NELLA SAT IN HER BEDCHAMBER and watched out the window. The Earl of Danvers had arrived nearly an hour ago and was still with her father. They were discussing the details of her marriage to Danvers. A marriage that would never take place.

Nella leaned her forehead against the window pane and let the glass cool her warm flesh. Autumn was coming earlier than usual this year. Even though the sun was out, it wasn't strong enough to warm the air. The days were cool and the evenings cooler yet.

Or, perhaps the coolness was a harbinger of the events of the day.

"Papa wants you to join him in his study, Nella," her sister Evangeline said after she opened the door.

Nella took two steps toward her.

"Oh, Nella," Evie said on a sigh. "You are the most envied female in all of London. Lord Danvers is the most handsome man in the world, and every female has been vying for his hand for the past several Seasons. I can't believe you will be his bride."

Nella didn't say anything. How could she? She hadn't won his affection. She'd won his hand through trickery and deceit. He didn't care for her. After what had happened, he probably even hated her.

Truth be told, he didn't even know who she was. He'd never paid her the least bit of attention. And wouldn't even now if he hadn't been drugged.

Nella made her way out the door and down the stairs. Over and over she told herself she only had to endure the next few minutes and this would be over. Once she refused his suit she could escape to the country and hide away for the rest of her life. Her father had already forewarned her that this would be her last Season. Nothing had changed except that for her, this Season had ended several weeks earlier than usual. She couldn't be terribly disappointed in that.

She reached the bottom of the stairs and walked to her father's study. She entered when a footman opened the door.

"Come in, Petronella." Her father walked across the room and took her elbow to escort her close to where Lord Danvers stood.

"My lady," he greeted.

"Lord Danvers," she curtsied.

Nella took a moment to meet his gaze. She only wanted to memorize his features this last time before she would never see him again.

Her breath caught. His usually devilish grin was tinged with sadness, his brow knitted as if he wrestled with some impossible problem. Yet even with these changes, she still felt his strength, still sensed his ownership of the space he occupied.

How was it possible for one man's features to be so perfectly formed? From her safe distances in grand ballrooms his features had seemed as if drawn on an artist's canvas. But here, practically within arm's reach, the life and health and color made his face alive with tense emotion. Her heart shifted in her breast.

"Sit down, Petronella," her father ordered. "Lord Danvers and I have been discussing your marriage arrangements."

"I'm sorry, Papa, but that is not necessary. I am not going to marry Lord Danvers."

Her father and Lord Danvers both looked at her as if they couldn't have heard her correctly.

"What did you say?" her father asked.

"I said I have no intention of marrying Lord Danvers, Father. It's not something I want, nor is it something Lord Danvers desires. What happened last night was a mistake. A horrible accident not worth ruining his lordship's future or my own."

"I'm afraid you don't understand, Petronella," her father said in a harsh voice. "You don't have a choice in the matter. Your future is already ruined."

"But I do have a choice, Father. I've reached my majority and can no longer be forced into a marriage."

"You obviously haven't thought this through, Petronella. You are a ruined woman. You no longer have any prospects for a respectable marriage."

Nella wanted to laugh. Was her father so blind he couldn't see she never did have prospects for marriage—respectable or no?

"It's my life you're talking about. You've brought me up to know my own mind and achieve what I want in life. Well," she said, turning to face him, "that is exactly what I'm doing.

"But—"

Nella turned her back on her father and moved to face the earl. "I thank you for your proposal of marriage, my lord, but I respectfully decline your offer."

An uncomfortable silence stretched through the room. Nella watched, fascinated, as strings of tension corded along the young earl's neck.

Her father swung around to glare at her with lips pursed tightly and a hardened look in his eyes. In her three and twenty years, she had seldom gone against her father's wishes, but she could see the disappointment on his face. And the anger.

"If you will excuse me now." Nella turned to walk to the door.

"Wait, my lady."

Nella stopped and turned at the commanding tone in Lord Danvers' voice.

"A moment, Lady Petronella," Danvers continued, then turned to address her father. "Lord Shelton," he said, seeming to stiffen his spine, "would you allow me a few moments alone with your daughter?"

The look on her father's face indicated this wasn't going as he'd planned and he wasn't sure what to do. Finally, he gave a sharp nod of his head. "Of course, Danvers. I will be right outside should you need me."

"Thank you," the earl said, then remained standing until her father left. When they were alone, the earl walked to the other side of the room and stood before the window. "Would you do me a favor, Lady Petronella? Would you please tell me what happened last night? You see, I'm having difficulty remembering anything past receiving a note inviting me to... to meet with a...a certain female of my acquaintance."

"You were drugged, my lord."

"By you?"

Nella took a deep breath. "No, not by me. It was merely my intention to—"

"Then who?"

The name was on the tip of her tongue. How easily it could spill out and she would be rid of the horrid secret. But just as she would not wish to be betrayed, she could not wish to be the betrayer. There had to be another way to make him see there was an honorable solution to their dilemma.

"It no longer matters, my lord. What's done is done."

He turned and walked toward her. She hadn't realized how very tall he was, but the closer he came to her the smaller in stature she felt. That was new, and she rather liked it.

"You realize we have to marry, do you not?"

"No, Lord Danvers. We do not have to marry. While I did not drug you nor have any part in the despicable ploy, it is still my fault you were put in this predicament, and I alone have the ability to save you from the consequences."

"And if I don't want to be saved from the consequences?"

Nella smiled. "Of course you do, my lord. This is not the time to be noble. Gallantry will not spare you...or me...from a lifetime of regret. Doing what only appears to be right will put us in an impossible situation."

"You realize you'll be an outcast if we don't marry," he said with a tilt of his head.

An outcast. She'd never used that word before, but she certainly understood it. The only difference between her current status and outcast is that she would no longer be among Society. Either way, she'd be invisible, just as she had always been.

Nella could do nothing but answer his accusation with another smile. What did he know of being an outcast?

"And you will be an outcast if we do marry, my lord."

"If we don't, you will no longer be accepted in polite society. Never again," he countered.

"That is something I'm resigned to live with."

His words didn't affect her. Her father had already informed her that since the youngest of her three sisters was to have her come-out next year, Nella would not accompany them to London. He could not afford the expense of outfitting all of his four daughters.

"You can save your words, my lord. My mind is firmly made up. You are not obliged to marry me. You may inform Society that you did what you were required to do and offered for my hand but were refused."

"Who do you think will believe that, my lady?"

"You believe you are that remarkable a catch?" Nella asked, then wished she could take back her words. They were hurtful and cruel and nothing that resembled her true nature.

"I'm sorry," she said, lowering her gaze. "I know people will at first doubt that your offer was turned down, but in time, they will believe you. My father will make it known."

Nella paced the floor and tried to come up with another reason to thwart his claim. "I have no doubt that at first all will believe you paid my father to avoid having to marry me, but that notion will fade in time. And…" Nella swallowed hard. She did not want him to think she pitied herself, yet she knew that was how her words would sound. "…and, no one will blame *you*."

An angry expression darkened his features. With long steps, he walked to her father's sideboard and poured himself a glass of Dutch courage. He took one long swallow, then turned to face her.

"Why are you doing this?"

"Because marrying me is something you do not want to do." She spoke the words with every bit of emphasis she could summon.

"Do you honestly believe that makes a difference?"

"Accept the out I am offering you, my lord. It's what you want, and it's what will be best for both of us."

He separated himself from her and turned to look outside. He stood with his legs braced wide, his white-knuckled hands clasped behind his back, and his broad shoulders rigid. He did not speak for what seemed an eternity, and Nella wondered why it was taking him so long to agree with her offer. He should jump at the chance to avoid marrying her, yet...

"We will marry, my lady. I will procure a special license, unless of course, you wish to have an elaborate London wedding."

Nella felt her temper rise. "I do not wish an elaborate London wedding, my lord." She took one step toward him. "I do not wish to have any kind of wedding at all."

"Then perhaps you should have thought of that before you compromised both yourself and me." He took another swallow of his drink. "I did not invite you to that room. You came of your own accord. Nor did I entice you to stay there until we were discovered. That, too, was a choice you made. If anyone is the innocent party in this debacle, I am. It is now incumbent upon you to do what is required in order for me to get my good name back."

Nella stared at him. It was he who pinned her to floor. It was he who resisted her attempts to get him out of the room in time. Yet, he was putting the blame for what had happened on her. He was demanding that she marry him as penance. She would die of embarrassment if she was forced to stand at his side. The ugly duckling and the handsome prince. Him the frowning beauty and her the cringing, hideous beast.

Nella walked to the sofa on unsteady legs and sank down with an unladylike plop. She stared at the paisley carpet that swam before her eyes and prayed it would stop moving. In time, she slowly lifted her gaze.

"If..." she said, "and it's a very uncertain 'if'..." She swallowed past the lump in her throat. "If I agree to marry you, what would you expect from our marriage?"

The earl leveled her a serious look. "I would expect you to be a wife to me in all ways."

Nella stared at her hands clutched in her lap and nodded in assent.

"And, I would hope that in time you would give me an heir."

She clutched her hands tighter and nodded in assent.

"And what would you expect, my lady? Or are your demands so numerous you cannot name them all?"

"*If* we were to marry, I would have only one demand, my lord."

His eyebrows shot up. "Only one? What, pray tell, is your single demand?"

"I would make you promise that after we married I would be allowed to reside in the country. You could go to London as often as you liked, and stay as long as you liked, but I would want your promise that I would not be required to accompany you."

"You would not wish to enjoy Society's revels?"

"No, my lord. I would not."

He lifted his glass to his mouth and remained silent as if evaluating her one demand. "Are you sure that is your only request?"

"Yes, my lord."

"Then I agree."

"What!?" She fairly jumped to her feet.

"I agree. I will procure a special license and we will marry at the earliest convenience. I assume you would like to hold the ceremony here?"

"No!" she replied more firmly. "Did you not hear me? I do not want to marry you! And why would I? Nothing happened!"

"But no matter what you or I say, the world believes otherwise. So hear me well. You don't have a choice. And neither do I." He raked his fingers through his hair. "I will repeat my question. Do I assume correctly that you would like to hold the ceremony here?"

There was nothing more she could say, and yet she had to. This outcome was untenable. She had to make him see the alternative. Make a united front and confess their innocence. Even as she opened her mouth to speak, she wondered what words would come out. But he stayed her with his hand.

"You may profess your innocence all you want, but either way, I am ruined."

It was in that moment that she saw desperation in his face. There were reasons he had not—would not, apparently—share, reasons she wished with all her heart she could discern.

He stood there, poised on the brink of a life neither of them wanted, begging.

Nella swallowed hard. "Yes."

His head jerked, as if he'd been hit by more than a mere word.

"Very well."

He turned to call her father into the room but Nella stopped him. She had to offer him one more opportunity to escape this marriage. "You don't have to do this, your lordship. I will gladly assume the responsibility for rejecting you."

"Would that were possible, my lady, but it is far too late for that."

Nella watched him step to the door and call her father back into the room. She sat quietly to the side while they discussed the remaining items in the marriage contract.

Even though she sat in stoic silence, she couldn't stop the tears spilling from her eyes. She'd never intentionally hurt anyone in her life, yet she had.

She'd hurt the one man she'd loved for years. The one man she would have done anything to save.

Chapter Four

In a blur, the week passed before his eyes, but it was finally over. He'd procured a special license and was now a married man.

He'd taken more ribbing than he thought he could endure. The usual congratulations and good wishes reserved for those getting married reminded him more of words of sympathy.

He'd been teased and harassed because it had always been assumed that he would marry a great beauty. Instead, he was marrying a female lacking beauty or popularity. He'd even heard it bandied about that more than one of his friends thought of him with a generous amount of pity. It was the greatest betrayal from his friends for them to laugh at his misfortune. But he could not deny the truth of their derision. He would wake up every morning for the rest of his life facing a completely unremarkable, plump female.

But the worst of it was over now. He and his new bride were on their way to his country estate. To Colworth Abbey.

"Are you comfortable?" he asked his bride.

"Yes, very. How much longer before we reach your estate?"

"Another hour or so."

"So your home isn't that far from London?"

"No. Little more than two hours away from the City."

His new wife looked at him and smiled. There was something very pleasing about her when she smiled, a gentleness that hinted at good humor. At least he could take comfort in that.

James hadn't really taken the opportunity to study her features before. Her face was round and her cheeks plump, but her big sapphire eyes shone with warmth. And occasionally, merriment. There was something enticing in the excitement he saw in her eyes when she looked past him out the window at the passing scenery.

"Do you have many tenants?" she asked.

"Eight. In a few weeks I will introduce you to the families that tend my land and livestock."

"Would it be impolite if I asked what dowry you received from my father?"

"Your father offered me a parcel of land neighboring Colworth Abbey. It will be a good addition to my estate and comes with three additional tenant families."

"Yes, I know it well. The Andersons, Baileys, and Waters are the families that live on the land."

"You are familiar with them?"

"Yes. I often went with my father when he made the rounds of his holdings."

"Then I will be sure to take you with me when I visit them."

"I would like that."

She smiled and James experienced a gentle pull towards her. But he easily resisted it.

"Is there a village nearby your estate? One large enough to have shops and a bookstore?"

"Are you a reader, Petronella?"

"Yes. I'm afraid I enjoy reading as much as almost anything."

"Then you will be pleased to know there's an excellent bookstore in Siding Cross. We'll visit there soon."

"Oh, you'll not have to accompany me, my lord. I'm sure I'll be able to find my way."

"James. Please, call me James."

She lowered her gaze as if she was surprised he'd invited her to call him by his first name so soon after they were married.

"Then you must call me Nella. It's what my family and friends call me."

"Very well, Nella."

James was grateful for her easy ways, though they were laced with more than a bit of underlying nervousness. What she had to be nervous about escaped him. She was withdrawing to the country, a wish she'd expressed more than once. It was he who would be braving the world and its unpleasant opinion of him. She, on the other hand, had absolutely nothing to fear.

For miles he worked to stow his resentment in a place where it wouldn't be a constant reminder of his former life. He concentrated on what this turn of events might mean to him not just as husband, but as earl. From this day forward he would face the world not as a wealthy bachelor, but as the settled lord of an enviable estate.

And that was a stunning thought.

Perhaps that was the blessing in all this. He would no longer be the free and easy unattached fellow with all its obligations to marriage-minded mamas. Now he could allow himself to lead with his more serious side. If that became true, he would welcome it.

James looked out the window and smiled. "We're here."

"Oh," she said, turning to follow his gaze. She released a sigh. "Your manor house is beautiful."

The carriage slowed, then stopped, and James jumped to the ground. "Allow me," he said, holding out his hand for her to take.

She took it and he helped her alight. He was surprised. She wasn't at all delicate, but even with her ample weight, she was graceful.

They walked to the front door that his butler, Covey, held open for them. James introduced his new wife to Covey, then to Mrs. Pendleton, the housekeeper, the upstairs maid Blackstone, the downstairs maid Elffing, then to Cook. They all bobbed prettily when they met the woman he'd married, but James couldn't help but notice the looks of surprise on their faces.

He told himself he needed to get used to that expression. It would happen often until everyone in the village and neighborhood had met her.

Everyone would wear a similar expression of shock and surprise when they met the woman he'd married. She wasn't what any of them expected. But, he told himself, in time the surprise would evaporate.

"Mrs. Pendleton, would you please show Lady Danvers to her rooms?"

"Yes, my lord. This way, my lady."

"Thank you, Mrs. Pendleton," she said, then turned to him. "Would you mind if I had a tray sent up, then retired early, my lord?"

James couldn't help but be surprised at her request. "No, my lady. Not if that's what you'd prefer."

"It is," she answered, then followed Mrs. Pendleton up the stairs.

When she was out of sight, James went to his study and closed the door behind him. He stopped at the sideboard and poured himself a tumbler of brandy, then took the brandy decanter with him when he sat behind his desk. He took a swallow, then set his glass on the desk and leaned back in his chair and closed his eyes.

"Bloody hell," he hissed through closed teeth. His earlier acceptance of his situation suddenly abandoned him. How had he landed himself in this mess? How was he to survive the rest of his life?

James thought of the multitude of beautiful women who'd thrown themselves at his feet. Why couldn't it have been one of those who'd drugged him? Why couldn't he have compromised one of them?

He thought of how his life would change now that he'd married the woman he had. His wife had made it plain that she would not be going to London in their lifetime. She would not be a part of the nobility that attended the most fashionable balls and social events, but he was allowed to go without her.

Bloody hell, was he really going to be *that* person?

How long would it be before his friends and acquaintances would wonder why his wife was never with him? They would, of course believe he was ashamed of her appearance and did not want to be seen with her.

Was that true? Would that be the reason he wouldn't insist she came to Town with him? Could he be that vain and shallow?

On the other hand, had she insisted upon remaining in the country to give him an excuse? To let him believe it was her choice that he conduct his London business without her so he didn't have to blame himself for abandoning her?

He leaned forward and took a long swallow of his brandy. He wasn't proud of himself, but he couldn't deny that a part of him was glad she insisted that she remain in the country when he went to Town. He wasn't used to having any female other than one of the most beautiful women on his arm. It deflected attention from himself, and he actually liked that.

He finished his glass of brandy and refilled it, then walked to the window and stared out into the waning sunlight. Little by little the brightness faded and the darkness wrapped around him like the fleece of a warm blanket.

Tonight was his wedding night. And he was terrified. As terrified as he was sure his wife was. How on earth would he ever survive it?

He refilled his brandy, then sank into a wing chair and drank it. Then drank another. And another. And....

Finally, he climbed the stairs and knocked on his wife's door.

. . . .

Nella heard the knock on the door and pulled the covers up beneath her chin. This was her wedding night and she knew that her husband would come to her. She only thought it would have been long before now. It had to be well past midnight.

"May I come in?" he asked from the doorway.

"Of course, my lord."

Nella had never been so nervous in her life. She'd never been more frightened than she was now. She held her breath, seeking to sink beneath the bedclothes.

"I brought wine. I thought you might like a glass before we...uh... go to bed."

"Yes. Thank you."

Nella sat up in the bed and watched the man of her dreams pour her a glass of wine.

He handed it to her, then sat in the chair beside her bed and stretched his long muscular legs out in front of him.

She took a swallow, trying desperately not to clutch the wineglass so hard that it might snap.

"I don't mean to embarrass you, my lady, but I must ask you one question before we lie together."

"Yes?"

"You'll excuse me, but I must ask if you are aware of what goes on between a husband and wife."

Nella felt her cheeks blaze. She thought she might die of embarrassment.

He spoke to cover her unease.

"My aunt, the dowager Countess of Newbury, suggested I ask you. She said because your mother died several years ago, it was possible your father was uncomfortable bringing up the subject of our wedding night."

Nella took a large swallow of her wine then choked on it.

"Did your father speak to you?" he repeated when she'd recovered.

"Yes. We had a brief talk," she whispered.

"May I ask what he said?"

Nella's cheeks burned even hotter. "He said that you...have had much experience in...what goes on between a man and a woman, so I should just...um... do what you...tell me to do."

"Bloody hell," he whispered, then took several swallows from his tumbler.

"Was that not what you wished him to say?"

The clearly annoyed earl rose to his feet, staggered, then took several unsteady steps until he reached the curtained window.

"Was there more he should have told me?"

"A great deal more."

"I see."

Nella thought she might die of embarrassment. "Could we just do this without you explaining what it is you expect me to do?"

Her husband took another swallow. "Yes, that might be for the best."

He removed his shoes and stockings, then stood and removed his jacket, waistcoat, and cravat.

Nella gasped and turned her head to look away from him. "Are you going to get completely undressed, my lord?"

"Yes, wife. I am."

"Am I to undress, too?"

"Yes, wife, you are."

"Oh."

"Unless you would like me to undress you?"

"No! I will do it, but could we please put out the candles? Can you do this in the dark?"

"Yes, I can."

"Oh, good," she breathed, then watched until he'd extinguished all the candles. "And the draperies, my lord. Could you close them, please?"

He walked to the window and pulled the drapery and the room was cloaked in welcome darkness.

With trembling hands, Nella removed her gown, then lay deathly still. She heard her husband remove the rest of his clothing, then pull the covers back. He sat on the edge of the bed and the mattress sank in the middle, rolling her close to him. With a gentle touch, he wrapped his arm around her and pulled her next to him. The feel of a man's hands on her naked body was something she'd never pondered. Strangely, it seemed to push her nervous modesty into the shadows and replace it with timid curiosity. She lightly laid her hand on his arm that was now resting beneath her breasts.

"I will try not to hurt you, wife. It's my wish to bring you only pleasure."

"Oh," Nella whispered.

His hand moved and she sucked in a startled breath. He drew his fingers slowly across places she'd not been touched before. His hands moved from one tender point of pleasure to another.

Nella lay still and let him do as her father said she must, startled to discover that the experience wasn't something she would dread repeating. In time, she thought she might even come to anticipate it.

And maybe, in time, her husband might not be so repulsed by her that he could endure to kiss her.

And maybe, in time, her husband would not have to be completely sotted before he could bear to make love to her.

Chapter Five

NELLA WOKE THE NEXT MORNING to find herself alone in her bed, with a place deep inside her feeling alive like it had never been before.

She rose and slipped on her robe before her maid Theresa came into the room and found her without her nightgown on. She blushed, thinking of the things she'd allowed her husband to do.

Theresa came in a short while later and helped her dress, then combed her hair. When she was presentable, she went downstairs.

With every step she took, she wasn't sure how she'd have the courage to face him. She told herself that thousands of women before her had done the very same things she and her husband had done on their wedding night, but that didn't make what she'd done any less embarrassing.

Nella thought she was ready to face him, but she walked into the breakfast room to find him sitting at the breakfast table with the food on his plate half eaten.

He rose.

"Good morning, my lady."

"Good morning, my lord."

"How are you feeling?"

How sweet of him to ask. But was that a worried look on his face? For a moment, modesty made her consider how to answer, but her feeling of bliss swept it away. There was only one answer to his question.

"Content, my lord." One corner of her mouth quirked up in a way that felt scandalously sassy.

He cleared his throat, clearly not having expected her candor.

"James. You promised to call me James."

"Very well, James." Why in the world did her voice sound so husky? Was she coming down with something?

Before the thought fully materialized, her husband smiled and her heart flipped in her breast.

"Would you like me to fill a plate for you or would you like to get your own food?"

"No need...James. Eat your food before it gets cold."

He sat and continued to eat as she moved to the sideboard. Once her plate was prepared, she sat down beside him and poured herself a cup of coffee. She added sugar and cream and drank the cup before it cooled. Then, she ate the sweetened ham and coddled eggs she'd taken.

"What are your plans for today?" she asked, not wanting to sit in silence.

"I've asked Wittal, my steward, to meet with me and fill me in on everything that's happened while I've been in London. How are you thinking of spending the day, Petronella?"

A ripple of pleasure fluttered up her spine. He's spoken her name only a handful of times so far, very formally, with little warmth. But today the way it spilled from his lips was so natural that she was quite taken aback, as if he'd just paid her a high compliment.

"I thought I would ask Mrs. Pendleton to show me the house, if that's agreeable with you."

"Of course," he answered. "This is your house now, Petronella."

"Please," she interrupted. "I prefer Nella."

It was positively ridiculous to interrupt him, but the way he spoke her name *Petronella* as if she were some sort of Greek goddess stirred her in ways that induced a constant raging blush.

"Nella, then."

Drat. Entreating him to use her shortened name proved no less stimulating.

"If there's anything you see that needs to be done, or anything you'd like to change, feel free to change it."

She dabbed at the corners of her mouth with the linen cloth.

"Are you sure?"

"Of course. Nothing's been changed at Colworth Abbey since my mother was alive."

"Then I must say your mother had elegant taste. So I think I'll wait until I have a feel for our home before I make any permanent changes to the house."

He stopped fiddling with his fork and took a sip of his coffee. "That sounds like a wise decision. Are you always this cautious?"

She considered his words. "I don't know what you mean."

"I only mean, you don't seem like a person who makes rash decisions."

No, she was not prone to make rash decisions. Nella lowered her gaze. Except for the night she chose to rush to his rescue. That had certainly been her most rash decision ever.

. . . .

Nella followed Mrs. Pendleton as she led her through each floor of the house. The third floor was made up of rooms for the servants, female staff members in the east wing and male staff members in the west.

In the east wing on the second floor, Nella was surprised to see the nursery, a playroom filled with toys and games and even a white wooden rocking horse with big brown eyes and lashes, and a bedchamber for the nurse. The west wing revealed several guest bedchambers.

Nella's suite of rooms as well as her husband's rooms made up the entire east wing of the first floor. The entire west wing of the first floor was lined with several more guest bedchambers, with a glass-ceilinged solarium at the end of the hall.

"Were all these bedchambers in use?" she asked Mrs. Pendleton. "Did Lord Danvers entertain much in the past?"

"Yes, my lady. He had guests in the house quite regularly. They were mostly gentleman friends of his and they would stay a week or more at a time. It was grand," she finished.

Nella thought of what her husband's life had been like before they married. She'd always known he had a multitude of friends, so she should have realized that since he had an estate not that far from London, he would naturally entertain his friends here.

She wondered if he would continue that tradition, or if he would live like a hermit as she had suggested she wanted to live.

She walked out of one bedchamber and looked upward. A rich oak balcony surrounded the outer rooms on each floor that looked down on the pink marble-tiled foyer. Above the foyer rose a domed ceiling with a round stained-glass window set at its center. The beautifully-worked glass allowed colored decorative panes to cast the foyer in a vibrant rainbow. The formal entry was rather breathtaking from this vantage point.

She turned in circles, marveling at her beautiful dwelling and wondering how she'd been so fortunate as to have a home so magnificent. A long moment later, Mrs. Pendleton walked to the stairs and led her to the ground floor.

"This wing is where his lordship spends most of his time when he entertains," the housekeeper said, then crossed to the right, to the west wing. The first door she opened was definitely a drawing room designed for the comfort of male guests. The colors were dark, the woods richly stained, and there were several decanters scattered throughout the room.

"This is the Blue Drawing Room."

"It's handsome," Nella said, not wishing to step into the very masculine domain.

"Next to it is the Rose Drawing Room."

"Oh, how lovely," Nella said, realizing that this room was decorated in more quiet colors.

"And next are the Billiard Room and his lordship's Gaming Room."

Nella stepped inside the first room and took in the large billiard table set with balls ready to be struck. On one wall were several cue cabinets with a variety of sizes and lengths of sticks from which to choose. There were also several round tables scattered throughout the room with four to six chairs surrounding each one. The wall beyond them was lined with several targets, no doubt for darts.

This house was, in every way, more grand than the home in which she'd been raised. And more masculine. She would tread very carefully into the realm of suggesting change.

"This brings us to the informal dining room. His lordship eats breakfast here with any guests he might be entertaining."

The room had felt immediately cozy, and Nella thought this was no doubt where she and her husband would take their meals as they had done this morning.

Mrs. Pendleton led her from the small dining room by a back exit. An enclosed hallway led them to the opposite wing. The east wing.

The first room at the very end of the hallway was the formal dining room—vastly larger and much more elaborate.

From the dining room they stepped into the library. It took up nearly a third of the hall with a library running the full length of one side and both ends, and a gallery on the other long wall. It was high-ceilinged and rich with carved woods. A truly magnificent room.

There were atlases and maps and law books, and books of historical battles, and poems. It seemed there wasn't any topic left unrepresented.

Nella walked the perimeter of the room and ran her fingers along the spines of the books. The room was cleverly lit, and the clusters of chairs and tables and sofas and settees scattered around the room were logically arranged. There were enough small tables on which to set books and tea cups and trays. Nothing seemed amiss.

"It's a beautiful library," she whispered in appreciation.

"Yes, my lady. His lordship spends a great deal of time here."

"I can see why," Nella answered.

From there, Mrs. Pendleton showed her the adjoining Orchid Room and the Music Room. The Orchid Room was done in lilacs and greens and lavenders, giving it a warm, homey look. The music room was done in lavish shades of burgundy, creams and golds. And, in the corner of the room sat an ancient clavichord posed next to a beautifully ornate piano.

"And finally, I'll show you his lordship's study," Mrs. Pendleton said, breaking Nella's concentration. "This is where you will most generally find his lordship when he's working on estate matters."

Nella peeked into the room and stared at the large desk that occupied most of the room's windowed end. She could imagine James working in here.

"Would you like a cup of tea, my lady," Mrs. Pendleton asked as she led Nella back into the hallway. "I can have a cup of chamomile brought into the Rose Room."

"Yes, I should like tea, Mrs. Pendleton. But would you please bring it to the library? I'd like to search for a book."

"Of course, my lady."

"And would you relay a message to the staff that I am extremely impressed by the care you and they have given to Colworth Abbey?"

A broad smile crossed Mrs. Pendleton's face. "Thank you, my lady. I will tell the staff. They will be most pleased that you noticed."

Nella watched Mrs. Pendleton leave as she slipped back into the library, then walked around the room in search of a book or two to read. After a pleasant hour, she wandered to the music room, knowing without thinking that this might very well become her favorite room of her new home.

She sat on the piano bench and pressed down on a key. The touch was perfect. The tone was beautiful. She placed her fingers on the keys and began to play.

. . . .

James walked through the front door after having met with his steward and paused. Unexpected strains of music drifted into the grand hall. He walked toward his study but didn't go into the room. Instead, he walked on to the next room. The Music Room. A room he seldom entered.

There had never been much use going in there. Music had never been a talent he possessed in any great measure. He only knew enough to recognize raw talent when he heard it. And he was hearing it now.

As he listened, the music grew louder, soaring and dipping, drawing him closer.

He opened the door ever so quietly and stepped into the room. Not wishing to disturb his wife, he simply crossed his arms over his chest and leaned against the doorway.

James watched his wife display a gift he'd not expected. Her head dipped and swayed. Her eyes remained closed, her hands lifting gracefully to linger a moment before they plunged back to the keyboard.

She was remarkable. She played with such passion that her entire body moved with each note.

James wasn't sure what she was playing. It was something he'd heard before. Something written by a composer of note, but he couldn't say who.

The piece ended, or perhaps it was only one movement of the piece, because after a suspended moment she continued with a different part. And the next part of the song was much faster and seemed incredibly difficult to play. Her fingers danced over the keys, hitting them with practiced ability, and striking them with precision and strength.

The ending of the piece raced on, accelerating faster and faster. Then, with a crashing final chord, she swept it to a powerful conclusion.

As her final notes rang in the room, James felt his heart tumble, then begin to slow. She'd drawn him so thoroughly into her music that his heart had seemed to take on a new rhythm of its own. She had done that with nothing but her lovely hands that expressed her incalculable gift. Her ability was beyond anything he knew to compare it.

She sat in stillness for several moments before she finally opened her eyes and gently ran her fingertips over the ivory keys.

"You have a gift," he said when she turned her head and saw him standing in the doorway. Her surprise caused him to smile.

She rose from the piano bench and stood to face him. "Thank you," she answered, "but I'm afraid I have just enough talent to realize how lacking I truly am."

"I don't find you lacking at all."

Her cheeks darkened as if she wasn't used to receiving compliments.

He walked toward her. "Did Mrs. Pendleton give you a tour of the house, my lady?"

"She did. And it's beautiful."

"It will suit?" he asked.

"Very much, my lord," she answered. "I could not ask for anything more perfect."

James held out his hand and escorted her to the drawing room next door. "Would you care for a glass of sherry? Or perhaps wine?"

"Wine if you please, my lord."

"I fear we are reverting in our attempt to use our first names. My lord and my lady are terribly formal."

She smiled and took the wine he held out to her. "Thank you… James."

James sat in the cushioned wing chair facing hers and took a sip of his brandy. He stretched his muscular legs out in front of him and turned his glass in his fingers. "What was the name of the piece you played?"

"Ah. That was Beethoven's Moonlight Sonata. I only played the second and third movements, although the first movement is the most well-known. Were you familiar with it?"

"Yes. I've heard it before, but wasn't so familiar with it that I could tell you its title."

He gave a sheepish grin and was taken off guard by his wife's answering smile. A euphoria that had most likely risen while she played still seemed to linger in her sapphire gaze.

It was both reassuring and unsettling. Reassuring, because her ability to lose herself in music showed her growing comfort with his home. Unsettling, because of the way it stirred him.

His pleasure in the moment lasted through dinner and then a drink in the library. James was pleasantly surprised at how comfortable he was becoming in her presence.

"I believe I'd like to go for a walk in the garden before bed," she said as she rose to her feet. "That is, before retiring."

He noted her furious blush at the mention of 'bed' and smiled.

"We shall go to our bed a thousand times in the years ahead, wife. I trust the mere mention of it won't bring you to a blush every time."

He paused and pondered what he'd just said.

"Then again, I might wish for it."

Now it was her turn to pause. She slowly turned and looked at him from beneath her hooded eyelids. "If a mere blush brings...energetic thoughts to mind, then perhaps I shall make a habit of it."

Her hand flew to her mouth as if she wished to recall the words. She turned toward the terrace door and fled, leaving James to find himself wondering if he should reprimand her speech or dissolve in laughter.

In the end he did neither and merely followed her into the garden where they strolled to a stone bench.

"I want to thank you, James," she said as she sat and arranged her skirts. For the second time since he'd met his wife he wondered why she chose such uninteresting colors. He was discovering delightful shades to her personality, but her clothing did not match it at all.

"Thank me for what?"

"For making our marriage bearable."

"Only bearable?"

She flushed again. "What I mean is, I wouldn't blame you if you had taken your anger and frustration out on me for placing us in a compromising position."

"What good would that do, Nella? It would only make us both miserable. And a lifetime is a long time to live with anger and hatred."

"Yes," she whispered, "but I regret that you are the one who experienced the greatest loss."

He was quiet for a short while, then asked the question that had been nagging at him since they'd been found together. "If I ask you a question, will you answer me honestly?"

"Yes," she responded after thinking a moment.

"If I hadn't been found with you, would I have been found with someone else?"

She kept her gaze locked on her clenched hands in her lap. "Yes."

"Was that person someone you thought was not desirable?"

"It doesn't matter who it was, James. Don't you see? The deception alone was unforgivable. I just couldn't...couldn't bear to see you caught in a trap."

"If I insisted, would you reveal what really happened?"

She thought for several long minutes. "If you insisted I would have no recourse but to tell you what happened."

"Then I would like to know. I don't want there to be any secrets between us and I think keeping this information from me could cause a rift between us."

He watched her wrestle with the dilemma. But at last she spoke.

"Then I will tell you. I had escaped to the retiring room and while I was hiding in there, three women entered. They didn't know I was there, and I stayed behind a screen while they began to talk. One of them was to give you a message arranging the time and place for an assignation. The other was to drug the brandy in your room. The woman who was set on entrapping you was going to wait until you'd had time to drink some of the brandy and the sleeping draught began to work before she entered."

Nella stood and walked to the edge of the pathway. "I've always known that she was probably the person you would end up at the altar with, but I wanted it to be your choice. I didn't want you to be tricked into marrying."

"Yet, that's what happened." He tried hard to keep recrimination from his voice, but sensed he didn't quite succeed.

"Yes," she whispered as she turned toward him. "Please believe me when I tell you that isn't how I intended it to happen. I wanted to reach the room before you drank the drugged brandy and stop you, but by the time I got there, you were well inebriated.

"I tried to wake you but couldn't. Then, I tried to lift you, but couldn't. That's when you fell on top of me. I couldn't move you off of me before the door opened and we were found."

"I see," James said on a sigh. "Thank you for telling me. And, thank you for trying to save me."

"But I didn't save you! I failed in that attempt and forced you to do something far worse."

James rose from the bench and walked to where Nella stood. "Then it will be our duty to make our marriage something that is not far worse."

"How can you be so understanding, James?"

"What good would it do if I were not?"

"None, but..."

"Before I came to see your father, I visited my aunt. She's the one who convinced me I should make the best of our situation. I decided to take her advice."

"I'm glad you did."

Of course, he didn't tell her his aunt had issued a threat along with her advice, but that was something his wife never needed to know.

A long while later, after Nella had gone to her bed and his brandy decanter was empty, he climbed the stairs and undressed. When he was ready, he stumbled to his wife's room and climbed beneath the covers.

Their lovemaking was much as it had been the night before and when he finished, he rose from her bed and went to his own room. The minute his head hit the pillow he was sound asleep.

Perhaps his marriage wouldn't be so bad after all. Perhaps he would learn to adjust to married life without too much of a struggle. Perhaps he could give her a child soon and much of this pretense would be over.

Perhaps...

Chapter Six

NELLA LOOKED OUT ONTO THE BEAUTIFUL AREA she'd discovered on one of her daily walks. It had been three weeks since she'd become Lady Danvers, and every day she and her husband settled into a more relaxed routine.

They rose every morning, breakfasted together, then James retired to his study to work on the estate accounts and Nella met with Mrs. Pendleton and Cook to go over the day's menu. After that, Nella was free to do whatever she liked.

Today she'd taken her art supplies and walked to a spot she'd discovered last week. She sat by the trickling stream and put down on canvas the lush landscape before her. She wanted to get the varieties of flowers still in bloom onto the canvas before the autumn coolness and shortness of days stole their vivid colors.

She'd always found peace and enjoyment in painting, using painting as an escape from everyday tedium. Most females used their free time getting ready for the endless rounds of parties and balls, or for visiting their numerous friends and acquaintances. But since Nella had never attended the number of events most females might, she'd found other hobbies to keep herself occupied.

She swirled her paintbrush through a particular shade of green she liked especially well and applied it to her canvas. She'd been happily immersed in her art for more than an hour when a snap of a branch behind her brought her to halt her brushstroke and turn.

"It's beautiful," her husband said from over her left shoulder. "Beautiful."

Nella smiled. "If you find it so, that is because of the location. It's a beautiful spot."

James stepped closer to her and bent down to study her painting more closely. "You truly have a gift, my lady."

"I'm glad you think so, but I know my shortcomings. I am only an average artist."

"As you consider yourself an average pianist."

"Yes, only average." Nella started putting her brushes and paints away. "How did you know I was here?"

Her husband reached for the basket in which she carried her supplies and opened the lid while Nella put the brushes and small jars of paints inside.

"If you must know, I went to the kitchen in search of a raspberry scone and was told in no uncertain terms that Cook had saved the last one for you." He smiled. "It seems she tucked it into your kit."

"My...my kit? I don't think so."

Oh dear lord, she prayed. *Please don't let there be crumbs on my lips.*

"Not to worry, wife. Cook had just pulled pumpkin muffins from the oven. I had two and made her promise not to share a single one with you."

Nella gulped, then cast her eyes upward in time to see his dramatic wink.

"You beast," she moaned. "You wish me to starve?" Nella pasted a mischievous look on her face, but inside she was reeling. Her whole life she had been secretive about what she ate. And never, no never, would she have mentioned so very casually that she might eat a frosted pumpkin muffin. Or suggest that she would not welcome that most desirable state known as starvation.

Was she getting too comfortable with him? Had she best watch her tongue?

Nella folded her easel and carried it to a clump of trees. She returned for the small stool she'd sat on while she painted and hid both items in the folds of a huge trunk where she knew she could find them. She was very conscious of him watching her as she secured a canvas cover over the lot.

"I hope you don't mind that I don't carry everything back each time. It's just easier to store my things here so they're handy when I come back."

"Not at all," her husband said with a smile. "That's very wise of you." He looked around the area then back at her. "Are you ready to return to the house?"

"Yes," she answered, and he picked up the basket with one hand and held out his other arm for her to take.

Nella looped her arm through his elbow and they walked toward home.

The feel of his muscled strength beneath her hand sent strange emotions tumbling through her. It was a similar feeling she experienced every night when he came to her bed—the heat that radiated from him, the strength he exhibited when he drew her close.

At first she hadn't been brave enough to touch him, but each night she became bolder. Each night she wrapped her arms around him and held him close. And she allowed her fingers to explore.

"I must make a trip to London soon," he said as they turned onto the homeward path. "It will only be a short one. I have to meet with my solicitor and pay a call on the bank."

"When will you be leaving?"

"In about a week. If you would want to—"

"Thank you, but no," she answered.

He looked down on her and Nella met his gaze. She tried to tell if he was relieved that she was still firm in her resolve not to go to Town, or if it mattered not to him one way or the other. But she couldn't tell.

"If there's anything you need, just let me know and I'll bring it back with me." He pressed closer. "Anything. Jewelry. Gloves. An organ grinder's monkey."

Nella laughed at him and he gave a boyish grin that made her heart skip in her breast. "The last monkey I had threw me over for a chimpanzee.

So no monkeys, thank you very much."

She leaned toward him a bit and looked up into his merry eyes. "But I *would* like a horse, if that's possible."

"You ride?"

The surprise on his face made her laugh. "Yes, but the horse will have to be a sturdy one to carry me."

He huffed, then leaned down and pressed his forehead to hers. "You are not that heavy, Nella. Any horse that can carry me, will also be able to carry you."

There it was again, speaking of her size with simple candor and no condemnation. His words touched her more than she could say. "If you are sure, my lord."

"I am."

And he kissed her forehead.

Nella missed a step and tightened her grip on his arm. It was the first time he'd kissed her since that awful night of betrayal. The first kiss since they'd wed. It hadn't been on her lips, but suddenly, that didn't matter. He'd kissed her. And in broad daylight.

Tears swam in her eyes and she blinked rapidly to brush them away before he saw the wetness that threatened to escape and run down her cheeks.

"So, what plans do you have for tomorrow?" he asked.

She coughed slightly to clear the tears from her throat.

"I thought if the weather was nice I would walk into town. I'm anxious to see the shops. Especially the bookstore."

"Ah, yes. The bookstore. I should have known." They walked a few more steps before he said, "I will accompany you, if you don't mind."

She stopped. "Are you sure?"

"Of course I'm sure."

He looked at her as if he couldn't believe she doubted he'd want to accompany her.

"Then, some day before I leave, I will take you with me to visit with the Colworth Abbey tenants."

"Oh yes, do!" she said excitedly. She was anxious to meet James' tenants. Anxious to be a part of her husband's country life.

They were nearing home and he dropped her arm, then wrapped his arm around her waist. And pulled her closer.

"It seems we have a busy few days ahead of us," he said. "A trip to town, choosing the perfect horse for you, then, of course, we'll have to take your horse out for a ride."

"Yes, we must," she said as they reached home.

How she wished life could stay like this forever. How she wished nothing would change between them, but that was not likely. Everything would change after he returned from London. After he realized how much he missed City life when he was in the country. Then, his trips to London would happen more frequently. And they would lengthen. Until he was away from her more than he was with her. And his life would not be one with her, but with numerous females fawning over him and she would be nothing more than a distant memory that he had to check in with every once in a while.

They hadn't discussed whether or not she expected him to be faithful, but the choice wasn't hers to make. He would be in London and she in the country.

Heaven help her. She wasn't sure if she could survive if she had to share him. She wasn't sure if she was strong enough to discover he made love to other women and pretend she didn't care.

Yet, the only demand she'd made of him had nothing to do with faithfulness. She would have to live with whatever happened.

· · · ·

James sat in his study and worked on the account ledgers for the estate. Ordinarily he had no trouble at all concentrating on the task. But lately he found his mind in a war with itself. From day one, he had been determined not to regard the woman who had tricked him into a loveless marriage with anything other than courtesy and, in truth, he felt he was doing just that. It was important that he keep their relationship civil.

He had but one goal where the lady was concerned and that was to get her with a child, then hie himself off to the City to regain his former life. He, of course, might have to spend a few weeks in her company every couple of months to ensure she became pregnant again in case their first child was not the son he needed, or to provide him with a spare.

James threw the pencil he'd been working with on the desk and leaned back in his chair. He hadn't anticipated the fact that every night with her created more memories. Memories he thought he could easily ignore and forget.

When they'd first married, she'd allowed him to come to her without any hesitation. She had quietly allowed him to make her his wife in the true sense of the word without any emotion. But, over time that had changed.

James filled his glass with more brandy and took a long swallow. Would that things had remained that way. Would that she had not begun to shyly participate. Would that she had never shown any emotion toward what he was doing.

Would that she had never found the need to wrap her arms around his body and hold him close. Would that her gentle moans would not echo in his memory.

He pushed back his chair and rose to his feet. With his glass in hand he walked to the window and stared out into the dismal rain. The weather had prevented them from traveling to town like his wife had wanted to do and he was trapped in the house with thoughts of her that he didn't want to entertain.

He emptied his glass then turned at the knock on the door. It was her. It was the female he couldn't shove from his mind.

"My lady," he greeted.

"Am I disturbing you?"

"No, not at all. Come in. Sit." He pointed to a chair near the fireplace. "What can I do for you?"

"You mentioned that in a week you would need to go to London on business."

"Yes."

"I wondered if I could ask a favor."

"Of course. What is it?"

"If I would pen some letters, would you see that they are delivered?"

"Of course. I imagine you have friends with whom you would like to keep in touch."

"Yes. In fact…"

She paused and James could tell her next request was difficult for her to voice.

"Yes, in fact what?"

"I was wondering if it might be possible to invite my two best friends to come for a few days."

"Of course you may."

Her loose whey-colored curls fell prettily across her white shoulders as she earnestly expressed her wish. How would one say no?

"I would understand completely if you would rather I didn't invite guests."

"No, Nella. This is your home as much as mine. I don't expect you to closet yourself away in the country, never to see your friends again."

She lowered her gaze as if she was overwhelmed with relief. Was he really so terrifying to her?

"Thank you, James."

"I have an idea. What would you think if I invited two of my closest friends to come at the same time? We could make it a house party of sorts."

"Oh, that would be perfect. Are you sure?"

"Of course I am."

Her eyes lit. "Then, I would love it. That would be marvelous."

"You decide on a time to host our autumn party and I will take care of inviting our guests."

James wasn't sure why he'd suggested such a thing, but when he looked at his wife and saw the wetness in her eyes he couldn't help but wonder what had caused such a reaction.

He bent to place his finger beneath her chin and lifted her head. "What? Are you crying? Why?"

She shook her head from side to side, then rose from her chair and raced across the room. She threw open the door and ran from the room.

"Nella," he called, then followed her. He didn't catch her until she entered the library and collapsed into a chair. "What? Why are you crying? What have I done?"

She retrieved a handkerchief and wiped the tears from her face. "I don't deserve your kindness, James. I don't deserve you being so lovely to me, so agreeable. Not after what I did to you."

He sat in the chair next to hers and reached for her hands. He held them in his and gently squeezed her fingers. "Nella, I won't pretend I'm happy about it, but I know your reason wasn't intentional. I know you thought only to save me from entrapment."

"Nothing worked out the way I thought it would, James. I never thought to force you into marrying me."

"I know you didn't, Nella. But, it's too late to cry over spilled milk. We need to make the best of the cards we've been dealt."

James prayed for the crying to stop. It helped nothing, and just made both of them feel worse.

"Do you know how special you are, James?" she asked as she wiped the tears that ran down her face.

A damn of guilt cracked somewhere inside him. Special? Him? Hardly.

He strove for a light-hearted tone.

"Of course I do, Nella. You've told me several times and I refuse to think you'd lie to me."

She smiled and he patted her hands. It was awkward. He'd made it awkward. Because he'd given little thought to her fears and conducted himself only in neutral ways, ways designed to make her comfortable within the box he wanted her to live in.

James rose.

"I have more work to do, Nella. Will you be all right?"

She gave him a smile, although the cheer wasn't reflected in her eyes. "Yes, James. I'll say goodnight."

She rose and left before he could form another thought.

She would be all right. She'd said so, hadn't she?

James went back to his study to work on his ledgers.

He didn't want her to feel bad about what had happened on that night that started the whole debacle. He thought of what a hectic life with someone like Lady Blanche would be compared to the genteel life he was experiencing with Nella and it startled him. Other than having a wife with a marvelous figure, he could think of no other benefits.

But life with Nella?

Well, it was certainly more congenial than he could ever have imagined.

Chapter Seven

NELLA SAT DOWN AT THE PIANO and lost all track of time. It's what she did when she was frustrated. When she needed to take her anger or annoyance out on something. Or someone. Except the only person with whom she was angry was herself.

Why was he being so nice? Why would he act the way he had? Agreeing to anything she requested. Supporting her with whatever she wanted: her desire to go into the village, her request for a horse to ride, her entreaty to deliver any letters she wrote to her family and friends, her suggestion to invite some friends for a country stay. Anything she wanted. As if he was eager to grant her every desire.

She pounded the keys as she played the most stormy piece in her repertoire. Then, she continued with a similarly thunderous piece. Nothing *pianissimo* or *dolce* would be among her choices today.

"Are you angry at someone?" he asked from the doorway.

Nella stopped playing and placed her hands in her lap.

"Me, perhaps?" he asked, stepping inside the room. He closed the door after himself.

"No. Myself."

"Ah," he said stepping up to her.

"Ah, what?"

"Ah, that explains everything."

Nella looked up at him, knowing his nearness would cause her heart to spiral. "It explains nothing! Stop pretending that you understand me.

That you know me. When you don't. You don't know the first thing about me. And if you did, you wouldn't have the first thing to do with me."

"Why would that be?"

Nella rose from the piano bench and moved to escape his closeness. She lifted a decanter and poured some of the contents into a glass. Before she could change her mind, she took a swallow and nearly choked.

He came up beside her and lifted another decanter and poured some of its contents into a glass. "Here. Drink this instead."

She took the glass from his hand and drank. It was wine. She recognized the taste and liked it much better. She was sure she could get drunk on wine as easily as she could on that other disgusting intoxicant.

"Come, sit down."

He brought the two decanters with him as he followed her to the sofa. He sat down beside her and placed the decanters on the table in front of them.

"Now, why are you angry at yourself?"

Nella lifted her glass and drank a long swallow. "It doesn't matter," she said taking another swallow.

Her glass was nearly empty and he refilled it.

"Why are you as you are?"

"Now, that's a complicated question. Probably for the same reason you are as you are."

"That's not an answer."

"No doubt because your question was not a question."

"It was, too."

"No, it was an accusation. As if you don't like the way I am."

Nella looked at him and a part of her melted. His bloody handsome face was serene. There wasn't one feature that she could find fault with, from his high cheekbones, to the square cut of his jaw, to the cleft in his chin, to his dark, penetrating eyes and his expressive brows.

Even his personality was near perfect. He was always kind to her even when she did not deserve it.

She lowered her gaze to her rounding figure, her thick arms and her never-been-willowy legs. She had nothing to recommend herself.

Nothing.

She drank the rest of the wine he'd poured for her. She didn't deserve to be his wife. She'd compromised him whether she'd intended to or not. And everyone would always know it. She would live with the shame of what she'd done for the rest of her life.

As he would live with regret for the rest of his life because of what she'd done.

She lifted her glass to her mouth, but it was empty.

He filled it for her.

"Why are you trying to lose yourself in drink?"

"I'm not," she said taking another swallow. "I won't."

"I'll remind you of that in the morning."

He leaned back in the sofa and stretched his arm around her shoulders.

"Don't," Nella ordered and shrugged her shoulders to dislodge his arm.

"Don't what?"

"Don be nice to me."

"Is sitting on the sofa with my wife being too nice to you?"

"Yesh, you know it is." She emptied her wine glass again. Her head was spinning and her vision blurred.

"Why is that?"

"'cause I don desherve it. Because you dinna even know who I was 'til I…"

"You what?"

"Nothing."

"No, Nella. You what?"

"If we wonna been found together."

"But we were."

"And I'm so shorry."

"Did *you* drug me the night we were compromised?"

She shook her head. "You know I din." She sighed heavily. "I'm tired, my lord. I wanna go ta bed now."

Somehow she got to her feet and even made it to her bedchamber without her husband's help. He followed close on her heels.

"I'll sleep in my own bed tonight, Nella."

"No," she said, holding on to him. "Sleep with me. Love me."

"You don't want that. Not tonight."

"I do! Yesh, James. Please."

It was the last thing she heard before sinking into the softness of her bed. The next morning when she woke, Nella wasn't sure if he'd slept with her or not. The only thing she knew for sure was that she felt like the wrath of God.

. . . .

James gave his wife's maid orders to let her sleep late the next morning. He knew when she woke, she'd feel horrible. And she did. He could tell by the dark circles that rimmed her bloodshot eyes when she finally came down the stairs. If her looks hadn't confirmed how badly she felt, the fact that she couldn't tolerate even one bite of food by lunchtime did.

"I blame you for how I feel, you know."

"Me? Why me?"

"Yes, you. I wouldn't have drunk nearly so much if you hadn't continually refilled my glass."

"That's hardly fair, dear wife. I daresay you would have drunk even more if I hadn't been there to stop you when I did."

She placed her hand to her forehead.

James placed his hand on her shoulder. "May I suggest we postpone our trip to the village today, as well as taking a ride on your new horse?"

"I think that's an excellent idea," she said quietly. "Perhaps I'll spend the day in my room writing letters."

"No letters. Not today. That's an order. Just rest. And lots of water. I'll work on my accounts and leave you alone. Let me know if you need anything."

"I won't. I'm perfectly fine."

James couldn't help but smile. He thought of her as an essentially brave lady. With a will of iron. Drinking until she was so inebriated was totally out of character for her, as far as he knew. He would ask her later about it and hoped she'd tell him what had instigated her mood.

But he doubted she would tell him.

He worked on his ledgers all afternoon, and when his wife came down for dinner, she looked much better.

"How do you feel?" he asked.

"I think I might live," she said.

He took her arm and led her into the small dining room. "I hope you don't mind, but I asked Cook to prepare something light for dinner."

"I don't mind at all."

He sat her at her usual place at the table.

"How do men do it?" she asked.

"Do what?"

"Drink night after night. Have too much to drink one night and repeat the process again the next night?"

A footman arrived with a light soup and a warm loaf of sliced bread. James buttered her a piece of bread then handed it to her. She thanked him and took a small bite.

"It takes years of practice," he answered. "That's how we do it."

"How do you survive until you become used to it?"

"I think one simply tires of feeling like bloody hell every morning when they wake."

She took another nibble of her buttered bread. "I dare say you won't have to worry about me relying too heavily on wine on a daily basis."

He laughed. "I'm glad." James dipped his spoon into his bowl of soup. "So, why did you drink like you did last night?"

She stopped with her bread halfway to her mouth, then continued eating as if he hadn't spoken. He was sure eating was a tactic to stop from having to answer him.

Before he could ask her again, a footman came in with a platter of cheeses, more warm bread, and a bowl of fruit.

"You haven't answered my question, Nella. What were you upset over?"

"I wasn't upset."

"Liar."

She looked at him with a cross expression on her face.

"I wasn't," she repeated. "I was angry."

"With whom?"

"With myself."

"Why?"

"Because," she answered. "Just because."

"I'm not going to get an answer from you, am I?"

She lowered her gaze and ate a few pieces of fruit. "No."

James gave up questioning her until she finally finished nibbling on her cheese. With a heavy sigh she dropped her linen napkin on the table and rose. "If you will excuse me."

James rose and pulled her chair back. She laid a hand on his arm, a companionable thing to do.

"I'm glad to see you feeling so much better."

She huffed.

"Well you are," he insisted. "But I'd feel better if I could see those dimples." He raised a finger to lightly touch her cheek.

His easy quip and gentle touch seemed to do the trick. James lowered his gaze and caught the smile he'd been hoping for. It changed her features. Made her seem younger... happier. Prettier.

He wrapped his arm around her shoulders and led her from the dining room. "I will leave on Thursday for London. If you will have your invitations written by then, I will take them with me and see they get delivered."

"Oh, thank you, James." Her voice elevated with a measure of excitement. "I can't wait," she said, then lifted her head and kissed him on the cheek.

Every muscle in her body stiffened when she seemed to realize what she'd done. She separated herself from him as if she thought something as simple as a kiss on his cheek was a step too far. As if she didn't have the right to show him unsolicited affection. As if he could come to her bed every night and use her body, but she didn't have the same rights.

Suddenly, James realized that he'd never kissed her. He'd lain with her. He'd made love to her. But he'd never kissed her, as if kissing her on the lips would indicate that their relationship had gone another step. As if kissing her on the lips represented an intimacy he wasn't ready to show her.

"I think I'd like to retire now," she said.

James turned with her. "Would you indulge me for a moment?" he asked as they made their way from the dining room.

"Of course."

"Would you play for me?"

"The piano?"

"No. TiddlyWinks." He winked. "Of course I mean the piano."

"Of course. What would you like to hear?"

"Whatever you'd like to play."

They strolled to the music room where James poured himself a glass of brandy and sat in the corner of the sofa. His wife went to the piano and sat. She breathed in deeply, then placed her hands on the keyboard and started the most beautiful, most melancholy melody he'd ever heard.

James couldn't speak. He didn't have the heart to interrupt something so pure, so elemental, so heart-wrenching.

When he had decided to ask her to play he'd wondered what song she would choose. He wondered whether it would be some fast-paced heart-pounding song that represented the frustration he knew she felt, or the slower, more melancholy song that tore at her heart and exposed her hurt and agony. The fact that it was the latter spoke volumes.

He sat in silence until the last tone faded into silence, then watched as she lifted her fingers from the keyboard.

"Why did you choose such a sad song?"

Her head swiveled round to face him. "No reason," she answered without conviction. "My life is not sad."

"What would you say it is, wife?"

She studied him, then looked away.

"I'm not sure. What would you say your life is, my lord?"

He smiled. "That's easy. Interesting."

He heard her small intake of breath.

"Is it?"

"Yes, Petronella. It is."

She rose from the piano bench and walked to the small table where several decanters sat. She reached for the wine, then pulled her hand back.

"You changed your mind?"

"Yes. I don't need fermented grapes to feel better. After last night I've learned it only makes me feel worse."

She turned and walked to the door. "I think I'd like to go to bed now." *There was that blush again.*

"Go ahead, Nella. I'll be up in a short while."

She nodded, then opened the door.

"Nella?" he said, stopping her footsteps.

She turned to face him.

"The day will come when we will need to discuss what's bothering you."

She opened her mouth but James held up his hand to stop her words. "No, there is something. Denying it only allows the problem to grow."

In the silence that stretched between them she turned and left him. And James refilled his glass.

Chapter Eight

NELLA HAD NEVER BEEN HAPPIER IN HER LIFE.

Every day of the past week had been perfect. James had taken her to Siding Cross and she'd spent hours in the bookstore purchasing far too many books. The next day they'd chosen one of the horses from his stable and had gone riding.

Another day they went to a dress shop and Nella chose several pieces of material she wanted made into new dresses. The lady who owned the shop, Mrs. Blankenship, was a marvelous modiste. She showed Nella patterns she'd never seen before and told her which styles and colors of gowns to avoid because of her shape. Nella was stunned. Most of the styles and colors she was told not to wear hung in her closet.

Each day she wrote letters for James to deliver, and then suddenly, Thursday was here and he was about to leave for London. She tied the letters with a ribbon and tucked them into his valise as he bade her farewell.

A few days later he sent word back that he would return in one week and bring her two friends, Lady Rosamonde Littleton, and Lady Patricia Bickerton with him. He would also be accompanied by two more guests, the Earl of Candleton and Viscount Pomeroy.

Nella fairly sang as she readied the house for their party. She spent hours with Cook, planning the daily menu for the two weeks their guests would be here, preparing adequate rooms for them, organizing indoor and outdoor entertainment for each day, and completing the list of things that must be done.

Nella would be glad when they arrived. She could finally stop her worrying. She wasn't so concerned with Rosamonde and Patricia. They'd been friends long enough that they were accepting of Nella and anything she had planned. It was Lord Candleton and Viscount Pomeroy that concerned her.

She paced the drawing room that looked out onto the front drive then stopped to look out the window. They should be here any time now. Oh, she wanted everything to go perfectly. She didn't want to embarrass James in front of his friends. She would die if anything went wrong.

Nella had dressed carefully in the first of her new gowns. Two more were promised by Saturday. Now that she understood exactly what making subtle, flattering style changes could do for her, she could scarcely wait to show off her new wardrobe. And the new upswept hairdo the modiste had recommended showed off the neck she'd not realized was quite as long as it was. Certainly not at all swanlike, but long, nevertheless. She resisted the urge to preen.

Suddenly, a carriage came up the drive followed by three men on horseback. She recognized James right away. He was the tallest and sat his horse as if he had been born astride the beautiful beast.

The other two men were tall, as well, yet not as broad-shouldered as her husband. Nella ran to the door to welcome her guests.

"Patricia. Rosamonde," she sang as she ran from the house and stopped before the carriage door. James had handed his horse over to a groom and was helping her friends dismount.

"Oh, Patricia," Nella said, wrapping her arms around her friend. "Rosamonde," she said, greeting her second friend. "I've missed you heaps and heaps!"

"It's been nearly two months since I've seen you," Patricia said, giving Nella another hug.

"Has it been that long?" Nella questioned. "I've been so busy I didn't realize it was that long."

Patricia turned Nella to face the carriage where a very lovely older woman was just descending.

"Nella, darling, you must meet my aunt, Mrs. Merilee Applebaum."

It was a complete joy to welcome the woman whose rosy cheeks and twinkling eyes hinted that she would be a most delightful addition to their party, even if she was the girls' chaperone.

"Mrs. Applebaum! Welcome!"

"Petronella?"

Nella turned to see her husband approach her, followed by two men she knew only by sight. She'd been introduced to them just once, yet she'd seen them often in her husband's company at balls and formal events.

She caught a strange look in her husband's eye that suddenly flustered her. Had his time in London been so satisfying that it had left that gleam in place through the entire ride home?

"Allow me to present my friends, Lord Candleton and Viscount Pomeroy."

"Lord Candleton," Nella greeted with a polite curtsy. "Lord Pomeroy."

"Lady Danvers," they both greeted. "It's a pleasure to meet you again. Thank you for your invitation. We've been looking forward to visiting you and your husband."

"Thank you, my lords. Please, come in."

James placed a proprietary arm around her waist and led her inside the house. Lords Candleton and Pomeroy extended their arms to lead Patricia and Rosamonde. When they entered, Covey took their cloaks and hats and handed them to the two footmen waiting in the foyer.

"Come," Nella said. "I imagine you're quite exhausted from your journey. Follow me to the drawing room."

Nella and her husband led the way, and when they reached the drawing room, James poured a glass of brandy or wine for each of the party. Covey followed with a tea tray and pastries.

When all had been served, Nella looked at her friends and smiled. "How was the journey?" she asked.

"We were both surprised, Nella," Rosamonde said. She was always the first to jump into any conversation. "Colworth Abbey is not all that far from London."

"No," Patricia added. "It took us barely two hours to get here."

"And I can't wait to show you the estate. It's very beautiful."

"So have you found areas to put on canvas?" Rosamonde asked.

"My wife has already painted several landscapes," James jumped in. "I will take you to see them later."

"You paint, Lady Danvers?"

Nella felt her cheeks warm. "I dabble in it."

"She does more than dabble, Pomeroy. She's an amazing artist."

"Have you heard her play the piano?" Patricia asked.

"Enough," Nella said. She was desperate to change the topic from herself.

"I force her to entertain me every evening," her husband said, gracing her with a warm smile.

"Then we can't wait to hear you," the Earl of Candleton said. "You can be our evening's entertainment."

Nella turned her gaze to where James sat. There was a hint of pride on his face, but there was something wrong. Something in the hooded darkness in his eyes said something was not as it should be. That's when she noticed it. The fading bruises on his knuckles. A faint bruise on his cheekbone beneath his left eye. As if he'd been in a fistfight.

A knot clenched in her midsection. James was not a man prone to fisticuffs. He seldom raised his voice let alone became angry enough to raise his fists.

What could possibly have happened to make him so angry that he fought someone?

Nella cringed. In the back of her mind, in a place where she wanted to keep her fears locked away and hidden, she knew that whatever it was, it had something to do with her.

She decided not to mention it now, but would ask James about it later. When they were alone. Right now there was too much to talk about.

Patricia and Rosamonde filled her in on all the latest gossip, the talk of the *haute ton* that she was grateful to hear had replaced the scandal she had caused.

They filled her in on who was rumored to be in love with whom. Even the men stopped talking horses long enough to listen.

What followed turned out to be a splendid evening. The meal was peppered with laughter and she managed to choose light-hearted music for their entertainment that followed.

All in all, the house party was off to a charmed beginning.

Nella undressed and climbed into bed. The first day was over. Patricia and Rosamonde had retired early to get enough rest to be ready for the events Nella had planned for the next day. James and his friends had remained in the card room to chat. Tomorrow was going to be an eventful day. Nella had it all planned.

After they rose and ate, they would go for a hike and picnic down by the stream Nella had discovered when she first came to Colworth Abbey. After that, they would lounge about. Then, Nella had board and card games planned for the evening.

What pleased her most was that her husband's friends and Patricia and Rosamonde seemed to hit it off splendidly. They seemed to enjoy each other's company. All through dinner there hadn't been a lull in their conversation. The laughter had been genuine, ringing in the halls and bringing smiles that lasted through the evening. Nella was glad.

She lay in bed reliving their day, then struggled to keep her eyes open while she waited for her husband.

Perhaps he wouldn't come to her tonight. It depended on how long he remained with his friends. But she hoped she might have a chance to speak with him before tomorrow. She was desperate to know how he got his bruises…and why.

She had almost fallen asleep when she heard him come up the stairs. He walked down the hall and stopped at her door. He hesitated for a bit, then opened her door.

"Are you awake?" he whispered.

"Yes. I was waiting for you."

He entered, then closed the door behind himself. He removed his clothes, then slid into bed beside her.

James reached his hand to cup her cheek, then drew it gently through the tawny hair she'd brushed for one hundred strokes.

"I didn't find an opportunity to tell you how lovely you looked today."

His quiet, husky voice seemed on the edge of sleep, but his words wakened every nerve in her body. In truth, she had felt lovely. She would pen a note to her modiste in the morning, with effusive thanks for guiding her choices in the new gowns.

"I particularly like this new gown," Nella whispered.

"I wasn't speaking of the gown, although I quite agree."

His hand found its way out of her lush curls and trailed across her shoulder. "It was your face. Your smile. Everything was alight. So...so exuberant."

"Exuberant?"

"Mm-hm," he said drowsily. "Like your music. Alive. Exuberant. I felt like dancing."

Nella tsk-tsked. "May I remind you, dearest husband. We do not dance."

"We do not?" He raised his head to peer at her. "Still, I stand by what I said. Perhaps we didn't move our feet, but tonight we definitely danced."

Nella smiled and felt the warmth of it linger in her veins. James was right. Today had been perfect. Harmonious. Joyful. Perhaps he was right. Perhaps there was more than one way to dance.

But he was distracting her, and she couldn't allow it just yet.

"Is there something else you wish to tell me?" she asked.

He rolled to his back and placed his forearm over his eyes. "I thought perhaps you might want to know about that," he sighed. "If I pretended to be obtuse, I would ask what it is you want to talk about, but I know you well enough to know what it is you want to know."

"Yes, I suppose you do."

Nella turned on her side and gathered one of his hands in hers and touched his bruised knuckles. She pressed the palm of her other hand against the faint bruise on his cheekbone. "Who gave you these?"

James drew her hand away from his face and kissed her palm.

"It was just a little skirmish."

"Over...?"

"It doesn't matter, Nella."

"I see," she answered, then shifted to her back. "I'm sorry." Her heart ached with such pain she could barely breathe.

"You have no blame in this," he said almost angrily as he came over her. "And we will not speak of it again. Wife."

He pressed angry kisses about her shoulders until at last his mood turned tender.

Nella held him, wishing for words that would make the *need* for words vanish. She wrapped her arms around him and gathered him to her, trying to keep the tears at bay, though she could not.

It was her fault his dear face was battered, his gentle hands scraped.

She should have allowed him to be discovered compromising Lady Blanche. At least he would not have to defend her honor every time he went to Town. Nor would he have had to stand up to the abuse and insults because one of the least appealing women in Society had tricked the most handsome man in all of England into marrying her.

. . . .

Nella rose early the next morning and went down to make sure the preparations for their picnic were in order. When everyone was ready and had leisurely breakfasted, she called for the coach and carriage to be brought around. Patricia, Rosamonde and she, and of course Mrs. Applebaum, would ride together in the coach. Their ladies' maids would follow in the carriage. With the men on horseback, they would proceed to the spot she'd chosen for their day. It wasn't until they were on their way that she was able to relax.

"Oh, Nella. Rosamonde and I can't thank you enough for inviting us to spend time with you. We've missed you."

"As I've missed you," she answered and reached out her hands to grasp her friends' fingers.

"Are you as happy as you seem?" Patricia asked.

Nella felt a blush rising to her cheeks. "I've never been happier. Lord Danvers is the most considerate husband. He is ever so kind."

"And he appears happy," Rosamonde said. "Patricia and I worried that he would resent you for...well, you know. But he doesn't seem to at all."

"Tell me, what is the gossip concerning our marriage. Has the shock and disapproval died down any?"

Her two friends looked at each other.

"Well, that's answer enough, isn't it?"

"There have been several other scandals, but you are still among the main topics of conversation. Your husband's appearance in Town only renewed the speculation surrounding your marriage."

"Well, hopefully, in time, another scandal will surpass the one our marriage caused."

Nella turned the conversation to happier subjects until the carriage came to a halt and the men came to assist the ladies to the ground.

Several Danvers footmen had arrived earlier to set up for their picnic. A large blanket was spread beneath a shade tree and several baskets were placed about, waiting to be opened.

"I suggest a toast," James said, reaching inside one of the baskets and taking out decanters of wine chosen from his well-stocked cellar. He passed the glasses as he filled them.

"To Lord and Lady Danvers," Lord Candleton said as he raised his glass, "for inviting us to spend time with them."

"Hear, hear," they chorused, then took a drink from their glasses.

"To my wife," James said, "for hosting our autumn party, and making this a most enjoyable day," her husband said.

"Hear, hear," they all echoed, lifting their glasses again, then taking a drink.

Nella couldn't help but smile when she looked at her husband. She'd never been complimented like this, especially by someone whose opinion meant more to her than anyone else's.

But it was more than that. Today, James' gaze lingered on her, as if assessing her and finding her most satisfactory.

Nella pressed a hand to the bodice of her new autumn-gold walking suit—the one that minimized in all the right places. She felt transformed. Almost, dare she say it, lovely.

"Thank you," she said studying his face and finding sincerity there. She turned her attention back to her guests. "Could I interest anyone in a short walk before we eat? It's a beautiful day and quite soon after breakfast. Perhaps a walk will make us more hungry for the extravagant meal Cook prepared for us."

"Excellent idea, my lady," Lord Candleton said, extending his arm for Patricia to take.

Viscount Pomeroy extended his arm to Rose, and they followed Candleton and Patricia from the pleasant glade. The ladies' maids stayed to tidy up the picnic while Mrs. Applebaum napped in the sun, content to let the young ones take their stroll.

"That leaves you, my lady," James said and extended his arm to her. "You are stuck with me."

Nella looped her arm through his. "I shall do my best to bear it," she quipped dramatically as they walked behind the other two couples.

"Do you know how happy and proud I am?"

"As well you should be, my lord. Your estate is expansive and beautifully cared for, your staff is thoughtful and meticulous."

James stopped abruptly, turned to look at her, then resumed their walk, shaking his head. "I wasn't speaking of the estate, silly wife. I was speaking of you. How proud I am of you."

Nella lifted her gaze. "I've done nothing extraordinary, James."

"But you have. In less than one day you've greeted our guests as though you've known them forever. You've made everyone feel welcome and at ease. And I think you've even caused your friends and mine to form friendships they weren't expecting to form."

"That was purely accidental, you know. I am not responsible for their friendships. We both are. You because you had the good taste to consort with such agreeable fellows. And me, because my two best friends are the most wonderful people on earth and thankfully your friends are wise enough to realize it."

Her husband tipped his head back and laughed heartily enough that the two couples in front of them turned to see what was so funny.

"You are quite remarkable, Nella."

She hugged his arm closer. "There is nothing remarkable about me. Don't ever think there is."

"And why not."

"Because whenever you fool yourself into believing there is, something will happen to force you into defending me."

He stopped walking and this time Nella was forced to stop, too.

"Don't," he said in a tone that was closer to an order than a request.

Nella regretted what she'd said. It made her appear self-loathing and that wasn't what she wanted him to think. She didn't pity herself. She was used to being the wallflower. She was used to sitting quietly on the sidelines while all the females were asked to dance, or take a turn around the room. No, she didn't pity herself. Quite the opposite. He was the one she pitied. And he deserved all her pity and more.

"Have I told you what I have planned for tomorrow?" she said in an effort to change the subject.

He went along with her change of topics. "No, what are your plans for tomorrow?"

"You and the other men will have to rest well tonight, for tomorrow afternoon I have arranged for all of us to go sailing."

"Sailing?"

"Yes. Covey has found three boats he has assured me we can use to sail about the lake. Should the wind not cooperate, you and your friends will do the rowing. Meanwhile, I and my friends will hold parasols over our pretty heads and recline against a hundred pillows while you show off your muscular prowess."

"Delightful," he said on a laugh. "You are truly delightful."

Nella looked at him and smiled. No one had ever told her before that she was remotely delightful.

Just as no one had ever laughed *with* her instead of at her.

Chapter Nine

ONE DAY TURNED INTO TWO, then two into four and before he knew it, one whole week had gone by. James could scarcely believe it, nor could he remember a time when he'd felt so relaxed, so filled with good cheer, so...cared for. Nella had something special planned for each and every day, and in her subtle way, she always managed to make it look as if he had orchestrated their adventures. He wouldn't be surprised if she suggested he even orchestrated the marvelous weather.

One day, however, they'd had to cut their outdoor activities short when a raincloud interrupted their croquet match, which was a good thing, considering Nella and her friends were trouncing James and his friends.

But that hardly mattered. The men gathered around the billiard table, showing off for the women and challenging each other in several entertaining games while they drank James's most smoldering brandy.

That evening, Nella entertained them again at the piano, and the talented Lady Rosamonde serenaded them with her rather saucy mezzosoprano. She had a lovely voice and Lady Patricia was even coaxed into singing a popular duet while Nella accompanied them.

It was engaging, and a far cry from the rather raucous entertainment in which his gentleman friends usually engaged—in this very same room. Tonight, James felt certain he had never heard anything quite so pretty yet laced with so much humor.

When the entertainment was finished, James stood. "There's a full moon tonight, my friends. Who will join me in the garden for a look at it?"

Without the slightest hesitation, the other five paired easily and followed him onto the terrace. He noted how casually Nella tucked her hand into the crook of his elbow, and he suddenly loved the ease and rightness of it. He drew his other hand across to gather her tucked hand with his fingers.

"So what's on the agenda for tomorrow, wife?" he asked as they were walking down the pebbled path.

"If the weather is agreeable, I thought we'd go for a carriage ride in the afternoon. The girls want to see the shop at that wonderful glass manufactory just beyond the village. Then, in the evening, we'll put a fire in the library and play whist. How does that sound?"

"Perfect. Candleton and Pomeroy just mentioned today that they hadn't seen all of Colworth Abbey. This will give me the opportunity to show off my estate when we take the south road over to the factory."

"Oh, good," she said. "Then, the next evening I thought we might dance."

James drew them to a stop, looked up at the moon, and smiled. "Wait a moment. You've told me repeatedly *we don't dance*."

"Well, that's true. We don't dance. But you do, and so do the rest. I'll play, you'll dance. With Rosamonde and Patricia."

"So who's going to play for *you* to dance?"

"Nobody," Nella smiled. "Because I can't dance."

He stepped in front of her, knowing disbelief was written all over his face. "What?"

"It's sad but true, husband. I cannot dance."

"Now wait a moment, wife. You paint like a professional artist. You play the piano as well as anyone I've ever heard. In fact, you play for the Queen. You organize events as if you've done it your entire life. And you have a personality that makes people feel comfortable after just meeting you. So please be so kind as to explain why it is that you cannot dance? I thought every young lady was taught to dance from the time they could walk. Isn't that the first thing you are taught, along with embroidery and painting and playing the piano?"

"Most females are, I'm sure. But I was the oldest of Father's four daughters. Mother had already passed away, and Father didn't have much time to devote to our social lives. Instead, he hired a dance instructor to teach us, but he didn't see the necessity of putting out money to pay for an accompanist when I could fill the roll. So, I was recruited as the accompanist. I played the piano and my sisters learned to dance. I suppose he thought I would learn by watching, but it didn't seem to work."

"Oh hallelujah! I'm ecstatic there is something I can actually do for you, then. Something which I will happily undertake. I will hire a dance instructor *and* an accompanist and you will learn to dance. Or better yet," he said without thinking, "we will go to London for the Season and attend every ball. We will dance every dance together and you will—"

The full moon came from behind a cloud and he saw the color leave her face.

"No. We will not."

"I'm sorry, Nella. I didn't think. I...forgot."

She was silent for several moments, then said, "We should continue. The others are getting far ahead of us."

"Yes, they are." He looped her arm through his. "Come. We'll catch them up soon enough."

Nella walked down the path as if she was racing to run away from his remarks.

James regretted his comments. After his experience in London two weeks ago, he would never put Nella through the humiliation. How could he have made such a ridiculous suggestion? He was a complete cad.

. . . .

Nella woke the next morning and raced across the room. She reached the washstand bowl just in time to cast up the contents of her stomach. Wary lest it happen again, she clutched her middle and went back to lie down. She wasn't sure she'd be able to get up, but whatever sickness had struck her left after an hour or so and she felt altogether better.

She was glad. She'd so looked forward to touring the estate. There were several places she'd not yet seen.

She dressed, then went down to break her fast.

Everyone had already eaten and had gone to the library to relax before it was time to leave the house.

"Are you all right?" her husband asked when he entered the room and looked at her.

"Yes, of course. I'm fine."

"You seem pale. And there are dark circles beneath your eyes."

"I…um…didn't sleep well last night. That's all."

"All the stress of the last two weeks is wearing on you, I dare say."

"No, I'm fine. Truly."

"Well, sit down and have some breakfast."

James led her to the table, then went to the sideboard and started to fill a plate.

"I'll just have some toast," she said. The thought of eating any more turned her stomach.

"Are you sure?"

"Yes. I'm sure."

"Perhaps you'd like to go up to your room and rest until it's time to leave."

The thought of doing just that was most desirable, but she couldn't. She had guests to see to, and her husband would only think her weak if she neglected her company.

James put his hand to her forehead then removed it. "You're not overly warm, Nella."

"Of course not. I'm not ill."

"Very well." He leaned down and kissed her on the cheek.

Her heart wanted to leap for joy when he showed her just that little display of affection. It was everything she'd wished for.

"Join our guests, James. I'll be there in a moment."

"Very well."

And he left.

Nella drank her tea and ate a bite of dry toast. By the time everyone was ready to leave, she felt much better.

She wasn't sure what she'd eaten the night before to upset her stomach so, but she vowed never to eat it again.

. . . .

James watched Nella as they rode in the open carriage. Her two friends were with her while he, Candleton, and Pomeroy rode their horses.

"What is that?" she asked from the carriage.

James rode closer. "What is what?" he asked.

"That stone wall over there." Nella pointed to the only remaining wall of a crumbling structure.

"It's part of the old stone quarry. They cut squares for the original part of Colworth Abbey here and hauled them to the manor house."

"And what is that?" she asked, pointing to a small cottage.

"That's where the overseer of the quarry lived. It's been vacant for years now, though."

"Might we go inside?" Lady Patricia asked.

"If you wish. But no one's been there for years so I can't guarantee what it looks like inside."

"That's all right," she said, prompting James to order the driver to take them to the cottage.

"Oh, look," Nella said when they entered the small cottage. "Are you sure no one's been here for a long time?"

"I didn't think so, but perhaps someone has. Or at least they've been here to tidy up."

"Yes, I think you're right," Nella said. "What a sweet getaway this would make. I think I could even paint here!"

James lifted her hand and kissed it. "Then paint away, my dearest. Paint to your heart's content."

Laughter bubbled up as a welcome tingle traveled up her arm.

My dearest. He'd called her his dearest. A kiss on the hand and sweet words. The moment seemed as near to paradise as Nella had ever been.

"Come along, you two lovebirds," Rosamonde sang as she swept out the door. "I want to see that glass factory!"

After leaving the small house they toured the rest of Colworth Abbey and spent a fascinating hour at the factory. There was so much to see they barely made it home in time for luncheon.

"Oh, Nella," Rosamonde gushed when they returned to the manor house. "Those hills were beautiful. I can tell you've already found a dozen more scenes to paint."

Nella looked at her husband and smiled. "More than I'll have time to paint in this lifetime. This has to be the most beautiful area in all of England. And just imagine how it will transform in the spring and summer. I'll never have enough paints to complete the scenes I want to put on canvas."

"Are you short on paint, Nella?" James asked.

They'd gone into the drawing room and were enjoying a few quiet moments before luncheon was served.

"Don't you know," she teased, "artists are always short on paint. Like readers are always short on books and embroiderers never have the right color of thread."

Everyone laughed. James was reminded again that his wife had a wonderful sense of humor and he loved anticipating what bit of whimsy might come from her next.

"Then I have an idea. If you'd like."

"What?" she asked, the excitement evident on her face.

"What if we took a short walk after lunch and went into the village. You can stock up on paints, then you and your friends can visit the bookshop while the men and I go to the Tobacco Shoppe. I'm running low on pipe tobacco."

"That sounds wonderful," Nella said when she looked at the excited expressions on her friends' faces.

That is just what they did. After lunch, they all walked to the village.

James was glad that he'd had the foresight to have the carriage follow them to Siding Cross. Not to transport the females, who he thought might need a ride back, but to carry all the items they'd purchased.

He looped his wife's arm through his and walked with her as they returned home.

"Thank you," she said when they were on their way.

"For what?"

"For...everything. For making this day possible. For buying me a necklace I didn't need but love nonetheless. For making my friends feel so welcome. For..."

She lifted her gaze and James suffered from the most exhilarating effect when she smiled at him. It was as if a rush of molten warmth wrapped around his heart. As if he was consumed by a joy he couldn't identify.

She smiled and their gazes locked in a way that confused him. He wanted to kiss her, but didn't. He couldn't. Not here. Not now. Instead, he wrapped his arm around her shoulders and nestled her close to him while they walked back to Colworth Abbey.

The sudden desperation to have his wife in his arms completely flummoxed him. This urgency to feel her lush body beneath him, to feel her arms around him while they made love, was new to him. And astonishingly welcome.

His mind told him to push these thoughts away. To push her away. But instead, he held her close, and for the first time since they married, he realized the depth of his good fortune at taking her for his wife.

Chapter Ten

THEIR AUTUMN HOUSE PARTY was nearly at an end. Everyone would travel back to London tomorrow and the house would be empty again.

Nella hated the thought of seeing her friends return to London. Especially since James had informed her that he had important business he had to take care of in Town and would be leaving at the same time as their guests.

She told herself she shouldn't let his absence bother her. She'd known when they married that he would start to spend more and more time away from her. He was born for the life he had in London and couldn't be required to stay at Colworth Abbey with her. It wasn't the life he wanted or…deserved.

She sat in the library with a book in her hands, yet she wasn't reading. She raised her head at a knock on the door, then smiled when her friends walked into the room.

"There you are," Rosamonde said as she and Patricia entered.

"Yes, you knew right where to find me. Sit down. I'll ring for tea."

"Please don't," Patricia said after she and Rosamonde sat on the sofa across from her. "It's nearly time for luncheon."

"We wanted to thank you, Nella," Rosamonde said reaching for Nella's hand and squeezing her fingers. "We've had the most exciting time ever!"

"Oh, I'm glad."

"Yes," Patricia added, "and Lord Candleton told me he looked forward to dancing with me at the military ball next week."

"Oh, wonderful!" Nella said.

"And Lord Pomeroy asked for permission to call on me when we return to London."

Nella could hardly contain her excitement. This was much more than she'd hoped for. Wouldn't it be wonderful if her friends married James' friends and they could see them regularly?

"Oh, do let me know how things progress," Nella said. "Write me often."

"We will," Rosamonde and Patricia said in unison. Then, their moods turned dour.

"What? Is something wrong?"

"We weren't going to tell you this," Rosamonde said as she gave Patricia a look.

"There was talk brewing before we left London."

"What kind of talk?"

"It seems that Lady Blanche has it in for you."

"For me?" Nella said clapping her hand over her mouth.

"Yes. She says it won't be long before your husband is free of you."

"Free? Of me? Why would she say such a ghastly thing?"

"She says..."

Rosamonde looked to Patricia for reassurance, then continued.

"She says she will forgive him and...and welcome him."

Nella rose from her chair and stumbled across the room. What did Blanche know? What could have given Blanche the idea James would leave his wife? Unless...

Nella shook off the horrid thought.

When she reached the opposite side of the room she placed her hands on the window ledge to steady herself.

"He wouldn't leave me."

Her dear friends rushed to agree.

"Of course he wouldn't! We've seen how much he loves you."

"We just want you to be aware she may still be plotting," Patricia said. "Just be careful."

Nella swiped the tears from her eyes and stared out the window at nothing. "I will. You will let me know what you hear when you return, won't you?"

"Of course," they both answered. "We'll write straightaway. But don't worry," Patricia added. "Lord Danvers loves you. It's obvious from the way he looks at you."

How could she tell her friends that his look was no doubt for show? That it was merely the way a well-bred earl had been taught to treat his wife. But he didn't love her. He couldn't even bring himself to kiss her. Nor could he bear to come to her bed unless he'd bolstered himself with several glasses of brandy.

And, the only reason he came to her bed night after night was to get her with child. Hopefully, a son. The heir he so desperately wanted so he wouldn't have to see her again.

That didn't indicate that he loved her. It indicated that he simply tolerated her. In the kindest way, of course, but still…

Nella masked her hurt and pain with the same expression she'd perfected over the years. She put a smile on her face and returned to the chair where she'd been sitting. She reached for her friends' hands and squeezed them.

"Don't worry about me, you two. I am confident of my husband's regard for me. There is nothing to be concerned over."

Patricia and Rosamonde placed their hands over hers as a bond of their friendship. Then Nella changed the topic to something light and frivolous as she always did when the hurt was deeper than she dared admit.

Even though she dreaded to see her guests leave, she was thankful she would be alone to sort out what she needed to do.

Except she had no idea what that was.

. . . .

A short few hours later they were gone. Everyone had left immediately after an early luncheon and Nella was finally alone. She sat at the piano and played for an hour or more every sad and melancholy piece she knew. Then, she went for a walk in the garden and ended up in the library to read. But how could she concentrate on words in a book when she had so much on her mind to haunt her?

She went to bed early, intending to catch up on the sleep she'd missed over the past two weeks, but couldn't close her eyes. She ached for James' arms around her and his warm body next to her.

She rose early only to race to the chamber pot and repeat the now familiar exercise of casting up the contents of her stomach.

She felt worse today than any day before. She was glad everyone was gone. She wasn't sure she could hide her sickness from her guests or from her husband any longer.

At last she dressed and went down to eat a piece of toast. That was all her stomach could tolerate. When she finished her tea, she instructed Covey to tell Cook she wouldn't need anything for lunch, then went to the library to stare at the words in her book.

It was difficult to focus, now that she was sure. She had suspected it during the house party, but was afraid to let herself think it possible. Now, in the quiet of the last two days as she listened to her body, she knew.

She was with child. And she could scarcely wait for James to return so she could tell him.

Today she had the library's comfortably cushioned wing chair moved closer to the fireplace and sat down with a book she was finding most illuminating. But even as compelling as the words were, it wasn't long before she nodded off.

She wasn't sure how long she'd slept, but she roused to a knock on the door and came awake with a start.

"A Lady Blanche to see you, my lady."

A chill raced down her spine.

She should ring for tea, but that would stretch the encounter out unbearably. She wasn't truly required to do so, as Lady Blanche hadn't shown the courtesy of arriving at an appropriate hour. Still, it was the civil thing to do.

"Show her in, Covey. And bring in a tea tray."

"Yes, my lady."

Nella stood by her chair as Lady Blanche entered the room. She stopped at the doorway, beautiful and fresh as if she hadn't been bounced around in a carriage for the last two hours. She stared at Nella.

There was a hard look in Blanche's eyes. Her hateful glare and pursed lips told Nella from the start to be on her guard. This wasn't a social call. There was nothing at all friendly about it. Her nemesis had come with her claws sharpened.

Just be on your guard had been Rosamonde's final warning. Now Nella saw why. The woman fairly bristled.

"Marriage hasn't changed you at all, Lady Danvers. You are still as frumpy and unattractive as you always were."

"What do you want?"

Blanche entered and walked past Nella to the fireplace. Before they could speak further, Covey appeared with the tea tray and set it on a nearby table. Nella didn't offer her guest a cup of tea. She had been prepared to, but after the woman's rude greeting, that time was past. The sooner her guest was gone the better she would like it.

"I see your husband has come to London several times since you married. No doubt that is because he looks for any chance to escape you. And look!" She turned and gracefully swept her arm in a full arc, taking in the empty room. "Gone again!"

"Why are you here?" Nella asked, stepping forward so she could clearly see Blanche's face. There was something vile in the way she looked at Nella.

"I came to confront you. I came to make sure you understand that I know what you did."

"And what is it you are accusing me of having done?"

"You know what you did, you bitch. You stole James away from me."

"I did not," Nella said. "I saved him from you."

"I'm carrying his child!"

Nella felt as though she'd just been thrown from a high cliff. The pain she experienced was unlike anything she'd ever suffered before.

"And if I don't believe you?"

"Oh, but you do. You know it's not only possible. It's probable. It's true. James would never have married you if he hadn't been tricked into it. And you will have to live with what you did for the rest of your life. You will have to live with the fact that you ruined any possibility for James to ever be happy."

Nella tried not to let Blanche see how much her words upset her but it was impossible. The pain was too raw. Her words too true. She would have to live with what she'd done to James her whole life.

"Can he even bear to make love to you? Or has he spared himself the embarrassment of looking at your ungainly body?"

Blanche continued to taunt Nella with a snide expression on her face. "I daresay, if he has lain with you, he leaves your bed before dawn. I'm sure he spares himself the horror of having to look into your face first thing every morning."

Nella felt her courage shrinking. She could not listen to much more of Blanche's insults. "Why are you doing this? Why have you come to rail at me?"

"Because I want you to know what is going to happen to your husband's babe. It is too late to get rid of the bastard or that would have been my first choice. So, I'm going to go far away to have it. Then, I'm going to leave it in the first back alley I come to. I want you to know that it's your fault your husband's child will grow up alone, unloved, and in squalor. I want you to live with the knowledge that your selfish action has ruined your husband's life and the life of his child."

"You mustn't!" Nella cried.

"Oh must I not? And who, pray tell, would want to raise the little bastard. You?" She hurled the words at Nella.

Nella recoiled. "I...I..."

Blanche gave a vile laugh. "The only way the child survives is if you take it and leave James. Forever."

"But I..."

Blanche drew a small note from her reticule. "This is where I will be in seven months. If you want to rescue the babe, you'll be there. You'll take the babe and then leave England."

Nella gasped.

Blanche threw the note to the floor and swept across the room to the door.

"It's on your ugly head now."

And she was gone.

Nella retrieved the note. A scant line of scribbles spread across the face of the letter.

Bellingshire House, Windermere

She sat unmoving for a long while after the front door had closed and the sounds of Blanche's carriage crunched away from Colworth Abbey. She sat even after the maid came to take the untouched tea tray. She sat long after luncheon was served and went uneaten.

What had she done?

And worse, how could she live with what she'd done?

. . . .

James finished his business as quickly as he could. He was anxious to get back to Nella. Something was wrong but he had no idea what it was that could be making her ill.

He rode out of Town, but first he took the time to stop at his aunt's home.

"Come in, James," his aunt said when he entered her suite of rooms on the first floor.

James went across the room and held his aunt's hands in his. "Hello, Aunt."

"I'd heard you were in Town and so hoped you would stop by before you left. Did your wife accompany you?"

James shook his head. "We just hosted a two-week house party and she preferred to stay in the country and rest."

"Please, sit down."

James sat in the chair beside his aunt.

"How is your wife? I've often thought of the two of you."

James sat forward in his chair. "That's the main reason I've come to see you."

A worried frown covered his aunt's forehead.

"Is something wrong?"

"I'm not sure, Aunt. At first, everything was fine. She was happy, I thought, and we were rubbing along well. Then…"

"Then?"

"For the past week or so she's been ill every day. She doesn't know I realize it, but she gets up each morning and reaches for a basin. She's barely able to eat more than a piece of toast for breakfast. Do you think I should call a doctor for her?"

The frown on his aunt's forehead faded, then there was a twinkle in her eyes and she laughed.

"What? What is it, Aunt?"

"Oh, you men. You know your way around a woman's bedchamber with undeniable familiarity yet you know nothing about women."

"I don't understand," James said, becoming more concerned by the minute.

"Your wife, James, is no doubt pregnant."

James fell back into the chair.

"What?"

He felt as if the air had been knocked from his body. As if every ounce of strength had left him.

"Your wife is with child," his aunt repeated.

"But…" James paused.

"Don't you dare ask how this could have happened, my boy. You are obviously well aware how that part of a marriage works."

"Yes, but I thought it would take a lot longer to… to…"

"It takes only once, you charming simpleton. And you have been married for nearly two months."

"Yes," James said as if his brain was trying to focus in a fog. "But, why has she not told me? Why has she kept this to herself?"

"Why do you think, James?"

"I can't imagine. She knows how excited I will be. From the beginning,

I've wanted nothing more than to have an heir to pass my holdings down to."

"And what were you going to do once you have your heir?"

"Why…" He didn't know how to answer his aunt.

"How secure is your wife in your love for her? Could it be that your wife is afraid of losing you? Could it be that your wife is not confident of your feelings for her and at the first possible moment she thinks you will hare off to London to resume your former lifestyle?"

"No, Aunt. In truth, I've grown quite fond of my wife. She's unlike any woman I've ever met. I even believe that I love her."

His aunt smiled. "Have you told her that?"

James lowered his gaze.

"Then how can she know that you won't leave her the minute you realize she's done her duty as your wife?"

"I—"

"What? Have you assumed your wife can read your mind? Do you think your wife knows how you feel without you saying the words?"

"I've been a fool, haven't I?"

His aunt smiled at him. "No more so than any other of your male counterparts, James. You've all made mistakes where women are concerned, no doubt because we're complicated people and we expect you to inherently understand us when we sometimes don't understand ourselves."

"Thank you, Aunt. I need to get home and have a long conversation with my wife."

"That's an excellent idea, James."

James rose on legs that trembled beneath him and left his aunt's town house. He mounted his horse as if in a dream.

He was going to be a father.

Nella was having a babe.

He'd never felt such excitement in his life. Everything was perfect.

Chapter Eleven

JAMES HANDED HIS REINS OVER to a groom and raced into the house. Covey stood there with the door open and James strode through the foyer.

"Where's my wife, Covey?"

He couldn't wait to see her. Couldn't wait to hold her and tell her he knew what her sickness every morning meant. But when he turned to face Covey, he knew something was wrong.

"What is it, Covey? What's wrong?"

"I'm so glad you've returned, my lord. It's her ladyship."

"What is it? What's wrong?"

James raced for the stairs, eager to get to his wife.

"She's not here, my lord."

James stopped on the third step and retraced his footsteps. "What do you mean, she's not here? Where is she?"

"We don't know, my lord. She went to her rooms to rest and when her maid went in to check on her she was gone."

"Gone, where?"

"We don't know. We've checked the house from top to bottom but she's nowhere to be found."

His heart thundered, beating wildly in his chest. A terror unlike anything he'd experienced before began to waken.

"What happened?" James called as he raced for the music room where he thought it was most likely she'd be.

The room was empty.

"Search the house again. From top to bottom. From the cellar to the attic. She couldn't have gone far. Check every stairway. Maybe she's fallen and is hurt and needs help."

"Very well, my lord. I'll give orders to search the house again."

Several footmen and maids scattered to do his bidding.

"Did anything happen to upset your mistress? Anything, man! Something must have happened."

"Nothing unusual, other than she had a visitor yesterday afternoon."

"Who? Who was here?"

"A Lady Blanche. She seemed acquainted with Lady Danvers. They chatted for a while, then the lady left."

The conniving woman's name made James instantly wary. What would Lady Blanche want with Nella? What possible reason could she have for coming all this way to see her?

"My lord," the stable master said rushing into the house. "It's her ladyship's horse. It's gone."

"Blast! Tell anyone who can ride to find a horse. Now! We need to locate her before dark."

James divided the men into three groups and they rode in search of his wife.

His first destination was the small grouping of tenant households. Perhaps there had been an emergency. She might have been outside when they came to the house for help and went with them in haste.

But no one had seen her.

He turned his horse toward the creek and found the tree where she stowed her paints. But they were tucked away. Now his worry escalated. With every pounding hoof beat he searched his mind. Where could Nella have gone? And why?

He imagined her going for a ride and having an accident. He could see her lying in a ditch bruised and bloody. Or falling into the stream unconscious and drowning.

And in the back of his mind, another question lurked. She shouldn't be riding in her condition, should she?

Bloody hell.

He didn't know. He didn't know anything about pregnancy. He didn't know what was safe for her to do and what wasn't. He didn't know what she should be eating and what she shouldn't. He didn't know how much rest she needed, or anything. What worried him most was whether she even realized yet that she was pregnant. If not, would she cast caution to the wind and throw herself into dangerous circumstances?

"Bloody hell," he growled as he rode over the countryside. He couldn't even see tracks to indicate where she might have gone.

He rode through the meadows and pastures. He went to the sheltered vale where they'd picnicked. But there was no sign of her.

Finally, it became too dark for anyone to see and he was forced to call a halt to the search.

James sat in his study with a decanter of brandy beside him and filled his glass time and again.

Where could she have gone?

And for what purpose?

Something was obviously wrong.

What possible reason might Lady Blanche have had to come see Nella? James knew well the flighty woman's careless tongue. Had she said something to upset his wife?

James knew if he hadn't married Nella he no doubt would have married Blanche eventually, although her personality didn't suit him nearly as well as Nella's did.

He filled his glass again and took a long drink. He knew he should thank God every day for putting Nella in his life. He should say a prayer of thanksgiving because Nella was his wife instead of one of the simpering debutantes who cared more for parties and balls and expensive clothes and jewels than for a beautiful piece of music or a picturesque painting.

James lowered his head and felt the first tear run down his cheek.

Where was she?

What if she was dead?

How bleak life would be without her!

He had never even told her that he loved her.

Why was that?

He was more at ease with her than he was with anyone. He appreciated the finer things in life when he was with her. The beauty of music. The magnificence in a painting. The enjoyment of a quiet conversation. Delighting in mutual friends.

He bounded to his feet and threw the remainder of his brandy to the back of his throat, then paced the room from one end to the other. What if she was out there hurt and bleeding? What if she'd been injured and had lost their babe? What if he never found her? What if she was lost to him forever?

James paced the length of the room more times than he could count. He couldn't sleep. And time seemed to have stopped. The clock on the mantel seemed not to have moved from one time he looked to the next. He couldn't wait for it to be light enough to begin his search again.

At last the pre-dawn light was faint enough for him to return to the stable and saddle his horse. Several stable hands milled about, waiting to join him in his search and he wouldn't turn down their help. The more men searching for Nella, the sooner they'd find her.

They rode away from Colworth Abbey, then scattered when they reached the end of the lane, each rider taking a different area.

James didn't know where he was going. He stopped on a small rise and assessed the options. As he was about to turn toward the village, he realized he'd been on this very spot with Nella. With their friends. The day they'd stumbled across the old stone quarry foreman's cottage.

Excited, he urged his horse to a full gallop. As they crested a knoll, the small cottage came into view. His hopes were high, but it was the smoke coming from the chimney that threw his heart into tumult.

The moment they drew near the cottage, James threw himself from his horse and raced through its small garden. He smashed his hand down on the door's latch and burst inside.

It was early in the morning, and from her looks, Nella had just wakened. Or she hadn't slept yet. Dark circles rimmed her red, swollen eyes and her complexion was a pale shade of gray. It was obvious that she'd been ill.

"Nella?" he said, cautiously stepping to where she stood next to a wash basin.

With one more stride he pulled her into his arms.

"No," she said, holding a wet cloth to her face. "Leave me."

"I'm not leaving you. You need someone with you."

She shook her head.

"Not you. Oh, God help me."

She clutched at her stomach.

"Not you, my lord. Not after what I've done to you."

"Sit down, Nella." He moved her to a chair next to the table.

She sat. Not because she was following his orders, he was sure, but because she was so weak she couldn't stand on her feet.

"Stay here. I've got to let the rest of them know I've found you."

James stepped out of the house and fired his gun. Moments later, several of the men rode into the yard and he told them he'd found her. He ordered them to return to the house and tell Covey to have a bath and food prepared.

When everyone had gone, he went inside to be with his wife.

She stood beside the basin as if she needed to be close to it in case she became ill again.

He closed the door and stood there for several moments. There was something about the expression on Nella's face that terrified him. An expression that told him something truly awful had happened.

"What is it, Nella? Why are you here?"

She shook her head, then turned her back to him. "I needed to think. Please, leave me alone."

"I'm not leaving you, Nella."

She walked over to the small table and sat on one of its two chairs.

"I think we need to talk."

She lifted her gaze. "Do you?"

"Yes, I do." James stepped over to the table and sat in the chair opposite her. "Please, tell me what's wrong."

"I need time, James."

"Time for what, Nella?"

"Time to work out what I'm going to do."

"What do you mean, what you're going to do?"

She didn't answer him, but sat in silence. At last she lifted her gaze and looked at him. "Are you hurt? Did you get into another fight while you were in London?" she asked, reaching for his hands. She ran her fingers across his knuckles, then searched his face for any evidence of bruises.

"There was no fighting, Nella. It was just that once."

She lowered her gaze and clenched her hands in her lap, then nodded as if his answer lifted at least one heavy burden from her shoulders.

"Nella, what's wrong? Please, tell me."

She lifted her gaze and James' heart shattered in his chest. Her eyes were filled with tears that were ready to spill from her lashes.

"I want you to know, I'll do whatever you wish. We haven't been married all that long. I'll agree to a divorce. You can claim whatever reason you want. Say I was unfaithful. Or that I wasn't a good wife. Or—"

"Stop it, Nella!" he said, bolting to his feet. "Why on earth are you talking about a divorce? We're married! You're my wife!"

James skirted the table and knelt on the floor beside her. He reached for her hands and held them.

Nella shook her head and pulled her hands out of his grasp. "I'm so sorry. If only I had known, I would have let things play out as they intended. But I didn't know. I didn't know."

"You didn't know what?"

"About Lady Blanche."

He was confused. "What about Lady Blanche?"

"Oh, James," she said on a moan. "I'm so sorry."

She lifted her face and looked at him. Tears she'd held at bay until now ran down her cheeks. There was so much hurt and anguish on her face and in her eyes, it ripped his heart from his chest. He'd never seen such raw pain in a person's eyes as he did now. As if his dear wife hurt to her very soul.

"Please believe me when I tell you that I didn't know. I didn't mean to hurt you. I only thought to. . ."

"Thought to what?"

"To save you. And now I don't know what to do. I don't know how to make things right."

"What things do you have to make right?"

"Everything," she said and stood.

"Is that why you ran away?" he asked. "Is that why you left Colworth Abbey?"

She wrapped her arms around her middle. "I needed to think. And there were too many memories of you there. I couldn't think."

"What did you have to think about?"

James gathered her close and held her as tightly as he dared.

"I should have just let it happen the way they planned it."

"But I've told you, Nella,—"

Her small cry stopped his words from spilling out as she struggled to calm her breathing.

"I didn't know she was carrying your child and she was desperate to marry you. I ruined it all, James. I'm so sorry. I ruined your life. And hers. And the life of your child."

James dropped his arms from his wife and staggered back a step. "Why do you think Blanche is carrying my child?"

"She told me," Nella said through her tears. "She was here two days ago and...and...she told me," Nella finished in a rush of sobs. "And it was...obvious that she's with child. Oh, James! I've ruined everything. She's going away to have your baby. She intends to give it away to the first person who will take it. Or leave it in some back alley. She's going to pawn off your baby as if it's a used piece of clothing or an unwanted pet. Unless..."

His heart froze. "Unless?"

She gulped. "Unless I take the babe after it's born and leave England. And you."

It was diabolical. He could strangle the woman for putting such an untenable burden on his dear wife.

"Nella, listen to me." James stood on shaky legs and held his wife. "If Lady Blanche is having a baby, it's not mine."

Nella shook her head. "You don't have to deny it, James. Everyone in the *ton* thought you and Blanche would marry. You were so well-suited to each other. She's the most beautiful creature in Society, and you're the most handsome. It was obvious from the start that you were well-fitted to each other and you wouldn't have given me even a first look if I hadn't tricked you. And now…now…oh, James. I'm so sorry. Tell me what to do to make things right," she begged.

James reached for his wife's hands and held them. "Nella, you don't have to do anything. Everything is perfect as it is."

"No." She twisted out of his grasp. "Nothing is perfect. I've ruined everything and I know you must hate me. You'll always hate me."

"I don't hate you. I have never hated you."

"You don't have to say that. I know you couldn't possibly mean it. And I can't blame you. I'm not the woman you wanted for your wife." She struck a fisted hand gently against his chest and took a step back. "Do you realize, James, you have never even kissed me? Do you think I don't know why? Do you think I don't know that you find it repulsive to kiss me?"

"That's not true, Nella." He reached to pull her back. He intended to kiss her until she was senseless, but she twisted out of his grasp.

"Oh, James. Do you think I don't know that as soon as I provide you with an heir you'll no longer come to my bed? Do you think me such a fool that I haven't realized you cannot even make love to me until you drink enough to give you the courage to touch me?"

James reeled at her words, yet he could only find truth in them.

"Is that why you haven't told me that you're going to have my babe?"

Her eyes opened wide and her mouth formed a quivering 'O'.

"You know?"

"Yes, I know. Why didn't you tell me?"

"I wasn't ready to lose you yet."

There weren't words that could have hurt him more than the words she'd just uttered. Perhaps in the beginning he thought he would leave her and go to London when he was assured she was having a child, but that was true no longer. Just as it wasn't true that he needed a drink or two for courage before he could make love to her. Most nights he couldn't wait to pull her into his arms. To have her beneath him while he made love to her. To hold her and feel her hands caress him.

"Oh, Nella. I'm so sorry. I never meant for you to doubt that I cared for you."

"How could you care for me?" she asked quietly. "I forced you to marry me. How could you want me?" She walked away from him. "Now please, go away and leave me be."

James looked at his wife. It pained him greatly to know how he'd hurt her. How unloved he'd made her feel even though he hadn't intended to. How unwanted he'd let her feel even though he wanted her more desperately than he'd ever be able to prove to her.

"Please come home with me, Nella. We have much to discuss yet."

She shook her head.

"Please," he said. He grasped her by the arms and locked his gaze with hers. "Please," he said, then lowered his head and pressed his lips to hers.

He couldn't fathom why this was the first time he'd kissed her. How could he have been so unfeeling? So unkind?

He kissed her once, softly, gently. Then, kissed her again.

There was so much he wanted to teach her. So much he was desperate to show her.

He wrapped his arms around her and gathered her close to him. When he had her in his grasp, he deepened his kiss. Not enough to frighten her, but enough to show her the depth of his feeling for her.

At first he feared she would not respond to his kisses, but on a soft moan she tilted her head and wrapped her arms around his neck.

"James," she whispered and he kissed her again.

Her voice rasped, and her breathing became heavy.

"Yes, Nella. Kiss me. Let me show you how much I love you."

She stiffened in his arms.

"Yes, Nella. I love you. I *love* you. I love everything about you. You are one of the most tender, most talented, most caring persons I've ever met. I don't care a whit if you can't dance. I'll teach you. I promise. Then there will be nothing you can't do."

He brought his mouth down on hers again and kissed her once more.

"I love you," he said when he lifted his mouth from hers. "Please, don't ever doubt that I do. I couldn't live without you."

She answered his kiss with a kiss filled with passion. He'd never doubted that she cared for him. If she hadn't cared for him, she wouldn't have saved him from Blanche's deception.

"Come now," he said. "Let me take you home."

"What about Blanche?"

"I can do nothing about Blanche. If she's carrying a child, that child is not mine. It's someone else's."

"Truly?"

"Of course, truly. I've never lain with her."

"Then why did she tell me she was carrying your child?"

"To hurt you. Because she's a spoiled, manipulative female who is used to getting what she wants and you ruined her plans."

"But—"

"But nothing, Nella. Marrying you was the best thing that ever happened to me."

"Why did you agree to marry me, James? I offered you a way out."

James smiled. "Yes, you did. But we have my aunt to thank for my decision."

"Your aunt?"

"Yes. She knew before I did that you would be a perfect match for me and persuaded me to take you as my wife. I will always be indebted to her. I've found a love with you I don't deserve. I've discovered a life I never thought I'd have."

A small sob spilled from Nella's lips.

"What?" he asked. "What has you so worried?"

Nella drew a long breath. "The child, my love. Blanche's child. It doesn't deserve—"

He placed a finger across her lips to hush her words. "We'll be there to get the child when the time comes, Nella. I promise. If we don't discover who the father is, we'll place the babe in a good home, with people who will love it. I promise."

As soon as she registered what he was saying, she threw her arms around him and hugged fiercely.

"James. Oh, James! You are the dearest man!"

James laughed and held her closer. He nestled her to him and wrapped his arms around her. He never wanted to let her go. "I love you, Nella. I love you so much I'm afraid my heart will break from the thought of ever losing you. You've shown me a love I didn't think was possible and I can't live without you."

"Are you sure?" she asked.

"I've never been more sure of anything in my life. Now, come with me and let's make a home for the child you're carrying. Our child."

"Gladly, James," she whispered as she leaned up to kiss him.

And he took her back to Colworth Abbey, where she belonged.

. . . .

James woke the following morning to the sounds of Nella quietly retching.

"Nella," he said when she came back into the bedchamber. "Come back to bed with me."

She didn't argue, but made her way back in the pre-dawn hours and slid into the bed next to him.

"I'm sorry I woke you," she whispered. She wrapped her arms around him and nestled her head beneath his chin.

"I only wish you wouldn't have to suffer so." He lowered his head and kissed her forehead.

"It's only your child telling me he or she is healthy and growing inside me."

"I've decided it's a little girl," he said as he nuzzled her chin.

"What makes you think that?"

"Because I want a little girl just like her mother. I want a little girl to paint me pictures I can hang on my study walls, and I want to listen to the sound of my little daughter practicing her piano so she can become as talented as her mother. And a little girl who can snuggle on my lap and listen while I read her stories."

"Oh, James," she said as she stretched lazily. "Actually, I don't care if it's a boy or a girl as long as it has your remarkable good looks. And doesn't slurp his or her tea."

"Ha. Can you believe we were fortunate enough to make another human being to carry on our name and talents?"

"It is quite remarkable, isn't it?"

"Yes. Quite." He drew her close again. "When I think of how our life together began, I consider it a miracle. Do you remember how you refused to marry me at first?"

"Yes. What a fool I was."

"Which reminds me," he said, changing the subject. "Have you written to your friends yet to tell them our good news?"

"No, but I will. And soon. I can't wait to hear if their relationships are blossoming with Candleton and Pomeroy."

"I think my friends were quite taken with your friends."

"Wouldn't it be wonderful if they found as true a love as we have, James?"

"Yes, wonderful indeed. It would prove that we have superb taste in friends. And I can't wait to tell them we're going to have a little girl."

"Yes do," Nella laughed. "That will just about guarantee that we'll have a boy!"

James kissed her fiercely. "Well of course we will, my love. Because I insist upon at least one of each."

"Oh, James," she said as tears ran down her cheeks.

He lowered his head and kissed her again. "We seem to have done an all right job of things, haven't we."

"Yes, we have," she smiled.

"Except for one thing," he said soberly.

"What's that, my dear perfectionist?"

James stretched his arms behind his head and gave a dramatic sigh.

"You, my dearest, have not yet learned to dance."

Chapter Twelve

Four months later

He was going to tie her to the bedpost for sure, he fumed.

"For the last time, it's not safe for you to travel."

"Oh fie! I'm barely six months, James, and I've never felt better. Please, let me come with you. I'll stay in the carriage. And besides, you'll need someone to hold the babe until we get to the vicar's home in Lancashire."

"I can do that just fine."

"Pish-tosh!" Nella gave him her most dramatic look. "And what if the infant requires a change of nappy. Hm? You'll do that, as well?"

James recoiled.

Bloody hell. He hadn't thought of nasty nappies.

"Nella, darling, I'll work it out."

She grinned. "You'll do no such thing. Because I'll be there." She hooked elbows with him and sidled close. "You know you'll want me with you." She turned her face up to him and delivered her most engaging smile. The one he could never resist.

"You're positively wicked, my little minx."

"Then I may go?"

She fairly jumped for joy.

"On condition that you don't set one foot out of the carriage."

Nella swatted his arm. "We'll be in Windermere, forgetful husband. You can't possibly deny me the opportunity to do a bit of shopping."

James sighed. Perhaps he should wish for a boy. He had begun to discover that as sweet as they could often be, girls were dreadfully hard to argue with.

"All right. Shopping only." He tapped her nose with his forefinger. "But you'll let me handle things at Bellingshire House."

"Absolutely, my love. I truly do not want to be anywhere near that woman. And the quicker we get that innocent babe out of her hands, the happier I will be."

"And that is forever my life's goal, my dear. Making you happy."

The kiss she surprised him with put their argument to rest.

"You'll have to come up with another goal, darling husband," Nella cooed, "because every moment of every day with you makes me happy."

He laughed. How he loved the way she made him feel like king of her world.

"Well, then, wife. Be ready at eight o'clock tomorrow. We are to be at Bellingshire House by noon. I won't have time to wait for any primping lassies."

"I shall come in my nightclothes, if need be."

James wheeled around, half shocked at her statement, half worried she might be serious. Her laughter reassured him. She would be ready. And fully clothed.

. . . .

Nella sighed. The coach to Windermere hadn't been nearly as awful as she had anticipated. A month before, James had insisted his coachman put new springs and gadgets on the coach's undercarriage so it would rock as gently as a cradle. The man had driven it around the countryside for hours breaking in the new hardware. And it had worked.

Once she alighted from the coach in Windermere, it took her only a moment to recover her land legs. Her maid, Treadway, fussed over her briefly until she was finally satisfied that Nella had made the trip unscathed.

"Crowley's is at the end of Portsmouth Avenue. I'll meet you there at two o'clock." James squeezed her hand. "Don't be late."

"I shan't," she assured him. In truth, she felt she could spend days here in the charming Windermere shops. But a couple of hours would have to suffice.

James backed away and returned to the coach, calling directions to his coachman.

On her own while James went to Bellingshire House to collect Lady Blanche's infant son, Nella led Treadway into *Windermere Mercantile.*

"I'll look for the china I wish to replace, Treadway. You look over there for some baby things. I don't want to leave Blanche's babe with Vicar and Mrs. Chancellor without a few necessary items."

Treadway nodded, pleased to have a mission of her own.

In truth, Nella already felt a connection to the child. While she believed her husband completely, the poor little thing's vulnerability as long as he remained with his mother had sealed within her a commitment to sponsor the child into his new life. How grateful she was that James shared that commitment.

The china she sought proved more of a problem than she'd expected. By the time she had narrowed the choices to only three, they had been in the store for more than an hour. If she were to get to the wonderful millinery shop she had seen, she needed to go now.

"Treadway? When you've finished purchasing the baby things, come to this counter and choose a china set. Twelve place settings will do. I can't decide, so you choose. Get both the tea cups and the demitasse cups. Have them wrapped and ask the valet to carry them with you to Crowley's. I'm going to pop into that darling millinery at the end of the street. I'll meet you at Crowley's at a quarter to. All right?"

Treadway beamed her assent.

Nella had no doubt she would choose the best set. The girl was masterful at matching jewelry with gowns. She would easily do as well with china. Besides, Nella liked all three sets of bone china equally well.

Free at last, Nella darted as ably as an almost-seven-month pregnant female could out onto the sidewalk. It took just minutes to reach the end of the street where the charming millinery shop was located. If the hats displayed in the window case were any indication, this milliner was top rung.

With nobody to hurry her along, Nella wandered the three aisles of the shop, collecting riding gloves and a hat that would go well with her herringbone riding habit. She stepped around a ladder where a shop girl was retrieving samples from a hundred button drawers that lined the wall. Once safely past, she stopped at a table laden with lace.

On impulse, Nella snatched up a charming bundle of lace remnants, sure she could use them on her own babe's growing wardrobe. As she turned to lay them on the counter, a voice from behind her froze her where she stood.

"You never learn, do you."

Nella whirled toward the voice and choked back a startled yelp as she saw Lady Blanche stepping toward her. The woman's face was frozen in a look even more hateful than Nella had seen months earlier.

And worse. She looked haggard, as if giving birth had stripped her healthy glow and replaced it with stark whiteness.

"You…you don't look well, my lady. You should sit down."

Blanche ignored her and took another step closer. Now she was near enough that Nella could see the milk stains badly soaking the front of the woman's gown. Knowing Lady Blanche's vanity, it was a shocking thing to see her in that state.

"How did you know I was here?" Nella asked, trying to keep her voice from trembling.

The woman cackled, a hollow, deranged sound. "I was just leaving Bellingshire House. Can you see it? Just there on the hill." She breathed a seething breath. "I saw the coach let you out down here, and then your bastard of a husband showed up to take the brat."

Nella turned and easily spotted the large house that sat on a knoll not far from the center of town.

"You were supposed to come alone. *You* were supposed to take the babe and leave James. That's all you had to do. Just disappear!"

With each statement she moved closer, gathering herself in a menacing way.

"But you had to bring him, didn't you. You just had to ruin my life all over again."

"Ruin? I don't—"

The woman staggered, knocking into a table and sending its display of hats flying in every direction.

"You brought him to humiliate me, didn't you."

Nella cringed at the pure hatred that flowed from Blanche's stiff lips.

"No, I—"

"You were to collect the brat and leave the country. That was our arrangement. But oh, no, you wanted to keep the brat and James, too." She cocked her head to the side as if hearing voices. "I couldn't understand why you'd take the brat, but now I see." She gestured at Nella's swollen stomach. "You're probably afraid yours will turn out to be a mongrel."

Lady Blanche let out a vile sound that seemed to start as a laugh and ended as a howl. Her eyes turned manic and Nella realized Lady Blanche had lost her grip on sanity.

"We're taking the child to a good ho—"

Lady Blanche struck out with both hands and pushed Nella back a step.

"You'll not touch the brat." She pushed again harder, forcing Nella to back into a display table. "You'll just leave. Now!" She slapped Nella. "Get out. Leave. Go anywhere you like, as long as it's far away from James."

With each word her anger escalated. "Now get out! Get out! Get out!"

She grabbed Nella and flung her sideways. Out of instinct, Nella reached out for support as she began to fall. She grabbed at Blanche and the two crashed into the table and tumbled to the floor. Nella tried to protect her babe, but the fall was bruising.

Nella was dazed, and clutched at her abdomen as if she could discern whether the unborn child was all right.

The proprietor of the store ran in from a back room, shouting orders to his shop girl. "Summon a doctor!"

Nella recovered herself and rose to her knees, grateful to know nothing was broken. But to her horror, she saw that Blanche had not fared so well. Blood was now seeping from her temple where she had struck her head as she fell. Her eyes rolled back, focused, then rolled back again.

"Are you all right?" The man asked as he crouched beside Nella.

"Y-yes. I...I think so. But this woman needs that doctor. Now!"

"No. No doctor." Nella heard the weak protest and turned to Lady Blanche.

It was clear the woman was fearfully injured, but as Blanche struggled to focus, she reached a hand to Nella. The least Nella could do was give the poor woman some comfort until the doctor arrived.

Blanche began to speak, but Nella had to lean close to hear her weak voice.

"You...think you're such a...a good woman." Lady Blanche coughed, leaving a red tinge in the corners of her mouth. "It's a pity he'll...never... love you."

Nella grasped Blanche's hand more firmly. It would be so easy to answer tit for tat, to spew vitriol at the woman as she had railed at Nella. But no words formed in her mind. Instead, her heart overflowed with pity.

"God be with you," Nella whispered.

And in what seemed the same instant, Blanche's breathing stilled, and James came crashing into the millinery shop.

"Nella!"

He rushed to her side and drew her away from the still figure on the floor.

"They said a woman was bleeding, and I thought...I was afraid...oh, Nella, I was so afraid." He softened his crushing grip and leaned back.

"Are you all right?"

"Yes, my love, I'm all right."

She leaned into him, and as the trembling began, blackness overtook her.

. . . .

For the next two months James watched Nella constantly, knowing he was being overprotective and finding it impossible to behave any other way. He'd thought he loved her as much as any man could, but seeing her crumpled on the floor of the millinery, then watching her cuddle and coo over Blanche's babe as they returned from Windermere had stolen his heart all over again.

Vicar Chancellor and his wife were thrilled to receive the baby they'd longed for, and James was satisfied that all in all, things had turned out for the best. Except for Blanche's tragic accident.

But he couldn't think of that now. All he could do was pace the room. From one side of his study to the other, he trod the floor like every expectant father before him had, praying for his own child to be safely delivered into this world.

"You're going to wear the carpet out if you keep pacing like you've been," Candleton said.

He and Pomeroy had arrived two weeks ago along with Nella's best friends for the arrival of their babe. The doctor was secluded with Nella and her friends and it took every ounce of James' willpower to remain in the library. He couldn't understand why he wasn't allowed above with her.

He walked the perimeter of the room, then walked from corner to corner and back again. Every few steps he would hear a cry of pain from upstairs and would stop and swipe his hand down his face.

Nella was having their baby.

Thankfully, Aunt Angela was with her along with the doctor and the nurse he'd brought with him.

James wanted to be with her, too, but he was chased out of the room as if he didn't have a role to play in the baby's birth. But he did. He'd been with her from the beginning and wanted to be with her now.

Nella was sure the babe was a boy, but James prayed it would be a little girl. A pretty, pudgy baby girl who looked exactly like her mother.

Another cry escaped the bedchamber. Aunt Angela had come down a few minutes earlier and informed him it was almost over—that the babe was nearly here. But it had seemed like hours ago. And there was still no babe. James didn't know how much more he could take. He hated to think of his wife going through this alone.

Suddenly, he heard a pain-filled utterance, then a healthy baby's cry.

James ran to the stairs and clutched the newel post. He wanted to run up the stairs, but his aunt said she would call him when his wife was ready to receive him.

He put one foot on the bottom step as if that would give him a head start when the time came. Finally, his Aunt Angela appeared at the top of the stairs. Her smile was broad and her eyes glimmered with excitement.

"Your babe has arrived, my lord. And is anxious to meet her father."

"Her?" he said bounding up the stairs. "It's a her? A girl?"

"Yes, dear boy," Aunt Angela said as he ran past her. "It's a girl."

James raced through the bedchamber door and stopped short.

Nella sat propped on the pillows with a bundle in her arms. It was the most beautiful sight he'd ever seen. He walked to the bed on legs that felt weak beneath him. The sight of her blurred before him and he realized he had tears in his eyes.

"Oh, Nella," he said, reaching for her one free hand. "My beautiful, beautiful Nella." He leaned over and kissed her.

She returned his kiss and cupped her palm to his cheek. "Come and greet your daughter, my lord. She has been most anxious to meet you."

Nella lifted the bundle in her arms and placed it in his.

The babe weighed nothing. Absolutely nothing, and he was suddenly terrified that she would break if he handled her wrong.

"Oh, James. Don't worry. She's not that fragile. She has a strong, substantial mother and a hardy, formidable father. She comes from sturdy stock. I only hope she grows up to have your fine form."

"And I pray she grows up exactly like her mother in every way."

James sat in the chair near the bed and held his daughter. He couldn't take his eyes off of her. She even clutched his finger when he held it close to her little chest, just above her happily beating heart.

"Oh, Nella. She's beautiful."

His wife laughed. "No, she's not. Not yet anyway. Your aunt tells me that no baby is born beautiful. They become beautiful over time."

"Well, our daughter is the exception. I think she's the most beautiful babe ever born. And," he said, taking his eyes from the baby to look lovingly at Nella, "I think she's going to have your beautiful hair."

Nella simply beamed and reached for his hand. "You're not disappointed then, that she isn't a boy?"

"I've never been happier in my life. There will be plenty of time for a boy. But, for now, a girl suits me just fine. After all, our boy will need an older sister to keep him on the straight and narrow path, won't he?"

Nella laughed tiredly. "I'm glad you're pleased," she said. "Now, what should we call her? Have you chosen a name?"

"I haven't thought of that. Have you?"

"If you don't mind, I'd like to name her after my mother. She would be so happy if she were here."

"What was your mother's name?"

"Eliza."

"That's beautiful. We'll call her Eliza." James looked down at his daughter and smiled. "Hello, Eliza Petronella. Welcome to your family."

James watched his new daughter for several wonderful moments, then looked at his wife.

"Have I told you recently how grateful I am that you chose to save me that night?"

"Quite often, husband."

"Then, let me say it again so you never forget. I love you, Nella. If I could live a thousand lives, I'd wish to live them all with you."

He lifted her hand and pressed a sweet kiss as a tear of joy slid from her eye. In that moment he saw exactly what he must do.

She'd saved him from the world.

Now he would give her back to it.

Epilogue

"I'VE CHANGED MY MIND, JAMES," Nella said as they neared the Marquess and Marchioness of Grantville's town house. "Let's return home."

Her husband smiled down at her, then reached for her hand and held it. "I'm right here with you, Nella. We won't be alone. Patricia and Rosamonde will be here and so will Candleton and Pomeroy."

"I know, but..."

"You'll be fine." He drew a finger down her cheek. "And you look beautiful."

Nella trembled like a leaf in a gale storm. This was the first time since they'd married that she'd returned to London. The first time she'd ventured into a large formal affair in the year and a half they'd been married, and she wasn't sure she had the courage to go through with it.

Everyone would be there—the ones who had ignored her, the ones who had shamed her.

Nella thought of everything that could go wrong: Blanche's two conspirators could turn their backs on her; the guests could snicker and giggle at her; there might be rude comments about how she looked in James' arms as they danced. Or gads, she might even fall on her face.

This night was bound to be a disaster. James could even get into a fight defending her honor like he had the first time he'd come to London after they were married.

Why had she let her husband talk her into coming to Town?

Nella knew his idea had taken seed the moment she'd mentioned to him that try as she might, she couldn't dance. Hearing her regret, James had taken it upon himself to hire a pianist. He'd moved the piano into the solarium where they would have a larger space, and he had taught her himself.

He was a brilliant instructor. Kind and encouraging.

She treasured every moment of those hours as she learned to float in his arms about the solarium. She'd stumbled over and over as she strove to put her feet where they belonged. And then he'd forced her to look into his eyes, to keep her gaze fixed on him as they moved. And magically, she began to dance.

He himself was a marvelous dancer, but she had known he was. She'd watched him every time he'd partnered one of the sought-after debutantes during several Seasons. She'd sat on a chair at the side of the room and watched with envy as he'd twirled female after female across the floor, imagining that she was the girl in his arms. And now she was and she was terrified.

She smoothed the gossamer layer of her gown with her hands gloved in silver—another of his gifts. He'd taken her to the best modiste in London who insisted she choose only certain fabrics—ones that would move and shift and float with each turn. And tonight, when James had presented her with the uniquely French silver gloves he'd ordered from Paris, she had simply melted. At first glance, they were a glistening white, but a second look showed the cleverly woven silver threads that caught the light in magical ways.

But it was the tiara that transformed her—the tiara that had been in his family for generations. It sat perfectly among her curls. When she looked in the mirror she scarcely saw herself, because the tiara drew her eye upward. She prayed it would do the same for others, drawing every eye away from her and upward toward its crowning glory.

Still, she couldn't help but feel uneasy this first time back mixing with the *ton*.

"But, what if—"

"There are no 'what ifs' Nella. You dance as well as you play the piano, and paint landscapes. You're as proficient at dancing as you are at being a mother."

Nella clenched her hands in her lap. "How I wish I was home with Eliza right now."

"You will be soon. We'll leave for Colworth Abbey at the end of the week. After tonight there's the concert and the opera, and then we shall wend our way home."

"It's been a wonderful three weeks, James. I can't thank you enough. I truly missed the music and the excitement of London."

"And the shopping?"

"Oh, yes. And the shopping. And the teas I was invited to. And seeing Patricia and Rosamonde again. It was nearly like it used to be."

"And just remember. We will have to return in three months' time for Rosamonde's wedding to Candleton, and Patricia's wedding to Pomeroy. Whoever would have thought our marriage could bring our friends together, too?"

"It's wonderful, isn't it?" Nella said.

"Now, get ready," James advised. "We're here."

"Oh, James."

"You'll be fine, Nella. I'm right here with you. Just be ready. I promised you a night of dancing." He skimmed a finger beneath her chin. "And you promised me the same."

Just as Nella was about to tell her husband he was free to dance with anyone he pleased, he leaned down and kissed her. "Remember, my love. My eyes are for you alone."

Nella felt a tear spill down her cheek. His dear declaration moved her more than any words he could have chosen. The feeling so overwhelmed her that she was certain she would shatter into a million sparkling pieces.

But at that moment the carriage stopped. James dismounted and took her by the hand to help her alight. Then without hesitation, he escorted her into the ballroom.

Everything was as she remembered, except for the memory of being ignored by the members of the *ton*. Tonight all eyes were focused on her. Conversation stopped the second their names were announced as everyone turned in her direction. Perhaps their focus was on James, and how unfortunate it was that the most handsome man in the world was tied to a frumpy, overweight wife.

She paused, nearly missing a step, but James kept her secure and leaned close to her ear.

"They're quite taken aback, my love," he whispered.

"By what?" In truth, she was ready to flee.

"By your transformation, of course."

He smiled and gave her the wink she'd never seen him share with another. She searched his face and found her heart soaring as she realized his sincerity.

If there had been a transformation, it was all his doing, and she loved him wildly for it. Transformation at his hands had given her the courage to step into her role as wife, to step into motherhood, to step into this room. She loved him all the more for it.

Rosamonde and Patricia, along with their fellows, made their way to greet them.

"Together again!"

The four greeted Nella and James with all the enthusiasm she would have expected.

"Let's find a glass of champagne for you, shall we?"

"I'm afraid it will have to wait," James said. "They're playing a waltz and I promised my wife we would dance every dance."

Nella blushed. Dancing away with the love of her life was exactly what she wished to do, and she was quite afraid that her face showed it.

James led her into the dancing melee and turned her into his arms. They went through the steps as masterfully as if they'd been born waltzing. With each turn, the gossamer layers of her gown stretched and flowed, clinging to her ankles then whisking away in graceful swirls. She had never felt more lovely.

They twirled across the floor and nothing could make her believe they were not floating on air.

"Do you see the looks of admiration, my love?"

Nella smiled. "Those are looks of envy, James. Can't you tell the difference? Every female here is envious because your arms are around me instead of them."

"I think not. I do believe they're astonished because no one realized how wonderfully you danced until now."

"And I have you to thank for it. Without you, I would be sitting along the wall."

"And I would have missed being blessed with the most perfect wife any man could ever hope for. I love you, Nella."

His words lingered in her ears, words delivered with tenderness and infused with truth.

He loved her.

Nella could not contain her smile. To think she might have missed this glorious night!

James leaned in and touched his forehead to hers. And then, without warning, he kissed her. Sweetly. Lovingly.

Before the whole world.

Making her heart beat wildly in her breast.

And neither of them missed a single step.

A half million pages of Laura Landon books
are read each month.
Read more by looking for
Laura on Amazon,
or at www.lauralandon.com.

Linger in the pages of a great love story.
Read Laura Landon Victorian Romance!

About Laura Landon

Laura Landon enjoyed ten years as a high school teacher and nine years making sundaes and malts in her very own ice cream shop, but once she penned her first novel, she closed up shop to spend every free minute writing. Now she enjoys creating her very own heroes and heroines, and making sure they find their happily ever after.

A vital member of her rural community, Laura directed the town's Quasquicentennial, organized funding for an exercise center for the town, and serves on the hospital board.

Laura lives in the Midwest, surrounded by her family and friends. She has written thirty Victorian historical romances, all of which are selling worldwide in English, one in Japanese, and several in German. Two are Scottish historicals.

Always beautifully set and with a mysterious twist or bit of suspense, Laura's books average a million pages a month read by her loyal readers.

LAURA LANDON IS A PRAIRIE MUSE PLATINUM,
KINDLE PRESS, AND AMAZON MONTLAKE AUTHOR

WWW.LAURALANDON.COM

SEASONS

Other Books by Laura Landon
Published by Prairie Muse Publishing

SHATTERED DREAMS

WHEN LOVE IS ENOUGH

BROKEN PROMISE

A MATTER OF CHOICE

MORE THAN WILLING

NOT MINE TO GIVE

LOVE UNBIDDEN

KEEPER OF MY HEART

THE DARK DUKE

CAST IN SHADOWS

CAST IN RUIN

CAST IN ICE

CAST IN SCANDAL (novella)

JADED MOON

THE DEVIL'S GIFT

ONE MYSTICAL MOMENT

BEWARE THE RICH MAN

BEWITCHED BY THE POOR MAN

BETRAYED BY THE BEGGAR MAN

BEHOLD THE THIEF

WINTER'S COLD HEART

SPRING'S TENDER HEART

SUMMER'S DISTANT HEART

AUTUMN'S WILD HEART

Published by Montlake Romance

SILENT REVENGE

INTIMATE SURRENDER

Laura Landon

INTIMATE DECEPTION
THE MOST TO LOSE
A RISK WORTH TAKING
BETRAYED BY YOUR KISS
RANSOMED JEWELS

Published by Kindle Press

THE SECRET ROSE
DARK RUBY
DECEPTION IN EMERALDS
THE TRAITOR'S CLUB

WHERE THE WOMAN BELONGS
NOVELLA

Published by Dragonblade
A VOICE ON THE WIND

SEE ALL OF LAURA'S BOOKS
AT AMAZON.COM

COMPANION BOOKS (series)
by Laura Landon

THE BROTHERHOOD
When Love is Enough | Broken Promise

RANSOMED JEWELS
Ransomed Jewels | Jaded Moon

SEASONS

Dark Ruby | Deception in Emeralds

THE REDEEMED
The Most to Lose | The Dark Duke

CAST IN SCANDAL
Cast in Shadows | Cast in Ruin
Cast in Ice | Cast in Scandal

THE TRAITOR'S CLUB
Ford | Hugh | Jeb | Caleb

RICH MAN | POOR MAN | BEGGAR MAN | THIEF
Beware the Rich Man
Bewitched by the Poor Man
Betrayed by the Beggar Man
Behold the Thief

SEASONS
90-Minute Reads
Winter's Cold Heart
Spring's Tender Heart
Summer's Distant Heart
Autumn's Wild Heart

All of Laura Landon's books on Amazon
Visit Laura at www.lauralandon.com

www.ingramcontent.com/pod-product-compliance
Lightning Source LLC
Chambersburg PA
CBHW071644260626
47170CB00001B/229